The Tail of an Angel

To Rhea, My Wonderful former Art Coworker !!

The Tail of an Angel

Jillian Verbicky

Faith brought me far, but destiny knew it all along. Thank you for being such an amazing coworker and friend to me and I hope you enjoy the novel. :) Reach for the stars!

Jillian Verbicky

Copyright © 2015 by Jillian Verbicky.

Library of Congress Control Number:		2014915317
ISBN:	Hardcover	978-1-4990-6543-5
	Softcover	978-1-4990-6544-2
	eBook	978-1-4990-6545-9

All rights reserved. No part of this book may be reproduced or transmitted in any form or by any means, electronic or mechanical, including photocopying, recording, or by any information storage and retrieval system, without permission in writing from the copyright owner.

This is a work of fiction. Names, characters, places and incidents either are the product of the author's imagination or are used fictitiously, and any resemblance to any actual persons, living or dead, events, or locales is entirely coincidental.

Any people depicted in stock imagery provided by Thinkstock are models, and such images are being used for illustrative purposes only.
Certain stock imagery © Thinkstock.

This book was printed in the United States of America.

Rev. date: 02/10/2015

To order additional copies of this book, contact:
Xlibris
1-888-795-4274
www.Xlibris.com
Orders@Xlibris.com
649653

Chapter 1

You might think it is crazy, but do you believe in destiny? An inevitable fate that is laid out for you perhaps by a higher power or what I like to call the *Forest Gump* theory: maybe we're like a feather floating on the breeze going wherever the wind takes us, but maybe it's a little bit of both. To be honest, I don't know what to believe about destiny regarding the fact if it's true or not. Whether you believe it or not, it happened to me . . . over two years. I learned a secret no average human should've ever discovered; for a while I wasn't even considered a human.

Let me tell you my story. And it all starts with swimming.

I swam in a competition group known as the Fairview Olympians, and we swam competitions against the opposing teams in the upper Alberta Region. Coming first or second in your races qualifies you—for certain races—to swim in the southern competitions, and then it becomes the real competition for finals and chances to get scouted for swimming teams or have an Olympian coach for the rest of your swimming career. Some swimmers on my team are as skilled as Michael Phelps but don't have the motivation to go all the way into a serious career. I had been a strong swimmer for many years, and even though my parents threw me into swimming lessons, I agreed mostly to swim with my friends at the time. I started swimming competitively when I was about seven or eight, and I was a great swimmer at that time. In my age group, I and a local boy legend I knew were always head-to-head in our practices, and we pushed each other to our limits both competitively and for the fun of it. As the years went by, my skill levels dropped; however I still held the record for holding my breath the longest. Meanwhile, this legend grew into an amazing Michael Phelps-like character—with a similar body structure—and a love for Lady Gaga. Now he's switched schools and is still a great friend of mine.

My heartbeat raced as I stepped onto the block—cold, dry, and ready to win this race. It was the fifty-meter freestyle, and I was in the second lane, nodding to my teammates for a silent good luck. The whistle blasted for us to pull back on the platform, and then, the air horn blew. I launched into the water, far too deep—at least halfway, but thankfully, I was halfway the twenty-five-meter length. It was no surprise that the water was as cold as ice and made me want to swim faster. This is purposeful because it's a technique used for exactly that—making the competitors swim faster for a more exciting and faster race. I sprinted for the wall as I front-crawled toward it and flipped in a matter of seconds and sped back into front crawl and was back into first place. I smiled as I saw the other wall a few meters away until I noticed my friend to the left of me catch up. He torpedoed the wall before I could even gasp in shock, and for air. I reached the wall second but smiled at him on his win. I was disappointed and cold. I never felt so good on getting the second place, and it was a first for me to get second place. I continued to sit in the icy chlorine water until the judges told us to get out; with one race down and three to go, I was excited to spend my day swimming with friends. After that race, there were the fifty-meter backstroke, fifty-meter breast stroke, and two-hundred-meter IM. I hated butterfly. I did my best to win this one, and I did. I was tired, exhausted, and sore—all those feelings you get after a full swimming tournament, knowing I kicked ass, but I wouldn't change it for the world.

It was the middle of summer. I woke up the following Sunday.

The sky was bright pink and orange from the sunrise. Small songbirds sang in the distance, and squirrels went nuts in the pine trees in the backyard. I got up, stretched, and yawned. I was feeling lazy and was still a bit sore from the tournament, while the sunrays dragged me back to my soft and warm bed. The bed sheets echoed, "It's so cold out there, baby. Come back to bed!" But I left the bed in a fit of determination to rise up and make some breakfast. My mom stole the remote to watch the newest episode of *Criminal Minds*; a little grumpy and annoyed, I rolled my eyes and watched pirated cartoons on my computer. After her show was over, I took my shower, made eggs n' toast for breakfast, and continued my morning routine as usual.

As a great start to my day, I started listening to my favorite album by Owl City, *All Things Bright and Beautiful*, and downloaded a few songs I had written down on a piece of parchment. I grabbed my iPod and went downstairs to catch a few Disney movies I hadn't watched in years. *Bambi, Mulan, Tarzan,* you name it, I watched all the classics. Plain enough as it is, I eventually got bored at about 10:00 p.m. and went to bed. The only thing that was different was I had a new reoccurring dream all night about a merman who watched over me while I swam in the deep blue sea. This worried me since the dream was stuck on replay all night long. I had a scaly, shimmery blue tail, and as a mermaid I swam into the sea with the ability to breathe underwater; I found treasures and gold in caves and shipwrecks. The merman, whose name I never learned, was devastatingly handsome and about seventeen or so by the looks of it.

But in the last replay of the dream, something different happened; he swam up to me, tucked my hair behind my ear, and pulled me closer to his tanned, strong chest. Before I got the chance to kiss him, I woke up. I gasped and launched out of bed. The sweat on my forehead showed I had too many blankets on my bed. A sad fantasy—a tear drizzled down my cheek and dripped on my pillow. Looking down, I fell back asleep with his bright green eyes still in my mind; the memory drifted away like the waves of the sandy shore I met him on. Little did I know, this summer my mom had planned a surprise vacation for me and my brother to Hawaii. It had been nearly ten years since my father left, with only a note to say how much he loved my brother and me. He asked us to remember him, but he couldn't stay. I had never heard from him since our last family vacation my father won in a lottery. It was on a small island in the middle of the Pacific Ocean and nearly impossible to find on a map; it was perfect for family. I was only four, and I cannot remember a thing. The only memory I have of that trip is a single photo of him and me with my first saltwater fish, smiling at me; we had a priceless sunset across the ocean as our background. Our family hasn't traveled since, or changed. Our home was nice, but the houseboat is all we can remember him by. I'm glad my dad won it on my parents' honeymoon. Hawaii sounded so nice to visit; I longed to travel the seas and surf and scuba dive with the fish and dolphins. I had no clue of her intentions until one day my mother took me shopping for a new bikini. I questioned her so, but she burst out and gave me a hug doing so.

"Which island are we going to?" I asked.

"Honolulu, can you believe it? I'm so excited! I even got fuel for the boat and everything ready to go!"

"Let's get two! I want to have one for the poolside and one for the ocean!"

My mom sighed but smiled in agreement to my decision. My brother had ditched us to hang out with his friends instead of shopping with us; he'd shop for Hawaii with them. Although it took hours to find new makeup and other island essentials, we finished with our feet sore, but satisfied. We passed my brother's car on the way home and rested up for a big day we would have tomorrow.

Chapter 2

At last, I happily invited slumber to a pleasant dream with the wonderful dream I was looking forward to. This time, the dream I'd grown to love turned into a nightmare. On our boat to Hawaii, a massive wave totals our vessel and everyone is thrown overboard. I manage to find a blow-up raft and float away while the rest of my family drift away from me. I float away into the night, alone and scared, into shark-infested waters. Something tips my raft, and then I wake up in a cold sweat. My heart was racing, and the covers of my bed were all over the floor. I wiped my forehead and took a sip of water, thinking that it was only a dream.

Still shaking, I told myself to go back to sleep and that I have a big day to look forward to, and I can't afford to be tired.

Somewhat calmed down, I softened my pillow and eventually went back to sleep.

Chapter 3

My mother stormed into my room, flicked on the lights, pulled up the window curtains, ripped off my blankets and screamed, "Get up! We're going to Hawaii today!"

I grumbled some gibberish about mornings to my mom.

"I know, now give me back my blanket. I'm tired, cold, and a little *grumpy*!" I shouted, grumpy at my mother and ripped the blankets from her grasp.

"How can you be grumpy for a dream tropical vacation? I've already packed your stuff, but all you have to do is pack your hygienic things after you've used them. Hurry! We can't miss our flight!"

As excited as I was, I was still very tired and hungry. I rubbed my eyes, scratched my back, and dragged myself into the shower. Thank goodness it was a hot shower; otherwise, someone would have got a fork in the eye. If you haven't noticed by now, I'm not much of a morning person. But I don't drink coffee, and a plain fruit such as an orange would do just fine. Anyways, as soon as I got dressed, I saw my brother—just as tired, but less grumpy—in the kitchen.

"Morning!" he muttered.

"Morning, how are you?"

"Hungry and tired. What about you?"

"Ditto, excited?"

"Yep."

"Same here."

I yawned again while reaching for some instant oatmeal.

"Do we have any maple and brown sugar oatmeal packets left?"

I rustled around the box for a minute before he answered.

"Only two. You can have them. I'm in an apples and cinnamon mood anyways."

I threw the packets he wanted at him while also starting up the kettle for the hot water, and, as a bonus, my French vanilla hot chocolate. Mom's coffee machine was beeping while I stirred the hot water into my oatmeal mix. I hadn't seen my mother this happy since she won the lottery with my dad; she was glowing like when my father was still here.

"Good morning!" My mother sang. "Are you guys excited or what?"

"Yay! Hawaii" I said sarcastically.

"Woo . . .," Josh grumbled.

"Good enough!"

My mom laughed as she grabbed a coffee mug and her ridiculous black coffee within it. I finished my breakfast quite quickly and packed the last of my things I needed for the trip. Alas, there was something in my bookshelf I felt I should bring: *My Big Green Purse: Secrets to Saving and Protecting the World and the Environment.* I wasn't a huge green advocate; it wasn't the book I was after, but the condom my friend gave me. I snuck it into a secret hidden pocket I stitched into my pants, which Mom would never find, and quickly tucked it in. I touched up a bit of my makeup, but I had to hurry since my mother yelled that it was time to go. I pet my cat Moxie once more before racing outside to get into the car. By this time, I began to feel a little more awake and slightly less grumpy. The time was about 6:45 a.m. and I saw about seven cars before we reached the airport. The car ride was nothing special, just Josh and I sleeping with my mom playing her *Hits from the 80s*. Thank God I was sleeping. I woke up again to my mom yelling at us to get up and grab our stuff. The plan was to fly to the coast of California, where one of my best friends, and his family, were already down there for a week, taking care of our boat.

I met him at a leadership skills camp, where he became my *best friend* while I played with his hair; we spent our last night there dancing and watching the stars. I hadn't seen him since then, and I was so excited to see him, even just to give him another hug; his hugs were the best, my favorite.

Besides Jay, our families are great friends, and my mom really wanted another family to join us on the week-long cruise to Hawaii. What better way to travel than with good friends? I remember some gentleman saying that he had an older sister with whom my brother was sure to get acquainted. The airport, to my surprise, was somewhat busy, definitely about two hundred people. It was a massive airport, and it wasn't packed either. The speakers called for our flight in perfect timing, the second we got through security, which was super boring. I never really had a problem with flying; before Dad left, we traveled often; he had a high-paying job, so vacations were a pretty regular thing, driving or flying. My first flight was when I was two. I don't remember it, but I was told that I was fine with flights. The only things I still don't like is landing and takeoff. It's the shaking, launching, acceleration. I hate the feeling more than turbulence or flying over thunderstorms. I never got used to that feeling, and I don't plan to anytime soon. I put on my sunglasses to hide my tired eyes, but I also looked really, really good since I was wearing silver hoops and a sort of celebrity-type outfit. I could pass off as a celebrity trying to hide from fans, but I really was more focused on finding my seat and who I'd be sitting with for a few hours. I had a window seat in the middle of the plane with my brother in the middle and my mother on the end. Crap. This was going to be a long flight.

The captain announced the weather conditions and for the staff to take their seats. The plane was speeding up fast, and I grabbed my armrest and closed my eyes for the takeoff. Thank goodness the plane launched quickly. I felt sick to my stomach even before the plane got off the ground. Anyways, the aircraft stabilized and leveled out in a peaceful and smooth straight line. "Only six more hours to go," I thought to myself. I'd packed everything I needed to be entertained in my purse—book, iPhone, DS, diary, sketchbook, Word Search, iPod, you name it. Everything was charged and ready to use. I grabbed my iPhone first to check my Facebook page. After discovering a new friend request and three updates about some new status updates, I decided to make one:

On the plane to California! So excited! Can't wait for the family vacation!

Within thirty seconds, Josh and my mom had already liked my status. Jay Adam San commented that he was excited too, but with a winky face. I turned off my iPhone and played sudoku on my DS for two hours, read for one hour, played iPhone games for another two hours, and wrote in my diary for one hour. I had a lot to write about, and I'm very detailed in my writing. I once had an entry of twelve pages back-to-back. It was worth the hand cramp. The time flew by faster than I thought when I was busy; I just finished writing in my diary as the captain announced our landing immediately. I yelled a little "woo," and the plane touched the ground and safely landed. I was excited to get off the plane; I stomped on Josh and trampled over my mom to get off the plane. Not to mention that I knocked down three children and pushed an older person and two grandmas. The worst part was I only said sorry to one grandma that I pushed. All I cared about was meeting Jay's family in the airport. I waited for my mom and brother to finally meet me at the exit of the plane. Once again, we had to go through the hell of airport security where I had to tell the guy at the metal detecting door that I had a metal wire bra on; he didn't believe me, and I had to lift up my shirt to prove it. I was so embarrassed and angry, but eventually they let me though. Josh and Mom got through just fine but I managed not to blow a gasket and keep calm while we walked out into the entry of the airport when I finally spotted the one thing I was looking forward to the entire time, Jay and his family.

"Hey!" I yelled to Jay.

"Hey, Jill! Over here!" Jay yelled back.

I increased the pace of my steady walk to a speed walk, then to a jog while I still pulled my luggage. Jay left his luggage in a heap of stuff by his family; in turn he sprinted toward me before he crashed into my chest, and I dropped everything and gave him a hug. I felt my back crack a few times when he squeezed me.

"Ow! That hurt," I whispered.

"Sorry."

"It's okay. My back was sore anyways."

"I missed you," Jay whispered in my ear.

"I missed you too, Jay."

Chapter 4

I smiled a stupid grin but squeezed him tighter for a good five seconds. His hugs were always my favorite, the same as I remembered the night he hugged me at camp after our dance together. Just as warm and inviting as always. I picked up the luggage behind me while Josh took a few bags that I couldn't carry and brought them to the mountain of luggage. I hugged Jay's sister and their mother and father, and then I grabbed as much stuff as I could out of the airport.

The car was really close to the exit; thank goodness because my stuff was really heavy. I threw my stuff in the back, but Jay and I had to sit in the way back to fit seven people into the vehicle. Jay's dad and his mom sat in the front, Jay's sister, my brother and my mom sat in the middle, while Jay and I had the backseat all to ourselves.

"The weather is supposed to be gorgeous for the next few weeks I hear. All the way up to the thirties!" Jay's dad told us.

"Good, I'd rather have it crazy hot, than cold and gloomy," Jay's sister commented.

Jay put his arm around my shoulders and pulled me closer to him. I smiled and put my head on his shoulder in return.

"So what have you been up to since you got here?" I asked.

"Oh, not much, just chilling, swimming, surfing—"

"Surfing!? Since when do you surf?"

"Since I got here," Jay laughed.

I laughed too, but I hadn't been surfing since our one trip to Mexico, where a huge wave smashed me into some coral and knocked me out, while, as a bonus, cutting up my ankle as I drifted to the shore. The salt water didn't help whatsoever.

"You got to teach me how to surf. It sounds so fun!"

"I'd love to. Also you should try scuba diving, and it's amazing."

"Absolutely! That sounds just as good, only if you're coming with me though?"

"Hell, yes."

Jay pulled me even closer and leaned his head on mine.

I quietly sighed and closed my eyes for a minute to enjoy the moment for a while. Before we could take the boat out, they had to get all the supplies for the trip, like food, fuel and other necessities, which would take at least one day to do. That meant that we could do nothing for a day, but I was thinking of something a little different. Once we got to the house Jay's family had down in California, I took my stuff to my upstairs room and changed into one of the bikinis I had bought and sunglasses to tan on the beach for a while. I found a lazy chair under a palm tree umbrella and got comfortable.

"Mind if I join you?" Jay asked as he walked up next to me.

"Not at all," I answered, lowering my sunglasses. "Is it just me, or have you been working out?" I asked because Jay looked incredibly tanned, toned, and extremely sexy.

"Surfing is great for the body, and I've been drinking nothing but smoothies and eating tropical fruits all week."

"You look good!"

"So do you."

I blushed a little and returned to my tanning position. Jay moved his chair right next to mine to tan with me, but way too close at the same time.

"We should go surfing in about two hours," I recommended.

"Agreed."

For once in my life, I was actually tanning instead of burning and peeling, which I hated. A cool breeze passed by under the hot sun, and the smell of the salty sea air was incredible. The people at the beach weren't terribly loud, which was nice. I caught Jay checking out a few women walking by, but I forgave him since a few guys winked as me as they walked passed. Suddenly, I wished I could stay and live by the ocean forever. I'm positive at some point in my life, I will. It's now on my bucket list.

Chapter 5

After the first hour, I flipped over so I could tan evenly. Meanwhile, Jay and I chatted about the most random things, like best e-card you've sent and the best flavor of ice cream. It was nice to finally have some time to ourselves and just talk about anything. I think I'd always wanted a best friend to just talk about anything with, share all my secrets with, talk about issues and problems, like a family member. I was pretty sure I'd found him, and I bet he'd been looking for a girl like that too.

I sipped on my piña colada while he took a drink of his virgin margarita. It was so calm and peaceful, like we were the only two there. I only wished I could've frozen that moment and lived it forever.

"Hey, Jay! Who's your lady friend?"

The moment ended.

A hippy-looking guy walked up to Jay.

"This is Jillian, and she wants to surf just as well as I do."

"All right, no problem. He learned all his moves from me, you know."

"Sounds like fun!"

The shaggy hippy took Jay and me to his surf shack.

"Let's get started! What board do you want to use?"

I saw at least hundred boards to choose from; lots of them were just beautiful. Finally, I was stuck on two amazing boards; one was purple-and-blue with a rose and waves on it, while the other was black with flames and a fancy heart in the middle.

"I can't decide on the blue-and-purple one, or the one with the flames."

"Definitely the one with the flames," Jay answered.

"The one with the flames please!"

"Nice choice! That's one of my favorites too."

I learned that the name of the hippy was Steve; it suited him and his personality as well. He grabbed my board while Jay picked up his board polish. Steve grabbed his board too and took us out to the ocean side.

"First rule is that you got to wax your board. Makes it totally easier to catch a wave."

Jay had already started waxing his board, and Steve handed me a buffing cloth to wax my own board. He told me how his family had been surfing for generations, and they had always dreamed of opening a surfing shack for years. His dad had a rich grandfather, who recently died and left his fortune to his father, where they opened the shop about a year ago. When he became a surf instructor and won a bunch of surfing competitions, his dad left the shop in his care. Ever since, he'd been teaching people to surf and selling his passion to everyone. A few weeks ago, Steve decided to start making surfboards. The one he was waxing, he made it himself out of zebra, cherry, and oak wood.

"I'm also doing a few custom boards for my family and friends. I'm not gonna charge you for lessons though, since you're tight with my bro Jay here. Any friend of his gets free lessons, and the board is half price."

"Lucky me! What if I'm his best friend?"

"Anything in my shop is on the house."

"Did I mention I'm his best friend?"

"It's true!" Jay added.

"You're welcome in my shop anytime."

I finished waxing my board, and Steve took us into the ocean.

"Just a few tips before you can start surfing: balance, strength, and endurance. Balance to stay on the board, strength to be able to pull yourself onto the wave, and endurance to be able to stay strong on the wave, and paddle your arms to catch a wave. Here comes an easy one. Give it a try."

He pointed at the ripple coming at us while Jay got a head start.

"Hey! Wait for me!"

"Hurry up! You're gonna miss it!"

I paddled as fast as I could to keep up with him, but damn he was fast. He must have caught a rip tide or something because I was still quite far behind him.

"Here it is! Let's go!" Jay yelled back at me. I finally saw the wave grow to a crazy height as I kept paddling.

"I thought this one was easy!?"

"Easy as in, easy for him. No one said it'd be easy for you!"

"Freaking perfect!"

"Get up! I'll be right in front of you!"

"Ha! Not for long!"

I finally caught up and passed him before the wave came up in front of us. I got up and nearly fell off the board, but eventually I balanced out. Now I was surfing the wave and felt the wall with the tips of my fingers. Just when I thought it couldn't get any better, I slowed down into the very end of the wave as I was sealed in a cylindrical saltwater room. I breathed in the misty sea air but laughed at the many fish that got swept up and rolled back into the sea. I touched the swirling roof of the watery chamber with salty ocean rushing beneath me. I'd never seen the true beauty of the sea, until I felt it rush beside me. I spotted Jay ahead of me, and I twisted and turned to catch up to him. I got so close that at one point I was right next to him.

"You're catching on really quick! Nice job!"

"This is amazing! Have you seen the end of this wave? It's breathtaking!"

"Just wait till you go scuba diving! The surfing is just a start."

"See you on the other tide! Ha-ha! Woohoo!"

I flew past him and accidentally sprayed him in the process, but I laughed as I did to make me feel better, 'cause I don't think it made him feel better at all. I saw the end of the line ahead, and I had no idea how to stop. I had no choice but to crash and swim; only it wasn't that easy. I fell face-plant into the wave, and my board whacked me on the head when I fell; for a moment, I was totally knocked out cold for a moment, until I opened my eyes and saw that Jay had pulled me up onto his board from the ocean.

"You didn't get off right."

"Well, no one told me how to stop. It's just like skiing lessons all over again."

"C'mon, we have some scuba diving to do."

"Thanks for not letting me drown. I'll buy you a drink when we get back to the shore."

"How about I buy you dinner?"

"That works too."

I saw my board floating away to my left, but I caught it, got on it, and swam back to the beach. Steve surfed on another wave while Jay and I grabbed some scuba stuff from the shack. All we needed were flippers, goggles, oxygen, and a waterproof camera. Once I got all my stuff on, Jay took me off the busy part of the beach to a private area where no one could bother us. I dived in and followed him to a breathtaking reef with rainbow coral and billions of amazing colorful fish. I took lots of pictures, but Jay gestured for me to join him in a cave. It was dark and scary, but he grabbed my hand to guide me to wherever he wanted me to go. Suddenly, it started getting lighter the farther we swam, until we reached a cavern stuffed with priceless treasure. There were gold chests of jewels and gems. Jay swam up to a hidden shelf and brought down a small clam.

"What's this?"

"I found this in a sunken ship when I was diving with Steve, but I want you to have it."

Jay opened up the plain tan clam, and a small, baby-blue pearl was inside.

"It takes decades for a clam to make a pearl, but a blue pearl takes over a hundred years to grow. It's the rarest of all pearls, so rare that this one is priceless."

"It's beautiful. Why do you want me to have it? You could sell it and become a billionaire."

"I'd rather you have it, because it reminds me of you."

I smiled as I picked up the clam; the pearl was so bright and blue, and I could swear it was glowing.

"How does a priceless blue pearl remind you of me?"

"It reminds me of your eyes."

He swam a little closer to me.

"It's flawless, beautiful, and bright, and it's smooth. It can take a lifetime to find one. Mostly though, it's priceless and it seems like it even glows, just like your smile."

I closed the clam and swam up to give him a hug.

"Thank you I'll treasure this forever."

I looked around at all the other treasures there. I was breathless at all the untold items he had recovered while diving. The shelves of the cave were overflowing with flawless gems and diamonds and sunken treasure from everywhere. I spotted something twinkling and green near to top and found a perfect peridot.

"I can't believe it!" I gasped as I picked up the gem. "A perfectly cut peridot! It's my birthstone, you know."

"I was saving it for your birthday, but you can have it now if you like."

"So what do you plan to do with all this treasure?"

"I'll keep some, give some away, and sell some, not too much."

"You found all this in a week?"

"I spent 80 percent of my time here diving and 20 percent surfing."

"You lucky duck."

"We better go. I still got to cleanup for dinner."

"Good point. Let's go."

It didn't take too long to get out of the cave and go back to the house Jay was staying in. It was quite nice actually; it had a beautiful view of the ocean and the beach for a backyard and away from the busy crowds and noisy neighbors.

"I'll take a shower quickly, and then you can get ready," Jay told me as he opened the door to the house.

I headed up to my room, which had a view of the sea of course and was right next to Jay's. I found my own bathroom and saw my stuff was somewhat unpacked. I was pretty sure whoever did it was bored halfway through and didn't feel like finishing. Luckily, I'd packed formal wear in case we were going to have a family dinner. In my case, I would absolutely be wearing formal clothes tonight.

It was a flowing red dress with a slit in the leg on the right side. It was a little sparkly and showed the perfect amount of cleavage. I had some amazing black high heels to match and a few black accessories. I laid out my outfit and makeup for the evening, and with good timing, I heard Jay's shower stop the second I finished.

Quickly, I took my shower, brushed my teeth, dried my hair, and put on my makeup and so on. It took only one hour for me to get ready before Jay yelled for me join him downstairs. As I walked down the stairs, I was surprised at what he wore for dinner. He was wearing an open-neck black T-shirt with a white tie and jacket, plus black pants and sneakers.

"Really? You're wearing sneakers? I'm wearing high heels!"

"Well, I put on a tie."

"Whatever."

He helped me down the last few steps, which I guess made up for him wearing sneakers.

"So, where are you taking me tonight?"

"It's a surprise."

"Is it a . . . Italian surprise?"

"Nope."

"Chinese?"

"Nope."

"Indian?"

"I'm not telling you."

"Okay . . . Do I know this restaurant?

"I think you might."

He didn't drive too far to get there, although I really didn't care where he would take me. I was just happy he finally wanted to buy me dinner. At last, he wanted to buy me dinner at Red Lobster.

"Oh, I love Red Lobster!"

"Not as much as you're gonna love the seats!"

I gave him a confused look but walked right out of the car anyways.

"Reservations for two, under Jay San."

A skinny French waiter looked in the little black book on his host table and said with an accent, "Ah, Monsieur San, your table is ready. Follow me."

"Why is there a French waiter in a seafood restaurant?"

"I don't know."

The waiter led us to the very back of the restaurant.

"What kind of seats are in the back of the restaurant?" I thought to myself. Then, he opened a door to the outside deck of the restaurant. I could see only one table for two on the entire deck, and a single red candle in the center. The view of the ocean was amazing. I gasped a little when I got outside.

"Your server will be here shortly."

Just as the French guy left, he flicked on a switch, and above us lines of little light bulbs lit up the entire deck and the table above us.

"Nice seats!" I whispered to Jay.

"The stars aren't out yet, so I improved it a little."

"Cool!"

I clicked on the wood floor with my heels as I walked to my seat; just as I went to pull out my chair, Jay beat me to it and pulled out the chair for me. "Touché on the gentleman-like behavior. Well played," I thought.

"So how did you get these seats anyways?"

"My dad's a good friend with the owner, and his son is also one of my friends."

"You've got lots of connections here! You know that? Free surfing lessons, scuba equipment, amazing dinner seats, who don't you know around here?"

"Just a few people."

Our server returned to our table to fetch us some drinks. I had lemonade while Jay simply got a coke.

"I'd like to make a toast!" Jay declared, raising his drink.

"What shall we toast to?"

"To a night you'll never forget."

"To us?"

"Okay, that too."

We clinked our glasses, and I looked back at the black leather menu in front of me. Obviously, I ordered one pound of crab, and Jay ordered the same.

"I bet the crab here is freshest here."

"Totally," Jay agreed. I placed my velvet red napkin on my dress; God knows I'd never get garlic butter sauce out of this outfit. Finally, we were back to ourselves, chatting about the day, laughing in agreement to our likes and dislikes. I quote a wonderful movie called *Forest Gump*:

"Me and Jenny was like peas and carrots again."

I definitely preferred talking with Jay rather than texting. Our conversations rolled together smoothly with no breaks of waiting to text back, or the agonizing want of someone to say, "I missed you too!"

Somehow, the conversation twisted to the coral reefs, sharks, Australia, and me being in Australia, Mexico, Spain, and to speaking Spanish and so much more. Everything came together like finding the final pieces to a puzzle. It just snapped in place effortlessly, and our conversation grew to be more and more enjoyable. I'm not saying I always knew that this would happen; I was just so glad it finally did. Soon our dinner arrived, and the steaming crab was presented with a souvenir bib and complimentary hand towels to wipe down the soon-to-be buttery fingers. I ignored the bib and reached for the crab cracker and dug right in.

"I'm a master when it comes to getting the crab out perfectly out of the shell, you know. Takes lots of practice," I said as I cracked open a claw.

"Oh really? Then I challenge you to show me your finest work, and we'll see who the real crab master is."

"You're on!" I laughed as I dipped the crabmeat into the dreamy garlic butter. I carefully kept my most prized meat chunks from the largest part of the crab leg for show. I was sure that it would not get cold, so I finished the other meat quickly and efficiently. Not a single drop of sauce touched my dress or napkin, but I was certain a good portion of it was on my face. With the tiny crab fork, I slowly enjoyed my mashed potatoes while Jay finished his crab as well.

"It seems as if I've finished dinner first! Ha-ha!"

I smiled as I took a final bite of my mashed potatoes.

"You may have won the battle, but I will win the war!"

"Bring it on!"

I selected my finest and largest nugget of delicious crabmeat, easily the length of my hand. I lifted my piece, and Jay showed me his. Thankfully, mine was twice the length of his; the look on his face showed that he knew he'd been beat.

"I win!"

"What do you want as a reward?"

"I'll bring the snacks for the movie."

"I accept!"

I dipped the last piece of crabmeat in the last few drops of butter, but savored it, as if it were the last piece of crab on earth. I was far too full for dessert, and the bill came only minutes after we finished. I knew one French waiter was getting a great tip tonight. Jay once again beat me to my chair, only to ask that I hold his arm on the way out to the car. I thought he'd never ask. The French waiter thanked us and greeted us a good evening on the way out of the restaurant. The radio did most of the talking on the way home. Sirius Hits 1 was on, and Jay only turned it off once to ask what movie we should watch.

"Totally a horror movie!" was my answer, so he rented *The Devil Inside* on the way home.

I changed into my slutty pj's that came with some cute short shorts and a low tank top—perfect for a scary movie. I grabbed a couple sodas and waited for Jay on the couch.

"By the way, I'm shutting off the lights. Makes the movie way better," Jay said while throwing the disk into the DVD player. I nodded because my mouth was full of popcorn; it'd be snowing popcorn in there if I said okay. He grabbed a big, soft, blanket and pressed Play for the movie to start.

"If you get scared or anything, it's okay if you want to snuggle up to me."

"I was going to do that anyways."

I put my head on his shoulder while he put his arm around me, pulling me closer to him. The first thing I noticed was that he smelled amazing, like a musky pine tree and smoke. It was so good. The closer I got to him, the better it got, mostly because I was huddled in his arms and neck. The movie didn't seem so scary with him there. I knew I was going to get scared though, but I was prepared. Fifteen minutes into the movie I survived; half an hour later, I was scared; after an hour and twenty minutes, I was "shitting my pants" scared. Surely, I was cutting off circulation in Jay's arm, but he said nothing. Some devil escaped a person but dragged out all the organs with it, and I hid myself in his chest and arms.

"You scared?"

"No, I was freezing, and the blanket wasn't warm enough."

"Sure, whatever you say."

He whispered in my ear that he'd tell me when the scary stuff was over. I had no problem being in his arms and almost asleep in his chest.

I didn't watch the rest of the movie, since it was all really scary. He was so warm; all my senses told me to indulge in slumber. All I heard was the faint voices from the movie and his steady heartbeat. All I saw was his T-shirt and blanket over his shoulder. His cologne, I was sure, made the entire room smell good, while I held my own hip with my hand and the side of his with the other. What's not to fall asleep in! I couldn't resist and fell asleep. I did hear a bunch of screams before I slept. I don't really think it was good a movie anyways.

"You can come out now. The movie's over. It was pretty scary."

I could only guess that he saw I was sleeping, but he didn't move. I felt him tuck the hair on my face behind my ear and place his hand on my cheek. It wasn't even sweaty; it was hot though, and relaxing. I smiled a little and nuzzled closer into his hand. I'm pretty sure I heard him chuckle, but he didn't stop. Instead, he brushed his two fingers down the side of my face and his thumb down the edge of my jaw. He lifted up my chin to have a better look at me and lightly touched his nose on mine. It wasn't long before he lifted up the blanket and carried me to my room. He gently placed me down on my bed and pulled the covers over me. Surprisingly, he crawled into the bed with me and laid my head onto his chest. This time he didn't wear his shirt, and I placed my hand on his upper chest while twisting my leg with his. I smiled, knowing I was again seeing him in my dreams.

Chapter 6

I woke up in his bed instead of my own and in his arms, my head still on his chest. He was still fast asleep, and I had nowhere to go. So I went right back to sleep. I felt him pull me closer into his chest, and I, in return, put my other arm behind him and around his bare shoulder. He was slightly tanned. I examined his neck and shoulders for the necklace I thought he wore, but he must have taken it off. I closed my eyes once more and heard him take a large inhale and exhale in my hair; afterward he breathed as if he were in a coma. I looked down in enjoyment and fell back asleep again. It must have been only twenty minutes before I heard my mom blow-drying her hair. Jay woke me up immediately as if an alarm clock had gone off and gushed that I go back to my room.

"Good morning to you too," I said as I left his room but stopped just before leaving his room. "Thanks for the movie, handsome."

I winked and laughed as I returned to my room to get dressed. I hurried to put on my makeup and touched up my mascara.

"Hurry up, you guys! We got to get up early if we want to make good time!" Mom yelled to me. I raced down the stairs like *The Brady Bunch* kids with Jay right behind me.

"Morning," Jay whispered as I got off the step.

My luggage awaited me next to the table. I made instant oatmeal. Jay had Frosted Flakes, but he ate it all so I couldn't have any. I think it took about forty-five seconds to eat my oatmeal, which frightened Jay and me a little. Anyway, I grabbed my bag and threw it into the car and hopped into the backseat. Jay climbed in right next to me. He smiled at me as I buckled up and blushed a bit as I looked down. I couldn't help but look up and smile. I always wanted to smile at everyone because I never knew who could be falling in love with it.

"Everyone got their things?" Jay's dad yelled to everyone.
"Yep!" my mom answered.
"Yep," replied Jay's sister.
"Yep," said my brother,
"Yep!" I continued.
"I got everything I need," Jay said, looking at me.
I glanced up at him, knowing he was talking about me.
"Off we go!"

Jay's dad drove on to the harbor. The weather was absolutely perfect—clear blue skies, with not a single breath of wind. The sea was so calm that it looked like we would be boating on blue glass. Finally, we reached the deck, and I grabbed my stuff, eager to see the boat. It turned out Jay and I were sharing a room. My brother and Jay's sister had a room, my mom had her own—the best room of all—and Jay's parents had the second-best room. The back had a small hot tub and a ladder that would let us swim in the ocean. The upper deck had a small bar and plenty of room to tan in the sun. The lower deck had a brilliant view and a guard bar at the front similar to the scene in the *Titanic* with Jack and Rose. I sprinted up to it to look at the view. Jay's dad took hold of the wheel and started up the boat and raced into the distance at the crack of dawn, 6:00 a.m. I couldn't wait to finally sit in the sun and swim as I pleased.

Chapter 7

    I thought the weather was going to be raining and miserable. So I had to change into something more comfortable. I packed my golden sundress with yellow and orange flowers on it. It really was beautiful, and it was light and flowing, and the neck came down quite a bit, about which I didn't have too much to complain.
    I had trouble zipping up the back, until someone behind me finished zipping it up for me. Plus whoever it was tied a knot around my waist and fixed the shoelace hoop, which I didn't do that well on my neck.
"You're welcome."
"Oh, Jay! Thank goodness! You scared me!"
"Sorry! You're terrible at tying up your own dress."
"If you ever wore a dress, you'd know how hard it is."
"Glad I could help."
"Thank you."
    He grabbed my belly and pulled me closer to him. I giggled a little bit like a kid who got in a tickle fight with one of their siblings. I grinned like an idiot as I pulled his arms against mine. I leaned my head back a little into his neck and chest. He closed his eyes and smiled back when he put his head next to mine and whispered in my ear, "You look beautiful."
    I don't think I blushed that much since my first dance with the hottest boy in our school.
"Let's go for a swim!"
    Before I could run off and race him to the water, he picked me up and carried me outside.
"Hey! What do you think you're doing? Put me down!" I yelled at him but smiled at the same time.
"Not until I take you out to the front of the boat."

The Tail of an Angel

"Why?"

"Just wait."

So I stopped struggling to escape and sat back to enjoy it; in fact, I put my arms around his strong shoulders and neck and crisscrossed my legs to get even more comfortable.

"I knew you'd like me carrying you!"

"Just because I have my arms around you and got much more comfortable doesn't mean I like it."

"Whatever you say."

Jay kicked open the door in front of him to the deck outside overlooking the ocean.

"Nice job. I would've kicked open the door, but you beat me to it," I told Jay. I figured out that he recognized the scene from *Titanic* as well. I laughed at the decibel level of a mouse when I knew that he and I were thinking the very same thing.

"Are you thinking what I'm thinking?"

"I think so."

He put me down gently and pointed his hand to the very tip of the boat. I raised my right eyebrow and walked up to the bar nonetheless. I leaned up against it and sighed when I saw the sun was already setting.

"What a beautiful sunset."

Jay joined me at the edge and put his arm around my hip.

"It's the second-best thing I've seen today."

"What's the best thing you've seen today?"

"You in that sundress."

I smiled as I looked down when he snuck a kiss on my cheek. For once I didn't blush but smiled back and put my head next to his. I put my arm around him too and stared off into the strawberry sunset. I sighed in sync with him, and he did the same when I laughed. Just when I wanted to lean forward and look down to the clam sea below, Jay picked me up by the waist and raised me up above him. I yelped as I got higher.

"I swear if you drop me, I'll kill you!"

"You really think I'm gonna let you go?"

"Don't let me go, Jack! Ha!"

"Nice, now just enjoy the view."

"Okay!"

I looked forward into the very eyes of what I'm pretty sure was God himself ahead of me. I say "the eyes of God" because nothing more touching or powerful was ahead of me than the very creator himself. I was only up there for a few minutes because I'm sure he was getting tired and wouldn't mind a view of the sunset too.

"I don't think I can lift you up."

"You don't have to. I can see everything I want and need right in front of me right here."

"Me too."

We smiled at each other, but I looked down again for a minute to simply enjoy this moment. He put his hand on my cheek again like the other night. I closed my eyes and leaned into it; it was warm just like the sunset on my skin, but less dangerous 'cause warm hands can't give you cancer or sunburn. I opened my eyes to see he was already staring in mine. He had such innocent hazel eyes, dreamy, sweet, and inviting. I think the eyes are really the windows to the soul. That day, I'm sure I could see the very characteristics that made up my Jay. An unknown author came up the most honest and truthful quote I will ever hear.

"When a guy is in love, you can see it in his smile. But when a girl is in love, you can see it in her eyes."

"You have amazing blue eyes," Jay smiled.

"And you have an amazing smile."

"Really?"

"You should really thank your dentist. He did a great job."

"I'll get right on that."

He brushed my hair behind my ear and sighed while I looked up at him. He put his one hand on my waist and the other behind my neck. About one centimeter away from him, I was so close to kissing him, until his freaking dad honked the damn horn.

"Better go to bed you two!" Jay's dad yelled to us. I laughed and looked down in disappointment.

I looked back and whispered in his ear, "Maybe later tonight."

I walked away but looked back and pulled my pointer finger for him to come and follow me.

"Oh jeez! I'm such a tease. You silly flirt," I thought to myself. He followed me to our room and I grabbed my pj's to go and change. I had my slutty pj's, ready to wear again, which of course I wanted to wear since we had to share a bed. I closed the door to the washroom, and I was just about to take off my bra when Jay walked in and—

"Hey! Get out of here! I'm changing!"

"My bad."

"Shoo!"

As I waved for him to get out of the bathroom, I was still a little angry that he "accidentally" walked in. I was just glad he didn't walk in when I didn't have my bra on. I walked back in to find that he wasn't even in the bed yet, so I crawled in, still curious about his whereabouts. Anyways, I curled up to the pillow and snuggled up to the blanket since my pajamas weren't that warm. I fell asleep very quickly and went into that level of sleep when people think you're dead—that kind of sleep. Believe it or not, even in my death-like sleep I was awakened when I heard Jay open the door, letting in the blinding light from the hall. I heard him try to find his way in the dark once he closed the door quietly, but failed. I peeked with one eye open to watch him stumble around the room like a drunk or blind person. He tripped over my bag and over his own, both times stubbing his toe and finally falling face-first into the bed and on my leg.

"Ouch."

"Sorry! Did I wake you?"

"I'm awake now."

"Oh, good."

I rolled away from him, showing that I was still upset from the bathroom incident. His ice-cold feet brushed my leg, while I shivered and whispered, "Damn, your feet are cold!"

"Oh, they'll warm up eventually."

He inched in closer to me, shirtless and still warm from the sunset. He reached with both arms around my belly and pulled me up against him.

"Are you sure you don't want to turn around for me?"

"Only if you promise not to touch me with your ice-cold feet."

"I promise."

I flipped around, fast, while he put his one hand behind my back and the other behind my neck.

"You're not wearing a bra?"

"Why would I wear a bra to bed?"

"Well, I was just thinking—"

"We're not gonna do what I think you want to do tonight!"

"Pretty please?"

"Maybe another night. Right now I'm tired, cold, and worried that a storm will hit us overnight and we'll sink and sharks will—"

"Don't worry. I'm right here, and nothing bad will happen to you as long as I'm around."

"Thank you."

He kissed me on my left cheek and placed his hand on my face again.

"You better have clean hands."

"Relax. I just washed them. Why are you so worried? Calm down."

I closed my eyes and exhaled slowly, saying, "All right," but when I opened my eyes, he seemed to be looking through mine. It was as if he could see the want in my eyes. For only a second, he looked down at my lips while I, at the same time, turned my head slightly and looked at his.

He pulled me closer with the one hand behind my neck, forcing me to lean forward. I looked up for about three seconds as if to say with my eyes, "Don't let me go," and looked back down when his lips were only centimeters form mine. I inhaled quickly but quietly, and to be fair, he kissed me.

Although it was warm and the taste of peppermint was on his breath, I didn't think he would get another opportunity to kiss me after his dad saw him and me. Jay was so gentle, passionate, and smooth, like a cool glass of water. I breathed out ever so slowly, while I wrapped both of my arms around his neck and relaxed shoulders. He pulled me so close that I was practically under him. I turned my head slightly to get more comfortable when he found this to be his chance to French-kiss me. You can't really stop a French kiss, and you may only go so far to simply enjoy it. I was a little freaked out at first by how moist he was, but to have someone's tongue tangled with mine was a bit of a turn-on.

Some people may find out their turn-ons are just making out or having someone kiss their neck, or maybe even someone's hands on their hips; mine was definitely French-kissing Jay.

"I wish I could freeze this moment right now and live it forever," I thought as I leaned in closer to him. It was official; that was obvious to me as he was now on top of me. Hey, I couldn't complain. I loved it, and I didn't want it to end. But as we all know, all good things must come to an end. Shit. Just when I wanted this to go on for the rest of the night, he stopped and held on to me for one last kiss before he looked into my eyes again. Smiling at me that smile only heaven could make, he turned over to go to sleep. I looked over at him kind of sad that he wouldn't roll back over so I could sleep in his arms. If only he knew how badly I wanted to wake up and see him holding me on his chest, just being quiet.

"Aren't you forgetting something?"
"Goodnight?"
"And . . ."
"Sleep tight?"
"Nooo."
"Are you cold?"
"You're getting closer."
"Do you need another blanket?"
"Sort of . . ."
"You want to snuggle, don't you?"
"Took you long enough, jeez."

Just as I hoped, he rolled over and slipped his arm behind me and pulled me so close. I put my head into his warm chest, one arm around his shoulder and neck, the other face down from where my head lay, simply on his stomach, soft and strong. I heard only his breathing and heartbeat while the scent of his incredible cologne still lingered around the room. I smiled and kissed his neck to say goodnight while he whispered, 'Goodnight, Jilly Bean.'

"Sweet dreams, Jay."

"You too."

And just like that, I had no trouble falling asleep because even though reality was better than my dreams, I never felt safer before then in his arms, all to myself.

Chapter 8

It was the perfect day for Jay and me to sleep in. I could hear the footsteps of everyone already on the upper deck. I couldn't make out a thing they were saying, but I could care less. I was still sleeping in Jay's arms, with his around me, and I wouldn't change it for the world. After about five minutes of just plain rest, there were three loud knocks followed by an angry shout.

"Get up, you guys! Breakfast is ready."

I could tell from the tone of voice that it was Jay's dad.

"C'mon, we got to get some breakfast."

"Mmmm, but I'm so comfy, plus I'm not too hungry."

"Well, we got to get some breakfast at some point."

"Meh."

"Ten minutes?"

"Okay."

Jay pulled up the blanket to cover my cold shoulders, and I nuzzled into his chest and fell back asleep for the longest ten minutes I had alone with Jay—only hearing his heartbeats again—matching my own—and the peaceful breaths he gave forth onto my hair. It was more relaxing than watching the ocean sunset and watching stars fall put together.

"I bet our breakfast is cold by now."

"I bet it's not the best breakfast either."

"Get up please."

"Do I have to?"

"Yep."

"Good luck."

"I wasn't going anywhere," I thought to myself. He flipped me over with ease, right off the bed. I crashed to the ice-cold floor with a massive thud.

"Hey! That hurt!"

"You dared me!"

"I was expecting you to gently flip me over and get up!"

"My bad."

"Well, at least help me up, you idiot."

"That's Mr. Idiot to you!"

"Whatever."

As requested, he helped me up as expected; only, the very second I got on my feet, he kissed me.

"I'm sorry. I won't let you smash into the floor again."

"Okay, or a wall. Believe it or not, it happens more often than you think."

"Really? That's so funny!"

"Only when it happens to someone else."

"I'd like to see that at some point."

"Yeah, maybe not."

"Let's get some breakfast."

"All right."

I kissed him back and left the room still in my slutty pj's. I couldn't go out to his family wearing that, so I had to grab my fancy housecoat. On the way out, I saw Jay look back to make sure we got to breakfast together. I tied up my belt and wasn't looking at where I was going and walked right into the hallway wall. Crap.

"Oh my gosh! I can't believe you just did that! Ha-ha ha-ha! Wow!"

"Shut up and make sure I don't walk into any more walls."

I could smell bacon and eggs cooking and freshly brewed coffee. To my right I saw that Jay's sister had made a bunch of breakfast smoothies.

"Oh wow! I'd love a smoothie! What have you made so far?"

"Ummm . . . Strawberry, banana, blueberry pomegranate, purple cow, and piña colada."

"Oooo! I'll have a piña colada."

"Coming right up!"

She could totally be a bartender; she made that smoothie so efficiently and neatly. I had my drink in less than thirty seconds. Awesome. I overheard everyone talking about fishing, sleeping, tanning, and being lazy. It was like that noise that Charlie Brown heard when he talked to his teacher.

Anyways, I wasn't too concerned about their ideas of laziness; I was busy watching Jay put on some sunscreen. He was talking to my brother about some sort of car they both wanted to drive. I cared less about cars and how to fix an engine; I sipped my wonderful drink and thought of a way to get his mind off cars and onto myself. No man can resist rubbing sunscreen on a soft girl's back, a well-known fact. I ran back to my room, finishing up my smoothie, and grabbed the sexiest bikini I had. It was blood red and had string ties around the neck and back, along with boxer-style shorts that almost let my ass peek out and a sexy butterfly on the front side of my hip. I looked stunning, thanks to working out again—flat tummy, clear skin, and long slender and slightly tanned legs; I was drop-dead gorgeous. Winking at myself in the mirror, I put my housecoat back on and sprinted to the upper deck.

Placing my empty glass on the bar table, I unfolded my sunglasses and walked toward a lounge chair next to Jay. I tossed off my housecoat and lay down, looking up. The good thing about sunglasses is that no one can see what you're looking at; in my case, I was looking at Jay to see if he noticed my figure as I sat right by his side. He turned his head once to notice that I had sat down next to him and looked back to my brother. It only took two seconds for him to quickly look back at me and check me out. I knew the final step to wrap him around my little finger and get him to put sunscreen on my back.

Flipping onto my belly I asked, "Oh, Jay, would you mind putting some sunscreen on my back? I don't want to burn, and I need a little help."

"Sure!"

I was glad to see how eager Jay was to help; smiling, I handed him the sunscreen beside me. Just before he put his hand on me, I stopped him.

"Just let me untie this first."

I pulled the knot of the top from the lower back to make sure my entire back would tan. I only guessed that he blushed when I heard him clear his throat and take a deep breath. I thought it was cute that he was a little nervous, but I guess that was because our families were right there. I really didn't care if they watched. It was about time they learned Jay wasn't afraid to touch or get physical with me. Wow, that sounded dirty.

Anyways, the sunscreen was warm from sitting in the sun all morning, and his hands were just as warm, and soft. I was amazed at how gentle he was; he didn't just slap it on and wipe it around like cleaning a window, and he carefully massaged the sunscreen on my back slowly and peacefully. It didn't take long, but it was the closest thing I was going to get to sex for a while.

"Could you tie my bikini back up please?"

"Yeah, that seems pretty important."

Just as I thought he'd walk away, he whispered in my ear, "Maybe tonight I could take it off."

Jay winked at me and surprise, surprise! I winked back, smiled, and blushed. He walked over to the bar for another tropical drink while I stayed in my chair and soaked up the sun.

Chapter 9

I wasn't tanning too long because I'd already tinted slightly from California. I stayed in the summer sun for only an hour or so. Flipping at half an hour, I finished my piña colada faster than I had hoped. Jay returned, texting someone while doing so. I took off my sunglasses and squinted, thinking he might be texting someone who isn't me. Putting my sunglasses back on, I got up and left the upper deck to put my hair in a ponytail. I wanted to take a dip in the ocean for a while before I changed into my regular clothes to relax and play board games all day.

I dumped almost everything in my purse of makeup and hygienic things on the bathroom counter. Mascara, lipstick, eyeliner, and various blush brushes fell to the tiled floor, clacking and clicking everywhere. Scrambling through the makeup mess, I found the condom I had snuck in uncovered, exposed. I prayed no one could see it from the room. I left it there for about five seconds when I found a bunch of twisted ponytails right beside it.

"Is that what I think it is?"

I turned my head while grabbing the condom and hiding it by my side.

"You think what is?"

"That was a condom, wasn't it?"

"Please." I rolled my eyes. "It's an alcoholic wipe, good for cleaning cuts and disinfecting stuff."

"I don't think cleaning wipes say 'Trojan's Lubricated Condom.'"

"It said 'Torgo's Lubricated Cleansing wipes.'"

"It said 'Trojan's Lubricated Condom.'"

"Fine! You got me, who cares!"

"Why did you bring a condom?!"

"Just 'cause."

"'Cause why? Were you planning for us to use that?"
"No."
"Then who?"
"Ummmm..."
"Look, as much as I'm glad you have a condom, I'm a little freaked out you brought it. Can you imagine what would happen if my dad or your mom found that?"
"I know! It's just—"
"Just what?!"
"*I thought if we were going to die, I'd spend my last night on earth with someone I've always loved!*"

My eyes widened at what I couldn't believe I just said. Jay looked equally surprised; shocked was more the expression he had. I gasped, looking twice as shocked as I was before. Quickly looking down, I ran into the bathroom, slamming and locking the door behind me. I thought saying it would take the weight off my shoulders, when all it did was double, and leave me having to face Jay again as just a best friend again.

My iPhone buzzed next to the sink, somewhat making me jump off the closed toilet seat I was sitting on with my hands covering my face. Picking it up, I saw a Facebook notification which said Jay had recently updated his status. Bringing the phone closer to my face, I read the status, "So happy to see my Jilly Bean again! These few weeks with her in Hawaii are going be some of the best days of my life, and something I don't think she will ever forget. And what better time to spend with her than a week before her birthday! <3"

I smiled and liked his status, my way of saying I'm sorry and that I made a mistake and that he may forgive me. I couldn't stay in the bathroom forever, so I unlocked the door and peeked into the room. Jay had left, and I walked out to the door that led to the front of the boat. I placed my hand on the door and slowly pushed it open. Jay was at the edge, looking down at the ocean. Looking at his phone, he realized that I liked his status. I didn't say a word when I took a step out to see what he'd do. All Jay did was smile and put the phone back in his pocket. He sighed and put his arms over the railing and leaned over to look at the sea ahead.

"You really meant it, didn't you?"
"How'd you know I was here?"
"I heard you open the door, but you really did mean it."
"I did. Every word."
"Why?"
"Camp with you was the best days of my life. I've never had anything like it happen since."

"But why did you say you loved me?"

"I love you for your personality and your smile, your looks, everything. No one has the perfect things you have that I've always been looking for. I've always wanted to tell you, but I was scared you wouldn't feel the same, or just be friends."

"We're already more than friends."

"Best, I know. I've wanted more than that since we left camp."

I walked up to join him by the railing, leaning forward to look at the sea with him.

"What would it take for us to be more than best friends?"

"Anything."

Jay reached down into his pocket and pulled out his phone and typed in something.

"What are you doing? Is this really the time to be texting?"

"Just give me a minute."

He put his phone away and unhooked the necklace he was wearing.

"I want you to have this."

"You're lucky wolf tooth necklace? I can't take this!"

"No, really! I have another one."

"Why give me your necklace?"

"Check your phone first."

I looked at him as if to say "What are you up to?" But I picked up my iPhone anyways; I was surprised to see that I had two notifications, one message from Jay and the other from Facebook.

"Check your messages first," Jay asked.

Despite the fact that he was making sure I look at my phone, it made me feel a little uncomfortable. I opened my messages to find that I'd been charged ten dollars for going over my monthly usage.

"You knew I had to pay ten dollars because I went over my limit? Thank you, I think?"

"Oh! Damn! It didn't work. Anyways, what I was going to say was . . . I have always loved you too. I was too scared to say it, thinking you wouldn't feel the same way about me as I feel about you. I love you, and nothing would make me happier than for you to be my girlfriend and that I can be your boyfriend."

"You . . . you love me?"

"Always."

"I don't know what to say."

"Say yes."

I looked down at the necklace and looked up at him and smiled perhaps the best smile I've ever given. I gave him a big hug and whispered, "Absolutely."

He lifted me up by my hips and spun me around twice to the middle of the deck before setting me back down. I put my arms around his shoulders and neck. I laughed and put my head below his neck and above his chest. With his right hand, he tucked my hair behind my ear.

"Can you promise me something?"

"What?"

"Please don't leave me."

"I never will."

I kissed his neck and returned to where I was before while Jay and I swayed in one spot for a few minutes. Jay pulled back a little bit and lifted up my chin to his level and took one hand off my back and placed it behind my neck. He pulled me closer, and I smiled just before he kissed me. I moved my hands behind his neck and enjoyed a kiss I would never forget. It was a good two minutes later he released me from his lip lock. We stayed a centimeter away from each other and kept our eyes closed, which made that moment feel like forever. All I could think of was that I was never happier to be with someone than I was with Jay right now. I wouldn't trade the world for this moment or for anything that I wanted. All I wanted now was to be with Jay now and forever, knowing that we loved one another; nothing could make me feel so wanted, loved, and beautiful than when I was with him and in his arms.

Chapter 10

"I was planning to go for a swim. You wanna join me?"
"Sure!"
I was all ready to go, but Jay had to grab his swim trunks. He met me out by the back of the boat two minutes later.
"Wait! I'll get my brother to take a picture of us jumping off the deck!"
"Good idea."
I fetched my brother and camera to take a picture of us and told him to take a couple of pictures. I was a little scared I'd trip and ruin it, but I was feeling much more confident when Jay grabbed my hand.
"One!"
I started.
"Two!" Jay said.
"Three!" We said together and ran. I could hear at least three clicks from the camera as we ran, and finally, still holding hands, we jumped off the deck with our hands together, feet tucked in the air, and yelling "Woohoo!" We looked at one another for the last second and smiled before hitting the cold water. I forgot to put in my ponytail, but I'm sure that would just make the picture look even better. I tucked in the water so I wouldn't torpedo deep into the sea. I let go of Jay's hand underwater and opened my eyes accidentally. I was surprised that I could see and saw Jay had opened his eyes underwater too. Still a few meters underwater, I swam up and kissed him while the bubbles from the jump surrounded us and sped to the surface. I let him go and started swimming up since I was starting to want to breathe again. Jay started coming up too; only he was much faster than me and passed me in a second. I had to deal with trying to see past the bubbles but finally made it to the surface, popping up like a balloon from underwater, bursting out of the sea.

The Tail of an Angel

"*Woooo*, that was fun!" Jay yelled.

"*Wooohooo!*" I repeated after Jay.

"How's the water?" my brother yelled down to me from the boat.

"Beautiful! Come on in!"

"I'll be right back!"

I looked over at Jay and smiled again from the kiss underwater. It wasn't as amazing as I thought it would be because it was really salty, and although the salt water didn't hurt my eyes, I still wanted to look at the fish under water and take a few pictures with the underwater camera.

"Hey! You wanna grab the scuba gear I brought and check out the fish?"

"I was just gonna say that! Let's go!"

I swam forward, and I felt a little odd the faster I swam.

"Is that your top over there?"

I looked back and saw my red top just floating away behind us.

"Oh my God! Please grab my top!" I yelled to Jay while covering my chest. He swam up to it and plucked it out of the water and threw it to me. I managed to get the neck tie on, but the lower back tie I couldn't reach, let alone tie up.

"Need some help?"

"Just with the back."

I heard him swim up behind me and tie the back together, while also doing a good job of making sure the ties wouldn't come undone.

"Thanks."

"No problem."

I swam up to the dock of the boat and waited for Jay to grab the scuba stuff. I pulled my top half on the deck and kicked my legs into the air as if I were a model. I placed my arms down, bringing my hands together for balance.

"*Cannonball!*" Josh yelled as he leaped over the edge of the deck, making a massive splash that hit me like a wave.

"*Wait for meee!*" Jay's sister yelled when she jumped over the edge too. It sounded like they were having fun. I could hear them cheering behind me and swimming up to jump back over the edge. Rolling my eyes, I looked up and saw Jay bringing the scuba stuff down to me. He smiled when he came down to the deck and laughed at the position I was in when he threw my stuff at me.

"You look . . . good!"

"Thank you!"

I pulled the rest of me on the deck to put the scuba gear on: oxygen, flippers, goggles and so on. I was ready in less than three minutes, and so was Jay. I didn't look too bad in the scuba gear as I saw from the reflection in the wavy water. I snapped the goggles on, put the oxygen piece in my mouth, and gave a thumbs-up to Jay to say I was ready to go.

"There's a waterproof microphone in the goggles, so we can talk underwater."

"Cool! How deep are we gonna go?"

"Doesn't matter, just as long as you do so slowly. If you go too fast, the pressure may kill you or break your oxygen tank."

"Anything else I should know?"

"Watch out for sharks, take lots of pictures, and stay close to me. If you get too far from me or the boat, you might get left behind."

"Sounds good. Let's go!"

I jumped in before Jay and tucked the camera into a pocket around my waist. It was built into the strap that was around me, holding the oxygen on my back. I waited for Jay to swim down next to me.

"You coming?"

"Just making sure nothing's gonna fall off or break."

"Well, hurry! The fish won't take photos of themselves!"

He descended next to me, and we began our decent into the teal blue salt water. I snapped a few pictures of blowfish, clownfish, regal tangs, and more. Already, I had pictures of over forty different fish and only three of just Jay looking at shells at the bottom. I was fascinated at how much light there was at the bottom of the ocean. I was pretty sure, though, this was just a high level of the ocean; the actual benthic part of the ocean was sure to be too deep, dark, and pressured.

"Let's get a picture together by that rock!"

"I'd rather get one by that chest thing over there."

"What! You found a chest!" I yelled at Jay in excitement and sprinted for the chest. I grabbed my camera and immediately took a picture of the chest, then another with us and the chest. Who knows what it might have inside, clothes, a mask that turns someone into a love crazy maniac, gold, gems, anything!

"What do you think is inside?"

"No idea. We should take it to the boat."

"You stay here while I take a look in that cave over there for more treasure."

"Okay."

I stayed, guarding the chest while Jay swam into a cave and disappeared into the darkness. I saw only darkness for miles, until I saw a shadow pass over me. I looked up to see nothing and looked back down at the sand, when another few shadows passed by. Scared to look up, I slowly raised my head and saw a group of great white sharks. At least five of them were circling above me; three were massive male sharks as determined by their darker gray color and larger fins, plus one female that was light gray and smaller than the males. There was also a baby shark swimming with the female. I forgot that it was the mating season for the sharks and that Jay and I were swimming right in the center of the traditional mating area. No wonder the chest was never recovered and taken to the surface; those people must have been eaten.

"Jay, you better finish up in there. There's something you better see."

"One second. I got to bring out a few more small chests I found in here. It's a gold mine! We're gonna have to make a few trips down here!"

"I don't know about that right now."

"Why?"

"Just get your ass out here and help me!"

"Is something wrong? What is it?"

"*Great white sharks! Ahhhhhhh!*"

"I'll be right out."

I tried to hide behind the chest, but it wasn't too big and the sharks were getting closer and closer.

"Hurry!"

Two of the sharks sped to the bottom right beside me; they were so close, the side fins of the sharks touched my shoulders. I closed my eyes, so scared and fearful I was going to get eaten.

"Oh my God! There's seven sharks!"

"What are you talking about? There's only five!"

"There's more."

"What do we do?"

"Very slowly swim to the boat."

"What about the chests?"

"Leave them! We can get them later."

"Look out! There's one behind you!" I screamed at Jay. The shark swam right up to Jay and nudged his arm that went right over the shark.

"Wait! These aren't great white sharks, they're just lemon sharks!"

"How can you tell?"

"The head has a bunch of dots on it. They're one of the friendliest sharks in the ocean."

"Where did you learn that?"

"It's shark week, and I watch Animal Planet all the time."

"So if anything, we're not gonna die?"

"No, they're really nice!"

"Awesome!"

Two big males swam up to me, and I petted them as they passed me. It was really cute how they came right up and played with us. I laughed a bit at how Jay played with the baby shark and a male shark by throwing rocks and watching the sharks go after them like a dog getting a ball.

"Since when do sharks play with people?"

"Since other people probably played with the sharks on their own boats. That or they have no reasons to hate people."

"Let's grab those chests now that we're not gonna die."

"Sounds good!"

The one we took a picture with wasn't too heavy, so I carried it, and Jay took all the smaller chests he found in the cave. The sharks pushed me over and swam away as a group. It seemed odd, but I could swear they were smiling when they left.

"Look! They left some teeth here!"

"Oh, wow! Let's grab a few to show everyone!"

I didn't have too much to carry, so I put a few in my camera pocket. Slowly, we swam up to the surface.

"Wait! I want to get a picture of the sharks! I'll be right back!"

Quickly, I caught up with the sharks and took a picture with each one, and when I wanted to take a picture with one new shark, it didn't cuddle up to me. I realized in horror that it was really a great white.

"Swim! Swim fast to the boat!"

"Why? What's wrong?"

"I took a picture with a great white, and it wasn't cuddly!"

"*Noooo!*"

The shark was speeding up slightly but not enough to kill him; I caught up but was still worried that the great white would eat us. It was indeed catching up to Jay and me, with pitch-black eyes, meaning he was ready to kill us.

"We can swim faster now since we're really close to the surface!"

"*Go, go, go!* It's right behind us!"

It was only a meter or so behind us, and the shark was coming faster and faster. I was so sure we were toast. I blasted to the deck of the boat and got out just in time when I saw the shark's fin dive back down, knowing it was not getting any person for lunch today.

"Get out of the water! There's a great white shark out there!"

My brother was a good swimmer, and Jay's sister was just as fast. Thankfully, they got to the boat just fine.

"Hey, what's that?" Jay's sister asked.

"We found some chests down there!"

"Well, then open them, of course!"

Jay ran to grab a hammer and smashed the lock on the big chest to break the lock.

"By the way, Jay and I get what's inside since we found it."

"Whatever," Josh and Jay's sister said.

I moved the chest off the deck and onto the upper deck so any contents wouldn't fall back into the shark-infested waters. I smashed the lock four times before it finally broke and fell off. Jay used a crowbar to pry it open and carefully opened the lid and revealed the treasure within. It was a bunch of gold jewelry, diamonds, gems, and a tiara fit for a queen. The other chests had gold, what looked like vials of potions, silver coins, and a journal with the name of a guy I couldn't read. We took all the treasure in our room and evenly divided it between us.

"I want the tiara!"

"Only if I get half the silver coins."

"Okay!"

This went on for about two hours, counting the quantities of treasure we had and admired the items we kept. I got the journal because I wanted to know who had written in it and why. Both of us were happy with our things, and we chatted about what we might purchase with this fortune.

"I'm gonna buy a diamond necklace, a car, and new clothes and save some of it for opening a cafe when I'm older."

"I'm gonna buy a watch, a car, and a party for all my friends and save some for college."

"Oh, right! I should put some aside for that too."

"And of course, I'll keep some for myself."

"Same here."

The day went by rather quick after that. I played Yatzee, Uno, Twister, Scrabble, and more games with Jay and my family for hours. No one went back into the water thankfully, but we took a dip in the hot tub, which was fun. Sipping on nothing but fruity drinks all day and devoting all my time to being lazy made the day perfect for spending time with Jay. Not much happened after our time in the hot tub; we just passed the time playing games, talking, and watching dolphins jump beside our vessel. Nothing could've made that day any better; then it ended as I watched the sunset again with Jay and closed it with a kiss.

"Isn't it amazing that we get to do this for five more days?"

"Totally! I'm never getting tired of this view."

"It is a nice sunset."

"I was talking about you."

"You're so sweet."

I'm pretty sure I looked good still wearing my bikini, but I put on a tropical silk scarf that I wrapped around my arms and back. I looked flawless when I twirled in the ocean breeze.

"So I think you should check your Facebook quick."

"What's with you and checking your phone? I might just throw it overboard."

"Trust me; you're going to like what's on Facebook."

I grabbed my phone and clicked on the Facebook app to see my notifications. Clicking on the world icon, I was taken to Jay's profile page when his latest status said, "In a relationship with Jillian Leigh Verbicky."

"You changed your relationship status?"

"You bet! Now everyone we're friends with knows that you're my girlfriend."

He kissed my forehead and smiled down at me.

"What about my status?"

"I changed it for you when you were playing Yatzee."

"Thank you! But what did your parents say? My mom can handle it, but I think your dad won't be as supportive."

"He was just fine with it, maybe even proud that you're my girlfriend."

Jay looked up to the upper deck to where his dad was nodding back at him and flicking something beside him. Suddenly, all the lights on the boat turned off and "I Don't Want to Miss a Thing" echoed from behind us.

"Can I have this dance?"

"This has got to be the most romantic thing anyone's ever done for me."

"Is that a yes?"

"Of course!"

Chapter 11

He grabbed my hand and pulled me into the middle of the deck and put both of his hands on my waist. I placed mine on his shoulders and smiled when he pulled me close to him.

"Is your dad okay with this? Or is he gonna watch us dance all night?"

"I don't know. Everyone could be watching us dance right now for all we know."

"No, we're not!" I heard my brother yell.

"Looks like they are."

"Doesn't matter. I'm just glad to be here right now. I don't care if they watch. All I know is that I want to spend tonight dancing with you."

"Would it be weird if you kissed me in front of our families?"

"Let's just wait until they leave."

"Good point."

One by one, everyone went to bed while more slow songs played. Everyone left but his dad, who, I was hoping, would leave soon. I looked up to him trying to say, "Please leave Jay and me by ourselves. I promise we won't do anything that involves either of us being inappropriate." Jay looked up at his dad right after I did; his face showed an obvious "Please go."

"Dad, please?"

I saw his dad cross his arms and squint at us. Jay shook his head at his dad, and in return his dad smiled and left.

"How'd you do that?"

"I'm just good at convincing people to do things for me."

"Like what?"

"Oh, I probably shouldn't tell you."

"How about if you show me?"

"Maybe when we get back to our room."

I grinned at him while the song ended and "Lips of an Angel" by Hinder began.

"Oh, I love this song!"

"I thought you would, but it's the last song on the list."

"You made a playlist of slow songs?"

"Believe it or not, my sister Kayla did."

"She has good taste."

"I bet you do too."

I raised my eyebrows, and just as the song ended, I put both my hands behind his neck. Once again, Jay put his hand on my face and ran his two fingers down the edge of my cheek and jaw. Bringing his hand on my cheek again, I leaned into it and put my one hand over it while looking down to the left.

"Is something wrong? You look like you're gonna cry."

"I'm not gonna cry. My eyes are just really dry, is all."

"It doesn't look like it,"

He wiped a tear from my cheek with his thumb and let it fall it the wooden floor below.

"That one just escaped, is all."

"Why are you sad?"

"I'm not sad. I'm just so happy I could be here, dancing in the moonlight on our way to Hawaii."

"Together?"

"Absolutely, everything seems so perfect."

"It's not perfect yet."

"What? Why not?"

"Close your eyes."

"Don't punch me in the face."

"I'm not going to punch you in the face."

"That's what my brother would say, and then he'd punch me in the face."

"Just close your eyes, and don't open them until I say so."

"Why?"

"Look, do you want me to leave right now? Or are you gonna close your eyes?"

"Eyes are closed!"

He put both of his hands behind my neck and used one to fix my hair and put it behind my ear. He played with the other side of my hair for a minute and put his hand back down on my hip. He stopped for a second and placed a flower behind my ear. I could tell because I felt the stem being pushed into the side of the hair and fixed to face forward. I felt him pull me closer to his chest and face, touching his nose on mine for a few seconds and inhale. He was so very close to my lips, only the cupid's bow of my lip was barely touching his. I opened my mouth a bit and inhaled too, almost breathing him in, and matched his lips on mine. So warm and moist! He put both of his hands behind my neck, bringing me closer while I wrapped my arms around his neck in return. It was so quiet; the screaming silence of the ocean was the only thing I could hear, and the breeze of the ocean twisted around me, blowing my hair behind me and out of sight from Jay's eyes. Even though I felt the flower blow out of my hair, neither of us saw it as both of us had our eyes closed. Completely by accident, he bit my lower lip; I stopped the kiss for a moment to laugh while he apologized, "Maybe I can make up for it."

"How?"

"Keep your eyes closed."

The very second I closed my eyes, he kissed me, returning to where we left off before he bit my lip. Jay pulled my neck, forcing me to turn my head slightly, and he slipped his tongue over mine. I thought I tasted something close to cherries, but I doubted it. I simply enjoyed it and French-kissed him back. Not only was he a talented kisser, but he knew all the buttons that turned me on somehow. He worked a few of his fingers into my hair and pulled another down my jaw very slowly. With one of my hands, I gently pulled his hair playfully, silently saying, "Don't stop." All I could feel was him touching every single inch of my neck, and I loved it. Nothing else could've felt more right other than what we were doing right now. He slowed down his French kiss to leave his tongue in twisted with mine for a little bit longer. I knew he would stop soon when he finally gave me a regular kiss; I lengthened the moment by French-kissing him once more. Barely nibbling his lip, I kissed him for only a few more seconds before leaving him with a final lock for five long seconds. Finally letting go, I kept my eyes closed for a second and opened them to catch him staring in my eyes. Little did he know, I'd already fallen in love with those hazel eyes long time ago. It wasn't hard to tell that he was falling in love with mine; light silvery blue and dark steel lines of sight is what everyone loved, and they showed the very inner beauty that was shown in a cover of bikini and golden brown hair. His jet-black hair reflected the moonlight shining above us, clear as day, yet black as pitch. I couldn't decide what looked better, Jay, or the clear night sky filled with stars and a full moon.

I looked up at the sky, resisting his addictive stare, and saw that the starry sky looked far better over the ocean.

"Wow," I whispered to Jay.

"You can say that again."

"I meant the stars."

"Ohhh, oops."

"Look!"

I pointed to the stars I saw ahead of the boat. For all I knew, those stars were there just for us. I'd never seen the moon so big and bright before then on that night. I was tempted to stand on the front of the boat and watch the stars, and I couldn't resist. Still in awe at the view, I left Jay in the dust behind me and stood at the railing at the front of the boat.

"I love stars."

"Me too."

I looked back at Jay walking up to join me at the edge; the look on his face told me he was in awe too. Only he wasn't looking at the stars, but looking at me, before looking up at the stars at the edge with me.

"Jay, are you crying?"

"No."

"You're crying."

I wiped the single tear that ran down his face with my scarf and asked him what was wrong.

"You look even more beautiful in the moonlight."

"You really mean that?"

"Every word."

"So how would describe this whole day then?"

"Perfect."

With both my hands over the railing, Jay grabbed the one closest to him and held it over the edge with me. I put my head on his shoulder, and he slipped his other hand on my hip and pulled me right next to him and placed his head on mine. He was right about it being a perfect day; nothing could've gone better. The ocean calmed down and leveled out as far as the eye could see. The wind picked up again and blew my hair around behind me again. It made my shoulder cool, which quickly became very cold. I shivered twice and tried to keep as still as possible, which didn't work. It was as if Jay read my mind and removed his arm from my hip and placed it around my shoulder. I smiled when I looked over and saw his arm around my shoulder, bringing me closer and into his chest where I felt safe and warm.

"Is that what I think it is?"

"It can't be."

I silently gasped just leaving my jaw to drop open, when I saw something green and blue dance across the sky. It goes by many names, but I simply knew them as the northern lights.

"That can't be right. The northern lights can't be seen this far south."

"I thought that too!"
"It must be really rare then."
"It's got to be."
"But why tonight, and in the middle the ocean?"
"Why not? And what better place than in the middle of the ocean?"
"It's kind of . . ."
"Nice?"
"Nope."
"Pretty nice?"
"Try again."
"Romantic?"
"There you go."

    I didn't have any words to describe it, but "romantic" was probably the best. The lights were so clear and colorful; it was like a rainbow across the sky, and the moon was shining through it all. They danced everywhere around us; it was like they had a mind of their own, going wherever they pleased. At one point, the lights descended lower and lower to the ocean, until they were so low that they touched to salty waters below. The lights slithered on the water, spreading like fire and infecting the water as it absorbed the lights and slowly making the water glow like the very stars in the sky above. I've never seen anything like it happen before; only that it was the most breathtaking thing I had ever seen. The lights still above the water started getting closer to the boat and rising up higher and higher on our vessel. I looked over the edge as much as I possibly could and looked in absolute amazement at the lights engulfing the entire boat in glowing light. The lights below where I stood twisted up around my feet, twirling around my entire body.

"What the . . ."
"Don't move! I'll be right back!"

    He sprinted to the door to the lower deck and popped out ten seconds later with my camera and his own.

"Smile!"

    I smiled perfectly as the lights made me glow as if I were on fire. He took a few pictures with my own camera and a bunch with his. It was so bright outside; he didn't even need to use the flash. When I didn't hear any more clicks with his camera still facing me, I was a little suspicious.

"What are you doing now?"
"Making a video."
"Why are you making a video?"
"Because this is the most incredible thing I've ever seen!"

I smiled and twirled, holding the scarf with two hands, and danced with the lights surrounding me. I must have looked like an angel when I did so, because Jay's jaw dropped as he said, "Wow!" After about three twirls in the light, I slowed down to let my skirt flow and flare around me. I stopped when I faced him at an opposite angle and smiled again and laughed at my own actions. I flipped around again but not toward the camera, but right to the railing where the view of the lights and stars was the best.

"Well, don't just look at me. Make sure you get a view of the northern lights!"

I walked up to Jay and pulled him by the collar of his shirt to the edge of the boat.

"Hey! Easy there. This is my favorite shirt!"

"Maybe tonight I get to take it off?"

"Maybe."

"Hello, sky's up there!"

"Oh, right."

Then he pointed the camera to the sky and the stars hiding behind the lights, all on camera for us to keep forever.

"Beautiful, isn't it?"

"Breathtaking."

"Flawless."

"Stunning."

"My girlfriend."

"Thank you! But you should edit that later. My friends would freak out if they saw that on video."

"And they wouldn't say anything to see you glow or that the northern lights are all the way down here."

"Probably."

"Why don't you put this on?"

Jay turned the camera on me and gave me the tiara we found in the chest. Still glowing, I picked up the tiara and only adored the beautiful emerald in the center of it. Jay plucked the tiara from my hands and placed it on my head. The northern lights twirled around me even more when he put the tiara on; only, the lights suddenly stopped in the air, and I began to rise off the boat.

"What the . . ."

"What are you doing? Come back down!"

"I can't! Do something!"

"I can't reach you! You're too high!"

"Help me!"

"Just stay calm! I'll think of something!"

He was still videotaping me. I stopped rising into the sky about four or five meters above the boat. I was still freaking out, and the lights around me moved farther away from me and spun all around in a circle until I saw nothing but bright light all around me. I was no longer glowing, but shining like the sun, which made me seem heavenly.

"What's going on up there?"

"I don't know! Whatever it is, it's really bright and warm for some reason."

The light turned from bright color to bright baby blue. It started closing in on me, and strings of blue light grabbed me and soaked into my skin. Looking at my hands and feet, I saw they had slowly turned blue and the blue light spread all over until the sphere of light around me engulfed my entire body, making me as blue as the sky. I shone like a sun, and it made my back really sore. It felt like two massive needles were stabbing me in the center of my back, and I was burning like I was being branded.

"Jill! Why are you glowing blue?"

"I have no idea! But my back is killing me!"

"You're never gonna believe what's behind you right now."

I couldn't see a thing behind me from the blinding light. I closed my eyes for a minute and opened them. I was looking at the camera and asking Jay what was happening now.

He said, "You . . . you're . . . Ummm."

"Well, tell me!"

"You're blue!"

"Thanks, Captain Obvious! Tell me something I don't know!" I yelled as I started to slowly float back down to the boat.

"You're floating back down!"

"I know! Thank God!"

I didn't feel any different from I felt before; only my back was incredibly sore, and I was still blue, but not as bright. Jay was still filming despite this crazy scene; only, the second I touched the floor, I think I passed out. I opened my eyes in Jay's arms, and he asked if I was okay. Saying I was fine, I got to my feet while Jay took two steps away from me.

"What? What's wrong?"

"I don't know."

"What do you mean, you . . . ?"

Suddenly I felt even warmer and looked down at myself to see my skirt had fallen off, and I let go of my silk skirt when I saw the blue light I was glowing in started receding up to my face. The blue light, one string at a time, pulled up from my legs and arms and skin; I slowly started feeling cold until my face was the only thing shining. Jay's jaw dropped again, and he nearly dropped his camera.

"What now?"

"Your eyes..."

"My eyes what?"

I looked down to the water over the edge and saw my eyes glowing bright neon blue, like the color I was before. I touched my face in awe at what my eyes looked like and gasped at what was behind me. A pair of white angel wings, the same color of my real eyes, at the tips, still shining like I was before. The reflection in the water was only half as good as I think I really looked in real life. I got up from my knees and rose to my feet and looked at Jay.

"What happened to me?"

"You're an angel!"

"I kind of look like one, don't I? What's with my eyes, though?"

"No idea, but you look amazing."

I examined the rest of my transformation into a flawless angel, wearing a flowing white dress that glittered at the tips with a blue neck that spread more blue designs as it got further down. The necklace had somehow changed from a tooth to a heart-shaped locket; it was silver and engraved with the words "The Blue Angel."

My eyes were still glowing because Jay kept reminding me that my eyes were still bright blue.

"How long is this going to last?"

"I don't know. How'd this happen?"

"I always wanted to be an angel, but I didn't wish for it!"

"Ummmm... funny story!"

"What did you do?"

I walked up to him, leaving a trail of blue footprints behind me, with a look of anger on my face.

"I saw a shooting star earlier, before we danced, and wished that I'd fall in love with an angel."

"And now I'm a freaky glowing angel because of that!"

"You have no idea how beautiful you look!"

"Let's just keep this video between you and me. No one should ever see me glowing with blue eyes."

"Agreed."

"So now what?" I thought for a minute.

I looked up at the sky again and saw the stars starting to move, something that almost scared me as much as my glowing eyes. The stars joined together to form a bunch of letters and then organized into three words. With the camera, Jay and I looked into the stars that said, "Kiss the Angel."

"You didn't wish for that, did you?" Jay asked me.

"Maybe."

Jay grabbed my hand and brought it up to his chest level, when a blue diamond ring appeared on my ring finger. I took my hand, still holding his, and looked in amazement at the flawless ring. Inside the diamond was a tiny golden halo, and I looked up at Jay and saw that his eyes were now glowing blue as well.

"Your eyes are blue too!"

"What? My eyes are hazel!"

"Look! Give me the camera!"

I videotaped his eyes, but his reflection was too small to see from the front so I pointed to the water below.

"Well! That's kind of freaky."

"Welcome to my world, hun."

He looked back at me and asked for the camera, saying that he wanted to try something.

"I want to see if this works."

"What works?"

"I think I know how to get you back to normal."

"Wait! Before you do, I want to see what's in this locket."

"Okay."

I took off the necklace and looked at the locket for an opening. I managed to find one and pried it open with my nail. I clicked it open and found nothing for a second.

"Wait, what's that!"

Jay pointed to something as a small blue ray turned on in the locket, and a small girl came out of it. It was a projection, of course, and I soon realized it was me, only that the girl spoke to Jay and me.

"Treasure the love you two share. Tonight is the night that love will be all you have for one another. Never forget the time you have together and this wish the spirits of the lights have given you. It is your choice, if you want to be like this forever, or return to be yourself with a kiss. You will return to be an angel one day, only for now are you given this blessing. Do not fear the future for you two, embrace it. Or face it alone."

The little angel floated back into the locket and it closed itself.

"That was on video, wasn't it?"

"Yep."

"Are you ever gonna shut off that camera?"

"Only when you decide."

"Decide on what?"

"Do you want to be an angel forever?"

"Of course not, I want to be a regular person with normal blue eyes!"

"Then kiss me."

I thought about it for a moment, thinking of my future as an angel or as a normal human being with Jay. I looked up and quickly kissed him. I began to feel a little better and opened my eyes when I let him go.

"Your eyes are still blue," Jay told me.

"Yours aren't."

"Maybe it didn't work."

"Look behind you!"

I watched my open angel wings start to lose their brightness and evaporate into the colorful lights I was surrounded with before. I felt my dress disappear, but my bikini top and skirt returned quickly; the silk scarf was back in my hands. The blue eyes I had were turning my skin blue again and leaving my body in the same strings as they had entered, only leaving behind the blue diamond ring to always remind me of this. I whispered to the sky, which was turning back into the plain moon and stars before the lights arrived. It was like it never happened to us at all.

"You can shut off the camera now."

"That is gonna make the weirdest video I've ever seen."

He finally put down the camera and made sure I was complete and back to normal. I assured him I was fine and showed him the ring left behind.

"Let's not wish on any shooting stars for a while."

"Oh yeah."

I walked back to the door with Jay, walked to my room, and crawled into the bed still in my bikini, with a video showing the crazy night we had together.

Chapter 12

I remembered I had to brush my teeth, so I had to get back up and go to the bathroom. My stuff was all cleaned up from earlier, except that the condom was missing.

"Jay, where's the condom?"

Never thought I'd say that.

"I don't know."

"Seriously, I don't want my parents to find it."

I mumbled as I spit out the toothpaste and rinsed out my mouth.

"Oh, your parents aren't gonna find it."

"Did you hide it somewhere?"

"Sort of."

"I'll find it later."

Jay was already sitting on the bed putting a hand on his back, showing that his back must have been sore. I knew just the thing to make him feel better.

"Is your back sore, Jay?"

"A little. It's nothing though."

"I know just the thing!"

"What's that?"

I walked up to him wearing my black tank top and red bikini shorts. Putting my hands down on either side of him, I said, "One of my legendary back massages of course."

"I don't think it'll work."

"Believe me, I give the best back massages."

"I guess I could give it a try."

"Oh, and you can't wear a shirt," I said as I grabbed the bottom of his shirt and ripped it off over his head, before he could even stop me. "Now roll over on your stomach."

"Why?"

"I can't massage your back just sitting up."

"What are you doing?"

"I forgot to mention I have to be sitting on top of you to give you the massage."

"This seems kind of sexual to me."

"Is that a bad thing?"

"Umm..."

"Thought so. Now just relax. Your back will feel much better in no time."

I climbed up on top of him, got comfy, and started my massage. I saw him try to move his head over to see what I was doing.

I looked down and whispered in his ear, "I don't bite... hard."

I got back up on my knees and worked around his shoulders and lower back.

"This doesn't feel too bad actually."

"I told you I'd make you feel better."

I continued working on his shoulders and middle of his back. I felt at least three knots in his back, two on each shoulder and one on the right side of the center on his back. It took a few minutes to fix them, but I finally got those knots out one at a time. I was sure there were no more knots for me to get out, so I just continued my freestyle massage wherever I pleased.

"Are you sure you don't know where my condom is?"

"Positive."

"Then what's this?"

I reached down under the pillow where a tiny orange square was sticking out. I pulled it out and showed the empty package to him.

"It wasn't me."

"You're wearing it, aren't you?"

"Nope."

"I don't believe you."

He flipped over onto his back and said to me, "I swear, I am not wearing the missing condom."

"How can I be sure?"

"Only one way to find out."

"I'm not having sex with you."

"Please?"

"No... Wait... you just admitted you're wearing the condom."

"Shit."

"I knew it!"

"So what are we going to do about it?"

"Nothing."

"Pretty please? What was all that on the deck then? That we both wished for something, and they both came true! Plus you had the most beautiful blue eyes."

"I still have blue eyes, Jay, not glowing or anything."

"I love you, Jill! And I just want to show it by spending tonight with you."

"I'd rather actually sleep with you than 'sleep' with you."

"I know you want to."

"I think you're a little tired."

"You're already on top of me."

"Only because you rolled over."

He pulled himself up to my face and pushed the hair behind my ear again.

"I want this to be a night you'll never forget."

"Forget about it."

"I don't want to forget what happens tonight for the rest of my life."

I whispered back to him, "I scared about my first time."

"Don't be. You'll be fine, I promise."

He put his hand behind my neck and pulled me down flat on top of him while he lay out on his back. I stuck my arms out beside his head on both sides to prevent me from lying completely on top of him.

"It'll be fun."

"I love you too, but I don't think I can do this."

"Believe me, I'm a little scared too, but we can be scared together."

"I can't do this, Jay! I just can't."

"Let me show you then. I'll do everything."

"I don't think you can do anything that will change my mind."

"I want to see how beautiful you look without that bikini on."

"Keep trying, babe. It's not going to work."

"I know everything that can turn you on."

"Nope."

"I can make you feel amazing."

"Nope."

"I'll show you all the tricks I know."

"You're a virgin. What tricks could you possibly know?"

"Most of it will be freestyle."

I got up on my knees; sitting straight up, I rolled over away from Jay, saying without words "I'm not having sex with you anytime soon." Jay got up from the bed and walked to the washroom.

"You may as well just toss that condom in the garbage."

"Just wait!"

I heard what I thought was some sort of spraying and saw him pick up his shirt from the ground outside the bathroom. I got up from my pillow and then the bed. I walked up to the bathroom door he had closed and asked what he was up to. I stood there for a minute, still waiting for an answer, until the door burst open and Jay picked me up and carried me around the room.

"Put me down! I'm in no mood to be carried right now!"

"Just relax."

"Do I look relaxed right now? I don't think so, so put me down!"

"Not until you kiss me."

"Fine, whatever."

I kissed him for all of three seconds and demanded I be put down.

"Is that . . . Chocolate Axe you're wearing?"

"How nice of you to notice."

"How did you know that's the only scent that turns me on the most?"

"Just a guess."

I was put down gently on the middle of the bed, completely flat, while he climbed on top of me on all fours.

"Please spend the night with me?"

"Only on one condition."

"Anything you want."

"You'll never leave me?"

"I will love you forever and always."

"You really mean it?"

"Every word."

I closed my eyes and smiled when I looked down to the side of the bed at the opened condom wrapping, thinking about whether or not I should really do this.

"You'll never forget this."

"I sure hope so."

"I'll do anything and everything you want."

"All I want right now is for you to take off my shirt."

He reached under tank top and flipped it right up and over my head.

"You're wearing your bikini top."

"I didn't say I was going to make it easy for you."

"Fine. Just means I get more time undressing you."

Lucky for him, under my bikini top was another bikini top and two bras, then another bikini top. I think it was gonna be pretty fun for him.

He untied first bikini and tore it off.

"Another bikini top?"

"Surprise."

"Am I gonna be doing this all night?"

"Wasn't that the plan?"

I raised my shoulders and chest up in a slow motion making it look like I was being lifted up by a string. He pulled off the second one with ease and discovered the bra beneath it.

"This is ridiculous."

I laughed and let him unhook the back with two hands. Congratulations! It's another bra.

"This better be the last bra!"

"Only one way to find out."

"You're such a flirt."

"Is that necessarily a bad thing? Also, show me that one-handed trick you're so famous for."

"I don't think it's all that famous."

"It is to me! It just so happens to be one of my biggest turn-ons."

"Really?"

I pushed him up and over on his back and sat on top of him, placing my hands on the head of the bed above him.

"Oh, and I happen to be really strong and flexible, just thought you should know."

"That's good to know!"

I lowered my face closer to his, and only inches from my belly, he put his right hand on my warm back, and clicked the metal hooks once or twice until I finally heard them snap off.

"How on earth did you do that?"

"I figured it out."

I kissed him, still above the rest of him while he pulled the bra off and threw it on the floor. I was still wearing my shorts, and he was wearing pants. The second he pulled me down on top of him I raised right back up and starting pulling down his pants. I couldn't pull them off since he was wearing a belt. The stupid belt got in the way, and I couldn't get the damn thing off.

"Having troubles?"

"Is your belt a Rubik's Cube by chance? 'Cause it's totally not coming off."

"There's a safety latch that you got to pull to unbuckle it."

"Where did you get this? Why not just put on a normal belt?"

"I didn't say I was going to make it easy for you."

"Well, isn't this fun! You're just lucky I'm really patient."

"Whatever."

I figured out the stupid safety latch and pulled the belt off and accidentally slapped him in the face with the tail of the belt.

"Oww! What was that for?"

"Ha-ha-ha! I'm sorry. It was an accident."

"That's gonna leave a mark!"

"Oh, you're gonna be getting a few more marks tonight, only not as painful I think."

"Is that a good thing or a bad thing?"

"First one, then the other."

"You're crazy!"

"And I'm proud of it. Sometimes you got to be a little crazy."

"I wasn't expecting my first time to be this crazy."

"Well, what were you expecting?"

"Not as painful and more, ummm, physical things."

"Be patient. This isn't going to take a few minutes you know. I wanna make it last."

"Wow! That sounded dirty."

"Just wait until I finish that over there."

I pointed to a package of cherry Jolly Ranchers and asked, "What are those for?"

"You'll see in a minute."

I grabbed the package and ripped it open, throwing away the wrapping around the cherry candy and tossing it in my mouth.

"Seriously, why are you deciding of all times to eat some candy?"

"Close your eyes."

I lay down on top of him and French-kissed him with his eyes still closed. It was warm and even better than before. As the candy melted on my tongue, I accidentally let it fall on his; getting it back was the hard part.

"Can I have my candy back please?"

"Nope. This one's mine. Get another one."

"I want that one back. I'm not getting up to get another one."

"If you want it, come and get it."

Jay smiled and stuck out his red tongue with the candy on it. I squinted and kissed him again, fighting to get it back in my mouth. I didn't even know there was such thing as a tongue fight, but it was really fun. Eventually, Jay kissed me like a normal person, and I dived right in and got it back on my tongue, where it belonged. I laughed as I said, "Got it," and pulled his pants right off.

"Hey, I want that candy back!"

"Too bad! 'Cause it already dissolved on my tongue. You're not getting it back."

"I can try!"

He flipped me onto my back again. I really tried to push him back over, but he had me pinned down by my hands. I couldn't get up no matter how hard I tried. I couldn't even kick because he was sitting on top of me. I was absolutely pinned under the grip of his strong hands.

He wasn't going to play fair, and neither was I. I pulled my chest up to kiss his neck and loosen the grip on my hands, I'm sure he'd get a hickey two minutes later. He still smelled like Chocolate Axe, which made me feel all right to be under him. I could only keep sucking on his neck like a vampire so that he might let me go. He let out a rather loud exhalation as he released my hands and brought them down to my hips. Finishing up on his neck, I looked up to see that he was busy trying to get my shorts off while I flipped him over twice, thinking he'd be on his back. But he went off the bed, and we crashed onto the floor.

"Ouch."

"Now I know how you felt when I threw you off the bed."

"Only I had a softer landing."

"Please get off my legs, it hurts."

"My bad."

"How strong are you? You managed to flip the both of us off the bed!"

"Thank my Zumba instructors."

"I will!"

I got back on my knees and threw Jay back up and onto the bed.

"Did you just throw me on the bed?!"

"Yep, so?"

"Wow, you're strong. Are you okay?"

"Maybe you could help me up. My shoulder landed on a pointy hook from one of my bras."

He grabbed my hand and yanked me up onto the bed.

"Which shoulder did you hurt?"

"My right one."

I twisted to show him the small indent the hook made in my shoulder that was starting to get really sore. He examined it and asked if it hurt when he touched it. I replied that it didn't hurt too much. He leaned down and kissed it, hoping it would make me feel better, which definitely did.

He worked his way up my shoulder and kissed my neck, similar to how I had done before I knocked us off the bed. I closed my eyes and put my hand just below his jaw and turned my head backward to fall on my back with Jay on top of me again. Thinking he would take off my shorts, he grabbed my hands and pinned them down again; only this time he made both of my wrists crack.

"Hey, take it easy. I don't want to wake up with something broken."

"I guess I don't know my own strength."

"Try to keep that strength under control, will you?"

"No guarantees."

Releasing the harsh weight of my hands, he still kept them pinned, and I couldn't get back up, but I didn't want to. He laid down the rest of his body on top of me when he switched to kiss the other side of my neck. The side he left felt warm and a little sore in one spot. I was pretty sure I was going to get a hickey there when I woke up tomorrow. Everything from his waist down was not even close to touching me. Even when I raised my hips as much as I could, I was still nowhere close to touching his. He got up from my neck and kissed me, still keeping me pinned and trying to get his hips down on top of mine. If only he would let go of my hands, I could push myself up enough to bring his hips down, and his shorts off; the last thing he was wearing. I could tell he wasn't planning to release my hands and arms anytime soon; I was trying to think of a way to get his warm and strong arms off my own. Still French-kissing me, I pushed my hips up as high as I could and finally fit them together; something clicked in his brain that he should take off his boxers, just as I hoped. I was the one who wanted to take off his shorts though, if he ever let go of my hands.

"Can you let me go now?"

"No, why?"

"I want to take off your shorts."

"Oh, yeah, absolutely."

He let go of my hands. I brought them together and rubbed my one wrist with my other hand. Twisting the wrist, I held the hand for a minute while opening and closing my hand, stretching and twirling it.

"Your hand is sore, isn't it?"

"A little bit. It's not as bad as you think it is."

"You'll be okay?"

"Just as long as you don't hurt my wrists anymore, anything else is okay."

"So I can hurt you anywhere . . . else?"

"Within reason."

"Sounds good to me."

I turned my head over to signal that he should get off me and roll over on his back. It was just another thing I didn't actually have to tell him; my body language was all the talking I wanted to do after that. Before he rolled over, his pulled the blanket under him, over me and slipped under the cover next to me. I rolled over rather quickly on top of him, smiling like I was a kid in a candy store, and started pulling down his boxers. He pushed up against me, up until the waist I was sitting on, and kissed me when I pulled off his boxers slowly as he French-kissed me. Pulling up my hips to slip off his boxers, I pushed him down with my one hand back on his back, both of us completely naked; nothing could've felt more right than me on top of him.

I returned to kiss his neck on the way down to lie on his stomach and pushed my waist on his. He worked his hands from my back to my hips and pulled my ass harder on him. Both of us inhaled in sync the second he pulled my ass on him; my eyes widened and blinked twice. That made me pull back off his neck.

"Whoa."

"I was just gonna say that," I whispered back to Jay.

He kissed my neck, exactly the way I did and pulled me down onto him. Stuck between his shoulder and neck, I gasped as silently as I could, but was far louder than I hoped. I was sure he heard or felt on his skin every breath I took. Hearing only his breathing and my own was the best thing I ever heard beside my favorite song. I was worried that our parents may have heard the crash earlier when we fell off the bed, but nothing indicated that they were coming downstairs to see what we were up to. He released the grip from my neck, giving me the chance to French-kiss him again; only he flipped me over by my hips. I laughed as he did so and looked down for a second to make sure he was actually wearing the condom whether it had broke; thank goodness he was wearing it, and it was in one piece. I'd never been so glad to see a condom. I couldn't believe what I was thinking. I also thought that I probably didn't need it since I was already on the pill. I shook my head slightly to get my mind back to right now and not on something else on my mind.

I wrapped my arms around his neck and pulled it down to me, maybe too hard I thought when I heard his neck crack a few times.

"That didn't hurt much, did it?"

"Nope. It actually felt good."

I smiled with my eyes closed and continued to bring his head down to kiss me again. I grabbed the scruff of hair behind his neck and pulled it up gently and playfully; it made him smile before he returned to kiss me, and I played with the rest of his hair. I ran my entire hand through the side of his hair and brought it up to the front, completely turning his hairstyle from stylish swept part to a mess that made it look like he just got out of a tornado. I realized then why everyone has such messy hair after they have sex. With one of his hands behind my neck, he pushed the other hand slowly down from my chest to my belly, hips, and behind my back, pulling it up to his chest. I felt like I was rising up like a vampire; I felt like there was nothing under me and something was pulling me into the air. I just forgot that he was lifting me up. He brought his face lower to where I couldn't see it. I turned my head sideways, like I was gonna say, "Whatcha doing?" He kissed my belly, lowering me down to the bed, and kissed it again. He slowly worked his way up my stomach and just above my cleavage, stopping at my neck. I knew then that he figured out that my neck was the one place that turned me on the most. He pushed his waist on top of mine again. I gasped the minute he put his lips a centimeter away from mine, taking my breath away. He just remained at the top of my lip, hardly touching it, and not close enough for a kiss. He only opened his mouth and breathed me in; he took my oxygen away without me trying to stop it. It was the best feeling I ever felt the entire night, just him breathing out and me breathing in. Only a minute or two later, he took a bigger breath, stealing my air again, forcing me to inhale through my nose when he kissed me. I thought this was one of the tricks he had mentioned before. I was impressed.

Again and again he pushed his waist on top of mine, making me gasp every time. Under the covers, it got so warm and sweaty; I felt a bead of sweat drizzle down from my forehead down to my cheek and slithering down my neck. It wasn't long before my chest was slightly wet and my neck was still dripping with sweat from my forehead. I saw the sweat rain down from Jay's head as well; only his gathered to drop from his chin and bottom lip. He pulled up for a minute to wipe the sweat off his head, and using a part of the blanket, he wiped the sweat from my head. Only when he returned to look at me, two drops of sweat left his lips and fell to my neck and down between my breasts. I brought him lower and gave him a normal kiss, with a hint of salt on my lips. Another drop of sweat fell to the bottom of my lip, but it was nowhere near entering my mouth; it simply slipped to the middle of my lower lip and didn't move down at all.

He used his pointer finger to wipe it off my lip, letting it fall to my neck below. I smiled at him, a way of saying "Thank you for not letting your sweat fall all over me," and kissed him the same way as before. His back was far sweatier than mine; since he was closer to the top, he got all the heat enclosed in the blankets. When I felt the sweat behind his neck drip down to his back, I brought my hand up to the back of his hair, slightly cooling his neck. He picked up the speed he kept on top of my waist, and I went crazy. I bit his lip a lot harder than I was planning to. I was sure it hurt him a little too much, but he only embraced it, laughing. I theorized that me hurting him only felt good to him. I don't know how he thought pain and pleasure were in the same family, but I didn't care, since if he liked it, I'd only hurt him more. My eyes rolled back into my head when he pushed my legs open and lay down on me harder than before. I squeezed his neck so tight that for a minute I thought I had strangled it.

"I totally didn't mean to strangle you!"

"Are you kidding? Do that again!"

I squeezed his neck, not enough to cut off his oxygen, but enough to make it a little hard for him to swallow; and then he whispered in my ear "Don't stop." I was quite concerned at his amusement to pain, or real physical pain. While I was still grasping his neck, he French-kissed me in a much harder and in a slightly different manner than before, twisting his tongue all around my mouth instead of just in one spot. I released his neck to enjoy the kiss, until he gently placed both his hands around mine, pressing down and choking me. I hated to admit it, but it felt really good.

"Doesn't that feel amazing?"

"It does! Why does it feel so good?"

"I have no idea."

He pressed harder on my neck. It was still feeling incredible. He grabbed a Jolly Rancher and tossed it in his mouth. I immediately rose up and kissed him to get the candy, fighting to get it in my mouth. He pushed me down hard onto the bed saying, "It's mine." He pinned my arms down again to make sure I wouldn't steal his candy; it wouldn't be his for long. I pushed up on his chest, forcing him to let go my hands and pull me up by my back, sitting straight up but still under him. I found my chance to steal the candy and took it in a matter of seconds.

I said, "Too slow," and lay back down on my back with my arms behind me, relaxing and showing my victory. He shook his head at me and literallyjumped on top of me and hit me hard at the waist. Instinctively I gasped, tilting my head back and closing my eyes for a second, when I felt him slip into my mouth and take back the candy.

I was starting to get angry, but I had no plans to take it back when I noticed him accidentally swallowing it and saying, "Shit." I wasn't gonna get the candy back, but he was gonna taste like cherries and I couldn't argue with that. I pulled my hands down his back; he was still sweaty but inviting since he still smelled like Chocolate Axe. He pushed his waist on mine much faster than before, and it felt so good; it was almost starting to hurt. This continued for about five minutes, and I could only hear him breathe out and in on top of me. I tilted my head to let him bite my neck. I thought he was gonna kiss it, but he bit into it like a vampire. I was likely to get bite marks on my neck. I opened my eyes and looked over at his neck and counted three hickeys I gave him and a bruise from the belt on a bite mark. The worst part of the marks was trying to hide them tomorrow. I had an urge to push up on him harder and faster and embrace his hands pushing down on my belly. My breathing slowed down but was louder than usual, his as well, but we continued to push our waists harder into each other.

Finally, he slowed down to just one more thrust into me, making me scream quietly; it sounded similar to a laugh mixed with a silent cry. His was far more quiet than mine—a plain silent scream just above my lips. I touched his chest which was the only thing that separated him from me as he had lowered the rest of his body over me. He placed his top lip on mine, closing his eyes the exact same time as me—staying there only for a minute to enjoy this moment as if it were our last, and sealing it with a kiss. He finally rolled back over and sighed as he put his boxers back on. I reached down to put my underwear back on and put my head on Jay's warms chest, which was still a little sweaty. He was breathing pretty hard, showing that he seemed to be quite exhausted.

"You tired, sweetie?"

"Duh, aren't you?"

"Not really. I have a much higher stamina than you."

"I can tell. Was it worth it?"

"Hell, yeah! I'm so glad we finally did this."

"Me too. Told you I could convince people to do what I want."

"When did you say that?"

"A second ago."

"Oh, right."

"And just like that."

"Shut up! And hand me my tank top."

I put my tank top back on and cuddled up to Jay and lay still on his bare chest. He pulled me closer to him for the final time tonight, while I placed one hand on his chest and the other on his shoulder. I kissed his neck and said, "Goodnight, Jay. I love you."

"I love you too, Jilly Bean."

He kissed the top of my head and turned his on the pillow to go to sleep; following him, I closed my eyes, feeling our hearts beating in sync. He took my breath away, I took his, and in the end, I should've said goodbye once more to him. I didn't know this would be the last time I'd see him forever. The moments in our lives shouldn't be measured by the breaths we take, but by the times our breaths are taken away.

Chapter 13

I woke up after what seemed like minutes, but it was really the next morning; time flies when you love the person you're with. I saw that Jay was still dead asleep, with no chance of waking up anytime soon. It was the best time to take a shower and smell amazing, just in time for Jay to wake up and see me, looking beautiful and smelling like a goddess. I moved ever so slowly to get up off his chest without waking him up. I looked back once, still getting up; then deciding that he wasn't gonna be getting up that easy, I jumped off the bed and ran to the bathroom, slamming the door. I stopped dead in my tracks to listen if he was getting up, but I heard no rustling from the room. So I undressed and went for the shower, shampooing my hair and conditioning it—the regular routine of my shower, when I heard Jay run into something in the room. I listened for a minute and heard nothing. Then I heard him slam open the door so fast I didn't even stop showering until he ripped open the curtain to the shower and hopped in.

"Jay! Get out of my shower!"

"Surprise!"

"Get out, or I spray shampoo in your eyes."

"Not if I kiss you first."

"You dare, and I'm gonna f—"

He kissed me and pushed me up against the wall of the shower, pulling my hips on his. I tried to pull away, but at the moment my muscles hadn't kicked in and I was like soft candy in his hands, sweet to taste, and melted in his mouth. He was stronger right now than he was last night. I was helpless and couldn't escape his grasp on my back and neck. The body wash that I had on a minute ago ran down my legs and chest, ending up mostly on Jay as he was squeezing me on top of him. I put my hands on his hips, with water being the only thing between us, washing the sweat off from last night and erasing the crazy hairstyles we had from under the hot covers of the bed.

Letting go of my lips, he stayed on top of my upper lip, while the hot water ran into my mouth from being slightly open. He closed his mouth for only a second, then opened it to let the water run over his face as well. I opened my eyes with the water still rushing all over me, making it hard to see the look on Jay's face.

"You should get out of the shower now."

"Aw! I don't even get to shower myself?"

"If you haven't noticed, this is my shower time, and I'd appreciate if you took your own shower."

"Are you sure?" he said as he grabbed a cloth and started washing my back.

"All right! That's enough. This is your last warning!" I yelled and laughed as I poured some shampoo into my hand.

"You dare and I'll throw that bar of soap at you."

"I'll take my chances."

I tried to throw the shampoo in his eyes, but he ducked and the entire glob of shampoo in my hand landed in his hair.

"Thanks for washing my hair. How did you know I needed to shampoo it today?"

"Very funny, Jay. Rinse it off and get out."

"Your hands are already in my hair. Why don't you just massage it in, and I'll get out."

"Fine! Whatever."

I worked the shampoo into his hair for a minute and turned him around to the showerhead to rinse off his hair.

"Thank you."

"You're welcome! Now shoo."

"Oh, and one more thing."

"What?"

"Close your eyes."

"Don't throw the soap at me."

"I'm not gonna throw the soap at you. Jeez, just close your eyes."

I closed my eyes, taking a step forward when he pushed me. I felt something cold on my head for a moment, and then his hands ran down my hair. He just put some shampoo in my hair and worked it into my scalp.

"I thought I told you to . . . to . . . Wow! That feels good."

"See? Isn't this fun."

"Mmm hmm."

He ran his fingers into my scalp all the way to the front and slowly, pushing his fingers forward, he brought his hands to the back, leaving my entire head in a thick lather of foam and shampoo. He reached around my tummy and pulled me up to him, directly where the showerhead was pointing and squeezed me like I was a teddy bear. I was tempted to smile and laugh a little while he pulled my chin around ninety degrees and kiss him again while the shampoo in my hair rinsed behind me, sliding down his back and legs. As the water splashed our faces, I kissed him back, even though the water was hot and steaming up the air around me. Placing his hand gently on my neck, he pulled me back to him for only one more kiss before he finally got out. I shook my head when I saw him steal my towel and laugh while he closed the door. I washed my face and got out, wiping my hair down a few times and twisting it to get most of the water out. My body was still dripping with water; I popped my head out of the bathroom and yelled to Jay that I needed my towel back.

"You really want my wet towel?"

"No, toss me a dry one please."

"What do I get in return?"

"I don't punch you in the face twice when I get out there."

"Ah . . . okay!"

He threw me a small hand towel from in the dresser next to the bed.

"Isn't there any bigger one I can use?"

"That's the last one," he said as he grabbed a big one and dried his hair.

"You don't even have that much hair to dry! I have way more!"

"But it's already wet!"

"You're being a real Moby Dick this morning, you know that?"

"And which one rocked your world?"

"Ugh."

I heard him laugh when I slammed the door with the tiny hand towel to dry the rest of myself off with. When I was finished, I tried my best to get the towel all around me, but it left a bunch of my belly exposed. I held up my towel with one hand and opened the door with the other hand.

"Does your towel fit?"

"Barely! Thanks for asking."

I walked up to my bag and stopped to think about whether or not I should bend over and risk my towel coming off.

"Why are you staring at your bag?"

"I don't want to lose my towel when I bend over to get my clothes."

"Do you want me to grab them?"

"That'd be nice."

He tossed up my clothes to me; I caught them one by one with my free hand but let one drop to the floor by accident. I reached down to pick it up, and the towel fell right off, damn.

"Don't look over here for a minute!"

"Why? Is there something . . . hello!"

"I said don't look!"

"Well, I've already seen you naked, twice actually."

"Three times in one day sounds a little slutty to me. Now throw me a bigger towel."

"I don't mind."

"Well, I do! Just toss me the one you used to dry your hair!"

"I don't know if I want to."

"Hurry up! I'm freezing!"

"I could warm you up if you want."

"By grabbing my towel."

"Fine."

He threw the towel at me, right in the face, and I wrapped it around me in a single second.

"You know, you look much better without a towel on."

"Sure I do."

"Really, you look beautiful. You don't need any wings to look like a blue-eyed angel."

"You really mean that?"

"Always."

I smiled and kissed him on the cheek before returning to the bathroom to get dressed. This was sure to be a good day after an amazing night and crazy morning. I just prayed that no one had heard us or would find out about the last night for the rest of the cruise and vacation.

The weather outside was slightly overcast; I put on a T-shirt and sweater with plain blue jeans. Jay was wearing something similar; only he looked better with just a T-shirt. I grabbed my iPhone off the dresser and found that there was a new status update from Jay on Facebook.

"What did you post on Facebook?"

"Oh, nothing much."

"If it has anything to do with last night or my shower, I'm gonna kill you with my bare hands."

"Well, you might as well read it first."

I opened Facebook and clicked on his update; it said, "Having the most amazing time with Jill on the cruise! Let's just say this is one vacation neither of us will forget for a very long time. I've never been more happy to be her boyfriend, and that's how it's gonna stay. Love you! <3"

"Awww! That's the best status anyone's ever posted about me!"

"I really meant it. I decided not to mention how beautiful you look without any clothes on 'cause our families would toss us off the boat and leave us there."

"Yeah, that sounds about right."

I kissed him before opening the door and looked over at him when I realized something was terribly wrong.

"Oh shit! You better cover your neck!"

"Why?"

"Here, I'll take a picture just to show you."

I took pictures of both sides of his neck and showed him the five hickeys and bite mark that looked way darker now than they were last night.

"I don't remember getting five hickeys!"

"I do."

"How many do you have?"

"Well, take a picture and show me."

"About seven and a bite mark, really? You get seven, and I have five!"

"Is that a bad thing?"

"It is if my or your parents see them."

"I have a few scarfs we can use."

"Do you have one that's not too girly?"

"Maybe. Let's go."

I ran back into the room, throwing all my stuff all over the place, searching for the scarfs I'd packed. One was black-and-white and a little sparkly; the other one was just plain gray.

"Take the gray one."

"Okay."

I wrapped mine around my neck, which covered every single hickey just fine. Jay couldn't figure out how to tie his scarf like mine, and I helped him put it on like a normal person.

"Didn't anyone ever teach you how to tie a scarf properly?"

"Nope."

Once I double-checked my scarf to see that everything was covered, I headed out with Jay to the upper deck.

"Morning, you two! What was that crash I heard last night?" my mother asked us.

"I rolled off the bed."

"Oh, you okay?"

"Yeah, I'm fine."

"Why are you wearing a scarf?"

I looked around for a moment saying nothing but um-m-m-m, while Jay said, "It was pretty cold by the lower deck, so I grabbed a few of her scarfs to wear."

"Oh, I see. I just thought you were hiding something, was all."

Jay's mom returned to her seat, while I sighed in relief that she didn't ask any more questions about last night. I sat down next to Kayla and Jay, who were sipping on some smoothies and chatting among themselves.

"So what's really under the scarfs?" my brother asked.

"Nothing."

"That's not what it sounded like from what I heard last night."

"You didn't hear anything."

"You guys had sex, didn't you?"

"Well . . . uhh . . . ummm."

"I . . . ummm," Jay and I both grumbled.

"Show me your neck."

"You can't tell Mom or Jay's parents. They'd kill us!"

"Sure, sure, now show us your neck."

I pulled my scarf down just enough to reveal three hickeys and a bite mark, while Jay had four on one side.

"Wow! You guys are crazy."

"You know those are gonna last for a week, right?" Jay's sister commented.

"Are you serious?"

"Yep, and we hit Hawaii in six days or so. You're gonna have some serious explaining to do when you guys take off those scarfs."

"Isn't there any makeup I can use to cover it?"

"Absolutely, but it's not waterproof."

"That will work! Do you have Jay's shade by chance?"

"Oh yeah. It's the kind that adjusts to anyone's skin tone."

"God bless you!"

I moved my hand in a cross motion while Jay asked my brother about what they were up to the other night.

"Umm . . ."

"You too?"

"Only we were quieter."

"You can't be serious."

"I'm serious. If my mom was on the lower deck, she would've known something was up in your room."

"I didn't think we were that loud."

I put my arm on Jay's shoulder and told him that we were pretty loud.

"Just keep it down next time, will you?"

"Sure."

I grabbed a smoothie from the bar and walked back to the table with Jay and played a game of scrabble. We were only twenty minutes into the game, when it started raining, ruining my hair. I pulled my scarf down as it got wetter.

"Bring it to the lower deck!"

"Why?"

"'Cause I said so!"

"Calm down. I'm bringing it."

Josh and Kayla brought the game while Jay and I ran into the lower deck and took off our scarfs. I tossed it into the room and walked into the room my brother was staying in, because ours was a mess.

"Oh wow! You guys have so many hickeys!"

"Jay got a little carried away."

I looked up at Jay and shook my head.

"Then why am I the one with seven, hmm?"

"Let's just play some scrabble."

I wasn't focusing too much on the game, just playing simple words because I was more worried about the rain outside and the shade of the clouds coating the sky. The game didn't take too long to finish up before I asked Jay to talk in private.

"Keep it down, you two! Ha-ha!"

"Shut up, Josh, or I'm telling you guys had unprotected sex!"

I heard a whisper from Kayla that she thought he had put on a condom. I laughed when I heard them start to argue and close the door.

"Really? I get to see you naked again? It's not my birthday though?"

"No, you idiot. I want to tell you about something that's been worrying me for the past few days."

"Well, sit down with me. You can tell me what's on your mind."

"It's stupid, but I've been having a terrible nightmare almost every night since this entire vacation began."

"Is that you that keeps twitching in your sleep? Why didn't tell me earlier?"

"'Cause it didn't seem important until it started to rain."

"I'm not following where you're going with this, but I'm listening anyways."

"Well, my nightmare starts out fine, good weather, tanning in the sun, nothing much, until it starts raining on the boat. It rains so much and the clouds turn black and the wind starts blowing waves over our boat. Soon we have to evacuate the boat, and you and I get stuck on board, and we jump off into the ocean and swim up to a raft."

"Good! We escape together and safely! What's so bad about that?"

"A massive wave tosses both of us into the water, and a current pulls you to a different raft with my mom on it while I get pulled away, too far to get back to where you are. Then the rest of it is just me floating away into the night in shark-infested water, never seeing you again."

"It was just a dream, Jill. It's not real."

"I know. I just don't want to lose you!"

"You're never gonna lose me, I promise."

A tear managed to escape my eye, as I looked away, trying to hide the fact that I didn't want him to see me cry.

"Please don't cry." He wiped the tear from my face and kissed my forehead.

"No matter what happens, I will never leave you. Look at me; do I look like I'll leave?"

"What if it's not your choice?"

"I will spend the rest of my days looking for you. I'll never give up on us."

"You really mean it?"

"Every word."

"You'll never leave me?"

"I promise to love you forever, and always."

"Always?"

"Always."

He kissed me and made all my troubles disappear. I gave him a hug and stopped the last of my tears from running down my face and down his shirt.

"I bet the weather has even cleared up by now."

"I sure hope so."

I walked out and went up to the deck to see that it had not stopped raining, but had got worse. The wind got stronger, and the sea began to get rougher the longer I watched.

"No . . . this can't be happening."

"It's not what you think it is. It's just a bit more rain."

"Does this look like a normal rainstorm to you? Those clouds are getting really dark! And that wind isn't going down anytime soon."

"We're going to be fine. I swear you'll be all right."

"I'm not too sure about that."

I gasped when a wave washed by my feet and another hit my legs on the deck.

"Come back in before you get swept away!"

I closed the door and ran back down to my room, where the floor was already a few inches deep in salt water.

"I'm just gonna pack my stuff, just in case."

"You're overreacting. Some water just happened to get into our room."

"Grab your things, guys! We're taking water on quick!" I heard my mom yell to us.

"This can't be happening! It just can't be!"

I packed my things very quickly; I was finished in less than two minutes when the water on floor was over knee deep.

"C'mon! We got to get to the top with everyone else."

The back deck wasn't too soaked with water, but the front was practically underwater. Another wave hit the very tip of the boat, making it turn eighty degrees on its side.

"Everyone get on the rafts!"

My mom got on her own raft with her stuff, Jay's parents were on one, and Josh and Kayla got on one, dropping into the water just fine. Jay and I got on one and dropped down; the raft spilled its contents and flipped us into the water. I looked around for Jay, screaming in the ice-cold water.

"*Jay*! Where are you?!"

He was floating on a suitcase, half conscious when I dragged him onto the raft.

"You . . . are you okay?"

"I'm fine. Just don't land on a suitcase next time."

I grabbed a paddle put of the water just before it started to sink and started heading for the group of rafts with the rest of my family. Jay just got up to sit up, when the worst was right behind us—a huge wave, sure to flip me out.

"Hang on!" Jay yelled to me.

I kissed Jay one last time and hugged him just before the raft was flipped completely upside down. I struggled to get to the surface of the ice-cold water. I blasted out of the water, freezing cold, screaming again in pain; only this time, the edge of a piece of luggage cut my arm, making it bleed far too much in the water behind me.

I looked around for Jay, who had not yet come to the surface.

"Jay!"

I swam back to my raft and flipped it up and threw my luggage in it; finding only my own bags made me worry more. I spotted Jay very far away, crawling into a raft with my mom.

"Over here! Wait for me!"

"There's a current pulling us back! I can't swim over to your raft!"

"I can't paddle over there! They sank!"

"You got to try!"

I tried using my hands, but it was useless against the strong current.

"You said you'd never leave me!"

"I won't! We will come back for you!"

"Don't leave me, Jay! I love you!"

"I love you too! But you got to hang on for a few hours. You won't be alone long!"

"I won't make it without you," I yelled, still crying.

"You got to be strong! I love you! And you got to hang on!"

"I can't do it alone," I said to myself, knowing he wouldn't hear it.

"You have to hold on, Jill, always."

It was the last thing he yelled before a wave pulled him out of my sight. I fell into a ball on the raft, giving up hope that he'd ever come back for me.

"Nooooooooooooo!" I screamed as loudly as I could, only hearing the heartless ocean in return.

This was it. My dream had come true. Jay was gone, and I was alone and freezing in the dead of night, watching the last of the boat finally swallowed by the evil blue sea; with a last flash of lights in the water, it was gone with no hope of being rescued. A flare was launched into the air about a kilometer away from me; they may find rescue, but I was doomed to a slow death in this godforsaken Pacific graveyard. The moon was the only comfort I could take in the journey I would continue by myself. I lost everything I ever loved—my family, my friends, my boyfriend—and nothing could give it back. Pulling the clothes out of my bag and changing gave me a bit more warmth; I put on my bikini underneath in case I needed to swim to rescue.

I looked up in the sky once more, straining to see another flare or a helicopter anywhere. The ocean had finally calmed down and was peaceful at last, the only time when I enjoyed the clear sky to the stars. I wiped a few more tears from my face, when something popped up out of the water: a chest that had all our treasures in it. Only I couldn't understand how it was floating. Nonetheless, I brought it on my raft and opened it. I found my tiara, the blue ring, the locket, the journal, and my camera plus Jay's. How this all got in the chest, I had no idea, but I was glad to have it with me. The one thing I was happiest to see was the locket. I thought it had evaporated with my wings. I opened it and found a picture of Jay and me, and on the back of it was written what wasn't on it before: "Always."

I cried tears of joy over the locket and whispered a thank-you to myself. A single beam of light, like the kind that surrounded me that night, escaped from the locket. Spinning around me once, it returned to the inside of the locket, closing it on its own. I put it on and laid my head down on some clothes for a pillow and fell asleep; I simply prayed that I'd be rescued by morning, with Jay holding me in his arms once more.

Chapter 14

I woke up curled up in my clothes, shivering; the sunlight was starting to keep me warm. I was in the middle of nowhere. I saw only the ocean in all directions; there was only one direction I wanted to go—home. I was really could tell where I was from time and direction on my own, looking at the position of the sun in the sky, I could make out it was eight in the morning, but with no compass, I couldn't tell what direction I was going. I couldn't even see if there was any fish I could catch and eat the best sushi I could ever get. I loved sushi, but I doubt I could even cut it open without a knife. I realized that I wouldn't be eating at all while I was on this raft, and even if I did catch a fish, I'd have to try and eat it with my bare hands and scale it with my teeth, which didn't sound like a good option.

Two hours went by, and all I saw was a bird, a few whales, and a group of dolphins that played together in the water, laughing and leaping around like the ocean was the best place in the world. Nothing could've cheered me up in the slightest, and I wished those dolphins would get caught and eaten in Japan.

I didn't say I was going to be happy on this raft; I hated everything that passed me, thinking this was the heaven on earth, and my slice of hell.

Time went by so much slowly as I was on my own; not even my iPhone could've helped me pass the time. iPhone? *Holy shit! My iPhone was in my bag! I forgot!*

I kept screaming "Oh my God I Oh my God! Oh my God! Oh my God!" until I opened my bag and found it in the sweater I'd packed in the last minute before the boat went down. I held it up in the air; it looked like I was holding it like an Emmy at the Oscars, letting the screen shine against the sun. I clicked the button on the bottom, and the screen lit up with 100 percent battery life.

"*Yes!*" I cheered and threw my hands in the air like on the cover for the movie *Platoon*. I was happier than I could even describe. I was speechless! I looked at the reception, and my joy diminished when I could get no reception signals. I tucked it away back into my bag, not using it once because of the risk that the battery life will drain, and I'd lose my chance of getting rescued. On my own, I grew even lonelier when three hours went by and the fish, whales, and dolphins disappeared. A terrible feeling in my gut told me it wasn't safe to be floating here, or that I was just getting even hungrier. The water here turned from light teal blue, to navy blue, and looked much darker and deeper. I had no weapons to protect myself from any danger I may face, like an unfriendly great white shark. I sat in the middle of the raft and tucked my legs in, shaking in fear instead of being cold, and wrapped my sweater around my arms. The water got darker and darker as the sun went down into the sky. It was about nine or so by this point, and I was positive something was under my raft. I looked around the edges and saw nothing, but something was stirring the water below. I should've gone back to the center, but I brought my head closer to the water to see what was in the water. I panicked for nothing when a small tropical fish splashed me beside the raft, and I splashed back in amusement. I almost lost my hand when a shark ate the fish right next to the raft, causing it to wobble on its side for a minute. I screamed for a second before it came back up to look for something else to eat. Unfortunately, it was lunchtime, and if I didn't get out of the way, I'd be next on the menu.

All I had for a weapon was some treasure, a tiara and some hairpins in my bag. I grabbed the hairpins and bent them to form a stylish knife with a handle made from a hair band and really sticky hair gel to keep it from falling apart. It was more of a spear at this point, because I tied it to a metal comb Jay had used but somehow ended up in my bag. I was ready to defend myself from anything that tried to eat me, and I would kill it and eat it first.

"Bring it on," I said to myself when I saw a shark fin rise out of the water and headed for the raft. I stabbed at the water, scratching the surface of the shark's head, when I saw three more fins circle my raft.

"Oh shit."

One shark bumped the bottom of my raft while I stabbed all around the raft, hoping to hit a shark. I felt nothing hit my knife in the water when I noticed a shark raise its entire head out of the water and try to take a bite of the raft. I turned to dodge its teeth and stabbed it in the eye, making it fall back into the water with its own blood starting to bring more sharks around it. Another shark took one more try at taking my raft down, but I sliced its head in one long cut, probably killing him since he stopped dead in his tracks and floated away on his back. It sank only moments later when the sharks started to rip apart the remains of the killer I stabbed. The frenzy made large waves around them, causing my raft to float away from the bloody waters that now stained the bottom of the raft, reminding me that I was not the biggest thing in this ocean. I grabbed my iPhone and played I Will Survive as I drifted farther from them, enjoying my victory over the sharks.

Being the highlight of my day, I watched the sunset as the warm sunlight left my side and the cool of night wrapped around me with the stars covering the sky once again. I fell asleep much easier with the knife by my side and an iPhone to give me light if I needed it. I made a pillow with my clothes and slept peacefully that night, feeling better about my safety even though my stomach roared with hunger. I'd catch something to eat tomorrow.

It was still dark when I woke up; the stars were still out meaning I slept for only a few hours or so. I don't know what woke me up, but I looked around the raft to see the growing length of the waves. I turned on my iPhone to look around at the water and put it back in my bag when it got harder to stay balanced. I started to panic more when I saw that there was something even darker than the sky in front of me, and I was heading straight into it very fast. At the very last second, I saw a huge rock and smashed into it, feeling water enclose me all around; then I blacked out in the water with an awful feeling of ice on my skin and the urge to fall asleep in the water. All I can recall is that I must have hit the rock, blacked out and sank into the water deeper and deeper while I felt the bubbles leave my mouth and rise to the surface; I closed my eyes and saw nothing else.

Chapter 15

I woke up, not in my raft with my stuff, but in a comfy bed, dressed in my bikini top and skirt. I got up, looking around the room in what appeared to be some sort of little cabin.

My head was sore, and I wasn't as hungry as I was the other night. I leaped out of the warm bed and ran around the room looking in my bags which had all my stuff in it and a note on the dresser, next to my charging iPhone. I sat down on the bed and read the note:

Dear Jillian,

You don't know me, but I know you. I've always known you. You nearly drowned after you crashed into a rock, knocking yourself out and sinking in the ocean. I saw that you were nearly dead, but revived you on the shore of this island. Your bags from the raft floated ashore, and the whereabouts of your raft I don't know. If you're wondering why you're in your bikini and skirt, it's because your clothes were heavy and freezing. If you kept them on, you would've frozen to death. You're welcome. Plus, the skirt looks really good on you. You're not the only thing in the sea you know. Don't swim in the ocean for a while, until shark breeding season is over. You have plenty of food in the kitchen if you're hungry, and a guitar to play if you get bored. I've looked everywhere for your family. I've found nothing so far, and I'm really sorry. Stay on the island, and you'll be safe here, and I'll do everything I can to find them, and make sure nothing bad happens to you, always.

Love, Seth.

Always . . . How on earth did he know about that? Jay was the only who said that to me; obviously this Seth guy knew me very well. I had no idea who Seth was nor had I seen him in a past life. I could sense this. "So, I'm rescued from a stranger in the middle of the ocean, who knows me well, even though I don't know him, and built a cabin on a tropical island for me? Who was this angel who saved me?" Whoever he was, I was thankful to him, and I needed to meet him. First things first though; I was starving and found the kitchen stocked with lots of food to eat. I discovered my favorite breakfast already made and steaming on the table, French toast and sausage with maple syrup. Where Seth had found this food in the middle of nowhere, I didn't know. What I did do was I dug right in and finished breakfast in a matter of minutes. If anyone had seen me eat, they'd say I looked like a hot dog-eating contestant, but with French toast and a single fork. Satisfied, I started to explore the cabin, which was more of an abandoned mansion by the looks of it. There were three levels to the house; the second level had a living room, my room, a bathroom, and a room with a piano. To my surprise, the piano was in tune, and I played an Adele song for a minute or two. I smiled as I left the second floor and walked up another flight of stairs to the third floor. There was only a couch, a flat-screen TV, and tons of movies to watch, some old, some new, lots of horror—basically every single great movie I'd seen and a few more. I ran as fast as I could down the stairs and looked around the first floor and the kitchen, with which I was already acquainted.

I found a room full of family-type heirlooms, treasures, and jewelry all in dusty glass shelves on the walls, and a clean picture frame with the photo of a shirtless teenage boy, standing by the ocean side at sunset; the photo looked similar to the one I took with my father. I guessed that it was Seth, and he seemed familiar to me, but nothing in my mind popped up when I thought of him.

One room was smaller but incredibly warm with just a chair and a sliding door that got warmer the more I approached it. I slid the door open, it looked out to a new deck that had a perfect view of the beach and sunset with a white umbrella, two lazy chairs, and a table. There were a few steps to get to the beach, and I walked down barefoot and dipped my feet into the warm waves on the shore. The cool sea breeze blew through my hair the way I loved, and transported me back to the memory of Jay and me watching the sunset. It was so clear in my mind; it was almost like Jay was right there, next to me just watching the sun go down, and the breeze messing up my hair, but all around me, leaving my skirt to sway as naturally as the tide pushes onto the sand and washes back out. I walked down the beach for a while, while I tanned a bit more in the summer sun, enjoying each step along the water's edge. I saw a flower not too far from where I was walking and picked it up to put in my hair. I looked back out to the sea and went out to about the depth of my foot, and held the lily in my hands. I closed my eyes and let a tear fall down on a petal of the flower, then splash into the ocean. I looked up and placed the flower in the water beneath me, letting it wash away in the ocean as a reminder that I was there. Alone and quiet, I watched the flower drift away slowly to the point where I could no longer see it. It went in the direction of the sun that sank into the sea itself. I walked back at twilight and reached the cabin at night, when I spotted only a single northern star. I gathered some wood from behind the house and started a fire on the beach. There was a match in the house, which came in handy. I ran inside and put on a sweater. I grabbed the guitar and walked outside and dragged a log as my seat.

    I was finally at peace with my anger at the sea; I was only strumming chords from "Summer Paradise" and humming along to the words that echoed behind me.

    "Singing La da da da da," was all I said in the entire song; when the chord came up, I heard a lower voice sing the same thing not too far away. I stopped humming and only played the chords to the chorus and heard someone singing the verse. I finished the song and looked back but saw no one behind me. I had a feeling that someone was on the island, singing a song I thought only I knew. I decided to call it a day. One thing was for sure, I was gonna find out where I was and who had been singing with me by the fire. He had a beautiful voice, but besides that, I didn't like being watched.

    I stayed in my bikini since the island was so warm; it was like Mexico all over again. I tucked the note into the drawer below it and saw the journal that I had from the chest. I didn't know why my curiosity peaked at that point, and I promised I'd only read one page tonight, since I was very tired.

    August 17, 2007, Friday

        I washed up to the shore of this island; my crew had perished in the ship I was traveling in. I had no trouble swimming, but the sharks were my biggest problem. I spent the last few hours building a shelter, quite small and a pathetic excuse for a hut. My bags washed ashore, and my radio needed batteries, so there was no way for me to hear about my disappearance. The plan was to find something to eat tomorrow; I have to rest tonight since the moon is the only comfort I can look at on my own. I won't give up hope of rescue this quickly.

This entry sounded a little similar to my story; only who wrote it was the real question. I wondered where they might be now. With that done with, I fell asleep with ease in the soft blankets and pillow I was glad to sleep on once again.

I woke up again, only feeling much better and well rested. I unplugged my iPhone on the dresser, with no bars for me to try and call my family. It wasn't hard to figure out that I wouldn't be getting any signals here anytime soon. With nothing better to do, I changed into exploring-type clothing to find out what else was on this island. I packed a lunch and other necessities as I was going to find out what was on every inch of this paradise. I found some sunscreen, since I'd built up a great tan already and took the door by the front out. The original exit led into a massive cave; it was so big and looked like someone had hollowed out a volcano, with the roof still a ways up from the roof of the house. It was still a little bright from a hole in the top and light shining directly at the sandy ground in front of the door. I decided to start with this cave and followed the sand to an exit carved out of the rock; before I went ahead though, I saw something off to my right. It twinkled when it caught my eye. I was drawn to it, as a moth is to a bright light; it went through a large tunnel and brought me to a cavern that had an edge before dropping off into a pool of water. I thought that it would lead to the ocean at some point, but it dropped down into something that must have resembled a grease trap, which, I guessed, was the light I saw a minute ago. I walked back to the exit and left the cave to the bright sunlight blinding me outside. I looked around at the breathtaking view, at a rainforest with all sorts of creatures running about. I took out my camera and walked forward, taking pictures of almost everything I saw. There was a path which was already walked on recently, and nothing passed the trail that that might trip me. Only vines and palm tree leaves fell to the ground ahead of me. I snapped a picture of a parrot sitting on a mossy rock; I tossed it a graham cracker from my bag and took a picture of it using its foot to eat it. I laughed and continued walking down the trail, snapping more pictures of beautiful flowers and birds flying over me. Something jumped on my shoulder and crawled across my back before leaping into the trees again.

"What was that?" I asked myself and looked around for a minute, finding nothing. I took two steps before something started playing with my hair, and I flipped around and saw a little spider monkey getting something out of my hair.

"What do you think you're doing?"

He pulled a small, scary-looking spider from my hair and ate it. Although it was kind of gross, I was glad to have a spider out of my hair. The monkey oohed and aahed a bit at me before stepping on my shoulder and sat there for a minute, playing with my hair some more.

"Well, aren't you friendly, you want a . . ."

I looked in my bag for some kind of fruit I'd packed and pulled out a banana. I didn't even have time to peel the banana before he wrapped around my neck and yanked the banana from my hands and leaped onto my other shoulder. It began to eat the banana.

"You're welcome! Can you show me if there's anything interesting on this island?"

He finished his banana and whooped at me; no translation was needed to tell me that he was saying thank you. He jumped down from my shoulder and yanked the bottom of my pants toward him. He ran forward a bit and turned his head back at me, so I followed him. He ran up a tree and started swinging from the vines above the path, forcing me to run to keep up with him. He took me into a thicker part of the path, while plants, branches, and flowers hit my legs, chest, and face with leaves shooting into my mouth. Spitting out all sorts of green junk, he stopped and screeched, hinting that I should stop. Taking the final pieces of fern off my face, I looked to where he was sitting and pointing to the view before my eyes.

"Whoa . . . this island seems much smaller earlier."

The view was of a huge forest with monkeys flying through the trees and a flock of Blue Macaws and tropical birds that flew up in a pink wave of feathers in the direction of the sea. This island looked about thirty kilometers long, and I couldn't see the ocean's edge from where I was.

"Any other surprises?"

He jumped on my shoulder and went back into the trees behind me. I followed him once more, while thinking of something to call him, a cute name, perhaps something that had meaning to me. He disappeared for a minute before he dropped right in front of my face, making me fall on my back instead of crashing into him. He turned around and pointed to a tall bush of grass. I pulled it aside and saw a bamboo shack that looked very new and had a Do Not Enter sign on the door. The monkey jumped in through the open window, which was only a hole in the bamboo wall while I opened the door to the shack. There was a light switch which I flicked on; the room took my breath away. The walls were coated with nothing but photos on shelves, and there was a smaller room which I couldn't see as the door was closed. I walked to the right of the room first, seeing what looked like photos of me, photos I'd sent to Jay and deleted later (How did he get those photos?). And there were more photos of my family, of my father.

I'd thought they were lost forever, assuming that my dad took them when he left; whoever had these must have taken them from my father himself. There was another one of me and my dad on a dock with my first fish; there was a photo of him and my dad next to it. There were even pictures of him and my brother. The left of the room had pictures of just one guy and what looked like his friends and family. I guessed once more that it was Seth, but I didn't recognize any of the people he was with. I saw a trophy cabinet with the lights off in the middle of the left wall and found the switch, and I quickly turned it on. Inside was something that took my breath away: a picture of me and my ex, a picture of Jay and me, and a far older one of what looked like Seth and me on a beach. I was no older than eight or so, and he looked about nine. Nothing I could think of made me remember the photo; it was at the top and a few things of mine were on shelves within it. The tiara I discovered, the ring, the necklace, and on a nail was the wolf tooth necklace Jay gave me. I was enraged that he took these things from me, and I even spotted my hairpin knife in the corner with the shark's blood still on it.

It looked like someone had been keeping a timeline museum of my life; I didn't know whether or not I should be scared, curious, or angry at this legacy. I heard the monkey yelling from the room with the closed door and hesitated to open it, wondering if my father would be in there, or Seth, or maybe even whoever I heard singing with me. I closed my eyes and slowly turned the doorknob; gently pulling the door open, I looked into the darkness of the room. Finally, reaching around the corner, I turned the light on. I saw the monkey sitting on a chair in front of a table and more glass trophy cabinets.

In this cabinet, I saw my flawless blue pearl, still in the clam and glowing like I remembered; the priceless and perfectly cut emerald I was supposed to get for my birthday but took home early; and Jay's camera with the video of our night on the deck together.

I grabbed a hammer off the table behind the monkey and smashed the glass in a fit of rage that this stuff was taken from me. The monkey got scared and ran out of the room as I grabbed what was mine from that shelf and tucked it in my bag. I walked out with the hammer and smiled like a joker at the other glass cabinets, just waiting to be destroyed. I was about to smash the box holding the photos of my boyfriends, but I stopped a few inches away it and dropped the hammer to the floor when I noticed the one photo just below the locket, a photo of us both as kids, at Christmas. Two photos actually, one of me holding the locket with another boy holding it with me, and the other of him kissing my cheek with the locket around my neck. I'd never seen the cutest thing I ever saw until now; the boy looked a little like Seth, but it couldn't be . . . It was the exact same locket I had the night I was an angel. I didn't recall ever getting this gift as Christmas, or seeing Seth there with me. I was so little, so young. "Is it possible he was with my family for Christmas? And how did he know my father?" I thought. I could only stare at the blushing smile I had on my face as a little girl and the big green eyes on Seth when he kissed my cheek. I couldn't remember a thing about that Christmas or about Seth giving me the locket; it was like it never happened.

I picked up the hammer again and threw it at the glass, I smiled when I picked up my stuff and grabbed all the photos I could, including myself. Ripping down the photos of Seth and his family made me feel better about him hiding my stuff in the shack. I looked back at the mess I made, and felt like the world had been lifted off my shoulders, and replaced with the monkey reaching for more fruit in my bag.

"I got to give you some sort of name, you know. 'Monkey' sounds kind of boring."

I swore that he nodded back at me while eating some grapes.

"How does Miko sound?"

He screeched right in my ear and ran around my shoulders, swinging around my neck and returning to my bag.

"I think that's a yes."

I called him Miko after the raccoon in *Pocahontas*; he was always hungry and often stole more food. It fit the crazy monkey perfectly. I turned off the light in the mess of papers and broken glass. I slammed the door and heard something else crash to the floor, probably more glass; I laughed a bit and started walking down to the path again. Come to think of it, it was the monkey that took me off the trail; I had no idea how to get back. With all the knowledge I had about the great outdoors, it wasn't enough to get me back onto the trail. If I walked in the wrong direction long enough, I'd never make it back to the house before the sun went down.

"You know how to get back, right?"

Miko stuck his tongue out at me; I smacked my head knowing it'd be difficult to get back home. Miko pointed to the grassy bush again, and I'd found my way from there. I started to get really thirsty a few minutes into the walk, when I noticed I forgot to pack water of all things. Even Miko looked disappointed when I found no trace of any drinks in the bag whatsoever. I looked around into nothing but trees and plants with no signs of water anywhere. If I didn't get some kind of liquid in my system, I would surely dehydrate quickly and grow even more ill as the day went on. Even worse, there wasn't much day left; I had only one hour left of daylight, and still a good two hours or so from my cabin I only guessed at.

I lost the track of time exploring the beauty of nature on this island, and I didn't have a watch anyways, and I'd left my iPhone at home.

"Do you at least know where I can find something to drink?"

Yanking on my hair twice, Miko flew into the trees and screeched a few times so that even though I couldn't see him, I could hear what direction he was heading in. I sprinted toward the sound of Miko, through all sorts of plant life that didn't taste as good as it looked. I sprinted for a good ten minutes and had to slow to running for five. Wheezing and panting like a dog I tripped over a vine and fell flat on my face on a leafy floor. Miko stopped swinging through the trees and laughed at me still on the ground while I wiped some dirt off my face.

"Very funny. Did you at least find some water?"

Miko jumped on my back and hit my head a few times, and pointed right in front of me to the oasis—the waterfall cascading fresh, clear blue water to the fantastic water below. I jumped right into the water, cold and refreshing and possibly the best tasting water on earth. I ripped off my clothes and left behind the bikini underneath and swam up to the waterfall, where the ground was higher and I could stand and shower under the cool water splashing all over me. Miko dipped his hands into the water to drink and only stepped in up to this little monkey hips. I splashed some water at Miko while he yelled and jumped out of the water, fixing his hair and eating something from my bag on a rock. I played with the water falling on me for a few minutes before diving into the deeper part of the oasis and having trouble finding a bottom. I came back up and grabbed my bag and took it down into the water with me. I had been swimming for years and had grown to expand my lungs from so many competitions that I could hold my breath for an easy two minutes. I added more seconds after my swimming tournament before we left to go to Hawaii (thirty-two seconds to be exact). I was so surprised at how well I could see in the water; the twists and turns I swam though seemed to never end, and I began to worry a minute and a half later with no sign of reaching an air pocket or finding out if there was simply a bottom. It seemed to be a waste of my time and maybe would kill me if I didn't get some air soon. I swam faster and faster into darker water, nearly at my breaking point for taking a breath of air; I swam upward and bolted into the air pocket. It wasn't an air pocket, but a massive underground crystal cave, and water pulling forward to a source I didn't know. I pulled my underwater camera out and started taking dozens of pictures. There were giant gems of every kind just waiting to be pulled out and hidden in someone's bag. The Swiss Army knife in my bag did just fine as I yanked out diamonds, emeralds, amethysts, opal, topaz, obsidian, peridot, quartz, rubies, sapphires, moonstones, sunstones, tiger's eye, jades, and garnets of every color. I fit gems the size of my hand into my bag, at least four of every kind.

My backpack was full of priceless jewels; it was very heavy and almost dragged me into the deeper water. I pulled the bag onto my back and felt something pull my legs forward. I tried to swim backward, but the current was too strong and yanked me deeper into the darkness within the cave. I twisted and turned around all sorts of corners, still a float in the water, with no idea where this was going, I could only guess it led to either a shore where I could escape or a deeper point of the ocean that was far deeper than a single two minutes of swimming. Either I was going to live if I made it to a shore or I would die a slow and terrible death at the bottom of the ocean, sleeping with the fishes in the unforgiving abyss of the sea. I was floating at a faster speed than before, and it was almost too dark to see anything at all. I felt around my bag for something to give me light. I felt something long and smooth and ripped it out to find a glow stick. I didn't remember having a glow stick but cracked it anyways. It lit up the entire cave. I threw my bag back on my shoulders and looked around the still twisting cave. I heard only water rushing louder in front of me and presumed that my ride on this underground water slide was gonna end. I was sure that it wouldn't be long before I splashed into whatever fate had thrown my way, and damn it, I was ready.

Chapter 16

My glow stick had shown me that the fun would end when I landed in a small cave, completely underwater with two exits in the bottom, and no chance of getting back up to the crystal water slide. I quickly took the exit to my right and went straight for a little while and curved around a few times, but I still had plenty of oxygen. Grasping the glow stick in my hand, I slithered around the corners with great speed and came up to something light gray ahead of me. I touched it; it felt soft; I grazed beside it and saw a pair of beady black eyes looking back at me. It was a freaking great white shark, and it looked like it had got stuck in here somehow, and judging by its small and bony body, it was hungry. My eyes widened for a second, and I swam forward for my life into an area I didn't know. I didn't dare look back knowing already that it was right on my tail. God knew if I would survive or end up in the stomach of the shark. I finally saw the end of the line, a wall that would surely be the last thing I would see, until I looked up and saw that the tunnel continued above me.

I pushed off the bottom and rocketed toward the top that led to a shore in another cave. I saw the shark fin get closer to the shore, and I leaped onto the land, looking back to make sure the shark won't shoot on the land like *Shark Night 3D*. Only it was really normal D; I didn't know dimensions that well. The shark dived back down to wherever it came from. I vowed from that moment, I'd be the one to kill that monster and make a necklace or two from its teeth. Never thought I'd ever say that, but I pulled my bag up and looked around the familiar cave I emerged from. It was the cave right outside my home! Following the tunnel out, I spotted the carved-out exit and looked back at my house, untouched and exactly the same. I ran back inside and leaped onto my bed and laughed in happiness that I was back home—well, the closest to home I was gonna get. I changed into my pj's and jumped into my bed, and then Miko leaped out from the covers, scaring the hell out of me.

"What one earth are you doing here?"

Miko yawned and crawled onto the pillow next to me, curling up in a little ball similar to a cat. I shook my head and walked into the kitchen with some fabric in a drawer and sewed a few pieces to gather to make a very wide blanket-like hammock for Miko. I hammered two nails from the ceiling and made a miniature swinging hammock for Miko not too far from my bed.

"You can sleep up there, Miko. It may remind you of the forest a little bit. Make it a little more like home for you here."

Miko screeched and oooed a few times as he jumped off my head and onto the dresser next to the hammock, then jumped in the comfy bed I made for him. He looked happy as he lay down and swayed a few times before falling asleep. I thought, "It wouldn't hurt to have someone here with me, before I lose my all social skills and start talking to a volleyball named Wilson." I took a peek at the journal again, reading one more entry couldn't hurt.

August 18, 2007, Saturday

I faced the ocean once more, so I could destroy that shark that came close to eating me. I made a few spears out of some wood I found and made sure they were big enough to kill that shark. It has been one hour since I killed the shark; it wasn't as hard as I thought it would be. The key is to make sure the spear goes through its head. Get that and the shark will be dead in minutes. I wish I knew that in the first place, because I tried to cut it open from the back along the tail and back of shark, which didn't work since he bit my leg, leaving it to bleed a lot on land. I didn't feel too good afterward, but I managed to stop the bleeding with a piece of my clothing, even though it is still dripping blood . . . and . . . Oh I don't feel very go—

I couldn't stop reading from that! I had to read what happened next!

August 19, 2007, Sunday

I woke up at night; I knew that I had passed out from losing too much blood. I looked at my hand, pale and white as freshly fallen snow. I removed the clothing from my wound and saw that even though it had stopped bleeding, it was infected and not improving, no matter what I did. Salt water, fresh water and even using the shark teeth to take the infected yellow skin off didn't help. I felt feverish and very nauseous. I had talked a little to the doctor on deck about shark wounds he had to deal with once. He said he treated patients on board and said if he didn't have any alcohol wipes or antibiotics, death would indeed reach the heart by blood that couldn't be filtered by the liver. Slowly, the heart would start to stop pumping, causing death by renal failure and cardiac arrest. There was nothing to help me here; I assumed I'd be dead in less than one more day here. It wasn't a happy ending, but I'd have one day left to do whatever I wanted for my last day on earth.

Seriously! I couldn't put the journal down now! There would only be one more entry left; plus it wasn't that late as I thought it would be. It was like I was reading something that someone had written as part of a book that eventually would get published and only included the journal entries as something to give the main character something to do! But what were the odds of that happening.

August 20, 2007, Monday

This morning I cooked up the shark for breakfast. It wasn't that bad actually, and I walked along the ocean side in my bare feet. I walked as far as I pleased, relaxing while my leg was still very sore. My fever had lessened and I was still very pale, but I knew then that the better I felt, the more blood would reach my heart and stop later on today. I walked into the forest, smiling at all the beautiful plants, animals, and flowers I passed; even a cute little spider monkey stayed on my shoulder as I looked around at the beauty of this place. This place was a tropical paradise all right. It was the perfect place to spend my last day, anyone's last day on earth really. I no longer feared death like I did earlier that day, seeing the flowers as bright as the sun in the sky and the birds as beautiful as my wife's face. I cannot even say good-bye to my family: my daughter, an angel; and my son, a brave and loving man. My day was almost done, and I sat down to watch the last sunset with the warmth on my face. My only regret is that I recently yelled at my son for getting suspended from school and yelling at my daughter for missing a class for science, even though she got on the honor roll with distinction.

My name is Simon Salderman, and I was the last person here on Crystal island. I found a gem cave under an oasis and took a few with me to where I might die, knowing I'd be left with a small fortune to bring with me on my way to heaven. I felt slightly calmer when the sun went down, the stars came out, and the moon greeted me on this last night. I even wished on a shooting star that someone would find this journal and read my short story. I left no legacy for my children, no riches in my hand for them, no will and testament to tell them what to inherit, but if someone is reading this, tell my kids, Jamie and Jack, I love them so very much, and tell my wife Mary, I love her with all my heart. I will miss them, but they should know my secret I've kept with me for years.

My crew was looking for a city called Atlantis, said to exist only in a mere legend. We found traces of evidence that proved it existed—pottery, jewelry, tools, everything—and we found its location not too far from the island. Only, something sunk our ship and it took in water far too quickly and in less than five minutes, killing over four hundred men and woman I knew and loved as my coworkers. Their secret went with them to the bottom of the sea, but I believe I was spared to write out what we found besides the city. I even took pictures of mermaids within the city. Mermaids are kind and beautiful and are known for their incredible voices. Very few Sirens still exist; most of them have been outsmarted by today's fishermen and killed for dragging other humans down into sea. It may be possible that Neptune, the god of the sea, could be the king of Atlantis. All we know for sure is that they exist; they could even breed with people and form a hybrid child. The offspring could live on land and be able to grow a tail underwater, being able to live as an average mermaid below.

One legend of the people of Atlantis is that any merfolk who are of royal blood can turn a human into a hybrid by simply giving them a kiss. Why a kiss, I have no clue; the only problem is that if mermaids were ever discovered by people, humans would overthrow the species, wiping them out and leaving no trace of mermaids for the future. This cannot happen since mermaids hold the secret to time travel, immortality, and weapons of mass destruction that could take out entire countries. If anyone is of royal blood or turned into a hybrid, they must take an oath swearing to never tell of mermaids or be killed by Neptune himself, and if they are part of any royal family by Neptune, they must only marry a prince or princess of Neptune's choice, and make the decision to stay in the sea with the merpeople, or live on land in isolation from the sea as two normal people forever. I knew one man that lived on land with his human wife; she married him knowing he was a hybrid and raised a family somewhere in Canada. Last I heard, he abandoned his family of four and had to return to the sea to ask Neptune for a favor, but instead he got locked away in jail somewhere in Atlantis.

That man's name was Jacob Liam Verbicky. He was a kind man, and I'm sure he is still in the Atlantis jail, waiting for Neptune to let him free. His two children might just be the ones to release him and find out his secret as well. Heck, if you're his son or daughter, he is indeed still alive and waiting for you. I knew him as a friend from high school, and we were great friends. I'm thinking now I have less than five minutes, so I tucked all my treasure in a chest behind me and will soon end this journal in a few minutes. The last thing I'll say is, if you so choose, a life married to a prince or princess under the care of Neptune will be a happier life as an immortal being, forever the age you are, the second Neptune gives you a crystal necklace that glows like a firefly and is as blue as the sky on a cloudless day. If I had any choice between a lifetime on land and an eternity in the sea, I'd choose the life under the sea. Nothing can hurt you down there, nothing can kill you, and there will always be a happy ending. No matter what.

The last page in the journal had a drawing of a heart-shaped locket; it was an incredible, realistic drawing, and under it, in beautiful handwriting it said, "Always."

I was thinking now that this "always" thing really meant "I will always love you." Jay had said it, Seth knew about it, and my father was the one who started it all. I started to cry; this poor man spent his last day alone and couldn't even tell his family good-bye. I didn't feel pity or the need to give condolences; I just felt afraid for this person. He died in a matter of minutes after he finished this last entry and told me a secret only he knew. He knew my father Jacob and the life of Seth and the reality if I never get rescued from this island, which he called "Crystal Island." I'd like to rename it "Crystal Paradise." That name suited it just fine, even though I was still very sad. I managed to tuck the journal away in the dresser and wiped the last tear from my face and went to sleep. I felt one last tear drop from my eye and onto the pillow, ending this day on a sad note, but I now knew what I should do, and that was to find out what was really the other thing in the ocean. And I wasn't talking about the sharks; there was something else, something that knew a heck of a lot about me.

Chapter 17

It was my third day on the island. I thought, "The date is August 15, a week from my seventeenth birthday." I vowed that I would kill the great white shark that tried to eat me and go on to kill as many of those devils as I possibly could. I didn't put them on the endangered list; I wanted to be able to swim freely again and find out what else was at the bottom of the ocean. I got dressed while Miko was still sleeping, took my shower and carried on with my morning routine. I grabbed some of my black eyeliner, and made two black lines under my eyes. I tied my headband around my head and looked exactly like the female version of Charlie Sheen in *Platoon*. I laughed a little like a villain in the mirror while Miko walked in and scratched his head at my odd makeup.

"So, you in the mood to watch me kill a great white shark?"

Miko jumped up and down and oohed and aahed a few times. I needed no translation to tell me that he said "Hell, yeah!" I ran out to the forest behind the house and broke down a few new trees, the strongest, for making a spear.

I grabbed the Swiss Army knife I'd tucked in my pocket and started carving out multiple long spears, perfect for jabbing a shark in the head with. It took me a good hour and a half to carve out about twelve spears about my arm's length long. I tied them all together with some rope I made from very tough vines in the trees above me. I was ready to kill a shark except that I had to leave out some sort of bait. I couldn't catch a shark with nothing, you know. Letting my leg bleeding in the ocean wouldn't be safe and would look stupid. But sharks can pick up the scent of blood a hundred miles away, or for you Canadians out there such as myself, 161 kilometers, which was enough to get a bunch sharks there for me to stab with my spears and use as bait to kill more sharks. With this idea, I was sure to kill at

The Tail of an Angel

least ten sharks. "More is better though, much better," I thought. I knew I had to get some sort meat to lure a shark here, and a little blood would keep them coming. I looked over at Miko for a second, but I could never hurt Miko; plus if he got an infection and died, I'd have no other friend to talk to or keep me company, and I'd be all alone once more. I couldn't let that happen, so I thought that I might have to use my blood for the bait. I looked around in the freezer for meat I could use, and thank goodness there was a small chicken in there, perfect for luring a shark to its doom. I threw it in the oven for about twenty minutes on the highest setting, just long enough to thaw it out and not to cook it, leaving it raw. I walked out with the chicken behind my back and some rope to hang it in the water. I felt Miko jump on my other shoulder and eat pieces of a banana. I smiled a little as I walked into the cave with the water just waiting to wash up red blood from the sharks. I happened to notice a perfect ledge in the ceiling that I could hang the chicken from. I threw the rope up and over the ledge on the roof and let the chicken fall into the water, just waiting for the fish to nibble the bait.

"You might not want to look over here for a minute, Miko. This is gonna hurt."

I pulled out the Swiss Army knife and flicked the knife out, while looking at Miko, a little scared. Miko put his hands over his eyes as I walked up to the shoreline and was still thinking of where I could get some blood without causing it to get infected. Then I remembered that diabetes patients prick their fingers all the time and never get any major infections. I looked at my left pointer finger and thought hard that it'd be very sore if I plucked it; ring finger it was. I quickly cut my finger the same way I would've tried to strike a match, and oh *gawd it hurt so bad! Ahhhhrrrrrggggg! Ermergerd!* I never knew true pain until today! Dayum!

"*Sweet baby Jesus! That hurts! Owwwwwww!*" I screamed, and my voice echoed all around the cave. I opened my eyes and watched my finger drip . . . drip . . . drip . . . drip more and more blood until I had a decent little puddle in the water. I sucked the few drips left on my finger dry. That was the most painful thing I ever felt in my entire life. I think it doesn't hurt that much for diabetes patients because they simply prick their fingers with a small needle, while I cut my finger with a slightly dirty Swiss Army knife. The cut was more of a gash. I think I cut too deep, and it wouldn't stop bleeding. I rinsed both the knife and my finger in the salt water, which was painful but not as bad as the cutting itself. I sat back with Miko a few feet from the water and waited for my trap to spring.

"You can open your eyes now Miko. It's not too bad, is it?"

Miko uncovered his eyes, and I showed him my still-bleeding finger. He shook his head up and down, showing that, in fact, it was really bad. "Anyways," I thought, "the trap will go off when the shark bites the chicken. There is a massive hook he will bite into, either sticking out through the top of his mouth, or preferably the side, making it impossible to get away from. Then I will pull the rope down and either bring him up out of the water, or forward toward me, depending on where the hook gets him. Any way is fine because he will be close enough to the spear. Either method I try, this shark will get no chance to escape. And now, the fun part everybody loves, the waiting."

One hour went by. I saw a single piranha try and eat the chicken, but I speared him in a single blow and tossed his dead fish body aside. Piranha doesn't sound that tasty, and I didn't want to try.

Two hours later, I sneezed and scared Miko. That was about it.

Three hours later, I saw something in the water, and a shark fin rose up to get the chicken. He waited only for a few seconds, and then he ate the chicken. I yanked the rope, pulling him forward on the shore of the water.

"It's about time!" I told Miko.

He jumped off my shoulder and hid behind a rock nearby while I grabbed one of my spears and ran toward the shark. It was the very same skinny one that tried to eat me yesterday, and boy, was I glad I was about to kill it. It tried to bite me when I got closer to it. Waiting for it to close its jaws, I raised my spear upward and thrust it down into its head, and I twisted it twice and waited for it to stop moving. I looked at its eyes, slightly black and frightened. I smiled as I watched it die by my hands, and I laughed knowing that it was the last thing it saw before it died. It stopped moving finally, and I sat down to take a look at my kill. There was very little shark blood that managed to bleed from the shark. I pulled it on the land, but wow, was this thing heavy. I removed the spear, and that was when I saw the rest of the blood flow back into the water, turning the entire dark blue exposed water there, into dark red blood, like the Nile when the seven plagues hit Egypt. I started cutting up the shark just as I wanted to, in the same way I would gut a fish, only bigger. Taking out the bones would be the hardest part. I cut the fresh meat into steaks for later. Taking off the head was the toughest part.

That thing was on there – The head that is -, and took me twenty minutes to get off. I may just mount it if I had some time, but right now, I sliced up that thing like a McDonald's fry slicer. After getting only the good meat off, there were only a few organs: its stomach, bones, tail and tail fins, and finally its worst feature . . . the poop sack. I couldn't think of the name for that body part. All I knew was it contained its excreted matter and wasn't going to be cooked up anytime soon. I dragged the much lighter parts of the shark out of the cave and into a deeper part of the forest. Then I ran back to the house, put on a Band-Aid, grabbed a shovel, and buried the rest of it. I sprinted back home, cheery and happy that I had killed it and managed to find something good to cook for supper. I found Miko touching the shark's head I'd brought back. I used my hand to make it close its jaw, scaring the crap out of Miko.

"Gotcha! It's dead. Don't worry, have a banana."

I handed him a banana from the table, and he took it to a chair and started eating it. Meanwhile, I started taking out the teeth one by one with a set of pliers, setting each one in a bowl of water to keep them clean. It took almost the rest of the day to get every one out, but there were three sets of teeth I had to pull, which are like our own teeth, times three. Plus, one row of teeth had like 40 teeth within it. That meant I had to pull out over 120 teeth. I had no use for the rest of the head, so I grabbed the same bloody spear I used to kill it and stuck its head back on the spear. Running outside with it, I placed it out on the shore of the beach outside my home, so if anyone saw that shark head, they'd know someone was here. Pulling those teeth really wore me out, and cooking up the meat didn't take as long as I thought it would. To be honest, it wasn't that bad. It tasted as if someone took the consistency of salmon and made it taste like sausage and bologna put together. I made a tasty dinner out of that shark, and the best part? I managed to save some of the shark's blood in a jar, which I just happened to grab before I caught the shark. With this shark blood, I wouldn't be cutting my finger anytime soon to catch more sharks. That was a good day for me. I could make a shark tooth necklace, and I had about a week or two's worth of shark for supper, and I had something fun to do for a few days. I was no expert, but I thought that the shark breeding season should be over in about two weeks, which was perfect timing for me to kill as many as possible. Miko jumped to bed right away, and I called it a night as well. Tomorrow was sure to be full of slicing up multiple sharks and plenty of more sharks' blood for me to kill more. These pleasant thoughts put me at ease as I went to sleep. Morning came at the perfect time; I was well rested, happy, and not too hungry and felt energetic for the day. I jumped up and out of my bed, flashed on my clothes, and made a quick breakfast of scrambled eggs. It was my fourth day here, and the date was August 16, I hoped. It meant I still had time to kill a bunch of sharks before my birthday, maybe even make a necklace for myself, since no one would be getting me a gift anyways. I was peppy and pumped and packed my bag quickly.

I was just about to leave the house and felt Miko race past my leg and out to the hunting spot. I followed him in the twist and turn outside my home and found the still body of water—clear and pure with no shark blood remaining in it, but a stain on the shore still. I planned to kill more than one shark today, at least three or four. I threw the shark meat back over the ledge and let it plop into the water and pulled the jar of shark blood out of my bag. I glanced back at my ring finger, still with a huge gash; it was clean but deep into my finger. I should've just poked it with my knife, like a needle, which would've bled far less. I couldn't change the past, but I knew the future; I would have sharks' blood on my hands and more shark meat in my fridge and in my freezer. I dumped a few drops of the blood into the water, making a puddle similar to I had of my own blood yesterday. Miko sat down behind me, emerging from the same rock he cowardly jumped behind the other day, and ate a peach.

"Seriously, Miko, are you just hungry all the time?"

Miko nodded as I sat next to him and grabbed a bunch of strawberries to munch on for myself. I could tell that today I wouldn't have to wait as long for a shark to take the bait; the blood was much more powerful in scent, and the meat was 100 percent raw and fresh. I bet I'd have a shark here in about forty-five minutes, and since it was the crack of dawn, they would be much more active and in larger numbers. The more of them die, the better I eat.

Forty-five minutes later, nothing touched the shark meat. Maybe these sharks weren't starved to the point of cannibalism. I pulled out the blood jar and poured some more blood into the water, making sure I didn't use it all. "It wouldn't be too long now before I get a shark on my line," I thought. It was only a matter of time.

Twenty-five minutes later, I saw something pull down on the shark meat. I was wrong! It looked like they did eat meat from their own kind. I yanked the rope down, bringing the shark forward again, and damn, it was a big one. It had to be at least eight feet long, or 2.44 meters long, which was still fairly big for a shark. I grabbed one of my spears once more and had a perfect shot at the head of the shark. I plunged the spear in, but it look like it wasn't dying. So I grabbed another spear and stuck it in its head next to the first spear and saw it slowly die. I stepped back since the shark was starting to move up farther on land, twisting and waving its head and jaws all around. This of course made it dangerous to be around the shark; waiting it out was the plan. It took about ten minutes to die, and I watched its blood flow back into the water. I managed to pull the shark up with the one spear and turned it to make the hole in the bottom start pouring out blood like a faucet and filled up the blood jar to the very top. I yanked out the second spear after I saw the rest of the blood return to the water. I dragged it up a little more onto the land and sliced up this shark quickly. Tying a piece to the rope, I tossed it into the water again while I threw the remains I didn't need in the same spot where I had ditched the other parts.

I checked on the trap on the way back and put the meat in my freezer. I came back to the bloody spot and dripped more blood into the water about five minutes later. If I kept up at this rate, I could easily have five sharks dead by the time the sun went down. I had no need for anymore shark teeth; I had enough to make a fortune in necklaces from the one shark alone, but I was sure the treasure I found in that crystal cave would make me a millionaire. "If I ever get rescued, I'm sure to have an amazing, upper-class lifestyle from now on, and I would be a trophy wife with my riches but have a heart of gold," so I've been told by my best friends and family. I was amazed to see the trap set off again in less than fifteen minutes.

I pulled the rope, and this time the shark went straight up and dangled like a piñata over the water. I had to throw the spears this time, but I had a better idea in mind for this. I swore there was a bow in the house, and I'd have a little archery practice now. A bull's-eye would be a headshot and fun way to kill this shark. I sprinted to my house, returning with the bow around my chest and back. I definitely looked like *Katniss Everdeen* now. I chopped up a few of my spears and made them into very impressive arrows. I had yet to make a quiver but picking them up will have to do. My first shot when right into its side fin. I huffed and tried again, nailing it in the throat.

"Oh, come on!" I yelled as I took another shot, and bam! Perfect 10 right into the head. The shark kicked around for a few minutes, until I finally saw its jaw open with the arrow in it and turn around very slowly like a man dead on a noose. I yanked the rope really hard to bring the shark forward, and let it go to make sure it wouldn't swing back over the water. The shark thumped on the sandy ground, while I left it right where it landed to cut it up. The stomach had something large within it; it was almost sticking out, leaving an odd lump bumping out. I pulled out the gut as much as I could and sliced the stomach open. If this were operation, I would've won the game by now. Anyways, popping out of the stomach was something yellow and shiny. I grabbed it with my hand and jerked it out, revealing a beautiful handheld harp. No strings were broken, but it was a little gross, covered with the food the shark was trying to digest. I ran my fingers across them, it sounded exactly like the music of the angels. My years of playing piano came in handy when I could figure out the notes I plucked on. I smiled and dipped it in the water to clean it. I set the harp next to Miko while I dragged the remains to the same spot again. I was getting so good at this; I chopped up the shark in less than ten minutes, including throwing the meat in the freezer.

Three sharks already were surprising to me, but I felt satisfied knowing I had every edible part to eat in my freezer. Miko looked at the harp in confusion; he plucked a string, and screamed as he ran behind his rock again.

"It's said that harps are the instrument of the merpeople; Sirens were known for using them and their hypnotic voices to lure fishermen to their deaths in the depths of the sea. This could only be from two things: a mermaid lost their harp or two, or there was a harp on the ship that went down that was mentioned in the journal. How the shark managed to eat it is the real question though. It's fine. The harp can't hurt you, Miko."

Miko looked over the rock and slowly came out and jumped up on my shoulder, playing in my hair again. I didn't feel any bugs in my hair, but I used a fruit extract shampoo. Miko must have liked it. I waited another hour for a shark, and just as I was about to drip some more shark blood into the water, the trap went off again. I had another shark on my line again in no time. This one was smaller, but it was still the perfect size to mount on a piece of wood in the living room. The head was just the right color and shape for being adored in front of a blazing fire. I had to find some way to kill it without damaging the head and fired my arrows at the soft belly. I had about ten arrows in the rest of the body, but I couldn't get the blood falling into the water at an alarming rate. By the time it died, all the blood had sunk in the water; luckily I had half a jar of blood to use. Once it was on land, I had so much meat as it was, I just cut all the meat off and threw it in the Bone Bush—and I nicknamed it—with the other un-usable parts. Wow, four sharks, and it was only one o'clock or so. "If I just killed one more shark that would be all I needed for today."

My wishes came true when I caught the last shark of the day; it was an easy kill when instead going up and out of the water, he pulled forward to the shore with one stab to the head. He was dead in a few minutes, and I cut it up for my supper in a record-breaking seven minutes. I was done killing for today, and I had the rest of the day to myself once I finished mounting the other shark head. I changed into my bikini top and golden skirt again. Grabbing a white flower from the tropical forest, I walked along the beach. The sea breeze blew my hair peacefully and was so warm. It reminded me of Jay again; his friends nicknamed him "Wolf man" since he was never cold and was as warm as the character Jacob from *Twilight*, or so I'd heard. I could only imagine how he smelled the last night I saw him; it was my favorite scent, Chocolate Axe. If only he was here beside me, on the beach of this island, enjoying the sunset and sunshine warm on my skin, the very same way I felt on the deck of the boat while watching our last sunset together. I kept walking barefoot and letting the water wash over my feet and pull itself out to the tide and spreading out onto the land again. Simple, quiet, peaceful, heavenly, I could go on forever of how it felt on that beach. The only thing I loved more than anything else in the world was a sunset on the beach with the warm wind in my hair. It would've been the most romantic thing in the world, but only if Jay was here. God knew where he was now, rescued and worrying if I was still alive, or still sitting in a raft, on the verge of death from starvation.

I couldn't bear to think of Jay dying in a raft and left for dead with my family and his own. I shook my head and tried ever so hard to forget about him, but it was impossible. It was like trying to remember someone you'd never met, truly impossible. I thought of something to make me feel better and only thought of the times we had together, good, bad, scary, fun, all of it. Even the night he convinced me I should spend the night with him, a night I knew now I could never forget. I only wished on a shooting star that he was going to be okay and safe in his real home, not like me, pretending that this abandoned mansion was my home now. This paradise wasn't anything like my home; in fact it was almost the complete opposite. There was nothing in Canada like this place. I could only dream of a Utopia like this. Who knew that I'd end up waking up here and have to live a life dedicated to leisure, occasional fishing, and picking the finest fruit from these trees as if I were in a garden of Eve? Earlier today, I saw Miko bringing back a pomegranate from the forest, one of my favorite fruits, and spend ages trying to open it, but I tossed it in the fruit bowl anyways. The pomegranate was said to be the fruit picked by the Goddess Aphrodite after she rose out of the sea and named it "the fruit of love." I loved pomegranates, which only fits because a pomegranate, in some cases, can keep the skin healthy and show real beauty from its juices, to show to those who eat it. No wonder I started looking better when I ate a couple of pomegranates.

The sun was almost down when I started thinking about pomegranates, and when I looked back, I thought that I should turn around and go home before it got too cold to walk on the beach. There wasn't a single cloud in the sky, which was perfect for a fire by the deck, and I already had some wood ready to burn for a fire anyways. I wasn't too far from home, and Miko was grabbing some small wood to burn as kindling. I had no trouble starting the fire, and with a black cherry soda I found in the fridge, I sat down with Miko, watching the stars come out. I saw a shooting star and closed my eyes, thinking of the only thing that mattered to me more than the chances of me getting rescued. I just prayed that a few other people I knew had found rescue. It was not a happy ending, but it was a good one. I finished my soda and put the last of the coals out by filling my empty bottle with water from the ocean and dumping it on the fire. I looked at the label Soda Pop Shoppe (the best soda brand there was besides Fanta). I learned to love it when I visited Mexico. I looked back at the ocean, thinking I saw something swimming around. It was far too dark to see what was in the water, and I was too tired to care. I put the soda bottle on the counter and changed into my pajamas. I thought of Jay and me the night I was an angel and remembered that I had Jay's camera with me. I fetched the camera and pressed Play on the video he had recorded. The stars looked so beautiful on the video, and the northern lights were brighter than the sun.

The lights started to come down around me, and I laughed at my dancing with the lights. I was shining like the stars and moon in the sky. Only when I started to float up into the air, I focused more on the lights as I was lifted up. Jay was yelling at me to come back down while I still went higher in the sky. In a few minutes, I watched how I was swallowed by the lights, and then I drifted back down, with my eyes glowing bright blue. I passed out and watched Jay catch me. I regained consciousness and heard his voice asking why my eyes were glowing blue and my skin was shining an even brighter blue. I watched myself freak out at why I was glowing blue, and suddenly I had wings. I ran to the water and adored the wings that I had. For some reason, I was wearing a beautiful dress and a flawless blue diamond ring and a locket on my neck. I read the engraving that said "The Blue-Eyed Angel" and looked amazing with the wings.

For a few seconds, Jay just kept pointing the camera at me, and my crazy blue eyes until I saw the stars start to move, and then he pointed the camera at the sky, where the words "Kiss the Angel" had formed. He somehow managed to hold the camera facing us, while his eyes glowed blue as well, and I opened the locket and heard once more the little angel inside tell my future. I felt really stupid not knowing what she was talking about, until now. When the locket closed itself, Jay had a great shot of my decision to remain a human, and kissed me. I watched the lights from before evaporate my wings and dress, returning my golden skirt and other clothes, and left my locket, tiara, and ring behind. I whispered, "Thank you," and the blue from my eyes and his disappeared. I looked up at the lights leaving the boat and returning to the sky; it was incredible, and when it was all over, I asked Jay to shut off the camera. The very last thing I heard was "You looked as beautiful as an angel." Who knew it'd be the last time I would hear his voice, or even be kissed by him.

I put the camera away and cut up the pomegranate on the table and munched on the seeds for a few minutes, handing a bunch to Miko, since he was the one who found the fruit in the first place.

"Can you show me where you found the pomegranate tomorrow?"

Miko nodded and jumped up into his hammock to eat his seeds, while finishing what I had left of mine in a bowl. I placed the bowl on the dresser, switched off the lamp on it, and nuzzled into my pillow for the night.

Chapter 18

It was my fourth night here, and the date was August 18; four more days until my birthday. I woke up feeling great and fixed a quick breakfast of a grapefruit and an orange. I got dressed and forgot about the *Platoon* makeup and just headed out with my bow, shark blood, plenty of bait, and my iPhone to kill the time if the shark were slow today.

I looked at my finger as I walked out of the house; it was healing quite nicely under the Band-Aid I used yesterday. The once-deep gash was now the depth and length of a small paper cut, but paper cuts hurt much less then slicing my finger with a Swiss Army knife. Miko sat on my shoulder again as I handed him a banana and asked him not to get any food in my hair. I returned again to the "shark graveyard" as I called it since many sharks would die here. I was aiming to kill another five sharks today, but I had enough meat to last me a month, so I'd simply just chop up these sharks and toss them in the Bone Bush.

To put it simply, I killed six sharks that day; the first three rose up straight out of the water, the next two pulled forward for an easy kill, and the last rose up again. Every single shark was a male, and a great white. My Bone Bush was getting awfully full, so I dug a hole right next to it and buried the remains nicely, and made room for more shark parts on top. I had an impressive collection of shark bones, and I could easily put together a puzzle with their bones. I thought maybe I would even mount a shark jaw in my room. I removed a few more teeth from the sharks, but only the biggest and the most clean, for my necklaces. It was only seven o'clock by the time I was done with killing sharks for the day. I looked over at Miko on the counter trying to open a pomegranate again by smashing it on the table.

"I'll open that for you. I just hope you didn't break too many seeds in the pomegranate."

I sliced it open after I washed the shark blood off my hands and gave him all the seeds to eat since I wasn't too hungry yet. I asked him where he got the pomegranate; he finished his seeds quickly and raced out the door, as I yelled at him to wait for me. Miko raced out behind the cave into the forest and jumped up to the vines above him, which gave me time to catch up and wait for him to shoot forward. He looked back to make sure I was following him and started to swing ahead of me, making me run after him. He went right along the path for about five minutes and took a sharp turn into Greenville, meaning I was eating random green plants as I ran into them and slapped into branches and vines that hurt my face so much. This lasted for another five minutes before I ran as fast as I could into a tree—ouch.

Miko tapped my on leg and pointed up to an unlimited supply of pomegranates above my head, while Miko jumped up in the tree and dropped one in my lap. I picked it up and looked at the perfectly ripe pomegranate; I could live off the fruit here for years if I picked it now. I had a few hours to kill, so I managed to find my back to the cabin and grabbed a few bags to pack the pomegranates back in. Miko waited by the tree, making a noise while dropping fruit so I could find my way back to pick up the fruit. The sun was still shining through the pomegranate tree, so I was still nice and warm while I picked up the fruit Miko dropped for me.

"Keep 'em coming. I have four bags to fill."

Miko dropped tons of fruit down, while I caught as many as I could with my hands; it was raining fruit, and lots hit me in the head. I filled up the first bag very quickly, the second took five minutes, and Miko even helped put the fruit in the third bag, while I filled the fourth. When I filled all the bags up with fruit, there was no longer any fruit on the ground and I had to take these heavy bags back on a ten-minute hike. I was gonna get a good workout from this for sure. Miko had a five-minute head start, and I took it slow and steady, making sure I didn't drop a single fruit.

"Who made pomegranates so heavy anyways?"

I made it home twenty minutes later, and the sun was starting to set. I put the bags in the fridge and walked outside to the beach again. I thought that by now if Jay hadn't been rescued, he for sure would've died at this point. Even my family and his own would've died by now, with only their things and each other to hold in their final moments. I stepped into the sea and thought of something that could make me feel better about their deaths. I cried as I ran back into the house and dried my tears when I grabbed a candle and a small foam plate. I wrote the names of everyone on the big candle, and Jay's name in the biggest letters with a heart next to it. I lit the candle and walked outside when the sun dried the final tears on my face. I had a pen in the side of my skirt, and I pulled an orange lily out from the bushes not too far from the beach. I walked back to the shore and stepped in the water up to the top of my feet. I watched the sun go down. Still holding the burning candle, I watched the sky go dark and the stars reappear. I wrote on the plate with my pen:

"Our time together was short, but it was the best time of my life. I will never forget you, and I will always love you. Always."

I placed the candle on the plate and looked at the name Jay for a minute; I closed my eyes, letting a single tear escape my eye. I looked up and opened my eyes to face the moon, which was almost gone, and stars twinkling back at me. A few shooting stars fell just for me, and I placed the plate with the candle in the water. I watched it float away into the sea; soon the small light slowly got smaller and smaller to the point where it no longer shined and left my sight.

"Always," I whispered to myself, reminding me of the two loves of my love I'd lost—my family and now Jay. All I could do now was find my father, who may or may not be alive at the bottom of the sea, and fall to my knees in the ocean and weep for my loss. I held my face in my hands when I felt the tears pouring from my eyes and into the water. I was in darkness, but I could still see the water, ground, and sky around me.

I sat on my back legs with the warm water up to my waist and decided I better go in before I get cold. I took off my skirt, feeling a bit of wind blow on my cold legs. Only in my bikini, I took a final look at the shore, swearing I saw someone standing out there where I stood before, but I was probably just seeing things. In the house, I was getting cold and took off my bikini in my room. Miko was sitting on my bed, and I told him to get out. I needed this night for myself and wanted to be left alone. Miko could find somewhere else to sleep; I dressed into my pj's and sat on the edge of my bed, looking at the pictures I took with my camera and the photos he took. My camera had photos of us tanning or watching the sunset with him wearing only a towel and his necklace. On his camera, he had dozens of pictures of me and him, but mostly me. I felt so terrible that I had his camera and that he couldn't see my smile one last time before he died. There were pictures of me in various situations: wearing a bikini, in my golden skirt, dancing in the wind with the golden skirt, tanning with him, surfing in California, scuba diving, the chest we found together, me as an angel, my crazy blue eyes, my normal blue eyes, wearing my tiara. My favorite picture was of me sleeping on his shoulder in the car. That was the best picture I saw on his camera. I saw that there were even more

The Tail of an Angel

photos: one of me and the northern lights, the sunset on the edge of the boat, me sleeping on his chest in our room, and finally the new favorite photos: one of him kissing my cheek while I lit up like the stars I saw outside my room, and the other was a kiss he surprised me with on the night we danced. I dripped one more tear on the camera and wiped it off quickly, hoping that it wouldn't ruin the camera at all and looked at one picture he took himself—just him wearing his swimming trunks and the wolf tooth necklace he gave me.

    I happened to have the wolf tooth necklace next to the lamp on the dresser, and I put it around my neck to keep him close. I needed this night alone to remember him and my family. Miko had all the time he wanted in here all day. I thought that maybe carving things from the shark bones might calm me down. I brought up a handful of bones and the Swiss Army knife and carved away, taking my time with each and every stroke. I remembered watching a special on how natives carved into stones and wore them as necklaces as their "Spirit Guide." Seven animals were chosen: The Eagle of Guidance, The Bear of Love, The Wolf of Wisdom, The Salmon of Enthusiasm, The Falcon of Adventure, The Otter of Independence, and The Rabbit of Friendship. I had an amazing artistic ability for which I was recognized all through school. I had tons of recommendations to embrace a career with an art major. I was glad I learned how to carve with a knife, which my father taught me, an art skill all its own. The bone shavings piled on the floor. Slowly the shape of the animal I was carving started to peek out and looked great. In about an hour, I carved a beautiful wolf totem. I felt a little sadder than I thought I would feel after carving it, but I tossed it on my dresser and started carving another. It took me only a few minutes to carve the next one, and I whipped up another totem, a cute little bear totem that I placed next to the wolf on the dresser. I carved every totem I could think of in less than an hour and lined them up neatly under the light of the lamp. Then I opened the door to my room to let Miko in. I felt a bit better, and now I had some cool totems to wear for six days of the week. I was thinking of what I could have on my neck on Saturday as Miko leaped up to his bed and fell asleep very quickly. I could only think of one more thing to carve before I went to sleep, and I carved it in about five minutes. It was an angel with long, heavenly wings. I felt much better now and could sleep with ease, peacefully as well.

    The next morning was warm and bright outside my room; it was August 18, and four more days till my birthday. I could hardly wait to turn seventeen; I'd be more excited if I had anyone at all to give me a gift. I had a bunch of pomegranates for breakfast and a banana fruit salad for Miko; he got some of the best breakfasts any monkey could have. I grabbed my things and turned my grieving and sadness into a happy obsession for killing sharks. I promised myself that I'd only kill sharks for one more day and then see what was waiting for me in the deep blue sea. I walked out with my bag and a smoothie I whipped up with some pomegranate seeds and a strawberry-orange frozen yogurt I made. It was like a healthy energy drink, perfect for a great white shark massacre. Miko took a sip of the smoothie while I yelled at him for getting monkey germs on my straw. I pushed him off my shoulder and threw my shark bait up on the roof ledge. I was hoping to kill about five sharks for the day, when I really killed only four. One rose up over the water, and the rest pulled up onto the shore for me, nice and easy. While I sliced up the sharks I wondered what I might find tomorrow. "Mermaids, treasure, and this 'Seth' guy, who knew way to much about me yet spent an entire Christmas with me I can't remember, my father, *who knows*!" I chopped up the head of a shark and thought, "Maybe my family and Jay were already rescued and sending help into the ocean as we speak." Now I could easily find where I came from because on a clear day, I could see the rock I smashed into that almost killed me. I doubt my raft was still there, but I could swim there with ease tomorrow. Throwing the remains in the Bone Bush, I made my way to the pomegranate tree and filled my bag for a weeks' worth of pomegranates to eat. Miko threw a few at my head for throwing him off my shoulder when he drank some of my smoothie. I think we were even as I rubbed my head and ripped the pomegranate open in half.

"And I'm not sharing this with you!"

I walked back with shark blood on my hands and a little bit more blood on my shirt. It seemed a much more beautiful today than it was a couple of days ago. I didn't know if it rained a little while I was killing sharks, or maybe I just didn't notice the forest's awesome beauty until today. I had no idea, but all I knew was that something had changed, and it looked good. Miko managed to beat me home again, but I stopped a few minutes away from home to see the flowers and trees that looked amazing at the moment. I picked up a rare-looking flower I'd never seen. It was like a white tiger lily, but the tips were a sea blue, and it was the perfect size to put in my hair or freeze and keep forever. It gave me a flashback to the night with Jay and my blue-tipped wings—which glowed brighter than the moon that night—and the lights that made it so. I blinked a few times a couple of minutes later, and that brought me back to reality. I immediately picked up the bottom of the stem and took the entire flower with the exception of the roots. I took the delicate flower with extra caution since I didn't want a single petal to break, rip, or fall off, and I wanted to remember the look of the lily forever. Miko was eating more fruit out of the fridge while I placed the flower in a glass vase, encasing the entire flower. I couldn't just leave it at room temperature; I had to preserve it somehow.

Then I thought of a way to keep the flower frozen for a very long time. I had a cooler in my room; I thought if the device that kept it cold was installed at the bottom of the vase with a lid on top, it could keep the flower exactly the way it was today. I carefully took the cooling device apart from the cooler and placed it at the bottom of the vase and built a white base to cover the device—from a large shark rib, of course. I had to make sure the cold would stay in the vase and had to make a wax lid since no lid could cover the vase, let alone last to keep it sealed. I melted some white candles and made a custom mould made from—you guessed it . . . bone. I didn't have to wait for the wax to solidify when I put it in the freezer. It took ten minutes max; I placed the lid on the vase and used a blowtorch to make sure no air cold ever escape. I took a final look at the finished product and thought it was missing only one thing, light. In one second, I cut a very small hole in the wax lid and put a bright blue Christmas light in the top. I attached it to a switch I could flip on and off, not affecting the temperature; if the light went out, it could be replaced with ease. I turned off the lights in my room and took the lamp off the dresser in my room and flicked on the light to my lily vase.

"Miko! Come and look at this," I yelled down to Miko, still eating in the kitchen. He thumped up the stairs and walked into my room. I heard him ooo as he jumped up on my bed.

"Nice, isn't it? I think so too."

Miko yawned and jumped up to his bed, even though it wasn't terribly late. I decided to play the piano and taught myself to play "Finally Found You" by Enrique Iglesias. It reminded me of better times, and I really got into singing the chorus.

"Because I finally found—"

Someone else sang "I finally found you," and scared me enough to stop singing, but I continued playing the rest of the song note by note. I heard whoever was singing with me, in harmony, over and over until I stopped and looked around for a few minutes and thought that I should probably play something else. I knew the only thing on my mind could be about that lily and something more heavenly, "Heavens Gonna Wait"—Hedley. I was surprised at how well I managed to sing on key to the song and still play every note perfectly like how the original version sounded.

I heard a voice sing the last few lines of the chorus only that this voice was closer than before, much closer. I continued with the song and nearly cried at the part when I sang "Only the good die young," reminding myself of the possibility that they really are dead. But I played on with the harmony in sync with my own voice, up until the chorus returned and only sang quietly like a background singer. I heard his overpower mine and played the very last few words acoustic to the piano and heard him finish the song.

"Seth? If that's you, leave me *alone!*"

There were a few seconds of absolute silence that felt like a moment in a horror movie, right before a killer chops through a door with an axe and kills whoever is inside.

"No one want to be alone, Jill."

"That's it! I'm coming out there!"

His response was only a room or two over, and I sprinted to the room and found nothing. I heard footsteps in the kitchen and the door slam. I ran to the deck where I caught him jump into the ocean and swim away, but I got a very good look at him.

"I hope something eats you!" I yelled to Seth as he made a quick dive and disappeared below.

"I'm so gonna catch him tomorrow," I told myself as I walked into the house and changed to go to bed. The lily lamp was still on, and I flicked it off and crawled into bed, with only one thing on my mind. It wasn't my hopes of killing more sharks, or thoughts of my family, Jay, Miko, or the strange change of the forest; it was simply Seth, and I wondered what I'd discover when I found him. It may have well have been my destiny to find whatever Seth was going back to, and why he sang along with me. "As God as my witness, I'm gonna discover whatever Seth didn't want me to see."

Chapter 19

It was raining outside today. August 19 was dreary, and my fifth night here wasn't looking as beautiful as always. I still had today to kill sharks and resume the rest of my days with leisure. I had three days until my birthday. I wondered what I might do for myself: make a necklace from those totems, bake a cake, decorate my room with birthday decorations—the possibilities were endless. Maybe Miko would bring me a new tropical fruit from the forest, and what I really hoped for was a small gift from Seth. With all this singing and dropping into my home very often, I had a feeling that he may drop off something for my birthday, and if not, I'd find a gift for myself in the ocean from a place called Atlantis. So far, I'd killed ten sharks and kept the teeth of about three, the heads of two, the meat of six, and the bones of nine. I might as well have kept some meat from two of the sharks. I had a few spots in the freezer I could fit it in; then I'd be set for at least four months of dinners and creative meals. I killed three that day, but the cave was very cold and damp. I hated it because I felt as cold as the meat I had in the freezer. I still waited an hour or two for the next two sharks and finished them off with ease.

"Well, that's it, Miko. My shark killing days are over. Do you eat meat at all?"

Miko shook his head and munched on some nuts he found in the forest, I guessed. They were cashews, and I loved cashews! But I wasn't that hungry and dumped the final parts of the sharks in the Bone Bush one last time. I stopped for a minute and adored my work over four days at this heap of parts and a few bones on top. I thought that maybe I should make it look a little better than just a pile of organs and crap. So I grabbed some of the bones and buried the organs that had begun to smell. I used two large ribcage bones and made a cross using some rope and tied them together and jabbed it into the ground. I hammered it down into the ground using a rock I found to make sure it could stand up. I had a little bit of shark blood left that I had no use for, and I poured it all in the cross. I looked around and placed a few flowers at the bottom and carved from a piece of bark "Here Lie 15 great white sharks, Taken during August 2012, by The Hands of Jillian Verbicky, The Bone Bush." I thought this looked really good; so ended my days of killing sharks. I headed back home and placed my things back where they came from. On the counter, I noticed a note beside the fruit bowl and picked it up while sipping on a berry smoothie.

The note read as under:

> Good news! Shark breeding season is over! You are safe to swim in the ocean again, but I recommend that you swim in the morning and not during the night. Swimming in the dark is dangerous, and you will most likely be eaten during that time. If you're wondering why you hear someone singing while you play the piano, it's me. You have a unique and beautiful singing voice, and I can't help but sing along with you. Very few people in this world have the talents you have. Just wait until you go swimming. You may be a little surprised at what you may find in the water though, and you should swim only during the sunrise.
>
> Sincerely,
> Seth.

Woohoo! And what good timing too! I could finally swim in the ocean as much as I pleased, and no one could stop me. Well, no one would anyways, unless Miko had a problem with it, which I doubted. "First thing tomorrow, I'm throwing on my bikini and taking a swim in the sea." Hopefully, the weather would clear up by then; no one wants to swim in the rain. The only thing I would in the rain is kiss someone, dance, or maybe just splash around in some puddles. But which bikini? The real question was, which bikini? The red one, the black one, or the blue with red flowers. I could decide this tomorrow, because first I had to make dinner. There was so much shark meat in my freezer, but I already had a bunch in the fridge, ready to cook. Only how to cook it was the real question: boiled, fried, baked, dried, grilled, the possibilities were endless. I was craving a shark Alfredo pasta, and I made a wonderful Alfredo sauce. I tossed in some angel hair pasta and stirred some milk into the sauce. The house started smelling so good; I sliced up the meat on a cutting board and removed all the bones in a single slice. Everything was running smoothly, and I even turned on my iPhone to listen to some music. I clicked through my music and played "Brand New Day" by Massari, and danced around the kitchen while still cooking. I strained the pasta and flipped the fillet of sharks, cut it into strips, and mixed it into the sauce. Boy did it ever smell good now. The sauce and shark was almost done, and I grabbed some pasta, dropped it in a bowl, and turned off the heat of the oven. I tossed the sauce in with the pasta, and in a symphony of spices, tasty juices, and pasta, I finished cooking my supper and brought it to the table. It was still steaming as I placed it down in front of me, and Miko oooed a few times on the ground next to me. I forgot to make supper for Miko.

"Oh, I'm sorry. What are you hungry for? You name it. I'll make it for you."

Miko jumped up and screeched, pointing at my empty smoothie glass by the sink, and I knew he wanted a berry smoothie of his own. I rolled my eyes and whipped up a berry smoothie very quickly and returned to my supper, still hot and steaming. I was so hungry, I dived right in, and believe it or not, the shark wasn't too bad. It was like a fish version of chicken! And it was perfect to eat with Alfredo sauce and a touch of zesty hot sauce. It was so tasty; it was the best meal I'd had in a long time. Miko looked satisfied with his berry smoothie, and I couldn't be happier with my cooking. I wonder if cooking is a form of art; if it is, then either I'm amazing at everything, or I happen to be talented at a lot of things. I savored every bite like it was my last, and the sauce melted in my mouth. Taking a nibble of the shark with it was infinite happiness. When I finished, I was kind of sad because that was a fantastic meal, and who knew what I might cook up next with even more shark. Miko took a final slurp of his smoothie when I placed my dishes in the sink.

"I'm thinking you liked that smoothie."

Miko nodded and handed me the glass; he had to pick it up with both hands. I didn't know Miko was such a smart monkey; no wonder he didn't want to go back to his fellow monkey-kind. They were really stupid, banana-eating monkeys; Miko was much better than all of them. Cleaning up for the first time wasn't so bad, doing the dishes brought me back to the days when I was really little and had to stand on a booster stool to reach up to the sink and dry dishes with my mom, and dad would put away the dishes after I dried them. It was an amazing time, and I blinked a few times to return to reality. These flashbacks were really interfering with me staying in the present. Stupid memories made me sad. "Just finish drying the dishes," I told myself as I put the last few plates away. I had nothing better to do tonight but just did anything I felt like doing. And I was in the mood to walk along the beach again.

Miko already beat me outside and played by the deck, throwing sand in the air and rock in the water. I had no idea what he was doing, but I didn't really care. It looked a little cool out today, so I put on a sweater and walked outside again; only, it was too cold to walk along the beach, and was perfect for another fire. Miko helped me start the fire by bringing me the box of matches, just as I finished building the tent-like fire. I wasn't in the mood to blow on the kindling for five to ten minutes, so I grabbed some flammable perfume I had and spritzed a bit on the moss on the bottom of the pit. I had to throw the match in the bottom because if I stuck my hand in, it would surely catch on fire. It started up nice and quick. I was warm in less than fifteen minutes, and Miko sat beside me on a log he had dragged up.

"Well, aren't you a strong little monkey! I could've got one if you asked."

Miko raised his hand as if to say "Whatever" and pulled up a banana from his other hand. Seriously? Miko was still hungry after that berry smoothie I made for him, stupid monkey. I grabbed another black cherry soda from the fridge, walked up to my room, and picked up all the totems I'd made plus some very nice necklace-worthy string. Placing my drink in the cup holder on my chair, I started making the totems I had carved into nice little necklaces. I started with the eagle, and since I didn't want to cut any holes in the totems, I tied a few knots around the neck of the eagle. One by one, I tied knots around the necks of each totem and tied the strings together in a double shoelace knot so that I could pull on and off the necklaces with ease. I finally got to the wolf totem one hour later and examined the wolf for a few seconds. I turned it around looking at the back, sliding my fingers across it to make sure it was smooth and no chips of wood were sticking out. I twisted it up and closer to the fire; it shone a little as I saw the fire reflect bright orange flames on the side of it.

It was really nice actually, no imperfections, no pieces of wood sticking out; it was a beautiful wolf totem to wear around my neck. The second I finished tying the knot around the back to make sure the necklace would stay as a necklace, I placed it around my neck. It fit just fine around my neck but was long enough for me to pull forward and turn around to look at the face of the totem. I looked at the fire while its silhouette glowed below it, and it brought a tear down my face, which dripped on the sand under me. Miko hopped on my shoulder and handed me a strawberry, but I said, "No, thank you," since I wasn't always hungry like him. Miko returned to his seat, looking a little sad; he took a bite into the strawberry while looking at the fire with me. I took a sip of my black cherry soda, but it didn't make me feel better. I looked back at all the necklaces I'd made and picked up the angel necklace and putt it around my neck, right next to the wolf. It was what should've happened, me and Jay, the wolf, next to me for the rest of my days.

Always. I tried to forget about "always," but it was impossible to do so. I sipped my soda again and watched the fire as I thought about it. Thinking about forgetting "always" made me even more sad, and a few more salty tears cascaded down my face and left a small puddle of tears soaking in the sand. I wiped the tears off my face, dried my eyes, and chugged back some more black cherry soda. I managed to accidentally chug back the rest of the soda and threw the bottle into the ocean. I stood up, suddenly raged, and walked up to the shore of the ocean, in my bare feet with water up to my shins and screamed, "You took everything from me! My family, my friends, my boyfriend, *everything!* I hate you! And I hate where you've brought me! I *hate youuuu!*"

I shouted to the sea as if it were an evil person and fell to my knees, crying with my hands holding my face and letting the tears pour into the sea. I just couldn't handle living on this island anymore. I wanted to sleep in my own bed, in my own home, with my boyfriend and my family a few doors down from my own. I wanted that life back! The boring, normal, and fun life I had back in Canada, with my boring friends and slightly crazy family. This damned sea took it all from me, every last thing that I loved, and the best part? I had no way of getting back home or getting found. It was the ocean that stole this life, the life I planned to spend with Jay . . . Gone. I didn't even know if he was dead or alive. The same was for my family and his too.

"Please stop crying."

"*Who said that?*" I screamed behind me. I was so sad I forgot who was watching me.

"You're gonna catch a cold out there. A few days ago you could've done that, but it's cold right now, if you haven't noticed!"

"Of course, it's cold. The sun went down a few minutes ago. Also, I'm waiting deep in the sea crying . . . Why do you care?"

"You can't afford to get sick here. There are no first-aid kits on the island."

"I know! That's why that guy in that journal died. I'm not stupid. Where are you anyways?"

"I knew that guy too. He was a really nice guy . . . Good friends with your dad."

"How did you know that? And how do you know my father?"

"I've known him a very long time, longer than you have actually."

"How?"

"I was only six when I met you. Of course you were five. So you wouldn't even remember me, but I knew your dad from his job actually. I was with my uncle, who happened to be Simon Salderman. He was great friends with him, and your dad started to really like me. I traveled with him a lot since my uncle didn't want to hire a babysitter, and he had his own kids to take care of as well, so he just left me with your dad. I went around the world with him when he was working. It's the few vacations he took with you. You traveled together. He told me all about your family as you were growing up. One Christmas, my uncle wanted a holiday to himself and his family, so your father invited me to your house for Christmas. I had a great time, and my uncle even got me a gift to give to you. He knew this because everything your dad told me, I told him. Anyways, it was a lot of fun, and I sort of had a crush on you. Your parents thought it was cute since we were really little, and your mom even took a few pictures. I asked her for a good chunk of the photos, and she kept the ones I wasn't in. That's exactly why I'm familiar to you, but you could never remember me because all the photos of us were taken by my uncle and your father, who both disappeared. I gave you that locket actually, but it didn't have any pictures or engraving of an angel. It was just a locket when you got it, and you gave me the most beautiful smile I can still remember today. You have a face that's meant to smile, you know, and I kissed you on the cheek in front of everyone. You lit up like the northern lights you saw on the boat. I kept that photo for myself because that photo would keep you with me forever. It wasn't long after that I had to go back to the ocean, twelve years later. My uncle disappeared and wrote in the journal, which I found only a year ago, and your father was locked up in our jail, in—"

"Atlantis?"

"How did you know?"

"Duh, the journal entry said so."

"Oh, right."

"Really though? My father had been down in Atlantis for years, and you never told me?"

"I think it'd be much more exciting if you found him yourself."

"Well, why is he in jail in the first place?"

"Well . . . your father is a . . . I just can't tell you, Jillian. Not yet."

"He's a what? Please tell me."

"Take a swim tomorrow, and I'll tell you."

"But why can't I know now? I've been waiting all my life to find my father! And you've kept him down there for years, knowing him longer than I have? How could you!"

"It wasn't my idea! My father locked him up."

"And who exactly is your father?"

"None of your beeswax."

I started walking into my home and raced up to my room, and saw nothing.

"I'm not in your house, by the way."

"Where are you? And why does it sound like you're in my house?"

"Why do you want to see me all of the sudden?"

"'Cause I just want to maybe . . . punch you in the face for never telling me about how I know you."

"I doubt that."

"Seriously though . . . where are you?"

"Take a swim tomorrow, and then we'll talk."

"But I want to talk to you now!"

"You are talking to me now."

"But I have tons of questions to ask you."

"They can wait. Besides, it's getting pretty late. I should go."

"I doubt that. Wait . . . you're singing with me every night, aren't you?"

"Duh, didn't you read my note?"

"I prefer talking. Notes is so immature, like I'm in grade school. Face me like a man, will you?"

"I'll see you tomorrow. Goodnight."

"Seth! Tell me where you are! I'm so tired of this! You're the only person I know here! I don't want to be alone again."

"You're not alone. I'm always with you. You know that, right?"

"What's with the 'always' thing? That was between Jay and I and my father."

I looked back down at my wolf totem and held it closer to my heart.

"Your father told me at Christmas. He told me that he was planning to see my father that year, and he said that he would probably never return. His exact words were 'Tell my family I'll be with them, no matter what. Always.' And it wasn't long before your friend Jay used that too, even though he didn't know your father was the one who started it all."

"Jay wasn't just my friend, you know! He was . . . different."

"Your soul mate? I seriously doubt that."

"You don't know me! And you can't tell me who is and isn't my soul mate! He's more of a man than you'll ever be!"

"You can't prove that!"

"At least he wasn't afraid to show himself to me!"

"I said I'd see you tomorrow!"

"So you're just gonna hide from your childhood crush for one night until she has to play hide and seek tomorrow? You're such a wuss."

"Fine then! Close your eyes, and I'll tell you when you can open them."

"You know the second I see you, I'm gonna punch you in the face, right?"

"Yeah, right. Okay, open."

I looked around and didn't see anything but darkness. Seth turned off the lights.

"Really? I still can't see you."

"One second, I still have to close the door."

"Turn on the lights. I want to see if I can recognize you."

All I saw, when I heard the door click shut, was a blue light on his chest, but it wasn't a light when I walked closer. It was a crystal on a necklace glowing around his bare chest. It was the exact same shade of blue my eyes were that night on the boat. I was awed at the crystal and brought it closer to my face.

"Where did you get this?"

"All the citizens of Atlantis wear a crystal necklace. It provides our city with life, technology, and longevity."

"Longevity? What do you mean 'longevity'?"

"When we so desire, the king can bless the crystal, and in return, we never age."

"So you're immortal? How long have you been this age?"

"Well, I'm only seventeen. This year my crystal will be blessed, and I'll be seventeen forever."

"Really? That's so cool! But I'd want to be immortal when I'm twenty-one, so I can drink in the States."

"Why be twenty-one forever in the States when you can be seventeen and immortal by the sea?"

"I want to see my family and friends again, though. I miss them."

I let go of the crystal and let it fall back onto his chest; it lighted up everything but his face.

"Why can't I see your face?"

"You can see the rest of me, can't you?"

"It's your face I want to see . . . and then punch."

"I can see yours, though."

"Exactly! It's only fair that you show me yours."

I looked at my iPhone on the side of my bed and saw my face was lit up from his crystal. I sighed and put the iPhone back down on the bed and looked back at the crystal.

"Why save me anyways? You could've just let me drown that day."

"I could've. You wouldn't be the first."

"Did you let my father drown?!"

"No, of course not! If anything, he's like me."
"And how is he like you?"
"We can both survive underwater."
"You scuba dive?"
"Don't need to."
"I don't get it . . . but you didn't answer my question."

I sat down on the edge of my bed and gestured for him to sit down next to me. I saw the crystal move forward a few steps, but he didn't sit down to join me.

"I couldn't just let you drown. I've been waiting to see you again for years. I grew up from the little boy you can barely remember, and the second I saw that boat with you on board, I was so happy to see you again. I couldn't forget the face that gave me the best hugs that Christmas. I knew there was a hurricane coming for your boat, but if I had come aboard and told you, you would've freaked out and feared me."

"You knew a hurricane was gonna wreck our boat? The thing that possibly killed my family and nearly killed me? *You bastard! How could you!*"

"Hey! I saved you! Aren't you glad about that?"

"*Why! Seth?*"

"I've . . . always loved you. But I could never have you. My father forbids me from falling in love with a human."

"You can't love me. You never have, and you never will."

"I always have. Only that you lived by the ocean once and moved to Canada, and I never saw you again."

"And why can't you love a human?"

"You can't know. I'm not really a human."

"You don't have a fish head, do you? I took a few photos from your hut, and you seem pretty human to me."

"I'm not happy about the condition about my hut either. It took me a few years to put that all together."

"And only one night to steal my things."

"They weren't yours in the first place!"

"Whose were they then, hmm?"

"My father's actually. They were his, and someone stole them and hid them in chests for him to bring to the surface at some point."

"It's why my father's in jail, isn't it?"

"I didn't say that."

I got up and heard him back up against a wall when I walked closer to him.

"Your dad thinks my father stole those from him?"

"My father is much more powerful than you know. He is only thought to be a legend."

"You talk of your dad like he's a god."

"In a way, he is."

"You're so full of it! My father is a great man and not guilty of these crimes. He's not a thief!"

Seth came closer, forcing me to back up onto the other wall.

"Your father didn't know that my dad could've killed him on the spot, and I was the one who saved his life! I saved you on his request that his little angel wouldn't suffer the same fate as he did!"

"You let him be killed!"

"*No!* I was the one who said he should be imprisoned instead of killed! I'm the reason you're still alive!"

"If you can't love a human, why save me if my father couldn't even save himself!"

"Because you're the only human worth saving!"

"I'm not the little angel everyone thinks I am. *This damn Island is hell! I hate it here!*"

Seth came up closer and put both his arms on either side of me, coming so close to my face that I could feel his breath hit my cheeks. It scared me a little.

"This island and I are the only things keeping you alive. If you dare try to break your father out of jail, I'll kill you myself."

"Ooooo! I'm so scared."

"You should be."

"I was being sarcastic."

"I wasn't."

"So first you saved me, just so you can be the one to kill me. That makes sense."

"I don't want to kill you, Jill. Just promise me you won't try and rescue your dad."

"What if I can prove he's innocent?"

"What do you mean? You don't even know what my father has lost."

"I bet you anything I have his treasures on the island right now."

"You're going to have to speak to my father then."

"Maybe you can back off also. You're kind of scaring me."

"So I scare you?"

"Only when you've got me up against a wall where I still can't see your face."

"You should be scared."

"The only thing that doesn't scare me is your necklace. It's very nice."

"I saw you made a few necklaces yourself. My favorite is the wolf."

Seth grabbed the wolf totem and pulled it up to his face, still as dark as the room behind him.

"Reminds you of your Jay, doesn't it?"

"Don't you ever call him that, Seth. That's all I have left to remember him by. You have no right to call him Jay."

"It's a cute nickname, but why a wolf to remember him?"

"His friends gave him a nickname 'Wolf man' because he was as warm as a werewolf, and never got cold."

"The Wolf of Wisdom, is it not?"

"Yes, but the wisdom is more my thing."

"Isn't that nice? I think the wolf is more like me because I'm the smartest person in Atlantis with the exception of my family."

"I really don't care if you're the smartest person in an underwater city. You can't replace the family and wolf I lost."

"Can't I at least make you feel better?"

"I'd feel better if you back off a little bit."

"My bad."

He took his arms off the wall and stepped back and apologized for pushing me up against a wall.

"I should probably go."

"I only have one more question for you then."

"What's that?"

"If you've always loved me, saved me, and kept me alive on this island . . . why bother with coming back up to the surface to sing with me and show me everything but your face?"

"I . . . You remind me of someone I lost too. My mother looked so much like you, and she loved to sing more than anyone else I knew. She was a pure mermaid, beautiful and immortal for only eighty years, but stopped aging at about twenty-five or so. At one point, she came to the surface to explore the world out of the sea. She sang to her heart's content and found the only thing that can kill an immortal mermaid. Sharks."

"How did her singing attract sharks?"

"She was near the surface too long, and it was the shark breeding season. She was right in the middle of it, and my father couldn't get to her in time."

"What happened to her necklace?"

"My father made her a unique crystal, one that no Atlantian has ever had. It was made from a peridot, which was perfectly cut and placed on a necklace for her. He lost that peridot and has grieved in secret ever since. Everyone misses her voice and the happiness she brought to Atlantis.

You remind me so much of her, and my father promised that day that it is forbidden to interfere with humans or the surface, let alone fall in love with one."

"Yet I can't see your face?"

"The only thing I want you to see now is my crystal. That is all."

"Can I have a crystal like that? It's very beautiful."

"It is to any mortal, but something that happened on the boat is why I'm here telling you. You can swim tomorrow and find out for yourself what I want you to see."

"Are you talking about the night I looked like an angel and had crazy glowing blue eyes?"

"Yes, it doesn't happen to normal people. It happens only to those who are . . . you could say, different."

"What are you getting at?"

"I've already said too much. I really got to go now. But what I told you tonight stays with you to your grave."

"Sure, whatever you say, Seth."

"Thank you."

Seth walked up to me and lifted my chin up with his hand and kissed me on the cheek. I smiled a little, but he didn't see it. I didn't even see his face after it all, and he stopped only an inch from my lips. I could tell he wanted to kiss me so bad and had to pull back, but he remained so close to my face. I knew that if I kissed him, he might just pull me closer and enjoy it. It was easily a full minute of just him holding my chin up to his lips and being tempted to kiss me, knowing that he shouldn't. He finally placed one hand on my face and the other behind my neck. I put my hand on the hand he had on my face, silently screaming, "It's okay! You can kiss me." I closed my eyes and nuzzled into his hand, which was surprisingly warm and soft. I opened my eyes for a second and saw his eyes glow bright neon blue, the exact same way mine lit up with Jay on the boat. I gasped ever so quietly and finally saw his face. It was so clear and bright. His face was sculpted and handsome. It was amazing, like he had the face of a model, yet he looked like a handsome man I might see in a movie. It was incredible how he looked at me. All along, one man I knew thought I looked like an angel, when all along, Seth was the one who looked like an angel. My eyes widened for a second when I saw his face glow brighter, and I knew that my eyes were glowing as well.

"Why are your eyes glowing?" I whispered to Seth.

He smiled and laughed a little as he looked down and back up with those amazing eyes.

"Let's just say it wasn't just me that saved you. It's what I did that makes us so similar. It's the reason I want you to dive into the ocean tomorrow and find out what I really am. I can't hide what I am anymore from you. You found my father's treasures, you sing like my mother, you discovered the journal, and you even found the secret of the crystals on the island. You . . . you're hard to keep secrets from."

"Are you saying this island is where the crystals of Atlantis came from?"

"If you want to, you can stumble on the biggest secret any person can discover with me, or stay on this island, eating pomegranates with Miko and singing along with the piano."

"Of course I want to see Atlantis, but will I ever be able to come back to this island if I want to?"

"Always."

I smiled, and his eyes finally stopped glowing, as did mine, but I could still see his face from the glow on his necklace. He smiled back at me and kissed me, pulling me close to his chest. I didn't exactly know what I might find tomorrow in the ocean. All I knew was that Seth would be the one to take me there. His crystal stopped glowing and left Seth to kiss me in the dark of the room; it only made the moment better, and he was a very good kisser. When he finally stopped kissing me, I only looked up at his eyes and looked back down to smile and blush. Why on earth was I blushing? I was blushing at someone who recently agreed they wouldn't kill me. Seth's crystal started to glow again, and he left without saying another word. I sat down on my bed and watched him walk on the beach in the middle of the night. His crystal lighted the way ahead of him and let me see him look back in my window for a second and dive into the sea. I only sat there, looking at my wolf totem. I took it off and left it on my dresser. I changed into pajamas and fell asleep right away. I could only think of his eyes glowing like mine the entire night. What it meant, I still don't know, but I had a feeling I'll find out tomorrow morning, somewhere in the sea.

Chapter 20

It was my sixth day here, August 20, and today was the day I would find out what lay in the underwater city of Atlantis. I leaped up out of bed and smiled a little when I found I still had the taste of Seth on my tongue. Miko fell out of his bed, scared from my sudden awakening, and raced down the stairs when I sang, "Good morning." Miko seemed a little jumpy, but I could care less since I finally would get to swim in the ocean again. I picked my red bikini to wear and threw on my golden skirt. I made a quick breakfast of berries and frozen yogurt and drank it all in a matter of seconds, giving me an awful brain freeze. I grabbed a pomegranate for Miko and cut it open, leaving the rest of the work for him to do. He had hands; he could do the rest himself.

"If you get hungry, Miko, there's plenty of fruit in the bowl on the counter."

Miko nodded and waved at me as I left and rushed outside; it was perfect timing to see the sun rise. It was a rather nice sunrise, but I started to step into the water. It was warm and clear, and it was a perfect day to go for a swim. I took off my skirt and scrunched it in a ball and threw it at my deck, since I didn't want it to wash away. The water was so inviting, and I dived right in, letting the sea soak my hair and wash all around me again. This time, I was glad to be in the water. It was so nice, and the second I got to the surface, I yelled "Woohoo!" I loved this feeling of freedom and warmth of sun on my skin again. I loved it! Only then something didn't feel right. My legs kind of hurt a little, and suddenly, staying afloat got harder and harder until I could no longer tread in the water and sank for a minute. I held my breath and felt my legs burn like hell, but it didn't make me gasp and swallow any water. I watched as my legs glowed bright blue again and pull together to give me one leg . . . and over the top, scales that shimmered blue and a touch of silver in the center of the scales. "A tail? I had a freakin' tail? No way..."

I inhaled the water, scared at first, but I wasn't drowning; it was like breathing in the freshest air I'd ever had the pleasure of breathing.

"I think I drowned, and this is heaven, maybe?"

I looked around and happened to notice that no bubbles came out of my mouth when I spoke. I didn't have any oxygen in my lungs, nor was any oxygen leaving my lungs when I exhaled; my lungs had either stopped working or were completely full of water. I had no idea what to do but freaked out and screamed as I swam around, looking at my tail and trying to figure out what on earth was going on.

"If this is heaven, why am I a mermaid? I can't be dead! I'd have wings... Do I have wings?"

I looked behind me and saw no wings.

"No... Okay then, why a blue tail? How am I breathing water? I can't breathe water? Lungs don't do that! What do I do?!" I yelled at myself until I realized I was talking as clearly as a bell, as if I was speaking on land. I wasn't amazed only at how I was still alive, but at how I could talk and even sing as if I was on the surface.

"Hello? Is anyone there?"

I looked around and even swam forward with ease, looking for Seth. I had never swum this way before. I didn't need to use my arms or ever have to swim to the surface for air; I just flipped my tail up and down and sped forward like I was wearing the best set of swim fins in the world. I saw nothing but clear blue water. The bottom of the sea got deeper and deeper, and a sudden hill of sand blocked my path. I peeked over the hill and saw a beautiful coral reef in front of me. I only said, "Wow!" to the wonderful sight before me and swam up to the squishy sponges, the hard coral, and the wavy coral that had fish going in and out of it everywhere I looked. I couldn't even count the fish that passed me as I touched all the coral. I even saw a dolphin laugh as it swam over me, and it made me smile. I'd never seen a dolphin this close before, and I couldn't help but swim up to it and play with it. It did a flip in the water a few times and disappeared in a cave, but I flipped in the water once and burst out of the water and dived straight back in, leaving a trail of bubbles behind me.

I never felt so good in my life. I got used to the tail after a few minutes of swimming and started singing. I sang a song I heard in *Tangled*, when lanterns were released into the sky and Rapunzel and Eugene sang "I See the Light." it wasn't long before I heard someone sing in harmony with me.

"Seth? I know that's you."

"Nope. Try again!"

I swam over to see the head of Seth but swam up behind him, being very quiet and sneaky. I blew it when I laughed a little and said, "Oh, darn."

"Well, don't you ever look nice?"

"I can't believe you didn't tell me I could turn into a mermaid! How did this happen? I didn't turn into a mermaid all the other times I swam in the ocean."

"To make a long story short, I happen to be a hybrid, which is a human/merman. I have the ability to swim in the ocean as a merman and walk on land as a human. I also have the power to turn any human I want into a hybrid such as myself."

"How did you do that?"

"The night I saved you—"

Seth swam up closer to me and grabbed my hands.

"You were so close to dying. I thought I couldn't save you, until I tried CPR a few more times, and you coughed up so much water on the sand. You must have been dead for at least five minutes, and you were barely conscious when you started breathing and basically just fell asleep. I carried you up to that house, took off your very heavy clothes still dripping with water, and placed you on the dry bed. Don't worry, you were still wearing your bikini, and I didn't take that off."

"Thank you."

"Anyways, you smiled when I lay down next to you, and you flipped over onto my chest and placed your cold hand on my stomach. I didn't want to move because you looked so peaceful and happy. I had no idea if you even knew it was me, but I stayed there with you for a few minutes until you were in a really deep sleep and got up. I looked back at you on the bed, and saw you turn on back and flip your head on your pillow toward me and smile. Your eyes weren't even open, but I walked back and kissed you. From that moment, I had given you the power to be just like me in the water, even though you didn't know I existed. I made sure every day you had food, warmth, and security, even though I risked my life every time to see you."

"So what was that kiss last night for?"

"Because I always wanted to, when you're awake that is."

Seth kissed me on the cheek, and I knew I looked the exact same as I did that one Christmas we had together. He told me to follow him, but he zipped away much faster than I hoped, since I hadn't had much practice at swimming fast. By the time I figured out how to swim much faster, all I saw was a trail of bubbles leading me somewhere bright, toward a massive hill of sand and rocks. I swam up and over the hill and saw a city glowing yellow and white with golden buildings and silver towers. I couldn't take my eyes off the mermaids swimming in and out of the city from above and the gateway that said: "Welcome to the Capital city of Atlantis."

I gasped as I swam into the huge city, seeing merpeople of all ages and sizes. I was awed at the children playing in a park and the colors of everyone's tails, which matched their eye color as well. I looked around at the hundreds of merpeople I was just dying to meet, and a mermaid, who looked about the same age as me, swam up and said hello.

"Hi! You're new here, aren't you? What city are you from?"

"There are more underwater cities? No way!"

"Yeah, there's like twenty . . . Wait . . . are you from the surface?"

"Yep. I'm looking for a friend of mine though. I lost him a ways back, and he said he'd—"

"No time! I hate to be panicky, but all hybrids must see the king first before deciding to join the city."

"Can I at least know your name?"

"Sure! I'm Akari."

"Nice to meet you. I'm Jillian."

"Cool! Let's go."

She swam up ahead of me, and I managed to follow her just fine through the twists and turns of the city.

"Has anyone ever told you how much you look like the queen?"

"Yes, I have actually. What was her name?"

"Augustina. It's scary how similar you two look. Do you like singing too?"

"I love singing, and I'm pretty good says my, umm, merfriend, if that's even a word."

"It is, but you should show the king that."

"Who's the king anyways?"

"Neptune."

I thought to myself, "If this was really the Neptune I learned about in a Greek Gods class, I don't think I'm gonna be going home in one piece tonight." Two guards stood at a shimmering silver gate and looked down with anger at Akari and me.

"I have a hybrid here to see the king."

"Oh! Well, go right ahead!"

The guards opened the gate and smiled as we swam by.

"Is Neptune a very nice king?"

"He is on one condition."

"What condition is that?"

"If you're from royal blood and you haven't met any of his sons."

"Oh dear," I whispered to myself as Akari stopped me beside her and called for King Neptune.

"I have brought a hybrid here who wishes to join our society."

I looked closer into the dark water and saw a massive merman swim forward with a trident in his hand and a crown with many rare jewels glittering at me. In a booming voice, Neptune spoke to me.

"What is your name?"

"Jillian Verbicky."

"Who turned you into a hybrid?"

"I'm pretty sure it was a merman named Seth."

"My youngest son, Seth?"

"Maybe! I don't know any other merpeople in this city, Your Majesty!"

"Bring forth my sons!" Neptune commanded and turned on the lamps around us, lighting up the room and letting him find his throne. For some reason, the lamps were burning with flames that I thought was impossible.

"While we are waiting for your sons, may I ask how it is possible for fire to burn underwater?"

"This fire burns underwater from the gases connected to the volcano not too far from here. These gases are too hot, and they burn like fire and light up my palace."

"That's really cool."

I saw Neptune's three sons come out of the side of the room and line up by their father's side.

"What appears to be the problem, Father?" the first son asked.

"Seth turned a human into a hybrid."

"Seth! How could you!"

The second brother hit Seth on the back of the head as Seth said, "Ow!"

"I'd like to introduce my three sons, my eldest son, Sedrick."

The first son kissed my hand, saying, "It is a pleasure to meet you." I nodded in return and didn't say a word.

"My second eldest son, Skylar."

The second son kissed my hand and only smiled, and I smiled back at him in return.

"And my youngest son, Seth."

Seth kissed my hand and smiled, but he winked at me, making me smile more brightly than I did before.

"Now why do you wish to join the people of Atlantis?"

"Do you want to hear the very long story of how all this happened, Your Majesty?"

"Absolutely, from start to finish."

"Okay, this all started when I was going on a weeklong cruise to Hawaii with my mother, brother, and my best friend, plus his family. The cruise was going just fine until the third day, when a hurricane sunk our boat and separated me from everyone on the cruise, leaving me all alone on a raft for two days. At the end of the second day, my raft crashed into a rock and knocked me unconscious, and I nearly died. However, I woke up the next morning, safe and in a warm bed. Seth told me the other day that he was the one who saved me and that he was the one who gave me the powers to transform into a mermaid or a hybrid as you all call it."

I saw Sedrick, Skylar, and Neptune scowl at Seth, as he scratched his head and looked down to his right.

"I was warned that I shouldn't swim in the ocean, since it was shark breeding season, and I stayed in the house for a day. Over the past few days, I've killed fifteen sharks, explored a few large parts of the island, and picked pomegranates with a spider monkey called Miko."

"A monkey? That's kind of . . . cute. Go on."

"At one point, I got lost in the forest and found an oasis that saved me from dehydration and led me to find an underwater cave full of crystals of every kind. I even filled my bag with as many crystals as I could and almost got eaten by a shark on the way back. Ever since that, I basically spent my time carving totems, making pomegranate smoothies, singing by the fire, and walking along the beach during a sunset."

"Did you say singing?"

"Yes, I've even heard Seth sing with me. I really do love singing."

"Seth? Singing? I've never heard Seth sing ever since his mother died. You remind me very much of her."

"I was told of how she died. I'm very sorry for your loss."

"Thank you, you have no idea how much I see of her in you. But it wasn't just my queen I have lost. I had three treasures I kept to always have her with me that I have misplaced. If you can bring me these treasures, I will let you become a citizen of Atlantis."

"What are these treasures, Your Majesty?"

"A blue pearl, which I found far out of our city, that I gave to Augustina for her birthday, her tiara, and a perfectly cut peridot gem that I made for her necklace. It was different than the blue crystals that what the normal merpeople wear. It was her birthstone and matched her bright green eyes. I really miss her so, and her spirit just isn't the same anymore. Her voice used to ring through the streets of Atlantis clear as a bell and her liveliness was an infinite joy and she had a warm heart. She brought something to the city that hasn't been found since. When she died, a part of Atlantis died with her. It's true we have many who can sing, but it's just not the same."

"If it makes you feel any better, I have these treasures on the island right now. Say the word and I can bring them to you."

"Really? Where did you find my treasures?"

"The pearl was given to me as a gift and the tiara I found in a chest. The peridot I found myself in a cavern when a friend gave me the blue pearl. It was a very nice gift."

"Thank you so much. You are welcome to join the people of Atlantis. But I want you to do one more thing for me."

"What is that?"

"Can you sing for me?"

"What should I sing?"

"Anything. I want to hear if you sing like her as well."

I thought hard on what I should sing for Neptune, and nothing popped in my head. I could only think of one thing to sing, and that was "Believe," just the chorus though. I didn't want to sing the entire song for him.

"'Cause everything starts from something, but something would be nothing, nothing if your heart didn't dream with me. Where would I be, if you didn't believe?"

"You sound just like her. Please . . .," Neptune swam up from his throne and up to me, "take this necklace. You are now a citizen of the city, of Atlantis."

"Thank you, Your Majesty. Can you tell me about these necklaces a little more though?"

"Absolutely. I have been the king of Atlantis since 360 BC, and I found these crystals on an island and shaped them into necklaces to wear. With my own powers, I used them for weapons, life, technology, and longevity. I thought that if anyone could choose their age to live forever, I'd have way too many young mermaids in my city, so I would give them a bigger necklace when they turned eighteen, and from that age, they can decide what age they want to remain forever. There are still many people in Atlantis as old as me. Only we've decided to stop aging at thirty or so."

"So how come I can still join this city, even though I'm not from royal blood?"

"I can see that my youngest son has grown to be very fond of you, and I want you to be able to explore my kingdom with him."

I smiled and looked down at the crystal necklace glowing around my neck, while Seth swam up to his father and told him, "Father, I believe that she really is from royal blood. I saw one of the signs occur on her boat and again last night."

"Are you sure of this?"

"Positive."

The Tail of an Angel

"It would seem that you may be from royal blood, but I'd have to see for myself if you are truly royal."

"To be honest, it's not something I can turn on and off."

"Are you sure? Because your eyes are glowing."

"Really?"

I looked down and saw the ground glow bright blue, and I looked over to a mirror on a wall and noticed they glowed the very same way my necklace did.

I tried to close my eyes, but they still glowed.

"Wait, this can't be right! This should only happen on land!"

Neptune's sons swam forward, but he stopped them from trying to reach me.

"Don't move! I have to see this with my own eyes."

I started to rise up, the very same lights I saw on the boat twirling around me again. I looked all around and saw my legs return; a white dress covered my bikini top and almost went past my knees, and it was so beautiful and white. I must have looked like an angel by now. Then I felt my back hurt again, and I knew this time my wings had returned, exactly like on the boat. I started feeling a little dizzy and then really, really hot. I felt like I was in a state of being half awake and half asleep, even though I knew exactly what was going on. It was like I was paralyzed, but I was still aware of what was happening and saw that I started glowing blue all over and felt my skin get harder, like a crystal. Feeling warm and seeing blue all around me, I saw the three treasures that belonged to the king appear in front of me and float toward the king, and he grabbed them from the bubbles that contained the treasures and popped them when he touched them. I closed my eyes and heard something coming from my necklace, a woman's voice, speaking in the brightest tone I'd ever heard.

"Protect this girl, for a part of me lives on within her."

"Augustina?" I heard the king ask.

"Yes, she is indeed from royal blood, only from another king in the sea. She is not a part of the royal family from your own. I can tell you I live in her heart, sharing her spirit, and her voice is very much the same as mine. I do indeed miss our sons: Sedrick, Skylar, and Seth. They will grow up to be the handsomest and wisest of men in all of Atlantis. My king, you will have to make a choice in the future that will put either Seth or this girl in danger. This choice may lead you to lose Seth or lose the girl with my spirit."

"Why are you telling me this?"

"Because I must give this warning that will change your life. The girl will soon be in danger and she must be protected from a great evil that is approaching. I never really left the kingdom you see, because I live on through this angel."

"Will you ever return to us, my queen?"

"I will always be with you, in the darkest of times, and be the shining light that you can face on your own. I will never forget my time here, and I will always love you."

"I will miss you so much, Augustina. I always will."

"Never forget me, my king. Always remember me and cherish your time and family here. Always."

I felt slightly less warm and I started to move back down on the floor, and then I blacked out, feeling my wings and dress bubble away and fall to the ground. I was completely out for a minute or two until I woke up with Seth holding me in his arms, asking if I was all right. I looked back down at myself and saw that my bikini top had returned and my tail was back.

"Well, that's never happened before."

"Are you gonna be okay?"

"Yeah, I'll be fine."

I rubbed my eyes and noticed they were still glowing blue, and the king's crystal as well as his sons' all lit up and got brighter while mine returned to normal. I blinked a few times, and when my eyes stopped glowing, their crystals returned to normal like my own.

"I see. You do know what this means, right?"

"Not really, Your Majesty."

"Somehow you are from a royal bloodline of mermaids, maybe a king, maybe a queen. Whatever it is, that could mean you are a princess and be able to marry a prince of your choice from any of our cities."

"How many underwater cities are there?"

"About twenty or so, which means you have lots of princes to choose from, including my own."

"What about what I heard from my necklace?"

"I was surprised to hear that my wife and queen Augustina is indeed still alive, but only within you."

"How is that possible?"

"You, in fact, have her voice and her spirit that lives on through your heart. She told us that you were in danger and must be watched to make sure nothing can harm you or suffer the same fate as my queen. Seth will take you on a tour of my kingdom and answer any other questions you have.

"Another point to be noted is that I was told I'd have to make a choice on whether or not to lose you or my son Seth. I'm not worried for the future if you are safe in the present."

"One more thing, I must ask you."

"What is that?"

"I read in a journal that my father is being held in a prison here. Why was he imprisoned in the first place?"

"Your father was the one who stole my treasures and I was going to kill him for his crimes, but my son Seth convinced me prison would be a better choice. He stole my treasures because he gave my blue pearl to his wife as a gift. His wife not knowing he stole it from me broke my rules of falling for a human on land, even though I forbid it."

"Really? How come your son isn't in prison because of me?"

"What?! Seth is involved with you?"

"Oops."

Seth looked up at his father and gave an innocent smile, saying, "My bad."

"I cannot throw my own son in prison, but I will not allow you to spend a night with Seth. If I find out, I will kill you."

"I understand, but why can't you release my father after I brought back your treasures?"

"I still cannot forgive him for living on land and falling in love with a human."

"Then why did he come back?"

"He came back to ask for forgiveness, and I showed no mercy."

"But you have your treasures! He's innocent and he returned to apologize for his wrongdoing."

"I've made up my mind, Jillian, end of story! Now off you go. Explore my kingdom as you please."

"Thank you, Your Majesty."

Akari waved good-bye as Seth and I left the room and swam out into the streets. I had so many more questions to ask Seth.

"So tell me more about Atlantis."

"Our city thrived once on land. We had life and technologies far beyond that of any other civilization. Immortal and free, our way of life was very much alive and growing in power. My father had some of the most powerful weapons of war, Only that was really our downfall. Our greatest weapon, the power of the crystal, grew to a size too big to control and grew a mind of its own, deciding things for the city the king couldn't stop. It is said that the gods thought this crystal could possess the same power as the gods in a few short days, and so they destroyed our city. The crystal formed a shield over the city and brought us down into the ocean, never to see the light of day again. I know this story because the elders spoke of it to me when I was a child. Everyone in Atlantis knows this story."

"So where does the mermaid part come in?"

"The crystal couldn't shield over the city forever, and so my father formed these new necklaces that allowed us to breathe underwater. It wasn't for a few years that we grew tails and began to . . . bear children with tails as well."

"So how does that work?"

"It's the same way fish do. Women lay their eggs and the men fertilize them."

"Eww. Humans are so much better."

"I agree."

"So tell me about the music of Atlantis."

"As you may already know, my mother loved to sing, and she wasn't the only one who fell in love with music. Before Atlantis was pulled down into the sea, we had all sorts of instruments to play: harps, trumpets, flutes, harmonicas you name it. It was an amazing time when my mother sang, and nothing but beautiful music echoed from every corner in Atlantis. When she died, everyone stopped playing the instruments, and the worst part is that the best players forgot how to play them again. With no use for the instruments, they were left to dust and were dropped everywhere in the city, but most of them were washed away or eaten by large fish."

"How could the instruments collect dust?"

"It's just really fine sand."

"Oh, okay. There are also a few more questions I have for you."

"Shoot."

"What do you do for fun around here?"

"Well, there's the library, arcade, and the park."

"You have an arcade? How on earth do you have an arcade?"

"We use seashells as currency, and we play Pacman, Super Mario Bros, and much more."

"What's in the park?"

"There's a statue of my mother in the middle of it. Trees, flowers, and grass surround it, and it's a really nice park actually."

"Can we go there?"

"Sure, is there anything else you want to see first?"

"I wouldn't mind seeing the castle."

"Absolutely! Follow me."

"So is the castle full of gold and treasure?"

"Yep."

"And where did you find it all?"

"Most of it we found in the ocean, but some is from the surface, where we conquered many rich cities and took their treasure."

"What cities have you conquered?"

"Lots, but we destroyed them, so you wouldn't know the names of the cities."

Seth swam up to pass the guards and led me to a massive ballroom, shining with silver walls and golden decorations.

"This was where the king would throw parties when we still had legs. Now it's just for show."

"It's beautiful."

"Just wait until you see our rooms."

"Awesome."

Outside the ballroom, Seth showed me rooms just full of treasure, another with instruments that had dust on them. A piano was in the back and I swam up to play it.

"Does it still work?"

"Yep, try playing something."

I played "Someone Like You" by Adele and sang along with it; it sounded even better underwater. I saw Seth swim over and sit on the bench next to me and sing in harmony during the chorus. I had a sense I was being watched by someone besides Seth, but I continued to finish the song.

"You guys should totally form a band."

I saw that Sedrick and Skylar were behind us at the door, watching us sing the whole time.

"Yeah, you rock at playing the piano!"

Skylar applauded and laughed as I got up to leave the room, and he joined us on the tour of the castle. Sedrick followed Seth, thinking he had nothing better to do; that was what I guessed. I was taken to a bright blue room, where the king kept his three treasures and other treasures that meant very much to the king. I saw many perfectly cut gems, golden jewelry, and so much more. Seth lifted up a red curtain which covered a statue about the same height as me. When I swam up closer, I saw it was the most beautiful statue of the queen, in pure gold.

"She looks so much like me."

"She does."

Seth put his arms around my shoulder and told me more about her.

"Same smile, same hair, same voice, same birthstone."

"Peridot I'm guessing."

"Yep."

Seth took his arm off my shoulder and asked me to follow him, but I stayed for a minute, looking at her hand that was flat. Reaching forward, I placed my hand on it, noticing it was the exact same size, same shape, and same nails. I looked into the eyes for a second before leaving the room and following Seth.

"So how old are you all then?"

Sedrick swam up to me so I could hear what he would say.

"I'm twenty, but I've been twenty for two years."

Skylar swam up in front of me, forcing me to stop swimming forward.

"I've have been twenty when I turned twenty on my birthday."

"Why didn't you want to stop aging at eighteen?"

"I didn't want to be a teenager for the rest of my life."

I smiled and resumed to follow Seth to his room. He opened the door to his room, and it was almost too bright to look at until my eyes finally adjusted to the shine inside. I rubbed my eyes for a second and then couldn't help adore the beauty of his room. There was a bed with a gold headboard and a silver footboard. He had silk sheets with silver stitching on it; it was simple yet breathtaking. He had a plain-looking dresser next to it with a golden rim and a floor made of white tiles. The walls were covered with frames of him and his friends and some with his family. On side of the room, there was a trophy case containing some necklaces, photos, and a photo of him and me. The roof had a white chandelier which lit up his room like the sun. I swam closer to the trophy case and saw a wolf tooth necklace, very similar to the one Jay had given me.

"I lost my wolf tooth necklace recently. You wouldn't happen to know anything about that, would you?"

"Wouldn't you prefer a necklace that glows and gives you immortal life?"

"That's my wolf tooth necklace, you know."

"Maybe."

"I really want that back, Seth."

"You already have a wolf totem."

"It was a gift from Jay!"

"Fine, I'll get it for you."

Seth swam up to the glass and opened the glass door, and he gave me back the wolf tooth necklace. I grabbed it and put it around my neck; it fell right in place next to the crystal necklace.

"So have you two been to the surface at some point?" I asked Seth's brothers.

"Oh yeah! I've been on the surface lots of times, mostly to Canada." Skylar told me.

"Really? What parts of Canada?"

"Mostly British Columbia, Alberta, Halifax, and Quebec."

"What part of Alberta?"

"Southern Alberta."

"Shame, the northern part is much more beautiful."

The Tail of an Angel

"I'll be sure to visit another day."

Seth escorted me from his room to the hallway, where I was thinking I would see Skylar's room next.

Once I walked in, I noticed right away his room wasn't as glamorous as Seth's, but was covered in posters of bands and movie posters I knew. It reminded me of my brother's room, covered with so many posters that you could no longer see any color of the wall behind it. There were still some treasures around the room and over hundred music CDs and movies.

"So do you have the animated Disney movie *Atlantis*? Sounds a little similar to what you have going on here."

"Granted, it is a little similar. It's a fictional story and only small bits and pieces relate to what is happening in Atlantis."

"And have you seen *The Little Mermaid*?"

"Yep."

"Doesn't her story sound almost the same as what happened to your mother?"

"Ah, her mother was killed by getting hit with a ship. Even though she liked to sing, it doesn't mean that it is the same thing that my mother used to do."

"But there's no music in Atlantis or instruments."

"Music isn't forbidden here. Everyone has just forgotten how to play music."

"Then why don't you play one of those CDs for everyone?"

Skylar looked over at his collection and swam over to pick up a CD.

"I collected these all when I was on land. This CD is my favorite."

I swam over to where he stood, and saw he wasn't holding a music CD, but a movie. I knew this movie too; it was called *Tangled*.

"This is your favorite movie?"

"Yes."

"Mine too! I even have the soundtrack!"

"Same here!"

Skylar grabbed another CD titled *Tangled: Music from the Motion Picture*.

"What's your favorite song from the movie?"

"'I See the Light.' You?"

"The one when her hair glows."

"The healing incantation?"

"Yes! That one! I even memorized it."

"Then by all means sing it for me!"

I looked over at Seth and Sedrick and saw them nod in return, encouraging me to sing.

"I might not remember the entire song, just a heads-up."

"Go ahead."

I finished singing and watched Sedrick, Skylar, and Seth stand still for a moment, their jaws dropping all at the same time.

"Is something wrong? 'Cause I know I'm off-key."

"Not in the slightest. That was beautiful!" Seth swam up to me and smiled.

"Are you sure? I've never had a single voice lesson in all my life, but I was in my school choir for a few years and we got silver at this one competition, even though I thought our choir sounded the best and—"

"You sounded amazing," Seth cut me off and told me to follow him to Sedrick's room.

"No wonder you decided to save the best for last."

"Seth's room was my favorite so far."

Sedrick opened the door to his own room and invited me to go inside. His room was entirely different from the others; his room made my jaw drop.

His room was bright green and blue with a floor of dark hardwood. His room was very organized and clean, and there were only a few pictures on the wall. I swam up to one photo and saw Sedrick and a girl . . . on land.

"Who is she?"

"When I was visiting the surface, I met a girl I won't ever forget. Her name was Sapphire. She had the most beautiful, dark blue eyes, much darker than yours."

"Aren't you forbidden to fall in love with a human?"

"Just because it's a rule, it doesn't mean it can't be broken."

"Tell me more about her."

"She loved to play guitar and play on the beach. That was kind of how I met her really. I was walking along the beach and saw her walking not too far ahead of me and asked if I could join her. She loved a sunset on the beach more than anything else in the world. It wasn't long before I asked her out many times, and every time was even better than the last."

"So why did you go back to the ocean?"

"It wasn't really my choice. I got in a car accident that nearly killed her and seriously injured me. I realized if I continued to stay on land, I would grow old and eventually die. I was nineteen at the time and spent one more year with her before I returned to the sea. It was an amazing year, probably the best of my life. It was the hardest thing I have ever done, when I said I had to leave her, but just before I did, we got our names tattooed on one another."

Seth pointed to Sedrick's upper chest on the left side, where I saw the name "Sapphire" written in dark blue and a light blue heart next to it.

"I asked for her name there because it's just over the heart, to keep her close. And even though the heart is on the left side, it's always right."

"Where did she get your name?"

"Same spot. Only a week later, I spent my last night with her on the beach,. It was definitely one of the best nights of my life."

"In other words, they did the dance with no pants on."

"Thank you, Skylar."

"No problem."

I laughed a little. I saw Sedrick take the photo of her and him off the wall and stare at it as if he was really with her again.

"What I wouldn't give to change her into a hybrid, but I just couldn't."

"Why not?"

"She wasn't a descendent of anyone royal and couldn't marry a prince."

"But you still love her?"

"Of course I do. Even if I did change her into a hybrid, she and I could never be together."

"Will you ever go back to her?"

"By the time I do, she will have already died."

"But you can give her a crystal necklace, can't you? She could still live as long as you if she has one, right?"

"If I gave her one, the powers still wouldn't work outside the water."

"Isn't there anyone else in the sea you might learn to love?"

"I've almost met every princess in the ocean. Most of them are narcissistic and vain."

"I'm just guessing at this, but I'm thinking that Sapphire was kind, maybe shy, loving, and had a pure heart."

"Exactly."

"Are you going to be all right?"

Sedrick put the photo back on his wall and looked down at the floor. I looked up at him and saw on his face exactly what I had felt when I realized Jay was dead. I gave him a hug; at least he got a hug when all I got was nothing but tears and the feeling of coldness. He smiled at me and said thank you. I knew that somehow I made it easier for him to tell me about Sapphire.

"So who wants to see the park?" Seth offered.

"I'll see you guys there!"

Skylar zipped out of the room, and Seth was about to leave, but he waited at the door for me.

"You want to join us at the park, Sedrick?"

"Sure, I'll be there in a bit. I just need a moment to myself."

I understood exactly what he wanted, and I knew he needed to be alone for a few minutes. I followed Seth out the door and out the castle to the city outside.

"You think he'll be all right?"

"Yeah, he only tells that story to people he trusts."

"But he just met me!"

"That just means he really likes you."

"Do you think the people here will like me?"

"Only one way to find out."

"Just out of curiosity, have you seen the show *H_2O: Just Add Water*?"

"Yes, why do you ask?"

"Same reason I asked about the similarities to the animated movie *Atlantis* and *The Little Mermaid*."

"In that case, they're just movies. All characters similar to people living or dead are purely coincidence and shouldn't be mistaken for anything in reality."

"Got it."

It wasn't a long swim to the park, but once I got there, I gasped and smiled at the beauty all around me. It was nothing like the parks in Canada: simple concrete pathways, signs on the wildlife in the area, and admission for tours of a stupid resort and gift shop. This park was the closest thing to heaven anyone could get; only that it was underwater.

I looked around and saw grass similar to fine seaweed, but soft as silk and the same color as a lime. The trees weren't anything like what you may see in British Columbia or in fact anywhere else. The trees were extremely tall and had trunks that twirled around like a braid and still considered bark, I think. The branches of the tree were weeds of some kind and weren't green, but mostly blue and white. I'd never seen any plant like this, but it was breathtaking. I didn't even mention the best part! The people there were so happy and content; I couldn't understand how happy they were, just sitting and chatting in the park with one another, even though no music was playing in the streets at all. I heard laughter and chatter all over the park, and it shocked me.

"How are you all so happy all the time?" I asked Seth.

"Everyone just loves it in the park. It was my mother's favorite part of the city, where she always sang to the people during time of music and joy."

"I haven't even seen the statue of her yet! Where is it?"

"I'll show you."

The Tail of an Angel

Seth said the statue was in the center of the park so everyone could see it, but this park was huge and I was guessing at least seven hundred people were here. Like I said, it was a really big park.

"Close your eyes. It's the best part of the entire city."

"I'm thinking this is a pretty impressive statue."

"You bet it is."

I closed my eyes like he asked and pulled me closer to the statue. I was so excited to see this, and I had no idea what to expect.

"Open your eyes."

I looked dead ahead and saw a golden statue of her, standing with a silver harp in her hand, and another right next to her, sitting down and singing with her arms slightly in the air. It was beautiful and frightening to see; beautiful in gold and silver, it was like she was encased in gold and frightening since she looked like an older version of me. I swam up to the standing Augustina and stood like she did, only I didn't hold a harp, and sat down next to the singing Augustina and touched her hand, twin like my own.

"Well, that's kind of freaky."

"Then don't turn around."

"Why do you say tha . . . whoa?"

Behind me was a massive crowd of merpeople of all ages and sizes just starting toward me. A small little boy, of only two or so, swam up to me and touched my face. I didn't move a muscle and only looked at Seth, thinking, "What do I do?" while he just looked at me and laughed a little.

The little boy looked at my tail and said to me in a squeaky voice that was sweet and innocent, "What's your name?"

"Jillian."

"Are you from another city?"

"No, I'm not. I'm from the surface."

I heard a few people behind him gasp and open their eyes even wider than before.

"Aren't you scared of me?"

"Nope, you remind me of the queen."

"Why do you say that?"

"You look like her."

I glanced up at the statue and back down at the boy.

"You want to hear me sing?"

"Sure!"

I looked up at Seth and at the people staring at me; they no longer looked surprised to see me, and I smiled, thinking they wanted to hear me sing. I was about to sing when a group of merchildren sat down in front of me in a circle, and a little girl sat on my lap. I laughed a little and suddenly forgot what I was about to sing.

"What should I sing?"

"Doesn't matter," the little girl told me. I remembered something I hadn't sung in so long. I knew they would love this one song I fell in love with, "I See the Light," from one of my favorite movies. I looked over at Seth and saw his brothers swim up next to him, just in time to hear me sing to the people of Atlantis.

I started singing, somewhat quietly, but strangely it could still be heard by everyone there. The children started to smile and couples in the crowd put their heads against one another, and very old mermen smiled as brightly as the children around me.

I heard Seth and Skylar join into the one part where the guy comes into the song and watched them sit down next to me, not moving the children, but simply joining me to sing. Seth even grabbed me hand before the last chorus, just like in the movie, making me smile and repeat the same song once more.

I sang in harmony with just Seth, and it sounded beautiful. I smiled and looked toward the crowd, wondering how they'd react. There was a moment of silence, and the little girl hugged me, surprising me, but I hugged her back of course. Following it, the massive crowd started to cheer and applaud. I laughed when I saw people whistle and celebrate.

"You sound just like the queen!" the little boy told me.

"Have you ever met the queen?"

"No, I haven't actually."

The boy gave me another hug and ran back to his parents in the crowd. I looked over at Seth and saw him smiling, and then he swam over to me.

"It sounds like everyone in Atlantis likes your singing."

"It sure looks like it."

Seth put his arm around one of my shoulders and kissed me on the cheek. I bet I looked like the little girl I knew in the photo during Christmas. The crowd cheered even louder when he kissed me, making me feel wanted and loved. A very old-looking woman afterward swam up to me. She must have been in her early eighties or was still aging and must've not wanted the immortality offered to her. I didn't quite know.

"Can you stand up for me, deary?"

"Sure."

I stood up from the statue and straightened my back to appear taller and more proper. She touched my face with her wrinkly hand on which large purple veins were sticking out. I didn't move, because I didn't know if she would hurt me, although I was still confused as to why she wanted to get a closer look at me. She looked down at my hands, soft and small; she ran her finger on my palm and on the lines of my hand. She asked me to spin around, watching my tail, and then she touched my hair. I looked over at Seth, wondering why on earth this lady was interested in me, and saw Seth put his arms up, indicating to say, "I don't know." Finally, she stopped and put two of her fingers to touch the bottom of my lip and her middle finger right next to my eye and then backed away from me.

"It's like the queen never left."

I smiled and nodded my head, indicating a silent thank you, and she turned to the crowd and smiled. The merpeople there went from watching this lady look at me to watching me thank the old lady, and something happened that I didn't understand.

"My name is Alana, and I knew the queen many, many years ago."

"It's nice to meet you, Alana."

"First of all, I wanted to live as an old woman many years ago. I'm about eighty-three, but I've been eighty-three for a very long time. I have acquired many skills over the years on land and in the ocean."

"What kind of skills?"

"I've been all around the world and learned so much from so many countries like China, Japan, Africa, Europe, Russia, you name it. I know almost every secret on the earth and skills only taught from various cultures, like palmistry, martial arts, dancing, and even more."

"Why are you telling me this?"

"I read your palm to see your future, and—"

"To be honest, I don't believe in psychics or someone having the power to tell me my future."

"Believe what you want, my child. I want to tell you what I read in your palm."

I sighed and agreed that she could tell me my future.

"Your life line is very long, but not as long as you may hope. Your love line splits into two, meaning that you will have to make a choice between the two men you love."

"Anything else?"

"You have many talents like singing, dancing, writing, drawing, and so much more. You are also so very alike our queen Augustina. It is no coincidence that you are so much like her, because a very long time ago, her great, great, great-ancestors created one of yours, which makes you from royal blood. Don't worry. You are not related to her or any of her family. Since it is such a long bloodline, it makes it too distant to be related to her. Because of this, you can marry any prince of your choice, even on land."

"Believe it or not, King Neptune already told me that."

"Oh, and one more thing."

"What is it?"

"You are in terrible danger. I see many things of hurt and even death in the future. There are sharks and storms that may kill you. I recommend that you stay on the surface in the future. You will be safer there."

"Can I ask you one more then?"

"Yes, dear?"

"Can you tell me if my family is okay?"

"Let me look at your hands once more."

I gave her my hands and watched her try to figure out the lines on my hands, and I simply prayed to myself that she would tell me my family was okay.

"To be honest, I cannot see them through your hand. I can tell you though that you will make it back to land someday."

"Really? Do you know when?"

"You will know when the time is right."

Alana smiled at me and swam back into the crowd, disappearing in the group of people. Sedrick handed me a harp and asked if I knew how to play it. The crowd gasped in shock, and someone ran into the castle, most likely to fetch the king.

"Where did you find this?"

"There are instruments all over the place. I'm just wondering if you could play a little something for us."

"I'm not too sure if I can play something on a harp, I'm more of a piano and guitar kind of person."

I looked at the golden harp and wiped the fine sand off the arm and held it up to my face. I plucked every string once to figure out what the notes were.

"I still don't know if I can so this."

"You can do it. Just play the first song that comes into mind, Verbicky."

I hummed to myself and looked up through my harp to see Kind Neptune in front of all the people, waiting for me to play a song. Suddenly, I knew the perfect song to play on the harp: "Halleluiah." I managed to get all the notes right, sounding like the music of an angel. When I finished, everyone chanted "Verbicky" and made the king smile.

I was a little scared to see the king swim up to me; he looked down with a smile on his face. I stood up and placed the harp down by the statue, waiting for him to do something. I just looked up with a flat smile on my face and blinked a few times, still wondering what he was gonna do. I saw him descend down to my level and bring his huge arms out from behind his back and pick me up with a hug.

I was so scared my jaw dropped open as I looked down to the crowd and saw them laugh. When he put me back down, I laughed a little as he stood beside me and announced to everyone there, "It is now official. The queen has returned through the eyes of this wonderful girl and has brought music back to our city. I couldn't be happier or more proud of her, and I'm glad that my son Seth has brought her to us. Tell me, do you not love this wonderful girl?"

The crowd cheered so loud my ears started to hurt, and the many whistles started to make me want to grab a set of earplugs.

"She is indeed from royal blood, and that means she can marry any prince in the ocean and become a part of our history as the princess who saved the capital city of Atlantis."

"I saved Atlantis?"

"Indeed you did."

I smiled so big and put my hand on my mouth in amazement as to what I really had done for this city.

"One more thing, Your Majesty."

"What?"

"Everyone?" I yelled to the people there, "My birthday is the 22nd of August. In two days, I will be turning seventeen. Would it be all right if maybe I could have a party here?"

"But of course, dear! It would be our pleasure to host a party for you."

The crowd clapped to the idea of a party; even though they looked very happy, I'm sure they would enjoy a party.

"Jillian, I don't want anything bad to happen to you, so I will have my son Seth make sure you make it back to the island safe and sound."

"Sounds good."

"But I have one condition."

"Anything you want, Your Majesty."

"If you and Seth get involved, I will kill you in the most painful way possible and feed your body to a bunch of great white sharks."

"I understand."

Seth swam up to me and grabbed my arm in the same way a grad escort would on prom night. I smiled as I slowly swam forward with him through the merpeople clapping as we left the city. I saw another little girl swim up to me and put her arms in the air toward me, squeezing her hands together. I picked her up and put her on one of my shoulders to sit on, and then I saw a little flower not too far from where I was swimming. I plucked the flower from the ground and put the flower in her hair. She looked so adorable. Seth had a little boy and girl on his shoulders. Both the children giggled when we swam a little faster, and finally we had to give them back to their parents. I waved back to the people when I reached the gate and smiled perfectly when they all waved back at Seth and me.

Chapter 21

Seth took me on a quick tour of the coral reef, not too far from the city, and showed me a route back to the island if he ever left me to do something back home. I followed him to a cave where I had encountered a shark; instead of finding a shark, I found the same tunnel I had taken to get to the shore line in the cave outside my home. The other tunnel led to my crystal cave, where I hid some of my treasures in a lit cavern. I didn't have that much, but it was at least something.

"Where did you find this stuff again?"

"In a cave under an oasis."

"Looks nice."

Seth picked up a few gems and held them up to the light in the top of the cavern.

"Have you been to the other secret cavern?"

"What other secret cavern?"

"Follow me."

Seth swam down to the bottom of the cavern and pushed at a rock on the floor, opening a large rock door for him to swim through. He swam through in a second, and I followed him right on his tail in a place so dark I couldn't even see where I was swimming and ran into the walls a few times. Seth grabbed my hand and guided me in the darkness. I didn't know where I was going, but I knew that whatever it was, it was gonna be awesome.

"How far is this secret cavern?"

"We're there."

Suddenly, the tunnel stopped going forward and went straight up to a higher place. The light got brighter and brighter the higher I went and finally ended when I burst out of the water with Seth. I looked around where I was. All I saw was a cave, a shoreline with sand on it, and a stone staircase, from where the light was coming. Seth swam up to the shore and I watched as he went from swimming with a tail to standing with two legs and walking on the sand.

"Don't worry. It doesn't hurt."

I swam up to the shore next and stood up with ease on my legs. I thought I wasn't wearing my bikini bottoms for a second, but they were there, thank goodness.

"You got to see the view from up those stairs."

Seth grabbed my hand and took me up the cold stone stairs; the light up those stairs was bright and hurt my eyes slightly. I had to close my eyes once I got out of the stair tunnel until my eyesight got used to the bright sun. It was the most fantastic view I'd seen, probably even better than the one Miko showed me.

I could see the entire island from up there and the ocean surrounding it; it was astonishing. The warm sea breeze flowed through every stand of hair on my head, and the sun kissed my skin. I looked around where I was standing and noticed a roof-like stone surface with a hammock on one side and a table for drinks not too far from it. I could sleep up here if I really wanted to.

"This is where I would sing with you."

"How on earth can I hear you so well if my house is so far away from here?"

"There's another staircase that goes right outside your cabin."

"That's not creepy."

"It's the best view of the island from here though."

"It sure is."

Seth walked up behind me and pulled me into his chest, holding me by my belly.

"How did you ever find this place?"

"Most of it I just found, others I made."

"You made the staircase to my cabin, didn't you?"

"Is that a bad thing?"

"Yep."

"I don't think it is. It just means you're not the only one on the island."

I turned around to see the sun and noticed it was starting to go down.

"The day's almost over already? Damn."

"Don't you like sunsets?"

"Of course I do. I'm just in my bikini though, and I wouldn't mind throwing on some different clothes."

"Then let's take the shortcut."

Seth waved his hand at me to follow him, and the staircase wasn't as long as the last one. The staircase stopped in the attic of my home; getting out of the attic itself wasn't that bad. When I got out, I was slightly dusty, so I sneezed.

"Bless you."

"Thank you."

I rushed to the kitchen to see if Miko had destroyed anything or injured himself. I found Miko sleeping on the counter with banana peels around him. He looked all right, but I picked him up and placed him in his hammock. I didn't even wake him up. I hurried to get a new outfit on since the sun was setting as I spoke, and I really didn't want to miss watching a sunset with Seth.

"Is it all right if I just throw on my pajamas and a sweater?"

"That's fine."

I brushed my hair quickly and walked out of my room, looking for Seth, but I heard him climbing a ladder to get into the attic. I rushed to get to the attic and saw Seth waiting at the staircase for me.

"Slow down, will you?"

Seth only smiled and started to walk up the stairs to the roof, where the sunset was waiting for me.

"Wow."

I looked at the sunset now and saw that the entire sky was orange, red, purple, and yellow. I'd seen some very nice sunsets in Alberta, but this one topped them all.

"Dibs on the hammock!"

I leaped into the big hammock and swayed back and forth while I watched the sun go down. I was a little thirsty, but I couldn't care less because the sunset was all I wanted to see right now.

I thought I felt something move the hammock, which wasn't me, and I felt something brush my leg. I looked behind me and saw that Seth had crawled into the other side of the hammock, and he waved at me as I looked at him.

"What are you doing in my hammock?"

"The sunset looks so much better in a hammock."

"Well, I do agree with you on that a little bit."

I felt Seth reach around my hips and pull me up against his chest again, and my belly was now wrapped up in his arms; he was squeezing me like a teddy bear. I didn't care if he wanted to cuddle with me; the sun was almost gone and I was a little cold. He wasn't wearing a shirt, but he was surprisingly warm. Not nearly as warm as Jay was, but he was still nice and warm. When the sun finally set, the orange and other bright colors I saw slowly dissolved in the sky and turned it dark blue. I rolled over on my back and watched the stars start to pop out. Seth put his arm over my shoulder, his hand on my upper arm, pulling me closer to him, but not so close that I was pushed up against his chest again.

"You really like cuddling, don't you?"

"Just a little bit."

One hour went by, and almost every single star there could be was out in the open to be seen. I pointed out some common constellations like the Big Dipper, the Little Dipper, Orion's Belt, and I even showed him where Venus was. He told me even more about the constellations of gods like Hercules, Pegasus, and horoscope constellations such as Leo which was mine and Gemini which was his. It was a pleasant conversation about the stars and was made even better when both of us saw a shooting star.

"Did you see that shooting star?" both of us said at the exact same time.

I laughed quite loudly, and it echoed for a second on the island, making him laugh in return. I turned to look back up at the stars, but Seth kept staring at me.

"So what did you wish for?"

"If I tell you, it won't come true."

"Bull, I've told other people what I've wished for, and those still came true."

"I doubt that."

"C'mon, you can tell me. It can be anything you want."

"I can tell you another time."

"Why not now, here in a hammock, under the stars? I can't think of a better place for you to tell what you wished for."

"I'll tell you first thing tomorrow."

"Do I really have to wait that long?"

"All good things to those who wait."

"What are you? A fortune cookie? Maybe rephrase that for me."

"You're going to like what I wished for later."

"How long is later?"

"Just watch the stars."

I looked at Seth and my smile changed into a frown, and then I looked back at the sky.

"Oh, don't get mad."

"Do I look like I'm mad?"

"Yes, you do."

"Well, I'm not mad."

"Then what is that face for?"

"You haven't told me your wish yet."

"Maybe it's a birthday surprise."

I opened my eyes and tried to hide my smile, but I simply couldn't. Seth laughed and squeezed my belly much tighter.

"Hey, take it easy. You're squeezing me way too tight."

"My bad, guess I don't know my own strength."

Something in my head clicked and instantly took me to the night I spent with Jay, and I even remembered how the Chocolate Axe smelled for the first time since I was taken here. I stopped breathing for a second and blinked a few times to bring myself back to the present.

"Are you thirsty?"

"A little bit. Why do you ask?"

"I grabbed a few drinks before you caught up to me in the attic. I made myself a margarita and made you a—"

"Please don't say piña colada. Please don't say piña colada," I thought to myself.

"Piña colada."

"How did you know I love piña coladas?"

"Duh, I saw you on the boat and—"

"You shouldn't have been watching me on my boat!"

I shot up off the hammock and threw the drink off the table, letting it fall down to the stone ground below and smashing into a thousand pieces.

"Why'd you do that?"

"It's not cute anymore about how you know me really well. It scares me and I hate it."

"I've known you for—"

"I know! You've known me since I was a little girl, and I didn't even know you until a few nights ago! Just go home, Seth! I don't want you here anymore."

"I'm going to come back."

"Come back in two days."

"You know I can't do that."

"You seemed to cope with not seeing me here for years. I'm sure you can handle a few days."

I raced down the stairs to my attic and straight to my room.

"Don't do this, Jill. I have to make sure you won't get hurt."

"If I can handle a couple of sharks, I can handle living on my own for two days."

"You can't say that! You're on an island with no medicine or antibiotics."

"Band-Aids helped me just fine."

"Band-Aids won't save you if you're attacked by a shark."

"Since when do you care, Seth?! You should just kill me! You said you wanted to!"

"I promised your father I wouldn't kill you."

"My father knows you better than he knows me. You're practically his son, so he won't miss his little angel anyways."

"*I won't kill you, Jill!*"

"Look! A knife! You can do it as quick as you please." I grabbed the knife off my dresser and handed it to him. "I dare you."

He threw the knife on the floor and looked at me with the angriest face I'd ever seen.

"I can't hurt you, I won't kill you, and I will never leave you alone on this island as long as I live."

"I bet you anything the sharks will get to you first."

I felt a hot tear run down my cheek and drip to the floor. I remained angry as I turned away from him and faced the window which showed no light for me to look up at; the moon was even behind a cloud, and the room was soon pitch-black. I looked back for a second and only saw his crystal and my own glowing, glowing blue on my chest.

"You should go."

"I'm not leaving yet."

"Well, if you're not going to be leaving, please tell me what you wished for."

"You tell me what you wished for first."

"I asked you first."

Seth walked up close to me, so close that the crystal around his neck was a few inches from my own.

"I wished that I could spend the night with an angel."

"No . . . please tell me you didn't just say that."

"A blue-eyed angel."

"*No!* You can't possibly know that! Well, it's not coming true anyways!"

"Is there something wrong?"

"I can't really explain it, but Jay took a video of it."

I managed to find his camera on my dresser and sat down on my bed to play the video. Seth got onto my bed and grabbed the camera so that we could both watch the video. The lights on the video looked as amazing as they were on the boat, and Seth watched it closely every time I twirled with the lights. I watched his face as the blue light on the camera lit up his expression when he saw I had wings and glowing blue eyes. At the point when the locket closed itself and Jay kissed me, Seth's eyes widened and he lowered the camera when the video was finished.

"You . . . looked like an angel."

"I have been twice now. It's not as fun as it seems."

"It didn't quite look like fun, but I told you my wish, so tell me yours."

I picked up the camera and clicked to my favorite picture of Jay and me, the one where I slept on Jay's shoulder in the car.

"I wished that my heart would always belong to Jay, no matter what."

"Always?"

I sighed and let my face fall into my hands.

"Yes."

"I think you should take a look at that locket."

"Why?"

"Here."

He handed me the locket from my dresser. I brought the crystal closer to the locket to see what was inside. I opened it and saw a photo of me and Seth.

"What the hell did you do to my locket, Seth? What happened to Jay's photo?"

"This isn't a normal locket. It shows a photo of someone you desire, even though your heart belongs to another man. But mostly it means you love someone."

"But I don't love you."

"I do."

"It doesn't mean I love you back! I still love Jay."

"I'm thinking your heart still does. Can't you give your heart a break?"

"I'm not agreeing to say I love you because some locket has a picture of you in it."

"Just because you don't say it doesn't mean you're not thinking it."

"All I'm thinking of right now is whether or not I should punch you or start crying."

"Please don't punch me."

I was about to punch him, but I started to cry instead. I really didn't mean to cry, but it just sort of slipped out. Seth put his arm around my shoulders and pulled me into his bare chest. I tried to pull back, but I was busy trying not to cry in front of him. He put his head on mine and tucked my hair behind my ear with his other hand.

"You'll be all right, Jill."

"No, I w-won't. I'm never gonna find . . . my family or Jay again."

"You will, you will. Alana said you will be on land again someday."

"She didn't s-say that I'd be w-with my family though."

"I promise you will."

I started to cry a little less, and there were just tears on my face after a while.

"Feel better?"

"A little bit."

I sniffed and wiped my nose with the bottom of my shirt. I took a big breath and exhaled when Seth let me sit up. I wasn't feeling all that happy about crying in front of Seth and told him I was going to get in my pajamas and that he could wait in the kitchen while I changed.

"So you're not kicking me out?"

"No, I will though if you try to have sex with me."

"I didn't say anything that had to so with—"

"Just wait in the kitchen."

I pointed at the door and watched him leave and shut it behind him. I hadn't done the laundry yet, and all I had to wear for pajamas was a tank top and shorts. I slipped on my tank top, and as I was putting on my shorts, I saw Seth's crystal outside my door.

"Seth! Kitchen!"

"Well, now you're dressed."

"How long have you been watching me?"

"I like your shorts."

I smacked my hand against my head and crawled into my bed. I felt infinitely better now that I was in a soft, warm bed. I saw Seth's crystal enter the room and sit down on my bed at my feet.

"Is it all right if I lie down?"

"I suppose."

Seth lay down next to me and looked over at me, since I could see his face in the light of my own crystal. I nuzzled into my pillow; only half my face was showing, and I looked up at Seth with one wide blue eye. He had beautiful green eyes; they were luminous and bright. It was almost scary the way he looked at me—like I was an angel.

"Why are you staring at me?"

"I'm not staring."

"Then what do you call a long look at my eyes?"

"Looking in your eyes."

"You're weird."

"You have amazing blue eyes."

"So I've been told."

"Has anyone ever told you there are silver lines in your eyes that look like a storm of blue ice?"

"I thought it was called blue steel."

"Either one sounds good."

"I've never seen green eyes like yours before."

"I'm sure you have."

I sat up from my pillow and brought my face close to his to get a better look at his eyes.

"There's a small lining of brown in the center, but it's more of a chocolate brown, and the green is like an emerald with lines of lime green from the center. It's really cool."

"It's just green eyes."

"Well, my eyes are just blue then."

"Mine are really quite plain. It's yours that look the best."

"Sure they do."

Seth put his hand on my face. It was hot. Not warm or room temperature, it was like "burn your hand on boiling water" hot.

"Your hand is really hot. It kind of hurts."

"I can't really stop it."

"Maybe take your hand off my face."

He removed his hand from my face, and I felt my face become warm as I sat up with my back against the headboard. I pulled the covers down a little because it was a little warmer than what I was comfortable with. Seth looked at me, and I looked at him, wondering why on earth he was smiling. He had an amazing smile, but it seemed like every other minute, he found a new way to freak me out.

"You really do have a nice smile."

"You're probably wondering why I'm smiling."

"I wouldn't mind knowing why, yeah."

"Your crystal is turning red."

"What?"

"Seriously! Look!"

He was indeed right about my crystal; it was glowing red instead of bright blue like it was earlier.

"Oh shit . . . what does it means if it glows red again?"

"Didn't I already tell you that?"

"No."

"I'm pretty sure I told you."

"Just tell me what it means again!"

"Close your eyes and I'll tell you."

I closed my eyes, hoping he wouldn't punch me, until I remembered that I was the one who wanted to punch him in the face, and I felt a little bit better. I didn't hear a thing, and I was thinking that maybe he had just got up and left. I was almost 100 percent sure he had left, and I took a breath through my mouth, just because my nose got a little stuffy. Then before I knew it, Seth kissed me.

I still wasn't too sure as to what a glowing red crystal meant, but I didn't even open my eyes to find out that his crystal could've been glowing red too. Whatever it meant, I couldn't care because I was caught up in his tongue, and he even bit my lower lip. He pulled me closer to his chest when he kissed me again, and I put my hands on his neck, for me to pull him closer to my own chest.

When he finally let me go, I opened my eyes and saw him smile, but then he looked down to his left. It didn't take long to figure out that he knew exactly what the glowing red crystal meant, but it didn't look like he was going to tell me. When I looked down to see why he had turned his head to the left, he quickly kissed my neck and pushed me down on my back. Just when I was about to sit up, he pushed my hands down by my hips, making me almost paralyzed on the bed. To be honest, I didn't want to get up; my hickeys were gone, and it didn't feel like Seth was going to give me one. I was just lying there, enjoying his lips on my neck, and he bit into it like a vampire; believe it or not, it really hurt and made me whisper, "*Ow*."

"Hey! That hurt!"

"My bad."

He continued to kiss my neck until I finally had to say something.

"Seth, as much as I love this, you have to get off me."

"Why? Aren't you having fun?"

"Sure, but I'm not going to be sleeping with you tonight."

"Why not?"

"Because I don't want to."

"Your glowing red crystal says otherwise."

"Seth! I said get off me."

"Please?"

I pushed Seth off me the second I pulled my hands out from his and flipped him over on his back away from me.

"What was that for?"

"I told you to get off me."

"Are you always that strong?"

"Yep, now I think it's about time you left."

I pointed to the door and sat up with my back against the headboard. I picked up my iPhone and looked at the reflection that Seth left on my neck.

"I really hope this bite mark will be gone by morning, Seth."

"I doubt it, but it should be gone by your birthday."

"Seriously? A whole day? Freakin' perfect. You shouldn't have bit my neck."

"My bad, it's just something I thought you'd enjoy."

"It was painful, not sexy."
"Well, shit."
"Out."

I tipped my head down slightly and waited for him to get off my bed and leave.

"Don't you know what it means if your crystal glows red?"
"You can tell me another time."
"You wouldn't be kicking me out if I told you right now."
"I don't care, Seth."
"Are you sure?"
"What part of leave don't you understand?"
"Fine, I'll go."

I pulled my hair back with my hand and looked down at my crystal necklace. I noticed it had stopped glowing red and returned to its regular bright blue. Seth had only taken a single step outside my door when he whispered to me, "Let's just say your locket was right. Goodnight!"

I finally realized what the crystal glowing red meant, and it made me stop and look at the door like a statue. I just let my jaw drop when Seth was no longer in my sight, diving back into the sea outside my window. "Is it possible that I was falling for Seth? That maybe his actions of saving me in the ocean, singing with me in my home and in Atlantis, and watching the stars earlier may have been the final key to my heart? That can't be right. I'd known Jay for quite a few years and took that friendship to the next level as my boyfriend, even though there had been a connection between us the entire time," I thought. Jay was the one who made me smile and blush on my worst days, and we even discovered a small fortune together. No one had ever made me feel that way since. When he kissed me, it was playful, warm, inviting and gave me butterflies in my stomach. That one night I spent with him was the best day of my life; if I could only live one day for the rest of my life, I'd take that day over, and over, and over.

Seth had known me in secret for almost my whole life. He knew me for longer than I knew him, and he even knew my father better than I did. He loved Seth like a son of his own, and he was treated like family around my parents. He even kept photos of me; when I moved into Canada, for about ten years, he still kept me in his mind when I had forgotten about him a very long time ago. How on earth he still loved me for so long still confused and inspired me. He rescued me from a terrible and slow death and made sure I survived on this island. Not only was I alive and well, he even sang in harmony to songs I would play on the piano; at first, he scared me, but later I enjoyed. When he pushed me up against the wall, even though I was scared he would hurt me, it reminded me of Jay when I felt his breath on my face and neck. The way Seth walked with me in Atlantis was fun, and I felt proud to be loved by the people of Atlantis; even the children on my shoulder and the two on his made me smile. Not the exact smile I had when I was with Jay, but one similar to that smile. But most of all, when he pulled me close to his chest while watching the stars and supported me when I cried, it changed the way I felt about him.

I didn't know whether I was just tired and angry or awake and upset. I just couldn't figure it out. On the one hand, I was still thinking if Jay and my family had been rescued or if they had died and the man I loved was sleeping with the fishes. If any rescuer had come looking for me, they would've given up on my search by now. I knew in my heart that if Jay was indeed still alive, he was doing everything he could to find me, even to his very last breath, until I was safe and sound.

Seth was, on the other hand, the handsome hybrid that had loved me for about a century and saved me from drowning. He was kind and great with children, loved to sing as much as I did, and not to mention a prince of Neptune's family. He promised that he would protect me from the dangers in the sea such as sharks and would make sure I made it back to my home someday; that could take years. What I felt tonight, under the stars and seconds earlier on my bed, must have changed something I loved. I loved Jay with all my heart and I always would. I have to admit though I loved Seth but not as much as I loved Jay. Nothing would change how I felt about those men: one human and dead or alive and the other hybrid and immortal.

I turned over and punched my pillow, making me feel better when I pictured the pillow as Seth.

"What's wrong with me, Miko? I can't love Seth!"

Miko jumped up on my bed and turned his head as if to say, "Whaa?"

"I've loved Jay more and longer than I've loved Seth. He's the one who's secretly loved me for years when I didn't even know who he was, like a stalker!"

Miko climbed up onto his bed, and it looked like he didn't really want to listen to my complaints any longer.

"Well, I should figure out the *pros* and *cons* of this situation. *Pros*—Seth can offer me immortality and a life to myself under the sea with him, bringing music back to Atlantis that the king would love. *Cons*—if I decide to find land again and live there, I won't be immortal and I could search for Jay again as a simple human being. *Pros*—if Seth finds Jay alive, I can live happily with the man I've loved for so long, with a normal life, and never see the city of Atlantis ever again. *Cons*—if I stay with Seth, I will never see land or anyone else I ever knew, and even though I'd be immortal, I'd not be with the man I've always loved, while Seth has loved me ever so much longer."

The math showed that I should try to find land and possibly find Jay, even if it risked my chance to become immortal and the savior of Atlantis. I loved Jay, I love Seth . . . I just started to get a headache in the end. This decision wouldn't happen overnight; at one point, I would have to decide between them and take a new path along the road of fate that had been destined for me. I flipped over onto my back and brought the crystal to my face. It was so bright and beautiful; I couldn't imagine giving this up, but I had enough time to think about it and finally decided to go to sleep.

Chapter 22

The twenty-first day of August was here, and it was my seventh day here on this island. I stretched to get up out of my bed and looked over at the sun through the window, which was shining on my skin and the covers of my bed. Miko rolled over in his bed and flipped out of his hammock, crashing to the floor with a loud thump. I laughed so hard I fell out of the bed myself and rolled on the floor in both pain and laughter. When I was finished, I got up and checked to make sure Miko was okay.

"You okay there, Miko?"

Miko got up from his side and nodded before storming out the door downstairs to the kitchen. Why else wouldn't he run to the kitchen? I wasn't expecting anything different. I walked downstairs in my pajamas, taking all the time I wanted. I had no rush to get anything done today. Miko had already opened and eaten two bananas and then started to eat a mango. How on earth could this little monkey eat so much in so little time? What a crazy monkey! I picked up the peels he left on the counter and tossed them in the trash. My breakfast was apples and cheese; it was small, but it was the perfect size for me since I wasn't incredibly hungry. Just as I turned around to sit at the table, I found Seth standing right in front of me, who said, "Good morning."

"*Ahhhhhhh!*"

I dropped my plate and heard it crash to the floor, while the contents spread all over the floor, making me step backward and hit the counter, hurting my back.

"Goddammit, Seth, you scared me. I kicked you out for a reason!"

"Just wanted to say hello."

"Well, you said hello and managed to ruin my breakfast."

"Sorry."

"Sorry doesn't bring back my breakfast or clean it up, so please leave."

"I'll help clean it up if you want."

"Whatever."

I grabbed a fork and stabbed at the dirty fruit and cheese on the ground and put them in the garbage one by one. Seth grabbed a rag and cleaned up the juice spatter from the apples and picked up the broken glass plate. If I wasn't angry last night, I was much angrier now. When we finished cleaning up the kitchen, I started slicing up another apple and grabbed the cheese out of the fridge.

"I dropped by to say I'm sorry, for . . . for everything yesterday and this morning."

"I forgive you, but last night got a little out of hand."

"I know. It's not very often that someone's crystal glows red."

"It doesn't change anything, Seth."

"Just be careful today, all right? Don't go swimming by the oasis or anything."

"Whatever."

Seth left me in peace, and I heard him dive into the ocean while I finished preparing my breakfast. The second I finished, I packed my bag with food and a weapon to take to the oasis. I wanted to get a few more gems from the cave. I didn't care what Seth said; I'd be just fine.

"You want a smoothie, Miko?"

Miko nodded as he grabbed a banana and a pomegranate and put them next to the blender. I smiled and quickly blended them with some vanilla and yogurt, pouring it into a tall mug. Before storming out the door, I wrote a note on the counter that said: "Gone to the oasis to gather more gems."

The trail to the oasis I had memorized, and I was there in less than fifteen minutes. I was a little concerned whether I would grow a tail in fresh water or whether I could have a tail in both types of water. The cave itself had a mixture of fresh water and salt water. Who knew, right? There was only one way to find out. I took off my clothes and stepped in, wearing my black bikini, carrying my bag on my back, the glowing blue crystal around my neck. I popped up to the surface and looked at the waterfall, and I noticed my legs were still there. I was glad I didn't have a tail in this water; if I made it back to land, I could swim in pools safely, only if they weren't saltwater pools. I took one big breath and swam down into the caves. On the way down, my legs melted together and became a tail just in time for me to reach the crystals and breathe in the saltwater. I could see the crystals much better with the glow of the crystal on my necklace. I smiled as I pulled off the crystals and placed them in my bag; unfortunately, the food I placed in bags started to float up and out with the current of the water into the darkness.

"Oops," I muttered to myself, but the food was in the bags, so the fish wouldn't be attracted to the area; mostly sharks were my worry. When I finished filling my bag to the very top with priceless jewels, I placed it on my back and swam with the current to the waterslide cave ahead of me. I was surprised at how much the necklace lit the way ahead of me, and it wasn't too long before I fell down into the cave with the tunnels that led to the cavern with my treasures, the sea, and the tunnel that would take me to the cave just outside my home. I took my time in the tunnel to reach the place where I had killed all those sharks; then I noticed a plastic bag on the wall, which was caught on something. When I swam up to it, it flew off into the rest of the water, but I really started to worry when I noticed the beef jerky I had packed was gone. I swam a little faster ahead, as I had a terrible feeling something was behind me. When I turned around at the wall just before the tunnel went straight up into the cave, I couldn't see anything coming for me and I swam up peacefully and slowly to the cave above. Just before I reached the surface, something bit down on my tail and pulled me down deeper into the water. The strangest thing happened when I saw my legs return; a shark had the bottom of my leg in his mouth.

Screaming in pain, with blood everywhere around me, I reached into my bag and pulled out my knife, at the same time trying to pull the leg out of his mouth. I was pulled back and forth, shaken like a dog toy, but I eventually stabbed it in the eye and side of the head to release me from his jaws. The heavy backpack made it difficult to get to the surface quickly, but the second I got there, I sprinted for land. I threw my bag on the ground and dragged myself out of the water, watching the pool of blood behind me get bigger and bigger the more I sat at the water's edge. I thought that slicing my finger was painful, but having a shark almost tear my leg off was so much worse. When I pulled the bleeding leg out of the water, I screamed in pain when I bent it slightly. The scream echoed all around the cave and hurt my ears; it was so loud. The bite marks on my leg, my poor leg, even though coated in blood, were very clear. The shark had almost eaten the bottom half of my leg and just over the kneecap; I counted ten holes in the bottom of my leg and twelve around the side and on the top. From each individual hole, blood was coming out as if they were all leaky faucets, letting out more blood than just a few drips.

It was one of the hardest things I'd ever had to do—getting up on both of my legs. Once I was up, I limped to my bag and quickly put it on my back. I had to use the stone walls to get out of the cave. I looked behind me and saw a trail of blood; that was more like thick puddles spread out on the sand. I pushed myself to get off the walls and walk on my own to my house.

"*Seth! You gotta help me!*" I screamed just before I fell through the front door. I was on my stomach and dragged myself on the ground to the kitchen.

"*Somebody!* Please help me."

I could no longer shout for help as my voice gave out on me. Of all times to lose my voice, why now?! The loudest I could talk was just between a normal speaking voice and a whisper.

"Seth . . ."

Miko ran down the stairs and started screaming when he saw the blood behind me and all over my legs.

"You gotta grab me a towel or something, Miko. Hurry!"

Miko, still screaming, ran to the kitchen and brought me a paper towel.

"I meant a shower type of towel. Does it look like a paper towel will clean my leg up?"

Miko put the paper towel on the puddle of blood at the bottom of the stairs and raced upstairs. If Miko got the right kind of towel, I could wrap it around my leg and maybe make it up the stairs to my room and wave out of the window for help. I sat down to relax for a minute, waiting for Miko to bring me the right towel and hopefully make it upstairs before passing out. I knew that if I didn't get a towel on my leg right away, I would pass out from losing too much blood, and with no treatment or the right care for the wound, I could die. I felt a little bit better when I heard Miko running down the stairs and threw the right towel at me.

"Thanks, Miko."

I wrapped the towel around my leg the same way I would wrap a towel around me after a shower, but I tightened the top and bottom so the circulation of blood would slow down a little bit, not so much as to cause a blood clot and not so little that it just soaked up the blood on my leg. I stood up and leaned on the rail on the side of the stairs, taking each step, one at a time.

I made it to my bedroom, but the towel was already soaked in blood and started to drip more with every step I took. If I kept walking, I would lose more blood, simple as that. I leaped to the window and opened it to shout out to the sea, "*Seth! Help me!*"

"Woo!" I thought. I could shout again, and I'm sure he'd be here in a minute if I called him one more time.

"*Seth!*"

I heard and saw nothing in the water, and I started to feel a little dizzy. I was guessing I'd have about five minutes before I passed out; it could even be my last five minutes alive. There was only one thing I wanted to see if these were my last few moments, something Simon wished he could see—the ones he loved.

I dragged myself over to my dresser on the other side of my bed and grabbed my camera. I sat down and put my back up against the side of bed. I might as well be comfortable for a few minutes. I clicked through the photos of Jay and me, my family, his family, and my favorite photos of Jay. I laughed at the silly pictures he'd taken of me and the even better ones he'd taken of himself; I was smiling, but at the same time in so much pain. When everything got slightly blurry, I flipped to the best picture of Jay and me and put on the angel wings totem I had made for myself. I bet I only had a minute left of consciousness before I passed out on the floor. I cried a little at the photo of me sleeping on Jay's shoulder in the car. I hadn't even noticed the next photo he'd taken. I was smiling a little when he'd kissed me on the forehead, my eyes closed. It was the exact same look I had in the photo of Seth and me at Christmas; I was ever so happy I saw that photo of me with Jay. If it was the last thing I saw, I'd glad it would be this. It suddenly got darker and darker; everything got really blurry. With only seconds left before I passed out on the floor, I held the glowing crystal in my hand and fell on my side, bringing the camera up to my face. I saw Jay's face one last time before everything went black, and I let go of the necklace in my hand.

Chapter 23

August 22, my eighth day on the island, was also my seventieth birthday.

"I'm not dead?" I thought to myself. "Why on earth am I alive and not bloody on my bed?"

I got up from lying down on something really warm, and it wasn't as soft as my bed. When I lifted up the sheets to reveal my leg, it was clean and soft; no bite marks were there because of the shark attack. Although my leg was still sore, it was somehow about 98 percent healed. I looked back at whatever I was resting on and saw Seth sleeping peacefully on his back, and his arm that was around my shoulder was now just stretched out on my pillow. I looked back at my leg and tried to get up out of the bed, but it was still very sore, and it was difficult to walk on my own. Trying to hold all my weight on my one leg was like trying to balance on a ball, even though I could walk okay when my leg had been bleeding.

I noticed Seth had made a pair of crutches from wood in the forest, and I limped over to them and fell against the wall with a thump too. I muttered, "Shit," under my breath, and I saw Seth roll over and open his eyes.

"Good morning."

"Morning."

"You really shouldn't be walking right now."

"Isn't that what the crutches are for?"

"Nope, I made them for when your leg is just about healed."

"Then can you at least tell me why I'm not in a pool of my own blood and dead on the floor?"

"Take a seat. You won't be able to stand for very long anyways."

"I seriously doubt—"

Thud. I accidentally let the crutches fall and I fell backward on my back. "Ouch."

"You all right?"

"Can't . . . breathe . . . that . . . well."

"Here, I'll help you."

Seth got up from my bed while I sat up carefully, trying not to move my leg. I sighed and put my hands by my side to hold myself up, waiting for Seth to help me to my feet. When I thought he'd simply pull me up to my feet, he picked me up by my legs and my back and carried me down the stairs.

"I thought you were going to help me get to my feet."

"Naw, you just have to rest. You'll feel much better afterward."

"Are you still gonna tell me why I'm okay?"

"After I make you breakfast."

"Oooo! What's for breakfast?"

Seth finally made it down the stairs safely and walked through the kitchen.

"Red Velvet Pancakes."

"No way!" I threw my hands in the air to show my excitement. "Way."

Just as I brought my arms back down to my belly, Seth opened the door to the living room and placed me gently on the couch.

"Happy birthday by the way."

"Thank you."

Seth walked out of the room and closed the door behind him. Good thing I had brought my iPhone to keep me entertained. Even though I had no service, I had plenty of applications to keep me busy while Seth made me breakfast. I was playing Doodle Jump for about ten minutes, when Seth came in with a plate of red pancakes, whipped cream, and cream cheese icing on top.

"That was fast."

"It was already cooking when you woke up."

"But . . . you were sleeping . . ."

"It was good timing."

"Indeed."

I cut up the pancakes on my lap and savored the first bite of pancakes with cream cheese icing on it. It was amazing.

"This is amazing!" I mumbled with food in my mouth.

"I don't know what 'miss a ma saying' means."

I swallowed my pancakes and told him what I had really said, "This is amazing!"

"Oh, thank you."

Seth made a few pancakes for himself, while I relaxed and enjoyed my birthday breakfast. Every red pancake tasted exactly like fine milk chocolate, and the rich and fluffy cream cheese icing was the perfect combination.

"How did you know that Red Velvet Pancakes are my favorite breakfast besides French toast?"

"Your father told me."

"Of course he did."

"My father," it echoed in my head, "still doesn't know what has happened to me over the past week." If any day I had to go see him, visiting him on my birthday sounded like a good idea.

"Speaking of my father, I must go see him today! There's so much I have to tell him."

"Not until your leg is feeling 100 percent better."

"Oh, come on, it's fine. Watch, I can still stand up on my own two—"

I put the pancakes aside and stood up tall and straight, noticing my sore leg began to shake a bit and grow weaker every second.

"Easy! You're gonna hurt yourself!"

I fell to my knee and held myself up with the one good leg and my hands, keeping me balanced while I tried to stand up again; it wasn't working.

"Just . . . take it slow or it'll get worse."

"Maybe you should've told me that before I fell on the hardwood floor."

Seth helped me up to my feet and I returned to sit and finish my breakfast.

"How would you like to go for a walk after breakfast?"

"Not until you tell me how I'm still alive!"

"Oh sorry, I completely forgot."

Seth put his empty plate aside and sat down next to me on the couch, pulling out the necklace I had in my hand that night.

"At first, I had the worst feeling in my stomach that something was wrong and I decided to see if you were all right. When I called for you at the front door, I didn't hear a thing and rushed into your room, to find that you were on the floor, lying in a pool of blood. I . . . I fell to the ground and rushed to see if you were still alive, while getting some of your blood all over me."

"My bad."

Seth laughed once, and he smiled for a second as he looked at the necklace and showed me the blood all over it. I touched the bloody part of the necklace and shed a tear when I felt that it was still warm and the blood had not yet dried.

"I could've sworn that you were dead and you were so . . . cold," Seth paused and held the necklace tight in his fist.

"What did you do?"

"The only thing I could do! I picked you up and placed you on the bed and cleaned up the blood on the floor, plus the blood on you. But I saw the necklace in your hand was still glowing. Even though the totem you carved was still soaked in blood, something told me you might still be alive."

"Why was the crystal necklace I had still glowing?"

"These crystals are very . . .," Seth paused and lifted his own crystal necklace to his face, "you could say magical, but I really don't know how to describe it. All I know is that the crystals can show if there is still a life force in someone."

"Life force?"

"I don't know—soul, whatever it's called. You know what I'm trying say."

"Yeah, I know, continue."

"So when I saw it glowing, I remembered how the crystals could heal any wounds, so I used it to fix your leg."

"But I was already dead. I don't get it."

"It's not just cuts or gashes it can heal. I saw someone restart the heartbeat of a person with a crystal. I don't know how the crystals can do such a thing, but it worked."

"So you started my heart again."

"Yep, I was amazed that it worked, and if it wasn't for the crystal necklace you had, you would've been a goner."

"Thank you for . . . saving my life . . . again."

"I'm not keeping count." Seth put his arm around me and kissed me on the forehead.

"Is there any way to make my leg feel a bit less sore?"

Seth was looking at his necklace again and raised his eyebrow before looking at me. "There is one way, but I'm not sure if it'll work."

"Might as well give it a try!"

I asked Seth to fetch my crutches so I could walk on my own outside. I hated the feeling of being unable to walk on my own or have Seth help me off the ground. Being dependent on an island I've had to survive on alone really builds up a necessity of having to be independent and strong. As I hopped out of the living room and up the stairs to my room, Seth asked if I had put on my bikini underneath.

"Seth, I can't swim like this!"

"It's just sore, isn't it?"

"Well, yeah I suppose, but I won't be able to . . . oh right . . . the tail."

"That's what I'm a little worried about."

"Does it mean I can't grow a tail again?"

"We'll have to find out."

I managed to get my bikini on just fine, but I fell over twice when I tried to pick up a crutch I dropped as I was slipping my leg into the bikini bottom.

"You all right?" I heard Seth yell from outside my room.

"I'm fine. I'll be right out."

Finally getting the crutch under my arms, I pushed the door open with my fingers and carefully stepped down the stairs. Seth was waiting at the bottom to catch me if I should fall, but I made it down in one piece.

"You know you're going to have to walk without the crutches before you get in the water, right?"

"I was just thinking about that."

Seth walked right by my side from the kitchen to the front door, to the sand outside the patio and a few feet from the shoreline. I looked at Seth and took a deep breath before throwing my crutches off behind me. I closed my eyes, thinking I would fall face-first into the sand, but I really stood balanced and straight up, as if my leg hadn't been sore at all. I opened one eye and looked down, and I noticed I wasn't lying down in the sand. Thank goodness!

"Be careful when you're walking."

"I know. Just make sure I don't fall face-first into the sand."

"Got it."

My first step was with my sore leg, and when I shifted my weight to stand on it, it felt like I had just dropped an anvil on my entire leg. Without even thinking about it, my other leg automatically stepped forward to regain balance.

"Huh."

"Looks like you can handle the rest."

"Are you sure?"

"I'm positive, just keep going."

Seth raced ahead about six steps before diving into the water, leaving me to fend for myself on the shore. Suddenly, I felt like I needed him there, just to protect me from falling down and having to stay on the ground waiting for him to help me up. I shook my head and convinced myself that I could do this; I could do this and make it to the water. With the same routine I did before, I limped toward the waves splashing at my toes, and with every small step I was about knee deep in the ocean; the cool water felt good on my sore leg. I dived forward into the sea, letting the water drench my hair, plug my ears, and release bubbles the deeper I swam. I stopped swimming for a minute, waiting for my legs to fuse together, but nothing happened. I opened my eyes, and in the blur, I saw Seth with his tail in front of me, waiting for my tail to grow too. I raised my hands and arms as if to say "I don't know," while I held my breath, just patiently waiting. About fifteen seconds later, I was starting to think that maybe I needed to go to the surface for some air, but my legs felt a little numb, and soon enough, my tail had formed. I blinked a few times, and I saw Seth crystal clear as I took a breath of the water and sighed with relief.

"For a second I thought my tail would never show up."

"Looks fine to me . . . wait."

"What? What is it?"

"You didn't have a scar on your tail before, did you?"

"Of course not, why would I—?"

I looked around my tail and realized that at the same spot where my sore leg was there was a long scar about twenty-five centimeters long. It scared me when it cut right through the scales that were once there; worst of all, it looked permanent.

"Please tell me this isn't permanent. You can get rid of it, right?"

"I don't think I can, but I know someone who will. Follow me!"

Seth swam quickly through a coral reef and twisted around until we finally reached the gates of Atlantis. Once we arrived, we slowed down to make sure we didn't run into anyone else on our way to the castle; every person we encountered greeted me a happy birthday. I smiled and waved in return, saying thank you, while Seth grabbed my other hand. I didn't mind, and I knew Seth could see it, as I waved to more people and continued to swim to the castle. When the greetings from people slowly began to stop and we were only a few feet from the gates with the guards, I looked down at my tail again, and my smile faded all the more at the scar.

"Don't worry. Your scar will be gone in no time."

"And what if my scar doesn't go away?"

"Then you'll just have an amazing story to tell with your scar."

"I almost died!"

"I didn't say it was a good story."

"But I can't even remember a large chunk of it."

Seth put his arm around my shoulder and pulled me closer to the side of his chest.

"Then I'll tell the story."

It was impossible not to smile just as the guards opened the gate for us. I nodded to the guards, and I felt a little bit better about my scar since they didn't notice it or point it out.

"Happy birthday, Jillian," one of the guards said as I walked through the gate.

The Tail of an Angel

Once I was in the castle, I immediately started to make my way to where Neptune was, but before I got out of the room, Sedrick and Skylar cut me off, scaring me to death, *"Ahhh!"*

"Happy birthday!" they said together with their hands in the air.

"Happy heart attack much! Jeez."

"Sorry, we just couldn't wait to tell you happy birthday."

Skylar laughed as he said sorry and gave me a hug. I laughed a little bit in return, but Seth laughed a lot more than I did when Skylar hugged me.

"Happy seventeenth, Jill!" Sedrick said when he hugged me next.

"What on earth is that on your tail?" Skylar asked.

"Oh it's nothing, just a long . . . boring story."

"I like stories!"

"Seth should tell you. I don't remember most of it."

"What? Tell me what happened!"

"It looks like some sort of scar," Sedrick pointed out.

"Unfortunately, it is."

"I didn't even know that could happen!"

"Seth . . ."

I looked over and bent my head down a little, widening my eyes, hinting he should start telling the story of the scar on my tail.

"Well, I can't tell the story."

"You can tell them about the shark part though."

"Sharks?" Skylar yelled.

"What sharks?" Sedrick put his hand over his mouth and gasped.

"Well, it started out when I spent a day collecting crystals in a cave and I brought a lunch since I was there for the entire day. I even packed some beef jerky to munch on when I got out of the water, but I brought the lunch bag with me underwater . . . And that's kind of what attracted the great white shark in the first place."

"Not a great white." Skylar shook his head.

"It was, and the shark snuck up on me just before I made it to the surface and bit my tail, and the strangest thing happened! My tail disappeared and the shark was trying to take off my leg. Instead, I sort of wiggled out of his mouth and stabbed it in the eye a few times until it finally let me go."

"You didn't tell me this part."

Seth looked in concern at the sad expression on my face as I told the story about the sharks. He put his hand on my shoulder and looked down and told me to continue the story.

"I'm sorry, but you were busy taking care of me."

"Anyways!" Skylar interrupted.

"Right! So I made it to the shore in the cave, and my leg was bleeding like you wouldn't believe. The water where I got out from started turning red from all the blood, and Miko started freaking out."

"Who's Miko?" Sedrick asked.

"Friendly monkey she keeps as a pet."

"Oh cool, I love monkeys."

"Can I continue please?"

"My bad. Blood everywhere, scared monkey, go on."

"So I told Miko to find help if he could, but I didn't see him for a long while. He's important though! And after I got out of the water, I managed to get to my feet and drag myself to the house along the cave walls, and I fell when I got to the front door with a trail of blood behind me."

"What did you do?" Skylar questioned me.

"I called out for Seth, but he never came that night."

"You idiot!" Sedrick punched Seth in the shoulder.

"Hey! Take it easy! I was there the next morning! Is that really the end of the story?"

"Nope, there are a few more things. When I got inside, I was only thinking if it was my last day on the island, I'd spend it somewhere I'd love for my last moments on earth. So I limped a lot toward the stairs, but I couldn't make it up the stairs without treating what I could of the wound. So when Miko finally showed up, I asked him to get a towel to wrap up my leg and I could walk on it somewhat decently and finally up to my room. I knew from reading a journal I found in a chest that I wouldn't have long without antibiotics, and since there were none on the island, I just sat in my room with my back to the edge of my bed, scrolling through photos on my camera. So I took off the towel to see the wound, and I figured I'd have about a half hour or so and yelled out of my window once more to see if Seth would help me."

Sedrick and Skylar glared at Seth, while Seth scratched the back of his hair, muttering, "Oops."

"So I sat back down at the edge of my bed and put a totem necklace I made around my neck next to the crystal one that was glowing brighter than before. And just before I blacked out, I flipped to a photo of my boyfriend and me and held the crystal necklace in my hand one last time, and that was all I could remember."

"So, Seth, what's the rest of the story?"

"Yeah, Seth, do tell."

Sedrick and Skylar crossed their arms and waited for Seth to start telling the story from the point where he came in.

"Well, my story starts very early this morning, when I called for her at the front door, and I immediately rushed to her room and found her on the floor, ice-cold."

I put my head on Seth's shoulder and looked down at the floor to the left. I really didn't like hearing the part about me being, well, you know... dead.

"But I remembered what the crystals could do about healing wounds and even restarting the heart! And if she wasn't wearing the crystal necklace that was just barely glowing, I would've thought she was really dead..."

"So?"

"So I took the crystal and fixed her leg and touched the crystal above her heart, and she didn't look as pale anymore. I was so glad she was okay, and I stayed with her until she woke up, but why her tail is scarred I have no idea."

"I think Dad can help," Sedrick suggested.

"That's exactly what I was thinking."

"Well then, what are we waiting for? Let's go!"

Seth moved his hand down from my shoulder to my hand and yanked me to follow him to see King Neptune. Sedrick and Skylar were the first to enter the room (as usual) and Seth and I were the last to enter.

"Father, Jill is here and—"

"Ah yes! Her birthday party is today! Happy seventeenth birthday, my dear Jillian!" King Neptune said in a booming loud voice as he swam up and gave me a hug.

"Ummmm, can he do that?" I whispered to Seth and his brothers, but they just shrugged their shoulders and muttered under their breath, "I don't know." When Neptune let me go, I grinned not just in surprise, but something told me that he thought I was family, especially when I needed family the most.

"Your tail!"

"Oh, I forgot to mention I was attacked by a shark."

"No!"

"To make a long story short, I managed to fight off a great white shark and make it home, but I've been told that I died... for a few minutes, I think."

"And your crystal was barely glowing."

"How did you know?"

"They can detect most forms of life, no matter how small they might be."

"How can a little crystal like this do so much?"

"Just because something is small doesn't mean it can't do great things."

At this point, Neptune sounded like some fortune cookie or some wise china man with many ancient phrases to share with monks or something.

"I bet that shark left quite a mark on your leg."

"Yeah, it's not my first shark encounter."

King Neptune grabbed the fin at the end of my tail and pulled me up, upside down, closer to his face to see the scar. I freaked out not only at how he pulled me up with ease to his face, but also that no one stopped him from doing so, while I had a miniature heart attack.

"Hey! It's still a little tender!"

"Hush! I just need to have a good look at the scar."

Seth yelled at Neptune as he held me upside down, "Father! Can't you see she's still healing from the attack and you're hurting her?!"

"She'll be all right in a second."

I was getting more and more sore the longer I remained upside down in his hand.

"I don't mean to stop you, Your Majesty, but can you please let me go?"

"Oh yes, I know exactly what I need to do."

He released me from his grip, and I swam up to stand straight while Seth asked if I was okay.

"I'll be fine as long as he doesn't lift me up again."

"My apologies. I just needed to see how deep the scar was."

"Why?"

"So I can fix it, of course!"

King Neptune reached behind his throne and pulled out a solid white crystal trident. It was beautifully carved and completely see-through, tinted white as if it was frosted. Around the center trident was the emerald I had returned to him on a necklace wrapped around the bottom of the trident connected to the staff below it. In a very simple conclusion, it was beautiful and was fit for a king such as Neptune.

"Hold still. You may feel some stinging in the lower half of your tail."

"Why?"

Seth and his brothers backed up when Neptune pointed his trident at my tail, yet I remained perfectly still. I looked at Neptune for only a second before staring in awe at the trident beginning to glow bright sky blue. It only took a minute or so before the glow began to be too bright to look at and my tail began to feel a little numb progressively like my tail was on fire. I didn't even think of screaming because I knew King Neptune would stop and the scar on my tail would never heal. I looked at Seth and his brothers, but they were already closing their eyes against the bright light, and I looked down to see my tail glowing just as bright as his trident and I was forced to close my eyes. Time went by ever so quickly, but the burning pain on my tail felt like it had been for hours and hours on fire, and when it stopped, I was just so relieved. I opened one eye to make sure that it was over and done with.

"Did it work?" I asked with one eye open.

"I don't see a scar anymore, so yes," King Neptune told me. I opened my other eye and examined my tail for the scar, turning around once and lifting my fin into the air to see even more of my tail. Sedrick, Skylar, and Seth stood where they were, just watching me trying to find the scar, and I could see nothing but healed scales and the sparkly glitter on them.

"Thank you, Your Majesty!"

"Anytime, my dear. As for your birthday party, I will call everyone to the ballroom in just a moment."

"What can I do to help?"

"You . . . can go to one of my son's rooms and wait until everyone has arrived."

"You can stay in my room," Seth suggested. Of course, I'd be staying in Seth's room. I couldn't think of a reason why not.

"How long will I have to wait?"

"Oh, ten or twenty minutes at the most."

"Really? That quick? I was guessing about an hour or so."

"Nope, the people in the city right now won't take long to arrange in the ballroom and the important guests are already on their way to the city. They just don't know where the party will be held."

"Who are the important guests?"

"The available princes from other cities around the world."

"The world? And they'll be here in about twenty minutes? That's amazing since I told him my birthday was a day or two ago."

"The cities that are really far away weren't invited."

I stepped into Seth's room and sat on the side of bed, and I lay down on my back, since the bed was unbelievably soft.

"How many princes are going to be here anyways?"

"Oh, maybe four hundred or so."

"Four hundred? That's insane! I'm going to be here all day talking to these guys!"

"Well, that's sort of the point."

"But I promised myself I'd see my father today."

Seth suddenly looked up at me and said nothing, as he sat down on the bed by my side.

"I don't know if my father will let you do that."

"Why not?" I asked, as tears began to fill my eyes.

"He's in jail for a reason, and he won't be getting out of jail anytime soon."

"I'm not asking for Neptune to release him. I'm asking if I can simply visit him."

"I'll talk to him about it."

"Thank you."

About ten minutes passed while I was talking to Seth, and then I heard a knock on the door.

"Everybody's here! Come to the ballroom."

"We'll be down in a second," Seth yelled to Skylar outside the room.

"Why can't we go now?"

"Close your eyes."

"Why?"

"Just close your eyes."

I closed my eyes, but I had no idea why I should. All I could hear was Seth walking around the room, and it made me a little concerned that he might walk out of the room and go to the party or even get completely ready while I just stood there with my eyes closed.

"What are you doing?"

"I'm getting something."

"What are you getting?"

"Be patient! You can open your eyes in a minute."

I crossed my arms and stood patiently while Seth walked a little closer to me. I wanted to back up a bit when I felt him so close to me. I could feel the heat from his breath on my chest. He wasn't standing straight up because I would've felt his breath on my face. I was just about to open my eyes, but I felt him put something around my neck. I heard a click of the object around my neck, and I found out it was obviously a necklace. Curious to what was on the necklace, I lifted up hand to feel the charm on my chest and felt Seth's hand on the charm instead.

"Can I open my eyes now?"

"Not just yet."

I let go of the charm and let my hand fall to my side, but Seth continued holding the charm on the necklace. Even though I couldn't see a thing, I could tell he was staring at the necklace and his face was much closer to mine, so close in fact his nose just barely touched mine, and I didn't even think of opening my eyes. I simply stood there for a few seconds, and when his lips just barely touched mine, someone opened the door to Seth's room.

"Hey, Seth, have you seen my—?"

I opened my eyes and turned to look at Skylar, the same time as Seth.

"I'll come back later."

I really tried not to laugh, but I burst out in such a loud laughter I fell down on the floor and continued to laugh. Seth didn't laugh until I was on the floor, laughing my ass off, which must have been hilarious to watch.

"So much for that."

"It was just bad timing."

I finally got up from the floor and sat up, fixing my hair.

"Let me help you up."

Seth easily pulled me up, right up to his face, and I smiled and kissed him on the cheek before asking him what he had put around my neck.

"It's the wolf tooth necklace Jay gave you."

"So you stole it. I took it and you stole it back to give it to me?"

"I never really thought of it that way, but yes."

"I don't know whether to thank you or get angry because you stole my necklace again."

"How about you just thank me?"

Seth kissed me on the forehead before I left the room with him to the ballroom. Before Seth and I entered the ballroom, Sedrick stopped us and told us to see Neptune first. Following orders, Seth and I found Neptune and Seth's brothers all waiting for us.

"How is your tail feeling?"

"Just fine, thank you."

"I forgot to mention that I will be announcing your arrival and a bit of your history before you entered our city. Is that all right with you?"

"Absolutely, I don't mind at all."

"Excellent! Follow my sons in after me and I will tell you when to step forward during your introduction."

Neptune made his way out the door and into the ballroom, and Sedrick, Skylar, Seth, and I followed after him. The second I reached there I saw the massive group of people there for my party; they cheered so loud it hurt my ears and made me laugh in amazement, since I'd never seen so many people at one party. Seth told me to stand next to him behind Neptune while he gave his speech.

"Can I have everyone's attention please?"

Neptune voice echoed through the room and the crowd became silent almost immediately.

"Our guest has arrived for her seventeenth birthday party."

Neptune indicated to me to stand next to him at the front of the stage, with a smile and a wave of his hand.

"This wonderful girl not too long ago survived a terrible hurricane with nothing but a raft and a few of her things as her family and friends drifted away from her in rafts of their own. She fought off starvation and sharks with nothing but a homemade knife and her bare hands, but she couldn't fight off a large rock that she crashed into and which nearly killed her. After all, she was only human."

Neptune gestured to his sons to join him at the front, and Seth stood next to his father, right beside me.

"If it wasn't for my youngest son, Seth, she would've died. And I'm ever so proud that he saved her."

Seth smiled at his father while Neptune patted him on the back a few times.

"Before she discovered our great capital city of Atlantis, she survived on an island not too far from here, managing to discover the secret crystal caves as well as plenty of food, shelter, and a monkey she cares for named Miko."

I heard awes and applause from the crowd.

"Not only is she very smart, but she even used her own blood to trap and kill fifteen great white sharks. Wow."

The crowd cheered but turned silent to hear the rest of the speech.

"It wasn't long before she stepped into the sea after shark breeding season, and she discovered she was a hybrid. And most of you know the rest of the story of when she swam into the gates of our great city, but for those of you who have not heard. Our beloved queen, Augustina, my dear wife, lives on in a part of her. She even has her eyes, her voice, and a piece of her soul. This means that she is from royal blood and may marry any prince of her choice, including my own sons."

The crowd went absolutely insane, and everyone was whistling, cheering, clapping, you name it. Something told me that a good chunk of this crowd were princes, who were looking forward to meeting me.

"We can be the family she needs today, while my sons and I will do everything to find her real family and other friends."

Remembering the loss of my family brought back an instant memory of the night our boat sank and the last time I saw Jay. I tried not to cry, but instead I let my head down, and Seth put his arm around my shoulder to make me feel better. To be honest, it did make me feel a little better, but not by much.

"Now then, it is my pleasure to introduce our guest of honor, who brought back the forgotten joy of music, and beloved angel of the land and sea, Jillian Verbicky! So let's show her a good time!"

The crowd was screaming just as loud as before; surely my hearing would get worse by the end of the day if this kept up. I looked up at the people cheering for little old me and thought of nothing better than to wave with Seth at everyone and speak to any of my other friends in the audience.

I noticed Seth was waving with me, and when the crowd settled down, I saw Akari with a few friends of hers waving at us to say hello.

"Hey, Akari!"

"Hey, Jill, I'd like to introduce you to Levi, Sky, Hunter, Kiara, and Tyler."

Kiara waved, saying hello, and Sky and Hunter said hey, flicking their heads up in the air; indicating through body language, Levi and Tyler gave a polite nod that was simpler than waving to say hello.

"Nice to meet you all."

"So you're turning seventeen today?" Sky asked me.

"Yep, another year and I can drink legally in Canada."

"You're from Canada? What's it like?" Hunter asked.

"Well, life on land is much different than in Atlantis. We breathe air and not water, and when people go swimming, they can't breathe in water and swim with legs, not tails."

"Wow, what's the landscape like there?"

"Where I'm from, there's lots of farm land that's wide and flat until the harvest, when canola or wheat grow to about waist high, and the canola would then glow a bright shade of yellow under a clear blue sky. But there are also lots of forests with pine and poplar trees that are home to all sorts of animals like moose, deer, rabbits, bears, and elk. Most of them are pretty tasty. And the summers are so warm, around twenty or thirty degrees, but the winters are the worst with tons of snow, frostbite winds, deadly slippery ice, and average temperatures of thirty and forty below. The snow where I live is so ridiculously deep one time I got stuck while jumping in the snow when it went up to my belly button, and I had to dig my way out."

"What's snow?" Kiara questioned, turning her head slightly to the left.

Jeez, it was like I was talking to a three-year-old; those people were smart, I was sure, but they could use a trip or two to Canada.

"It's frozen water that forms in clouds on a cold day and falls from the sky as a snowflake, but every single snowflake is very beautiful and unique. In fact, no two snowflakes are ever the same."

"What about spring and fall?"

"Spring is slightly colder than summer, but has lots of new life and water everywhere from heating up the winter snow. Plus, everything smells so good and it's green with plant life all around. It really is breathtaking. Then in the fall that comes after the summer everything gets much colder, but not as cold as the winter. The leaves turn colors on the trees, like orange, brown, yellow, red, and in a valley not too far from my home, I can't even describe the beauty of that place. Breathtaking is not even close to what it looks like. Finally, when the trees are stripped of their leaves and the winds blow every last bit of them away, everything freezes and it begins to snow."

"So why did you leave this wonderful place to live in the sea?" Hunter asked with a smile.

"It wasn't really my decision to end up down here. My mother thought it would be a good idea to take a vacation to Hawaii, but you kind of know the rest of the story. I can only hope that she is okay."

I dropped my head and expected a warm tear to roll down my cheek, but then I remembered I was underwater and that it would just dissolve into the water all around me.

"Hey, I bet they're relaxing and safe at sound at home right now."

Akari gave me a sideways hug, putting her one arm on my opposite hip.

"Omigosh! I forgot to tell you about the princes!"

"Princes?"

"Neptune would like you to meet the princes from the other underwater cities."

"Why?"

"Think about it! You're a princess, and he was hoping that—"

"I would marry one of the princes? That's crazy."

"Like it or not, there are four hundred available princes here, happy to meet you, and Neptune should be lining them pretty soon. I better ask him."

"Oh no, no, no, no, no! You don't have to do—"

"Your Majesty, may I speak to you please?"

Neptune swam over to us. "Yes, what is it, Akari?"

"Don't you think it's time to gather the princes to meet Jillian?"

"Oh, thank you for reminding me! Attention, everyone!"

I thought to myself that I might be here all evening if I had forty princes to talk to.

"Akari, I don't want to be here all day. I still want to see my father and have time to talk to him," I whispered to her.

"Relax, just talk to each prince for about seven minutes or so. Besides, Neptune's orders are for them to tell you about themselves, families, where they're from and so on."

"So I'll be here for about five and a half hours?!"

"Good thing it's only 9:30."

Neptune finally started his speech. "I would like all the princes here to gather outside of the ballroom to meet Jillian immediately."

I watched a large group of men pass me without so much as a hey or hello, and I found it to be a little bit rude.

"Do I really have to speak to every prince here?"

"Yes, and among your favorites will be a husband."

"There are really only four hundred princes in the entire sea?"

"Nope, there's thousands! The ones that are here are just good friends of the king and who could make it to your party in time. Believe it or not, only thirty or so are married; and all the men here are single and ready to mingle!"

"How many of them are hybrids?"

"We'll have to find out."

"Can I meet more than one prince at a time?"

"Absolutely, how about you and see them in groups of four, so you only have to do it ten times?"

"You can't be serious."

"Oh, it's very serious. It's an order from the king and can't be ignored."

"Akari, you have to come with me!"

"Why?"

"I can't talk to all these men by myself! I need someone else to help me keep the conversations going."

"I'd be glad to."

"Thank you! You're such a good friend."

I gave Akari a big hug. I didn't think she knew how much this meant to me, as for me to face all those guys by myself and have something interesting to talk about would take a freakin' miracle.

"Best friend?" Akari asked me.

"Definitely."

I felt much more confident on having Akari to join me, and I asked Neptune to order all the princes in groups of four. I looked up at the clock on the wall and took a big breath, fixed my hair, and walked forward to the first group of guys closest to Akari and me.

"Hey, my name is Alex. This is Peter, Shawn, and Lucas."

"It's a pleasure to meet you all."

"The pleasure is all mine," one of the handsomest guys said as he lifted my hand to his face and kissed it.

"Well, that's Lucas. He's a bit of a hopeless romantic."

"Really? Me too! Tell me more about yourself, Lucas."

Alex, Peter, and Shawn folded their arms and sighed in disappointment as I turned to chat with Lucas.

"Well, my full name is Lucas Dane Lafayette."

"What a beautiful last name."

"Thank you. I'm from the coast of the Adriatic Sea."

"Funny, I thought you would have a bit of a Greek or Italian accent."

"Well, I am slightly Italian, but I rarely visit the surface to see some of my family."

"So you're a hybrid too?"

"You bet!"

"That is so awesome! Am I the only one who thinks it burns a lot when you first get in the water with your legs?"

"No way! Me too! The first time I starting breathing underwater, I thought I died."

I couldn't be more impressed with Lucas. I had a very similar opinion of him, and so far, I wanted to find out more about him.

"What else can you tell me about yourself?"

"The city I'm from is called Lumina Nocturnale, and a few people in my family live there. Most of my large family is from the city I live in underwater, with my elder sister and little brother."

"Aww, what's your little brother's name?"

"Flynn."

"I myself just have one older brother. I really hope he's okay as well."

"My sympathies, Jillian."

"Thank you for your kindness. Is there anything else you wish to tell me?"

"You won't believe this, but some of the princes here and myself possess unique . . . gifts."

"What do you mean gifts?"

"More like powers really."

"Well, tell me about these so-called 'powers' you have then."

"Mind control, invisibility, precognition, telepathy, and invulnerability."

"Damn, but then why were you so surprised at my opinion on growing a tail in the water?"

"It requires a lot of focus to use my powers, and I wasn't all that focused."

"That's so cool!"

"Indeed."

"Well, I certainly would like to get to know you better, but I have five hours of talking to other princes to do."

"Are you serious? That's insane."

"Maybe it's a punishment for breaking one of the Ten Commandments."

"Which one did you break?"

"The one that forbids sex before marriage."

"You're thinking of the seventh commandment: 'Thou shalt not commit adultery,' and that only applies if you're married."

"Oh right, then I don't know why I'm being punished."

"You shouldn't think of it as a punishment. Was it a bad thing that you met me?"

"Of course not! I just have 399 princes left to talk to."

"When you're finished with everyone, come chat with me again if you're up to it."

"Sure, it was great to meet you, Lucas."

"You too, Jill."

Lucas kissed me on the cheek and smiled as he turned away and disappeared into the group of guys behind me. Next were the other three guys, who had been chatting to themselves patiently while I was chatting with Lucas. I thought I might as well get it over with.

"You're Shawn, right?"

"Correct."

"Tell me about yourself."

"My name is Shawn Dante Stone, and I'm from the coast of Greenland."

"Oh wow, wouldn't the water there be really cold?"

"Oh yeah, I don't see much of my family though since they've adapted to the cold water there and I always get sick when I visit. I really miss them too."

"That's so sad. Don't you have any other family nearby?"

"I do, but at the moment my friends are my family right now."

"What else can you tell me?"

"I can control the elements any way I desire."

"Show me."

Shawn raised his hand and it started a fire, only in a small ball somehow protected from the water, but it put me in awe as I watched. The fire glowed for a few seconds and froze, leaving the fire to freeze in the shape it was still on his palm. It was beautiful, and I was about to say wow. Before I could, the fire-shaped piece of ice melted and left an orange lily in its place; the lily had such bright orange and red highlights on it that I named it a fire lily, as it took my breath away.

"For you."

Shawn placed the lily behind my ear and tucked my hair behind it.

"It's beautiful. Thank you, Shawn. Any more surprises for me?"

"Nope, that's about it. All I can really tell you is that I've never really been to the surface, and I don't plan to."

"You're a hybrid?"

"No, I've never been anywhere above the water, not even to look at the sky."

"You really should. You're missing out on a really beautiful place."

"I'll take it into consideration. It was great to meet you, Jill."

"You too, see you!"

I smiled as Shawn started to walk away, and he winked once before he blended into the crowd of guys, like the last guy I had met.

"That's a beautiful flower Shawn gave you."

"Thanks. If all the guys here are as good as the first two, I'm gonna have some trouble picking out my favorites."

"Oh, believe me, some of the guys here shouldn't be princes at all."

"Like who?"

"See that lovely acne-covered gentleman over there?"

Akari pointed to a group of dorky-looking guys in the corner of the room, laughing among themselves; then the worst-looking one noticed me watching him. I had to resist the urge to say "yuck" and make a disgusted face. This guy was the exact definition of a nerd, with his large set of braces, an unattractive, scarred, and acne-covered face, curly red hair, and paler than an albino person and a vampire combined. I didn't want to be rude, but he was really damn ugly.

"That's the worst-looking guy I've ever seen."

"That's not the worst part."

"There's a worst part? Please don't tell me it gets worse."

"He smells bad, not very hygienic, and is allergic to almost everything."

"Ewwww."

The very second I said "ew" to Akari, the gross nerd guy waved at me and said hellooo. I couldn't have been more grossed out than was right then. I tried to be nice and waved back with a fake smile, and he lit up like the Fourth of July. So bad!

"Me next! I'm Alex!"

"You seem very eager to meet me, why's that?"

"My father never lets me go to parties, but to be invited by King Neptune here changed his mind, and I'm *so* excited!"

"I can tell. Tell me more about you."

"My name is Alexander Oakley Cato, and I'm from the coast of British Columbia in Canada."

"Oh sweet! I'm from Canada too! Alberta actually."

"I just love Canada, and on an off topic, do you enjoy *The Hunger Games*?"

"Absolutely. Is it just a coincidence that your last name happens to be the same name as one of the tributes?"

"Actually, I never really thought about it. Cool!"

I laughed and enjoyed his sense of humor and attitude that was similar to my own. The fact that he was Canadian made him even more fun to be around.

"So what of your family?"

"My family is all in BC and I have only my friends in the underwater cities. The surface is a much better place than in the sea I think. Even though it's beautiful down here, I miss the sunsets, walks on the beach, and just about everything in Canada."

"Why don't you go back to the surface?"

"I had a fight with my parents and ran away one night. I was all over the city looking for a place to stay and found a home to stay in, but later that night the house caught fire, and I escaped. But the papers said that I had died in the fire. I wanted to go home again, but I was afraid they'd still be angry at me. So with absolutely nowhere to go, I decided to go for a swim on the coast, and I grew a tail and stayed in the water from that moment on, living peacefully in the underwater cities."

"How long ago was this?"

"About five years ago."

"You should go back to the surface someday."

"I will, but that will be a few years down the road."

"You know what I would do in your situation?"

"What's that?"

"Volunteer as tribute."

Alex began to laugh to the point he was holding his gut and turning red in his cheeks. I thought it was cute to see how much I could make him laugh; something kept telling me to keep talking to him, even though I had many other men to get acquainted with. I didn't want to go.

"You're much funnier than I thought you would be."

"I was going to say the same thing to you, Alex. Do you mind if I call you Cato?"

"Ha-ha, no, I don't mind. Why do you ask?"

"Well, to be honest you look a lot like him."

"You really think so?"

"I don't think I mentioned he was my favorite tribute."

I sounded a bit flirty, but I meant it in the best of ways.

"That changes it up a little bit then, doesn't it then?"

Alex came a little closer to me and fixed the bit of hair that was covering the lily behind my ear.

"Do you do that to all the hybrid birthday girls?"

"Just the really beautiful ones."

He put his hand on the side of my face and kissed my forehead. I actually smiled a little, but tried to hide it from the other princes; they'd be super jealous.

"Times up, Jill. Let's meet the next prince then. Nice to meet you, Alex!"

Akari grabbed my arm and yanked me toward her; it made my arm crack actually.

"Say bye to Alex, Jill."

"But he's so nice. I'd like to chat with him some more," I whispered to Akari.

"Your five minutes is up. Let's go."

"Bye, Alex! Nice to meet you!"

"My pleasure, Jillian!"

I couldn't believe Akari had to drag me away from Alex to see the other princes. I knew now that it was going to be a long day.

Peter was a nice guy, who was quite shy to the point I did a good portion of the talking; I didn't enjoy him as much. Guy after guy, I started to speed up the stories they explained to me, agreeing they were all very cool and interesting, but really I was bored out of my mind. Akari joined into a few of the conversations since she knew a few of the princes there. Sure, a few of these princes seemed like they'd make some good husband material—good with kids, sense of humor, very kind. Only one or two I considered to be among my favorites; both of course were hybrids.

"I'm so bored of talking to people."

"I know, me too, but it should go by faster if these guys are fun and entertaining."

"Okay, let's get to it."

Back to chatting with the guys, I was pleased with a group that all had a thing for surfing all around the world. They surfed in almost every surfing area in the world, and one of the guys had recently surfed a hurricane wave. I was very impressed.

"You wouldn't believe this one wave. It was at least like two hundred feet high. It was so rad when Ricky caught that hurricane wave and lived to tell about it."

The guy high-fived Ricky and continued telling stories about surfing, until I finally look at the clock and finished up with these guys.

"How many more guys do I have to talk to now?"

"We should be at about two hundred or so."

"Oh great! I'll never finish."

"Oh shit."

"What?"

"Nerd alert."

I looked over at a group, and there they were—nerds. I overheard one talk about how *Aquaman* sucks. I found it funny that they would talk about that since they lived underwater.

"Just suck it up, be nice and—"

"Smile a bunch until they stop talking. I got it."

I walked up to the most disgusting one first and tried so hard not to laugh at his ridiculously squeaky voice. Everything he told me seriously sounded like a chipmunk, and his braces gave him a lisp that made it even funnier to listen to. Akari was snickering to herself, so I nudged her to shut up and listen to what the nerd had to say.

"So this guy was like, you can't be serious, and I was like, you want me to use my fists? 'Cause I can make that happen."

"Oh jeez, this is going to be the longest five minutes I will ever experience," I thought.

"That's . . . interesting. What else can you tell me?"

"I'm a level eighty-seven mage warrior on this fantasy adventure game on a website called—"

"I meant more about yourself, not so much what you like to do in your spare time."

"Of course! I'm partially Russian and I have won many dance competitions."

"What kind of dancing are you in?"

"Freestyle!"

Then out of nowhere, he dropped to the ground and starting spinning his tail around on the ground, lifting his hands so he could spin around more; finally, he stopped and laid his down, his head resting on his hand and the other holding his chin, trying to look like some sort of gangster. Akari, seconds later, burst out into laughter. I nudged her with my elbow to be quiet, but Akari would only stop laughing if she disappeared. So Akari left me by myself with the few nerds to talk to; I could handle the next set of nerds since they couldn't be any worse than this guy. Time went by much faster with the other nerds, but they were much more mature and smarter than the first. Finally, after hours and hours of chitchatting, hand shaking, and smiling so much at all these guys, I was free to enjoy the rest of my party and get away from the princes I didn't enjoy or I simply found weird.

"Akari! I'm finally done talking to every prince here!"

"You missed about thirty of them though."

"No! I'm through talking to princes for today. There's not one guy I wish to talk to right now."

"So it didn't go that well, did it?" Seth said behind me.

"I totally forgot about you guys. If I would have known better, you and your brothers would be the first ones I'd speak to. Damn, it's good to see you all."

I gave Seth, Sedrick, and Skylar a hug; I completely forgot that I could have Seth and his brothers along with my group of men who would be eligible to be my husband.

"So did you happen to meet any decent princes?"

"Actually I did, but I didn't pick as many as you might think."

"Well, how many?"

"Five."

"That's it?"

Skylar dropped his jaw and laughed for a minute before Sedrick smacked him on the head.

"It's still quite a bit to choose from for a single husband."

"Don't be so sure I'll choose someone from that group of guys. You're in the group too."

"All three of us?"

"You bet."

"Woohoo!"

Seth cheered and gave me a hug while Skylar blushed a bit and tried to hide a smile. Sedrick gave me a hug too. Skylar just stood next to Seth; he looked a little shyer than usual.

"Come here, Skylar!"

I gave him a hug, while his brothers laughed a little since Skylar was blushing even more.

"So now what do I have to do? Just pick a husband today? 'Cause I don't think I can today."

"Of course not, you'll have about a week to decide."

"A week?"

"Don't worry. For the entire week, you get to know the guys better and have a kick-ass wedding party and everything."

"I don't know about this, Seth. I'm only seventeen. I can't get married this young!"

"My father knows the rest of how it all works. Let's go."

Seth grabbed my hand and found Neptune so we could speak to him.

"Have you chosen among the princes that were here?"

"Five, Your Majesty."

"Only five?"

"Well, five and your three sons, of course."

"Wonderful! I'll make an announcement!"

The Tail of an Angel

I whispered to Seth, "Why does he always have to make announcements?"

"He doesn't make as many announcements as he used to. Besides, he loves making speeches."

I couldn't believe how many people were still there after five hours and not even getting to see me. These were the most patient people I'd ever met!

"Thank you so much for waiting patiently, everyone, but our guest of honor has finally chosen her suitors from the four hundred princes that attended this party today. Come forward and tell us who they are."

Neptune looked at me and smiled, so I stepped forward and spoke to the large crowd that was glaring at me with a hundred eyes and was dead silent, waiting for me to speak.

"Among the four hundred princes I met today, I have chosen five, as well as King Neptune's three sons."

A roaring applause followed.

"The names of the five men I have chosen are Lucas."

Alex came up to the stage and winked as he lined up beside Neptune.

"Shawn."

Shawn stood next to Alex and waved to the audience below.

"Alex."

When Alex got to the stage, he did the three finger salute, and I laughed a bit when he looked at me.

"Peter."

I felt that I'd get to know him better if I had a week to meet the more confident and sweet guy under that shy and kind exterior.

"And finally, Damian."

I hadn't mentioned Damian to be one of my favorites, but I had to pick another one and it didn't matter who it was. I just picked him because he had a rocking body. The second Damian got to the stage and waved to the crowd a group of women in the front swooned and some fainted. Oh good Lord!

"But don't forget that Neptune's sons are also in this group, and I'll give my decision of a suitor in a week's time I think."

"You're correct, but you missed a part," Neptune told me.

"She will choose a suitor and marry on her eighteenth birthday, on such a date, when she will be given the gift of immortality!"

The crowd was going crazy, and I joined them since in a year I could be immortal! I ran up to Neptune and gave him a big hug, which made everyone laugh and say "aw" at that the same time. Once I finished with my celebratory cheering and jumping up and down, I returned to look at the guys and Neptune with another million-dollar smile.

"So do I just hang out with everyone for a week or what?" I asked Seth.

"You will have to spend each day of this week with one gentleman, and since you know Seth so well already, it leaves you a day with each of these men to yourselves. And after this week, you will pick one of the seven men to date for one year and marry after you've turned eighteen," Neptune announced to me.

"Only a week though?"

"Is there something wrong with that?"

"No! Of course not. It's just fine."

"Good, I will choose who sees you on each day then."

"Oh, and after the party can I ask you for a favor?"

"Sure, but we still have a few things to do before the party is over."

Neptune yelled at someone from outside the ballroom, and someone brought in a massive cake with dinner rolling in behind it. How on earth food was cooked down there I had no idea, but it all looked really good. The cake had simple three tiers, with blue and green fondant covering it and edible jewels all over it. It looked almost too beautiful to eat, and I was so grateful for the cake and for everyone celebrating my birthday with me. Right as I was going to make a speech about how wonderful this all was, they began to sing happy birthday, and I forgot about it minutes later, as I blew out the candles. Another strange thing was how fire could burn underwater. I could care less, but I had to say something when they all looked at me.

"Thank you so much for everything and patiently waiting while I was chatting with the princes for five hours. I don't know about everybody else, but it was sure tiring."

The crowd laughed a little. I bet they were pretty tired too.

"Right now, I should be in Hawaii, enjoying a tropical sunset with my family and friends, probably sunburned since I can't tan whatsoever. But I'm not. And I can't thank everyone here enough for being here for me, when my real family can't. Today, you're all a part of my family enjoying this party with me and watching me blow out these candles underwater, which I still don't quite understand, and finally, I will eventually choose someone to be my husband and spend the rest of my days with. Everyone here will be invited, and I will hopefully spend the rest of eternity with you all here in the great capital underwater city of Atlantis."

Everyone was just as excited as I was and I think that was the best speech I ever gave, and I was damn proud of it. Seth cut the cake for me, and as I took the first bite into the cake, everyone looked at me like I was the queen of England. I looked around at the eyes watching me with the cake a few inches away from my face, and even though I wasn't too hungry, I quickly ate the piece and screamed that it was absolutely decadent. It was a combination of blue raspberry and chocolate. It was just sweet enough to melt in mouth and not be so sweet that it was like eating straight sugar—a perfect balance of sweet and chocolate bliss, so good.

Dinner was good, but it didn't compare to anything like the cake. Dinner was a simple sashimi and sushi buffet type of supper, but it was the freshest sushi and sashimi I'd ever had. How the hell I managed to pour soy sauce on my sushi was another question I had to ask Seth later. When we were all finished, I finished chatting with all the guys and said good-bye to the guests I didn't know, and the ones I did know, I thanked each one personally for attending my party today. In fact, I noticed one or two people leaving the party really drunk. (I thought it was funny because when they started hiccupping bubbles started coming up, and it was cute to hear the girl with him saying, "Dammit, Frank, pull yourself together.") It didn't take too long for the guests to leave, but the princes requested to stay in the castle to get to know the other princes better; it turned out they were all pretty good friends and wanted to hang out with Seth and his brothers for the week, so Neptune set them up with their own rooms in the castle. With everybody gone and the princes in their rooms, Seth and I could finally talk to Neptune about something that'd been nagging for years and years.

"Your Majesty, I believe you have my father in prison right now."

"Well, here's what I can tell you. When I finally got my lost treasures back, I was happier than I was when I found out you were from royal blood. But when your father made a family on the surface with humans, he betrayed my rules, and I cannot release him for such a crime."

"But I proved he didn't steal your treasures for the one crime you sentenced him for. What will it take for you to release my father?"

Neptune took a moment to think before answering my question, "The only way I would ever release that criminal is if he went to the surface and never returned to the ocean again."

"What if he could never find land again?"

"Then he will stay in prison until he dies."

"My father is no criminal, and how come he can't live forever like the rest of the merpeople?"

"He doesn't deserve to live forever, and I will never give him the gift of immortality!"

"Nooooo! You monster! How could you?!"

Seth was holding me back from attacking Neptune, and I didn't see it, but two guards were holding my arms back as well, so I must have been really angry.

"Just because it's your birthday doesn't mean I'll release your father."

Seth was telling me to calm down, and I finally took a breath of fresh water and the guards released me; Seth was still holding me back.

"May I at least see my father?"

"You may see your father, but if you dare trying to break him out of prison I will kill you. Are we clear?"

"I understand. I have only one more thing to ask."

"What is it now?" Neptune sounded angrier than usual.

"If I do choose to get married in a year, can he at least attend the wedding?"

"I suppose."

"And I request that a team of your best policemen search for my family and friends that were on the boat, alive or dead. If they aren't in the water, I want those men to look for my family on the surface."

"I don't have that many hybrid police men to search for—"

"Then hire some, I don't care. I must know if my family is alive or dead."

"And what if I don't?"

"Then I'll leave your little city of Atlantis, find my family, and never . . . come . . . back."

Neptune's angry face turned instantly into a face of fear, grief, and worry that I'd never seen in Neptune before. I felt much better knowing I could make him feel the same pain I felt when I lost my family, all with the simple thought of me leaving Atlantis.

"I'll send a crew first thing in the morning. Now please, my guards will escort you from my palace."

"With all due kindness, I can leave your palace on my own, and I would like to know where your low security prison is?"

"*Why, you little—*"

"Okay! I'll take Jill to visit the prison, and you can calm down with a piece of cake and I'll see you tomorrow."

Seth told me to wave good-bye and he pulled me to get out of the palace.

"He seems a little angry."

"Yeah, he gets a little angry when you threaten his security, break his heart, and ask him to send his security on a hunt for your family."

"I liked the part where he decided to send those guys to the surface even though he was really pissed."

"You're enjoying this too much. The prison isn't far from here."

Seth pointed to a gloomy and dark place, all in a cave not too far away from the palace; it was a place I wasn't looking forward to visiting.

"I'd like to see my father on my own. Just stay here and wait till I come back out."

"All right, the guards will take it from here."

Two very large men swam up behind me as I went forward into the poorly lit prison. They were using bioluminescent creatures in tanks on the walls for light; cool to look at actually, but I could hardly see any of the prisoners. There weren't those many prisoners, but the ones that were there definitely looked like they belonged in prison. At the end of the prison, there was a very well-lit and clean cell, and there was a man sitting on a bed facing the wall.

"Wake up, Verbicky. You got a visitor."

The cell had a clear Flexiglass barrier blocking me from running up to hug my father I hadn't seen in years.

He got up tail first and faced the wall opposite to me.

"Who are you?"

"Dad? It's me."

He turned around, and I could almost recognize him under the beard and scruffy hair that had once been short and slightly curly; from his eyes I knew they were my father's.

"Jillian?"

He swam up to the glass where a patch of glass had been removed for bars to be placed, and he could get his meals from right beneath it. I swam up to it so I could see his face better and so he could see mine. He brought his hand out of the cell and held it up to my face, and for a moment, he looked into my eyes as if I were a complete stranger.

"Don't you recognize me, Dad?"

"It's been so long . . . And you were so young."

"I'm seventeen now, Dad."

"I know it's your birthday today. I'm so sorry I wasn't there."

"It was fun. Neptune is pretty good at throwing a party, believe it or not."

"Can you convince him to let me out?"

"Believe me, I tried, but he's quite angry about you going to the surface and raising a family."

"He's still mad at that?"

"Very . . . Wait, aren't you surprised that I have a tail?"

"Not too much. I'm just glad you're alive and well. How did you find me anyways?"

"Well, it's a long story, but it started when—"

"Guard? Can you grab a chair for my daughter please?"

"You've been all right, Verbicky. I'll grab a chair."

Shortly after, the guard brought me a simple stool to sit on; I thanked him. My dad had already brought a chair up to the bars in his cell, patiently waiting for me to start telling him the whole story.

"Mom thought it would be a good idea to take a family vacation to Hawaii on the boat you won from the lottery."

"Go on."

"But she didn't want to go alone on the entire vacation with just Jay and me, so we invited the San family to join us. The flight down to California wasn't that bad actually, a little bit of turbulence, but it didn't bug me. The landings were a bit worse, but I could handle it."

"Anyways..."

"Right! So we relaxed for a day while stocking up the boat with necessities and all, but the day we launched was beautiful and perfect for a cruise to Hawaii... Unfortunately, two days into the cruise, we ran into a hurricane and the boat sank."

"Was everyone okay?"

"Oh yes, everyone made it onto the rafts just fine. But since the waves were so big and powerful, it separated me from everybody else. It wasn't long until I was floating around on my own with nothing but the few things I packed, a treasure chest my boyfriend and I had discovered, and an iPhone with no service."

"Boyfriend?"

"I'll explain later. Anyhow, I crashed into a rock during the night and I nearly drowned, until a merman named Seth rescued me."

"That Seth is such a good man, you know. I knew I could trust him."

"After he saved me, I lived on an island where I killed a bunch of great white sharks, found a friendly spider monkey I named Miko, found a journal that told me everything about Atlantis and told me to find you here."

"It was Simon who wrote the journal, wasn't it?"

"Yes, but he died."

"Never much of an outdoorsman that Salderman."

"But recently, I discovered that I'm from royal blood, and I may choose any prince in the sea to marry. Even though Seth saved me again from a shark attack, I still miss Mom and Josh and the San family."

"I do too, but Seth is the right man for you, and you should stay here with him."

"But I don't love him, Dad. I love someone else."

"Jay can't give you immortality though."

"I'd rather have one lifetime with Jay than a thousand with Seth."

"But Seth can protect you here. This Jay guy couldn't even save you on the island."

"I know he's still alive, Dad. I bet you anything he's spending every waking hour looking for me right now."

"And how is he supposed to find you when you're deep underwater?"

"That's not the point."

"All I'm saying is Seth can give you more than you could ever dream of here in Atlantis. Jay could never compare to what Seth can do for you."

"Since when do you care about who I'm with? You weren't even there for half my life! Why should you be the one to decide whose best for me?"

"Because I care about your future! Since your mother and brother aren't here to help you, I will."

"I don't need your help, Dad. I can look out for myself just fine."

"I just don't want to lose my little angel."

I lifted my head to see my father's eyes, as he reached out of the bars to give me a hug. Even though the tears from my eyes dissolved, I was crying in his strong arms, realizing that he had finally recognized me after all these years.

"I may have not been there for you for a good portion of your life, but Seth can."

"He can't be in my life forever, Dad."

"But I will, always."

"Visiting time's up."

The guards approached me and stopped directly behind me.

"I'm gonna get you out of here, Dad."

"Don't worry about me. I'll be fine. Enjoy your birthday, sweetie, and I recommend you get to know Seth a little better."

"You're not gonna die in jail, Dad, I promise."

"Everything is gonna be all right, Jill."

The guards were now pulling on my arms to get me out of the prison, and I had to go while my father pressed his hand against the glass and smiled under his thick beard. He finally returned to his bed and the fish lighting his cell were set free, leaving the room pitch-black behind me. I asked the guards to let go of my arms. They released them the second I reached the entrance to the prison; my arms were a little sore from being squeezed too tight.

"Well, how did it go?"

"Really good, actually, he didn't know who I was for a long time, but he finally recognized me."

"What else did you talk about?"

"Oh not too much—how I found him, how I got here, and so on."

"Anything about me?"

I stopped and had to really think about an answer. I didn't want to tell him a word of what my father had said about him, and I didn't want to in the future.

"Nope, nothing at all."

Chapter 24

I thought it was night by now, but it appeared so only because the prison was so dark. There was time to enjoy the sunset and maybe even have a fire if I wanted, but Seth wanted to take a swim by the reef instead.

"You wouldn't believe the view of the reef around this time of year. Everything's in full bloom and it is just so . . . awesome!"

Seth sounded very excited, and I was suspicious.

"You sound a little more ecstatic than usual. Is something wrong?"

"No, I'm just pumped to show you the reef . . . and your birthday gift."

"I don't want anything huge, Seth. I have plenty of jewels and necklaces. There's really nothing else you can get me."

"I beg to differ."

The reef was so colorful and bright it was worth it to swim by and see. The fish were so wacky and unique; I'd never seen these species before, but they were wonderful nonetheless. Even though there was so much reef to see, Seth only showed me the best parts with small caves and marine life I enjoyed swimming next to; there was a dolphin that swam with us to the island. As soon as I saw the tunnel to go back to my home, Seth yanked me toward the route to my cavern of treasures.

"Uh, Seth? Home is that way."

"Your birthday present is in here."

"I already told you I have lots of treasures. I don't need a gift!"

"You're gonna like this gift, trust me."

Seth told me to close my eyes the second I reached the cave, and I did so as I heard him swim up into the cavern and rustle around in some sort of box. I heard a bit of clinking and a thump of Seth dropping some sort of box.

"What are you doing?"

"Getting your gift. I found it, but don't open your eyes yet."

I heard him swim down to the ground again and come closer to me. He whispered in front of my face, handing me a little red box, "Open."

"This better not be what I think it is, Seth."

"It's not. Don't worry, just open it."

I lifted the lid of the little box, and inside was a diamond and peridot necklace, in the shape of a heart, and a ring in the shape of a rose, all carved into a diamond and a green ring surrounded by glass thorns.

"Seth . . . I don't know what to say."

"Thank you?"

"How on earth did you find a ring with a rose cut diamond?"

"I have my sources."

"And the necklace is breathtaking."

"Oh, it was nothing."

"It better not be an engagement ring though."

"It's not. It's a casual ring for wearing around anywhere."

"But it's too beautiful to just wear like nothing. I'll save it for when it'll look best."

Seth gently pulled the necklace out of the box and placed it around my neck. Then when I tried to look down at the necklace, he placed the ring on my finger, which fit perfectly.

"Why am I wearing this now?"

"Why not?"

"But I can't see how it looks on me without a mirror."

"Then let's go check it out in the house."

I followed Seth out and up to the cave, my legs a little sore from swimming all day, and I made my way into the cabin, beating Seth to the front door. I heard him laugh as I raced to my bedroom and stood in front of my mirror. The very second I got there, I only stared at how beautiful the necklace and ring were; frankly, my hair was pretty knotty and I was still wearing my black bikini. I would've looked much better if I was wearing normal clothes and had brushed my hair.

"You look beautiful."

"This jewelry is beautiful. I have to clean up a little bit anyways."

"Don't you want to stay in, relax, and maybe have some hot chocolate?"

"Sure, but I'd like to watch the sunset first."

I kicked Seth out of my room to quickly change and rinse my hair, but he was waiting outside my bathroom since he was ready to go already.

"Can we go now?"

"Just about done. I'm brushing my hair."

"Oh, I think the sun's almost down."

I blasted out of the bathroom and down the stairs to the deck in front, while Seth, taking his time behind me, came down slowly into the living room.

"Why are you so slow? I'm missing a great sunset."

"I just said that to get you out of the house."

I gave him an angry look and started to walk along the beach, wearing my skinny jeans, a low-cut T-shirt, and plain sweater; I wore what was comfortable if I was out after the sun went down. I started to walk along the beach until I found the perfect spot to sit down and watch the sunset.

"How about here?" Seth suggested.

"Maybe a little further. There's a rock in the way of my view."

We didn't walk long before I found the perfect spot to relax and watch the sun go down.

"This is just right!"

I made a square with my hands and sat down on the sand.

"I wouldn't mind sitting on something not covered on sand though."

"Wait here!"

Seth sprinted into the jungle behind me, and I waited about five minutes or so, hearing nothing but rustling and snapping as Seth ran through trees and bushes to find me a log to sit on. The second I looked back at the sunset, I noticed the entire sky had turned orange and pink, and the reflection on the peaceful and clear water made it look like another world was sitting on top of the other. I stood up and walked to the shore to get a better look at the water; it mirrored the sky above it flawlessly, and I muttered under my breath, "Wow."

"Wow, indeed."

"How the hell did you hear me say that from all the way over here?"

"I don't know, but I found you a chair and some wood for a fire if you want."

It was a bug-free, sturdy log to sit on, and it stretched out like a bench to sit on. There was a pile of wood to burn when it would get dark.

"Why don't you tell me a few stories about where you live?"

"Oh, I don't even know where to begin. There's so much beauty in the small place I'm from."

"Tell me about it then!"

"Well, a quad ride and a hop skip away from my home is a place called the Peace River. But the valley part of it is called Dunvegan. It's an area where a glacier went through a couple million years ago and was discovered by explorers who traded peacefully across the river aka Peace River. Quite recently, only about a hundred years ago, a bridge was built and connected the sides of the river, and a campsite was built there to attract tourists, outdoorsman, and so on. But where I visit the valley is a ways down from the busy bridge and far away from noisy campers and rich folks relaxing in their cabins. You could scream at the top of your lungs and no one would hear it—well, maybe the animals. The route at the top of the valley has a beautiful view of the river and both sides going south into British Columbia and down into the states, but the part where I'm from has the most beautiful view, far more beautiful than any other parts of the river in Canada and in the U.S. Anyways, my family and I go down to this part of the valley to stay and fish by the riverside or pick out vegetables on a farm and drink from the water in the hills that is clear as crystal and more pure than any fresh water in the mountains.

"Sure, mountain water's good, but this water is life-changing—true story. Sometimes when my father and I went down into the valley, we'd pick saskatoons and wild strawberries in a bunch of buckets while avoiding bears and deer hiding in the underbrush. Also, a bunch of wasps and bees are within the bushes, which I hate to this day, and I escaped every encounter I had with those damn bugs. But the best part of all wasn't winter or spring that looked the best. Sure winter was pretty, and spring was green. Even summer wasn't the best time to be in the valley, but autumn was the best of all. The valley would be warmer than other places and everything was brown and red, orange, tan. Everything was the most stunning sight you could ever see.

"The animals can be a little active and dangerous if you threaten them with guns or offspring, but otherwise it is the best place to go for a fire with the family or simply get away from the city for a little time of quiet and just block out all your problems and enjoy the beauty of Canadian wildlife and nature."

"Sounds amazing."

"Amazing doesn't even come close to what this place is like."

"Have you been anywhere else with such an effect on you?"

"Only three places: Mexico, Haida Gwaii, and the Queen Charlotte's at the time."

"What part of Mexico did you visit?"

"Puerto Vallarta."

"What was so amazing about this place?"

"Puerto Vallarta was a very beautiful place, and I can't ever forget the sunsets from the beach I saw there. Every single night, I watched the stars on the beach with my parents while my brother splashed around in the cool, salty water, getting our clothes wet and sandy. I hated how the sunsets were extremely short, and it made me think of how lucky I was to be there. In less than two minutes, the sun dipped down into the water, and the dark of night spread like fire to the rest of the sky. I didn't focus that much on the resort's restaurants, pools, bars, or theatres for entertainment. I was too busy having fun playing in the water, boogie boarding, and watching whales swim up to the surface from a boat and occasionally from the shore."

"That place sounds amazing. I wish I was there with you."

"I already told you a bunch of my stories. Tell me a few situations that you've been in."

Seth looked down at the fire and scratched his head. I was curious to hear how exciting or interesting his stories would be.

"I remember once I was swimming along the reef outside the city and a bunch of fish was missing from the area. Obviously I was concerned, so I followed the fish that were there to find out what was wrong. After following the fish for a long while, a huge wave of them surrounded me, and I got stuck in a pile of flashy and colorful fish with no chance of getting out. When I finally got out, I saw a great big shadow above me, and when the fish moved out of my sight, I realized it was a fishing boat. I knew this place is dangerous to swim around, but I had no choice to see what the fishermen wanted and why they were fishing there. As I swam up to the side of the boat, they threw a net over the edge to scoop up the group of fish beside me and just missed my tail. I thought I was in the clear until I felt something pull my arm. The net had slipped right over my hand and was pulling me to the surface. I was still a ways underwater, so I still had time to get out and remain unseen. I don't know how, but my arm and hand was knotted between the fish and the net, and the net was getting closer and closer to the surface. Since I couldn't get my hand out of the net, I had to bite my way through the strong string and wire. Just a few inches away from being seen by the fishermen under water, I got my hand back, but it was bloody and cut up from escaping the net. There was quite a bit of blood in the water, but I was thankful I was free, and I created a hole for the fish to escape along with me."

"Wow, did any sharks find you after all that?"

"No, but the fisherman left shortly afterward since they were too lazy to fix their net."

"Any other interesting stories?"

"Well, I do have one more, but I don't think you'll like it. It sort of involves you."

"I don't mind."

"It's about the hurricane."

I instantly felt a shot of grief and misery at the very word hurricane. I closed my eyes and breathed out slowly just before he began to tell me the story.

"The night the hurricane hit, the water in the ocean pulled apart many of the structures within the city and in the current of the storm. It ripped away fish in the reefs, people from their homes. Even a sunken ship was torn to pieces and buried in the sand beneath it. My family was sheltered in the castle, but I was out swimming to the island to build a shack on land."

"You never told me how you built that shack anyways."

"I will, just let me finish this story first."

"Okay."

"So when I felt the current pulling me all over the place, I knew the storm was occurring on the surface, and something told me I should see if anyone was up there. Some sense that I had told me something was very wrong, and when I popped up above the water, I heard a huge explosion and saw a loud crash of flames not too far from where I was. I rushed as fast as I could to the area, but all I found was some luggage and debris from a boat. I can only assume that whatever happened here was because of this hurricane and whoever was on the boat had gone down with it."

I looked up at Seth, curious as to what he would say next.

"I was about to swim back down to Atlantis, to see if everyone was okay, but I heard someone scream and followed the voice until I saw someone sitting in a raft, with nothing but a few things and a camera in her hand. Little did I know, I could've helped her right then and there, but I didn't."

"Why didn't you? I was practically dying and you were there the whole time? What did you do?"

"I didn't know who you were, and I didn't see any reason to help you since my father had warned me never to help humans."

"So why save me, if you were warned not to?"

"You've seriously got to let me finish."

"My bad."

"Anyways, I watched you for days and days. You were smart to fashion a knife out of the things in your bag and you seemed like you knew exactly what to do in your situation. The only thing I was concerned about was whether or not you were going to die of starvation or give up and jump into the water and let the sharks have you."

"It was something that crossed my mind, but after all that I just gave up, period."

"I'm so sorry I didn't help you when I could've. You would've been safer, and the entire experience is my fault."

"It's not your fault. I can't help the fact that I ran into a huge rock in the middle of the night. The only fault is that I could have stayed awake long enough to see it and jump off the raft in time to save myself."

"Even if you did, you would still have to face the sharks, starvation, and drowning at some point."

"I've thanked you so much by now. I feel like I owe you something for saving my life multiple times."

"All I want to do right now is spend time with you. I don't want you to leave. Is it so hard to just stay here with me and talk?"

"Of course not! I like telling stories, but I love hearing stories even more."

"Then you're okay with the shack story?"

"Absolutely."

"As you may already know, I built that shack when I spend almost all my time on land. I really did like land much more than the sea. There's so much to do, much better sites to see that I could ever imagine in the ocean. Your family and my uncle were the best things that ever happened to me. The photos I had in there took me years and years to gather and bring to the island. The friends I made there have forgotten me years and years ago. All I had left to remember them by were those photos and the objects that were of great importance to me."

"That explains the stuff inside, but what about the actual construction of the shack?"

"The shack did not take long to make. I gathered all materials from the island, and putting it all together only took me about a day or so. Really, you're not concerned about the years of pictures I had in there?"

"I like to think of it as an invasion of privacy from the wall that had pictures of my family, but I didn't even know. I could care less about the wall with all the photos of your friends on it. It's the wall that had hundreds of pictures of my family and my father that I never even got to see that bothered me."

"How could you say that? Those pictures were all the memories I had of my life on land, and I can never get those back!"

"Just calm down, Seth. I think I did you a favor."

"Favor!?"

"I made room for even more memories if you go back to land."

Seth sighed and covered his eyes with one hand; it was obvious to me that he really cared about the friends he had made on land. I had no idea that Seth cared so much about these people, and when he finally sat up and wiped a few tears from his eyes, I felt pity for him when I remembered how many of my friends I missed and how they had probably forgotten about me.

"I think I know what will cheer you up," I told Seth.

"What's that?"

"Stay right here!"

I bolted back to the cabin and grabbed the guitar from the living room. It would definitely cheer him up if maybe we sang a little bit by the fire. And I knew exactly which songs he would love to hear.

"What's that?"

"It's a guitar!"

Seth began laughing, and the tears I saw seconds ago were replaced by tears of joy. I sat down next to him and placed the guitar on my knee and asked him what song I should play first.

"I have no idea. You're the one with the guitar, so you should pick the song."

I already knew "As She's Walking Away" by Zack Brown Band, "Billionaire," "Candy Store," "Cruise," "Good Time," and a few others. By the time I finished playing guitar, Seth was in such a good mood that he grabbed the guitar and told me he would play a few songs for me.

"What songs could you possibly know that you could sing for me on the guitar?"

I couldn't believe he knew this song! Rhythm of Love? I knew this song like the back of my hand and I began to sing with him.

We sang together for the rest of the song, laughing in the parts we didn't know and singing along to other songs. He played many more songs than I did, and for the ones I didn't know at all, I listened and watched him play the guitar peacefully. He played "Good to You," "Cupid," "I Don't Wanna Miss a Thing," "I'm Yours," and "Just the Way You Are."

"You got to sing in harmony with me for these next few songs."

"What if I don't know the song?"

"A cappella!"

"What's that?"

"A cappella is basically making the same noise as instruments, but only using your mouth."

"That sounds like fun!"

Seth sang along with me to "Lips of an Angel," "Next to You," "Perfect," "She Will Be Loved," "Your Body is a Wonderland," "21 Guns," and "Wanted."

"This last one is my favorite."

"What song is it?"

"It's a surprise!"

I heard the first few chords of the song I didn't know and I couldn't even do a cappella part to it.

"

The Tail of an Angel

I remembered this song! Of course he sang Summer Paradise by Simple Plan. It was the perfect song to play on the beach in front of a fire. It sounded even better with him playing it for me, even though one chord of the song was something I had yet to share with him.

"_

Before Seth could finish the last line of the song, I quickly kissed his lips and stopped his singing instantly.

I whispered the last line of the song when I finished kissing him. Seth smiled when I sang the last line and put down the guitar from his knee to the side of the wood he sat on.

"Told you it was my favorite song."

"I can tell," I whispered to Seth.

Seth smiled even more as he put one hand on my hip and lifted my chin up with his other hand. I bit my lower lip and looked down at his hand, while he looked at my eyes. My cheeks had grown warm, and I smiled once more before he leaned in closer and kissed me. Seth squeezed my hip and pulled me closer, and I leaned my chest closer to his. When he stopped, he opened his eyes and smiled, looking at the coals of the fire.

"I don't know about you, but I'm really nervous about this whole marriage thing."

"Why do you say that?"

"I'm too young to get married."

"Seventeen isn't that young."

"Nope. Romeo and Juliet were too young for marriage."

"Good point."

I laughed for a minute or so.

"I just don't want to be forced into marriage so quickly."

"How long were you hoping to spend with these guys?"

"At least four dates each."

"Well, that's not such a bad request. I mean how can you manage to get to know your future husband in one date?"

"Exactly!"

"Well, there's not all that much you can do about it."

"There is one prince whom I'm not really looking forward to dating though."

"Really? Who?"

"Damian."

"So why did you choose to date him out of almost four hundred other princes?"

"He had a rocking body."

"Is that the only reason you chose him?"

"Perhaps."

Seth laughed so hard he fell off the log face-first into the cold sand. I giggled when he tried to get the sand out of his eyes.

"Do you feel ready to accept immortality in a few weeks?"

"Absolutely not. I don't know if I can spend immortality with one person. Are there other immortal mermaids that I could've talked to about it?"

"I hate to say it, but my father only offers immortality to citizens of Atlantis. It's one of the reasons why we were named the capital city, since our citizens are some of the oldest merpeople in the world. A couple of them were at the apocalypse of our time on land, when Atlantis sank all the way down here."

"Did you all just turn into mermaids to adapt then?"

"No, no, we still all walked on land. The prisoners drowned and the few drowned shortly after."

"So how did everyone survive?"

"Well, I think it was because of these crystals. My father told me they instantly turned blue to give oxygen to whoever wore them. The prisoners and people who temporarily had their crystals off didn't make it."

"I'm so sorry! How many died?"

"Two thousand."

"Oh, Jesus."

"Don't worry. There was still lots of people who survived the catastrophe. These crystals have been with us for thousands and thousands of years."

"How many were there that are still in Atlantis today?"

"Oh, a couple thousand. It is them who know Atlantis and its history better than anyone else."

"Was your father there when Atlantis was first started?"

"Nope, he is a king of our past kings. I can't remember all of them, but there were at least twelve."

"If the crystals give immortality, how come so many died?"

"Some gave up the kingship, other died defending Atlantis, and a few didn't wish to be immortal rulers of Atlantis and destroyed their crystals."

"How do you destroy the crystals anyways?"

"Why do you ask so many questions?"

I laughed to myself and finally stopped asking Seth lots of questions. I found the city of Atlantis to be an interesting topic since I was probably the first human to know of its actual existence—besides the few other hybrids of course.

"So all the other mermaids die of old age?"

The Tail of an Angel

"I hope that's your last question."

"It is."

"Mermaids in other cities live just as long as people do. The average life span is about seventy years, but the disposal of the dead is extremely important."

"Can you imagine if the body of a mermaid was found? There would be a documentary on it and they would become lab experiments in army facilities and never survive."

"Exactly, so certain mermaids, who can travel to the depths of the cold north or near volcanoes, toss the bodies in with weight to the bottom of heat vents or underwater volcanoes. There the bodies are evaporated and never seen by humans. Once a body had gone missing in the early 1700s and it became a roadside attraction. It was horrifying to see the body of one of our species in a glass box for humans to see. It is a fear of most mermaids to be seen by humans, but they mostly fear sharks and oil spills affecting the children of the people."

"Incredible, so what about hybrids like you?"

"I like the people on land a bit better than the ones in the sea."

"Why's that?"

"Because I got to meet you."

Seth smiled and poked around at the fire that slowly dimmed to barely flaming coals.

"Did I ever tell you sometimes I wish I wasn't a hybrid?"

"Oh, why not? You get the wonderful opportunities to live on the land and in the sea! What could be better than that?"

"A mortal life on land."

"I hate to crush your dreams, but land isn't all it's cracked up to be."

"People aren't meant to live forever. We are given only so many years to explore the world. That's the gift of life and they're meant to die. I actually know a few people that are perfectly content being four hundred years old."

"Who are they?"

"That's not the point. The point is that I rather have a mortal life on land than an immortal life in the sea. I'd trade that any day. We're a dying breed as it is."

"Hybrid mermaids?"

"Yes, Lucas and Alex are some of the very few hybrid mermaids left in the ocean. Compared to the mermaid species, they play a role of 3 percent of all mermaids."

"So why don't you just do what you did to me to make anyone a hybrid?"

"The crystals can only do it once. The king is the only person who can grant immortality, but it's sometimes dangerous to make someone a hybrid. A mermaid must choose carefully who they make a hybrid since they might tell someone what they can do in the ocean."

"So how did you become a hybrid and your brothers?"

"I was born into it. Someone on my mother's side was a hybrid, and the gene passed to me. Sedrick wasn't, and my mother made him a hybrid. Skylar was born into it as well."

"Lucky, you guys!"

I punched Seth's shoulder, smiling as I did so.

"Sometimes I wish I could just stay on land."

"Why don't you?"

"I can't."

"Sure you could!"

"I wish, but believe it or not I have a large role to play here."

"Seems like you have a pretty good life to live here." I smiled and touched his hand. "In my view, you are one of the richest princes in the world with something every prince on land would kill for—immortality. You really are a sweet man, and things are going to turn out just fine for you."

I snuck a kiss on his cheek and watched a smile creep out from under his lips.

"Thanks, Jill."

"I have one final question for tonight, Seth."

"What's that?"

"Why mortality?"

"Why be mortal?"

"Yes."

"I'd rather have a mortal life with someone on land than be alone with no one for eternity."

"What if a girl was immortal with you?"

"It'd be worth it."

It was a very romantic idea that stuck in my head for the remaining last minutes by the fire.

"The fire is just about out. Do you want me to get some more wood?"

"Actually, I'm pretty cold and I wouldn't mind going back to the cabin."

"Okay."

Seth put out the fire and buried the remaining coals within the sand. I picked up the guitar and stood next to the log while Seth washed off the sand on his hands in the ocean. I started walking back with the guitar thrown over my back, but Seth caught up in a second and snatched the guitar out of my hands. Looking back at Seth, I shook my head and grinned when he quickly stepped up next to me and put his arm around my shoulders.

"Aren't you cold?"

"It's not that cold, and we just left the fire!"

"I know. It was just an excuse for me to put my arm around you."

Seth kissed the top of my head and pulled me right up to his hip.

"Take it easy. As much as I love your confidence, it kind of hurts."

"Aw, did I bruise your hip?"

"I think so actually."

Seth lowered his head to my ear so close that I could easily feel his breath on the side of my face and whispered, "You know I could kiss it better."

Seth snuck a kiss on my cheek, and instantly I raised my eyebrow. I looked over at Seth for a moment before returning to look ahead to where I was walking. One thing I noticed was that I wasn't really walking straight.

"You okay? You're walking around like you've had a few too many drinks."

"Um . . . I'm okay."

It wasn't that I had swooned a little and couldn't walk normal, but Seth didn't realize that every step; he pulled me up with him, thus making it difficult to walk at all.

"Maybe if you could let go of me so I could walk. That would be great."

Seth stopped and let go of my hip, and I could balance and walk on my own again.

"Sorry, I have to work on controlling my strength."

"It's not that big of a deal. You just have to be a bit gentler."

"Think you could show me?"

If I wasn't mistaken, I was thinking that I would sleep with Seth tonight. I didn't say a word to Seth after that, but only smiled and walked back to the cabin hand in hand. When we were only a few feet away from the cabin, it turned completely black, and my eyes weren't adjusted to the darkness of the night.

"Seth, I can't see a thing."

"That's because I tucked my crystal necklace in my pocket."

Seth pulled out the necklace from his shorts and put the necklace around his neck. I could see just about everything in front of me in a luminescent blue glow. Seth walked inside quickly and put the guitar away, leaving me in the darkness of the house.

"Would you mind coming back downstairs so I can see where I'm going?"

"Just a second."

I could hear Seth running all over the place upstairs, and I had no idea what he was up to. I walked around blindly for a bit, feeling around the house to make my way to the kitchen as I was feeling slightly hungry for some fruit. With no light, I walked around the kitchen for the fruit bowl like a blind person and stubbed my toe multiple times trying to find it. I heard Seth coming down the stairs, and I also heard a second set of footsteps coming down the stairs with him.

"I just had to grab a lantern from upstairs."

"What was that sound from behind you?"

Seconds later, Miko jumped up onto the table and leaped up onto my shoulders. Miko started screaming and jumping up all over the place; Miko seemed quite excited I was home.

"He's just hungry."

"What a strange monkey."

Seth put a candle on the table, and I grabbed a pomegranate from the fruit bowl and gave it to Miko. Miko returned from running around the living room and into the kitchen again, and he finally came back to the table where I gave him the pomegranate and watched him run outside. I laughed under my breath when I heard Miko screaming off into the distance. When I returned to grab a fruit to munch on myself, Seth blew out the candle on the table.

"Hey, I'm trying to eat some fruit here!"

"Are you really that hungry?"

"Yes, I would love some supper."

"How does . . .," Seth paused, "seafood Alfredo sound?"

"Sounds great!"

Seth instantly looked in the freezer for the meat for seafood Alfredo; he found shrimp and a few other things and then started sautéing some onions for the sauce.

"Do we have any cream?"

"A bit."

How on earth Seth managed to get cream all the way out here in the middle of nowhere puzzled me, but nonetheless he managed to make a wonderful Alfredo sauce. He chopped up some veggies and cooked the meat in no time at all and mixed it all in, in less than half an hour.

"Smells good."

"Thanks, it's a pretty easy meal to cook and I've mastered Alfredo sauce."

"I can tell."

I put a finger into the sauce to taste and Seth scowled at me.

"It's delicious!"

I attempted to take another dip with my finger, but he whacked my hand with the stirring spoon he used to stir the sauce to perfection.

"Supper is almost ready, no double dipping."

I sat back down, and Seth made two plates, still steaming, with a meat I didn't recognize.

"This is a great seafood Alfredo, but what's this mystery meat I can't name?"

"Shark."

I paused as a flashback memory of the great white shark biting my leg popped up before my eyes and made me drop the knife—accidentally of course.

"Are you okay?"

"Yes, I'm fine. The shark is delicious."

I finished half my meal before the flashback of the shark attack stopped me again and made me lose my appetite. Words started popping into my head, which reminded me of the attack—shark, blood, fear, white, shark, knife, eater, shark, scream, scar, bite, and shark.

"I'm sorry but I've lost my appetite. The meal was so good."

"Glad you enjoyed it."

I reached for a mango on the table that I could much on later, since I would want a snack.

Seth took off his necklace and picked me up before I could take off with the mango, and I dropped it back onto the table. I playfully screamed and laughed when he flipped me around to hold up my legs and back.

"What the hell, Seth?!"

"Oh, c'mon, I know you're enjoying this."

"I'd rather be enjoying a tasty mango right now."

"I doubt that."

I crossed my arms as he looked up at the staircase and walked up to the first step.

"Don't even think about it."

"I swear I won't drop you. I've done this like one hundred times."

"I'm perfectly capable of walking up the stairs myself."

"Too bad! I'm carrying you up these stairs!"

"No!"

Seth sprinted up the stairs, and I wrapped my arms around him so I wouldn't fall onto the stairs if he happened to drop me. When he got to the top, I unhooked my arms from around his neck and scratched the back of my head, motioning that I wished to be set down. Seth gently stood me up and held my back as I stood up straight.

"See? Wasn't that fun?"

"Yeah, not really."

I walked up to my room and opened the door with Seth right behind me.

"And what makes you think you can come in here?"

"I left a few things in your room."

"Okay, fine, whatever."

I walked over to my dresser to take off my sweater, and then I felt Seth stand right behind me and wrap his arm around to pull down the zipper on the front of my sweater.

"Not tonight, Seth," I whispered.

"Why not?"

"I can't sleep with you tonight."

"That's not a very good reason."

"Can't we just have a regular night together?"

"But it's so boring."

Seth pulled off my sweater and tossed it onto the floor next to me.

"That's all you're taking off tonight, Seth."

"I wouldn't mind putting something on."

"If there's anything you're putting on, it's a shirt."

"Now where's the fun in that?"

"No means no, Seth."

Seth sighed and crossed his arms.

"Is there anything I can do?"

"Actually, there is."

"And what is that?"

"Stay."

"Simple enough."

I turned around.

"I'm scared, Seth."

"Aw, scared of what?"

"Sharks. I had a little bad moment when the night I was attacked by a great white shark came back to me. It scared me."

A tear leaked out from my eye; that sneaky little bugger.

"Please don't cry."

"I'm not crying. My contact lens are dry."

"You don't wear contacts."

"Shut up."

Another tear escaped my eye and slowly rolled down my cheek.

"Please stop crying, Jill. What can I do to help?"

"I'm still scared of sharks, Seth."

"There's not much I can do about that."

Seth came up to me and gave me a hug; it must have been my body language that said I really did need a hug.

"I'm so sorry I let that happen to you."

"It's not. It's the fact I brought jerky swimming."

"I promise . . .," Seth let me go and held my head with his one hand, "I will never let that happen to you again."

"Are you sure? What if you get attacked by sharks?"

Another tear managed to sneak out of my eye; I didn't even feel this one run down my cheek.

"I can handle myself. I'm strong enough."

I smiled when he wiped away the other tear with his hand.

"You want some dessert? I have some downstairs if you're up for it."

"What's for dessert then?"

"Coconut meringue pie."

"I'm good, thanks."

I had nothing against the coconut pie, but the sharks had made my appetite disappear. I simply stared out the window as the stars began to peek out and the echo of the thump-thump of Seth going down the stairs followed. I hadn't seen the sky so clear and bright for ages, so I snuck out to go see them. I could only think of one spot that would be perfect for watching the stars; unfortunately, it meant I would have to swim. I snuck out just fine from Seth's view and walked to the water cave, the same cave where the shark had attacked me; the blood on the rock was still there. I figured it was now or never and that I should face my fears. I jumped in, clothes and all. The water was dark and the crystal on my neck was the only light to see where I was going. A few feet underwater, I regretted it and swam for the surface. I smacked myself as I took a breath of air and said to myself that there was nothing below but water and gems, repeating this to build up confidence to go to the perfect place to watch stars.

I sighed and dove back down underwater in an instant splash; before I knew it, I was in the tunnel to the cave and up in the darkness before I knew it. I smiled to myself for facing my fear, giggling when I got out of the water onto the stone stairs. My giggle echoed a lot more than I wanted it to, and I whispered, "Oops." That echoed too. I realized something was steaming a little way off as the next breath of air I took was humid and hot; it was a bit steamy in the cavern, much more than usual. By the time I reached the top step, it was a steamy sauna and made me slightly drowsy, though sleep eluded me. I wasn't here to sit in a cave all night when a full moon and clear starry sky waited for me. I reached the hammock outside, and it was comfortably cool. I sat down in the hammock and rocked myself with one foot. Alone and at peace, I watched the stars with the sounds of tropical birds in the background; it ended when Miko showed up.

"How did you get up here?"

Miko pointed off the ledge to a long vine of branches that grew up the side of the cavern; Miko jumped around very excitedly and eventually climbed onto the hammock next to me.

"You seem a little excited. Did you meet a girl or something?"

Miko stuck out his tongue at me for the second time.

"Fine, fine, don't tell me."

Miko snuggled up to my shoulder and fell asleep with ease; poor little Miko must have been exhausted. I stopped rocking and let the warm summer breeze slowly sway my hammock. It was wonderful.

"Whatcha doing?"

I screamed, and Miko jumped down the vines back to the ground and toward the cabin.

"Dammit, I wanted some time alone, Seth . . . Did you make me a Caesar?"

"Yes, I did and a margarita for myself."

"Well, since you brought drinks you might as well stay."

"I thought you might say that. Here."

Seth handed me the Caesar with a large piece of celery in it and a pale green rim of celery salt around it. It was very nice of him to make me a drink; how he got it up there I had no idea.

"Hope you don't mind if I watch the stars with you."

"Not at all since you made me this fine Caesar."

"I'm glad you like it."

"How did you know a Caesar was my favorite drink?"

"I didn't. I'm glad I made your favorite though."

"What are you standing there for? Come sit."

"It's a one person hammock though."

"Oh pish-posh, I'll make room."

I wiggled over as much as I could and Seth had to snuggle in. I thought he would fall out, but he managed to fit just fine.

"What a nice view."

"I know! That's why I came up here."

"So why did you sneak out anyways?"

"I was hoping to have one night to myself before I'm surrounded by men for a week straight."

"Is that a bad thing?"

"Not at all, but I just enjoy the time I have to myself every now and then."

"Nothing wrong with that."
"Of course."
A moment of silence passed.
"They're beautiful, aren't they?"
"What's beautiful?"
"The stars."
"And why do you think they are so beautiful?"
"Some of the best times I've ever had have been under the stars."
"Really? Like what?"
"Oh, just my first kiss, first love, first time—"
"First time without your family."
"I suppose."
"First time facing sharks."
"That's not good."
"First time alone on an island."
"You're starting to make me sad."
"I can save your life, but I can't make you feel better?"

I paused and didn't respond as I had another flashback of the night I lost Jay and my family; they were probably dead by now. Nothing at the moment could make me feel better.

"There's got to be something I could do to make you feel better."
"Unfortunately not, I've lost everything, Seth."
"If it's your iPhone . . . I have it."
"Not that! My family, my friends, my boyfriend—"
"Boyfriend? You had a boyfriend?"
"Yes, his name was Jay. He's dead now."

A tear rolled down my cheek once more.

"How can you be sure he's dead? I bet he's at home right now missing his girl."
"How long has it been since you rescued me, Seth?"
"Since the shark attack or when I brought you to the island?"
"The island."
"I think it's been around 367 days."
"I've been here for a *year*?"
"Yes."
"You're kidding. Please tell me you're kidding?!"
"I'm not kidding. If I was joking around I'd say a horse walks into a bar and the bartender says, 'Why the long face?'"
"It's really been a year?"
"Well, yes."

I sputtered to say my next words and only freaked out worse as time passed.

"Don't freak out."

"T-t-t-t-t-*too late*."

"Just calm down, Jillian. You're not dead out at sea like you would be by now if you hadn't washed up on the beach."

"I ran into a rock. The last thing I remember I woke up in a strange room fully clothed and dry."

"It was a much more different side of my story."

"Why don't you tell me it, your day, until you rescued me?"

"Sure, my father had sent me to clean barnacles off the reef since they were starting to kill some of the rare coral, and a shadow fell on me that blocked out the sun that was shining on me. It was a girl whom I didn't recognize at first. It was just a floating silhouette with long hair. It scared me at first, so I swam up to see that you were and I recognized that face I had seen when I was young and said to myself, 'Jillian?' Obviously you didn't respond because there was a scratch on your head. I figured out that you were unconscious and had drowned. I died a little inside when I realized that. You floated down peacefully into my arms, and you were smiling even though you were very pale. I looked around and swam to the surface. You still weren't breathing and CPR didn't work. I couldn't live with the fact that you were dead."

"I wasn't dead! I don't remember being dead."

"I didn't finish the story."

"Oh, sorry."

"You were as dead as a doornail, pale and blue. I cried when you wouldn't breathe and I looked at the crystal on my neck. It was glowing blue as usual. I had promised another woman I would make her a hybrid on the surface, but saving you was a much better deal. My father taught me how to use the crystal to turn you into a hybrid, and the second I finished, a wave washed over you and you instantly had a tail. When it washed out, you were breathing again. You were still unconscious though and I took you to the cabin, and I was happy you were alive as the color returned to your face and your lips went from pale blue to rose pink. Becoming a hybrid saved your life, with a bit of my help."

"Why didn't you ever tell me this?"

"Saving it for a good time. Why not under the stars?"

"Good point, and I was really dead?"

"You still looked beautiful."

"Well, aren't you sweet? I couldn't have been dead long because I got no glimpse of heaven."

"What makes you think you would go to heaven?"
"What? A little blue angel like me belongs there."
Seth laughed to himself and kissed my forehead.
"You'll go to heaven, I'm sure of it."
Our conversation ended for a brief moment before he spotted something in the sky.
"Hey! Shooting star! Make a wish!"
"You spotted it. You make a wish."
"But I'm giving you this one. I'm sure I'll see one later on tonight."
"Fine, I made my wish."
"What did you wish for?"
"I can't tell you. It won't come true."

Seth coughed and pointed up; another shooting star fell shortly afterward, and I told him he could have it.
"So what did you wish for?"
"I wished we'd have a terrible night together."
"Well, now it won't come . . . aw."

Seth laughed; something told me he had meant to do that for the exact reason that it wouldn't some true—that we would have a wonderful night together. It turned out it was wonderful up to that point. We were sipping on drinks, chatting under the stars; Seth's wish had already come true.

"So if you love stars so much, why don't you show me where a few constellations are?"
"Oh, there's so many, Seth. I can only spot a few."
"Okay, I'll give you an easy one. Show me the Big Dipper."
"Oh, that's an easy one. It's right over there." I pointed directly at the Big Dipper, until I realized it was really the Little Dipper.
"I think that's the Little Dipper."
"Yep, I was wrong."
"Show me a different one."

I started to lean over Seth to point to Orion's Belt, but I stopped when he kissed me. He was a very strong kisser, and I couldn't back away; the taste of lime and margarita on his lips was delicious. Seth attempted to roll over, but he flipped the entire hammock; the crash of our drinks on the stone followed.

"That was a good Caesar."
"That was a tasty margarita. Want to try again back at the cabin?"
"Yeah, but I want a margarita this time."
"Sure."

Seth and I cleaned up what we could of the drinks and picked up the shattered glass in two handfuls; it was shattered enough so that it couldn't be fixed but large enough to carry in the palm of the hand. I had both shattered glasses in my two hands and I started to walk down the stairs; now the stairs were warm from the steam.

"Is it hot in here or is it just me?"

"No, it's really steamy in here. It started the second I got here."

Sweat started running down my neck and down my shirt.

"It'll be nice to jump in the cool water."

"Definitely."

Seth dove in and didn't surface right away, and I jumped in carefully afterward so as not to drop the glass in the water.

I dipped my foot into the water and it was warm.

"Jesus, Seth! The water's hot!"

"I know! It's amazing. Get in here!"

"Seth, I can't swim and hold all this glass by myself. Come grab your share."

Seth didn't return right away. From where he said that, I didn't know; he wasn't even in the cavern. I was a little concerned when all I saw was bubbles rising to the surface but no Seth.

"Seth?"

He still didn't show until a large fin rose out of the water and there was a massive splash, although I couldn't see a thing. Splash! And Seth whispered, "Boo."

"Dammit, Seth, I thought you were a shark! That's not funny!"

"Oh, c'mon, did I scare you?"

"Yes! Now hold your glass."

Seth started swimming in a circle around me, singing the *Jaws* theme song, laughing as he did so. Before disappearing into the water, he snuck another kiss on my cheek at the end of the song. I laughed and then saw something sparkle in the water. Seth return.

"Wow."

"Wow what?"

"Look up."

The entire ceiling of the cavern was encrusted with all the jewels and gems you could possibly think of. I even saw a bunch of peridot in the corner.

"I can't believe I never noticed that before."

I nodded in agreement to Seth, and the air was getting warmer.

"Me either."

I was looking dazed at the sparkling gems on the roof with the plain stone behind it; the jewels were dripping with water from the steam in the cavern.

"What is that like . . . $200,000 dollars of treasured gems up there?"
"That sounds about right, but you'd never reach the top."
"Good point."

I continued to stare at the ceiling, but Seth had finished and he slowly swam toward me. I didn't notice him swimming until I looked down, and then he kissed me again. I couldn't stop; the heat of his skin was equivalent to that of the temperature in the cavern, so it was really hot. Seth quickly flipped off my shirt before I could say a thing, I didn't mind at all since he saw me in a bikini top every day. I dropped my share of the glass in the water so I could wrap my arms around his neck. The echo of the water trickling as I lifted my arms was the only sound in the silence of the cavern; it was incredible. Just as Seth was about to unhook my bra, I stopped him.

"Don't even think about it, Seth."
"Think about what?" Seth laughed and kissed my neck.
"Don't even think about unhooking my bra."
"I wasn't."
"Says the man who's already unhooked the first level of my bra."
"Maybe I just wanted to take off a row."
"Sure you did. I'm still in the mood for a margarita."
"Of course."

I swam over to the edge and grabbed my shirt; it was too warm to put it on, so I felt no shame in swimming back in my bra.

"Is there any point that you'll let me take off your bra though?"
"Not tonight."
"So any night but tonight. Sounds good by me."
"I didn't say that!"
"Ha-ha, okay. Let's go get some drinks."

The swim back was brighter with Seth and his brighter crystal ahead of me. It was easier to find my way around and I felt slightly safer with him here.

"So what night can I then?"
"If you keep asking, I won't let you."

Seth became completely silent during the swim back. It was a quiet swim back to the cavern and an even quieter walk back to the cabin.

"I didn't say you couldn't talk."
"I just can't ask anything at all."
"Exactly, however I miss conversation."
"So I just can't ask about whether or not I can take off your bra?"
"Bingo."
"So what can we talk about?"
"How about those drinks?"

Seth smiled and opened the door to the cabin, following me in shortly behind. I headed straight to the kitchen and threw my wet T-shirt in the sink to rinse off the sand from the beach; it was easy to rinse it off. I felt no shame in letting Seth see me in my bra; he saw me in a similar bikini top almost every day. Seth ran into the kitchen and picked up the last pomegranate on the table. Just as he was about to slice into the pomegranate to get the juicy seeds within, Miko jumped up and stole it from his palm.

"Hey!"

"Calm down, Seth."

I instinctively put my hand on Seth's chest to hold him back. He hadn't even noticed the fact that his crystal was glowing red once more.

"Are you really in the mood for drinks?" Seth asked me.

"Not really."

"Neither am I."

"Seth, your crystal—"

"Oh, sorry about that. I know. We already talked about how you're—"

"Would you mind joining me in my room?"

Seth agreed and grinned, as I grabbed his hand before going up the stairs and into my room; I thought Seth would never guess my real intentions with him. The second I set foot in my room, Seth instantly grabbed me and kissed me. I wrapped my arms around his neck as he pulled me closer into his chest. His crystal was glowing bright red once more, mine wasn't. When I felt his hand crawl up to my back and behind my bikini top, I stopped him.

"This isn't exactly why I invited you to my room, Seth."

"Then what did you invite me for?" Seth smiled and kissed my neck.

"I'm scared."

"Scared of what, angel?"

"Scared of sharks. Just bringing them up again reminded me of the night I was attacked. I know I'm not going to get a good sleep tonight if I keep having nightmares."

"Aw, I'll stay here with you tonight if you like."

"Thank you, Seth."

"But I won't stop kissing you!"

I laughed when Seth kissed me on the cheek and I fell onto the bed. I smiled as I realized he had one hand on my stomach and the other behind my neck. It was fun for a while until I told him I was starting to get tired.

"It's getting late, Seth. I have to get a good sleep for tomorrow."

"All right."

I got up from the bed and took my shirt off, revealing my bikini top underneath.

"No peeking! I'm changing."

"I won't peek."

Seth's crystal was glowing such a bright red that even I could notice it from behind me. I was sure Seth was aware of it by now but could care less. I slipped off my bikini top and put on my pajama tank top.

"I peeked."

"Seth!"

"What? I barely even saw your bare back."

It wasn't a big deal; it was not like he had seen me topless or anything from the front. As I looked for my bottoms, I realized I had a bathroom at the last minute, where I could've changed in the whole freaking time.

"I'm so stupid."

"Why's that?"

"There's a bathroom I could've changed in the whole time!"

"Then I wouldn't have got to see you're bare back."

"Oh, Seth."

I flashed into the bathroom and slammed the door behind me; I looked at the bottoms I had grabbed. It was the last pair of clean pants I had—a pair of my skimpy shorts that matched my top.

"Shit," I whispered to myself before slipping them on and walking out of the washroom, scratching the back of my head.

"Nice shorts."

"It's all I had left that was clean."

"Well, they look good."

"Thank you."

I attempted a curtsy as I thanked him and crawled into bed. Seth jumped right in afterward and tucked himself right in, snuggling up to me. I rolled over with my eyes closed into his chest and felt an arm being placed upon my back and pulling me closer. Seth didn't notice the brightness of his crystal glowing red in the darkness. It seemed he was casual at this point about his crystal glowing red. I remembered that before that it had been a far bigger deal to him; it meant that I was the one. To me it was rubbish. The glow of red on my face did have a soothing effect as it was a warm glow before I fell asleep; the comfort in Seth's warm and bare chest was relaxing as he breathed in and out harmoniously, and I felt a quick kiss on my forehead before I slept.

Chapter 25

 I woke up warm and snuggled into Seth's chest, the same way I had fallen asleep. The air was warm and inviting and the sun in the window was shining on Seth and me. The sandman brought me no terrors of nightmares that night but sweet dreams instead. I got dressed while Seth was still sound asleep. I snuck out of the room and made myself some breakfast with the freshly picked pomegranate seeds on the side; my supply of pomegranates was finally running out. A year later, I could run out of pomegranates, who knew? I finished my breakfast and headed upstairs to wake Seth up. The second I opened the door, I saw Seth in the bathroom, fixing his hair.
 "Good morning, how did you sleep?"
 "Great."
 "Nervous for today?"
 "A little. Who's the first guy I'm seeing today?"
 "Well, I think the order is alphabetical, so Alex, I think."
 "Oh, I love that guy! He's awesome!"
 Seth coughed.
 "Don't worry, you are too."
 Seth smiled and started walking to the door.
 "Then go get 'em, tiger."
 "What's with all the nicknames, Seth? I like Jill or Jillian."
 "What's wrong with angel?"
 "You said tiger."
 "Tiger, angel, does it really matter?"
 "Yes."
 "So why are you uncomfortable with angel?"
 "I'm no angel, that's why."

"You don't think so, but I do."

I smiled as we stepped down the stairs and toward the front door. I laid my shirt on the patio before sprinting for the water.

"He's pretty cool actually. He's a little crazy though with those gifts."

"Alex?"

"Yeah."

"So what's the deal with these guys and gifts? How the hell do they get these powers anyways?"

"It's genetic. It's very rare for mermaids to receive certain gifts from their family histories. Kind of like if you were a descendant of a witch, you would have certain abilities with potions and a skill for science."

"So their parents have the same powers?"

"Depends. Sometimes the powers skip some generations, sometimes they don't."

"That's so weird. Are they as rare as the hybrids?"

"Surprisingly no. They are about 10 percent of the mermaid species."

"Why are there more gifted mermen than hybrids?"

"The genes are in their favor. It can be passed on to children, so the population spike of gifted merfolk has gone up. Becoming a hybrid is extremely rare."

"Race you to the water!"

"Nope."

I raced off anyways.

"I said nope!"

"I don't care!"

I splashed into the water, but Seth it appeared was the first to dive in. It looked like he had won the race. I stopped when I was about waist deep and then dove into the water. Seth had already made it; he was a couple of meters ahead of me.

"Wait up. I'm still iffy on the exact direction to Atlantis!"

"Even after a year?"

"Yes, even after a year."

I watched Seth stop swimming as I caught up to him and swam up to his side. Seth and I passed the reef which was in full bloom today with colors of thousands of coral that popped brighter than a rainbow flower garden. The shining tropical fish that passed me swam out and about around the coral in the thousands; it was a network of life and beauty within the reef. It took my breath away as we swam away from it and toward the deeper and darker part of the ocean. The only other things we saw before reaching Atlantis was a whale and a few playful dolphins. Once we reached Atlantis, it really seemed to glow today a green hue. We reached the gates in a short time, and Kiara was there to greet me shortly after Seth and I entered.

"Hey, Jill, you nervous for your first date today?"

"A little bit. I'm glad the date won't be too long though. Seth and I were going to—"

"I hate to be the one to tell you this but the date lasts until ten tonight."

"Really?"

"Well, I suppose it'll be better if the date is too long than not long enough."

"You do have a point, Kiara. I'm feeling pretty good about this long date."

"But we were going to see the reef in bloom today!" Seth complained.

"Don't worry. The reef should be in bloom for two weeks. We can go next week."

Kiara laughed and swam with Seth and me to the castle. Kiara seemed excited that I was dating these seven princes; she kept going on and on about some of her long-term relationships with some of the princes, some of whom she was really close to.

"Alex and I were really close friends for a while, but my parents thought he was a bad influence and I couldn't see him at school anymore. I mean like, seriously we smoked weeds together once and suddenly he's a bad influence. It was my idea in the first place. It was my choice and I should've been punished, not our friendship. I was so—"

"Ah! Here we are! The castle. Can Kiara come with us?"

"Unfortunately not. The dates are confidential, so she can't come in to see you with one of the princes."

"Aw, you're no fun, Seth. Okay, have fun, girl! I'll see you later."

"Thanks, Kiara! See you."

"She talks a lot, doesn't she?"

I whispered to Seth, "She's always been like that."

"Seriously?"

"Yep, I think Alex is inside."

Seth opened the door to the castle, letting me go in first. The entire castle was decorated in bright silver jewels and tassels; lights of every color shone brighter than any star that I'd ever seen. The lights were glowing in colors I couldn't even name and it was nothing short of beautiful. The tower of the castle had bright white jewels encrusted into the stone slabs on the side of the castle. How light managed to glimmer off the crystals this deep into the water puzzled me; it was still beautiful to look at. The swimming path to the castle had the same jewels on the walls of the castle; only that every so foot, there was a bright bloodred ruby that lingered out of the white jeweled pattern. Nonetheless, it was easy to see how rich the capital city really was. It didn't take long to get inside where Alex was patiently waiting for Seth and me.

"Good morning, Jillian."

"Good morning, Alex, how are you?"

"I'm doing great, thanks."

Alex grabbed my hand—that made me gasp in silence out of surprise—and silently kissed the back of my hand, maintaining eye contact, then smiled afterward. I blushed; no one had kissed the back of my hand since the party with the princes, but I enjoyed the favor anyways. I looked out of the corner of my eye at Seth, who had gone from his usual tan to green to even. His face had melted to a red that was almost as dark as his crystal would glow when he kissed me. It wasn't hard to see how jealous Seth was.

"Well, I'm ready to go. I don't know about you."

"Sure, I'm good to go."

Alex stuck out his arm in a half-crescent shape, and I quickly grabbed it and said good-bye to Seth.

"See you later, Seth!"

I waved good-bye to Seth with my free arm.

"So do you mind showing me the island you live on?"

"Oh, I'd love to! It'll take all day, but it'll be worth it."

"This is why I love being a hybrid."

"Me too!"

I laughed as we left the castle with my arm still held in his arm. The streets of Atlantis were quieter than usual, but I didn't really mind.

"So, Cato, why did you dye your hair blond?"

"Oh, I dye my hair blond all the time. Keeps up the nickname you call me."

I smiled when I suddenly realized how much he really did look like Cato with blond hair—the same smile, tanned skin, cheekbones. He looked a good blond.

"Do you have a name for the island?"

"A name?"

"Yeah, surely you've nicknamed the island by now."

I had never thought of giving the island a name before. Why would I give my home a nickname in the first place? Then I realized exactly what I was thinking. It was my home. I was in silent shock about the truth. This was my new home. Where else could I go? There was nothing but ocean all around me and there was no way of knowing I'd make it to the right coast after being hurled into the center of the Pacific Ocean. And it just wouldn't be home anymore without my family there to greet me. It was certain that a year later, without rescue, they would be all deceased.

"Maybe you and I could nickname it after today."

I regained my color and smiled at Alex, who smiled in return.

"Oh, and I should warn you. There is a sort of pet there that may surprise you on the island."

"I love animals! What kind of pet is it?"

"I'll let you find out for yourself."

The swim back to the island was scenic as we got to pass the reef in bloom once more. It was just as beautiful as that morning, only that it was brighter than before. I even swooned a little at the brightness that made me swim sideways.

"Are you okay, Jillian?"

"Yeah, I'm okay. The brightness of the reef distracted me."

"Sure, the reef made you swoon."

"It's true."

"Although the reef is a little bright, isn't it?"

"It is."

It didn't take long to reach the entrance to the island; the very first thing I wanted to show Alex was the treasure cavern.

"Is this some sort of entrance to the island?"

"You could say that, but there's something I want to show you first."

I told him to follow me as we entered the dark tunnel to the treasure cavern.

"I can't see!"

"Relax. Just feel your way around if you need to."

"How do you know there are no sharks in here?"

"I don't."

"That doesn't sound good."

I laughed as the tunnel twisted and turned into the light of the sun from the island not far above, which made all my treasures sparkle.

"This . . .," I swam to the top of the treasure cavern, "is my treasure cavern."

"Oh, you're so lucky. Where did you get all this treasure from?"

"Found it, stole some, not much but some."

"You steal treasure?"

Alex paused.

"That's kind of hot."

"This is nothing compared to what's ahead."

"I don't know about that. The view from here is very beautiful."

"Yeah, the treasure here is pretty nice."

"I wasn't talking about the treasure."

I smiled as I swam past him and gestured to him to follow me again with the flick of my fingers. I decided I'd show him the steamy cavern; hopefully, by this point it would have cooled down by now. The second we got there I noticed the cavern hadn't cooled down by a single degree.

"Wow, hot in here, isn't it?"

"Yeah, it was hot in here earlier. No clue why though."

"Kind of like a sauna in here. You really do have everything you need on this island, don't you?"

"Everything but a man in my life."

I glanced over at Alex and smiled as we both got out of the water and waited for our legs to form.

"I always hate that feeling of numbness in my legs whenever I get out of the water."

"I thought I was the only one with that issue! I'm so glad I'm not the only one with that issue."

"Omigosh, yes! Thank you for not being the only one."

I laughed as I showed him the stone staircase.

"You're going to love the view from up here."

"I already do."

I simply thought to myself how much I was enjoying this date with Alex. I loved how much he complimented me; I could spend an eternity with that.

"You can see the entire island from up there, you know," I said as we reached the top of the stone stairs. The view today was brilliant and beautiful as it always was—the bright blue ocean side, shining white sand, tropical forest that echoed with bird calls. It was beyond utopia for me and even past peaceful as I sat down on the hammock.

"This is an amazing view."

"Never gets old for me."

I told Alex, "Pop a squat, Cato."

Alex laughed to himself under his breath and sat down gently next to me, slowly starting to rock the hammock with his feet.

"So what do you do up here for fun?"

"Watch the stars and make out."

"Thank you for being so honest."

"You're welcome. Mostly watching stars though."

"Yes, it is quite romantic."

There was a short moment of silence before we gave out a duet of synchronized sigh as we gazed out into the tropical forest. Suddenly, there was a rustle of branches, and seconds later, Miko jumped down and sat in front of Alex and me.

"Don't freak out, Miko. This is Alex, but I call him Cato."

Miko jumped around, squawking in his monkey language, and launched at Alex.

"Will he bite me?"

"Not if he doesn't like you."

Miko climbed on top of Alex, scrambling onto his strong shoulders and up to his head to inspect his head, then back down to his shoulders. Alex remained motionless—to my surprise—and let Miko walk all over him.

"How long does this usually last?" Alex calmly asked.

"Only about a minute. He'll tire out any minute now."

Miko continued his routine of inspection and crawled over Alex's head some more. When Miko finally stopped, he rested on Alex's lap to rest because of the excitement.

"So does he like me?"

Miko immediately sat up and showed his tiny sharp teeth in a smile.

"I've never seen Miko do that before. I suppose he likes you."

"Aw, you have a pet monkey that likes me," Alex said as he petted the top of Miko's head. "Where did the name Miko come from anyways?"

"Have you ever seen the Disney classic *Pocahontas*?"

"Yes, I have."

"In the movie, there's this little raccoon friend of hers that does nothing but steal and eat food. When I first met Miko, he stole some food of mine, and so I called him Miko. Afterward, he showed me some fruit."

"That's the perfect name for a monkey, but where did he get the fruit?"

"I can show you if you like."

"I'd love to."

I got up first from the hammock and made my way down the steep stone steps, still a bit warm because of the steam in the cavern.

"It's nice in here."

"It is, but the steam makes me a little drowsy though."

I told Alex as I wiped some sweat beads off my forehead. The cavern was warmer than last time because of the temperature of the now hot water.

"Any warmer and this water could be a hot tub," Alex commented as he dipped his feet in the water.

"All we need is some bubbles and drinks, although you are right, the water is getting hotter each day."

"Shouldn't that be a good thing?"

"I never said it wasn't. I like how hot it is in here!"

"Me too."

Alex splashed into the warm water, splashing me with it as I dipped my feet in and jumped in. I surfaced right away to gaze at the ceiling once more.

"What are you waiting fo—?"

I presumed Alex looked up with me and noticed the crystal roof, something I had yet to nickname.

"That's breathtaking."

"It is, isn't it?"

"How did those crystals get all the way up there?"

"My assumption is that this entire island was under ground and water for millions of years, and all the pressure caused the gems to form until the water and ground disappeared, leaving all this wonderful treasure to look at behind."

"That's a pretty good assumption."

"Thank you. Whether or not it's true is the real question."

"Speaking of questions, would you mind if I asked you one?"

"Go ahead, Cato."

Alex was silent for a minute and laughed to himself, probably because of me calling him Cato.

"Can I—?"

Alex stopped mid-sentence and couldn't quite finish. I raised my eyebrow in anticipation for what he would say; still Alex said nothing.

"Would you—?"

Alex paused once more, and I smiled. I think I knew what he was going to ask and smiled bigger. Without uttering a word, he kissed me. Something was different about Alex when he kissed me; it was a far different feeling than when Seth kissed me here. I didn't mind the fact that he kissed me; in fact, I rather enjoyed it. He lifted his arm out of the water to gently place it around my neck and the other was on my waist. He pulled me closer as the water trickled and echoed when I wrapped my arms around his neck. Held in an embrace, I didn't let go and I didn't want to. When he stopped, a silent "aw" echoed in my mind. I never wanted to let him go. All he did was smile as I did in return when he put his forehead on mine and laughed to himself.

"What's so funny, Cato?"

"Easier done than said."

I laughed to myself as I asked him to follow me out of the water.

on the way to the back of the cabin. I figured I'd pack us a lunch if I was to try and find those pomegranates again. It might not even be the right season for the tree to bear its fruity goodness. Miko also might not even be in the mood to show me where the pomegranates are. The sand was cold coming out of the warm water, and I didn't mind that Alex held my hand once our legs returned. Alex opened the door to the cabin, and I walked in and headed straight for the kitchen and began to pack a lunch.

"Why are you making lunch?"

"Because it's going to take a while to find my way to the fruit trees. I'm not even sure I know the way."

"So we're going out somewhere where there's lots of fruit—"

"Lots of fruit."

"But you don't know where it is?"

"Miko knows."

"The monkey?"

"Yes, the monkey. We're completely out of fruit and Miko will help us find some more fruit."

"What makes you think he'll join us?"

"He's a good monkey who loves fruit."

Miko suddenly leaped on the table to eat the last fruit in the cabin. I threw in whatever snacks I could and grabbed a few other things. Miko finished the fruit faster than I expected and I finished making the lunch as it was anyways.

"I hope you know that was the last fruit, Miko."

Miko licked the juice off his tiny brown fingers.

"I hope you know you're going to help us find some more."

Miko stopped licking his fingers and launched for the door; it was closed, so he stopped.

"Miko loves his fruit," I told Alex. I threw all the lunch things in a backpack and walked toward the door. Alex put on a pair of running shoes that fit him well; unknowingly, the shoes were Seth's. Miko raced out the door the second I opened it and headed for the trees.

"You'd better keep up. He's a fast little monkey."

"Fast? Monkeys can't run that fast."

"Who said he would be running?"

The second I heard the rustle of the trees, I knew that Miko was already on his way. I sprinted for the forest with the backpack on my back, Alex right behind me. Miko gracefully swung above me in the trees at a great speed; Alex and I had to run to keep up. Miko took turns into forested areas I didn't recognize. I think we had been running for at least ten minutes straight; we ran past so many unfamiliar areas I wasn't too sure we would be able to find our way back. Sure enough Miko brought us right to the pomegranate trees.

"No way."

"What is it?"

"There's a mango tree here! I haven't had a mango in a year."

I raced over to the mango tree and found that I was too short to reach the juicy fruit above.

"You can't reach the fruit, can you?"

"I would love some help to reach the fruit."

Alex was just taller than me and walked up to the tree. With ease, he stretched up and grabbed the mango above and took a bite of it.

"Tasty."

"I was hoping to save those, Cato."

"Whoops."

"You got a little juice right there."

I pointed to his cheek, and he quickly wiped off the juice and laughed as he took another bite of the mango. He started reaching for some more mangos, while I watched Miko climb the nearby pomegranate tree. Miko was looking at me with a silly little grin on his face.

"Mind helping me out, Miko?"

It seemed as if he knew exactly what I was thinking as he started to rip down pomegranates ripe and ready off the tree.

"Watch out!"

Alex grabbed me and threw me on the ground and fell down with me covering his head and trying to ignore the falling pomegranates.

"Alex! He's supposed to do that!"

"Oh, sorry."

He helped me to my feet as a pomegranate bounced off his head and fell to the ground. Miko had already knocked down at least thirty pomegranates, which was more than enough to fit in my backpack.

"That's great, Miko, but we got enough."

Miko stopped ripping down fruit and dropped to the ground and crawled onto my shoulders.

"Good job, Miko. Here's one on the house."

I handed Miko a pomegranate out of my bag and watched him run off to where we had come from.

"Any idea how to get back?"

"Only one but it's fun."

I knew this pomegranate area well, so I knew exactly where I could show him the billion-dollar crystal cave; plus the waterfall was pretty romantic. The only issue was that there had better not be a great white shark there again. Alex followed me after he grabbed about twenty mangoes for me. With a flick of his wrist, he tossed the mangoes into the bag.

"You've been carrying that bag for too long. Let me carry it."

Alex grabbed the backpack right off my back and placed it over his. I didn't mind that he was carrying the bag since it was now at least fifty pounds heavier. I asked him to follow me into the bushes as I led the way to the unsaid waterfall.

"So where do you want to have lunch?"

"I know the perfect spot."

It took fifteen minutes to find it, but I finally recognized the bush before the waterfall would appear.

"How's this?"

I pulled back some bushes and revealed the hidden oasis within. It looked absolutely stunning today as the sun was shimmering off the water.

"Beautiful."

"Isn't it?"

"I wasn't talking about the waterfall."

"Well, aren't you sweet?"

I snuck a kiss on his cheek and raced over to the water for a quick drink; the cool water was nice on my chapped lips.

"Why are you drinking that water?"

"It's freshwater. It's 100 percent safe to drink."

Alex raced over to the water and grabbed a drink with me. It was perfectly cold on a hot day like today and it was just what I needed. I stood up after my drink and started unpacking the lunch I had packed under a palm tree in the shade. I first reached inside the bag for a mango and bit into it after washing it in the water. The juice ran down my cheek and neck, but the mango was so delicious. The tart of the fruit made me smile as I took another bite. Alex grabbed a pomegranate out of the backpack and started tearing away at the hard outer core that I myself would need a knife to break into.

"So why did you take me to a waterfall for lunch?"

"It's not the waterfall I wanted to show you, Cato. It's what's underneath."

"So what's underneath?"

"It's a surprise."

I smiled as I took another bite into my juicy mango. I was getting mango juice all over me at this point; I was a sticky mess in such a short time.

"You got a little something right there."

The Tail of an Angel

Alex pointed to my neck. Before I could even attempt to wipe my neck, Alex leaned in closer to me and kissed it, getting the dripping juice off my neck. I giggled when he kissed me because it tickled, but I liked it. He started to rip out the seeds in the pomegranate after smiling at me and placed the seeds in a bag so as to not let any bugs get at them. He ate all the beef jerky to my relief, at ease that the meat wouldn't attract another great white shark.

"So, Jillian, tell me a bit more about yourself."

"I play the piano."

"Really? How well?"

"I never finished my entire piano lessons since I was more dedicated to my school marks."

"You gave up piano because you wanted to raise your marks?"

"You bet!"

"What songs can you play?"

"Oh lots. I can pick at any song by ear."

"That's really cool! What other instruments can you play?"

"Recorder and guitar."

"Do you have a guitar here?"

"Yep, I can play it later if you like?"

"Sounds good to me!"

I finished the last of my mango and threw the core aside whilst wiping juice off my face. Alex was still picking away at his pomegranate, but he was nearly finished. I grabbed a peanut butter and jelly sandwich out of the backpack and took the first glorious bite. The jam was cold and wonderful with the warm and creamy peanut butter.

"I love peanut butter and jelly sandwiches."

"You brought peanut butter sandwiches?"

"I sure did."

"Why didn't you say so?"

Alex quickly finished peeling the last of the seeds in the pomegranate, getting a few squirts of pomegranate juice on himself and in his eye. I laughed as he scrambled to find a sandwich in the bag and one put, looking at it as if it were gold.

"Do you know how long it's been since I've had a peanut butter sandwich?"

"How long?"

"Four years! I'm so happy to see peanut butter again!"

Alex ripped the sandwich out of the bag and took a whiff before savoring the first bite of the sandwich.

"How can I thank you for this sandwich?"

"No need to thank me, Cato. Just enjoy it."

Alex ran up to my side and kissed me on the cheek before sitting down next to me and enjoying his next bite into the sandwich. I smiled before getting up and taking my shirt off.

"Ummm . . . Jillian? Why are you taking your shirt off?"

"I do it to feel human again."

I smiled as I took off my pants, revealing my bikini bottoms, and raced to the water and jumped in with a cannonball and an echoed *woohoo!* I popped up shortly with a sigh of enjoyment as I dipped my head back into the cool water.

"Aren't you supposed to wait half an hour before swimming?"

"I don't get cramps, never have after eating or swimming and never will. Come on in, Cato. The water is fine."

"I better make sure you don't drown. Wait for me!"

Alex raced to the water as I did, taking off his shirt while doing so and jumping into the water.

"Why do I still have my legs?"

"My theory is that we only get our legs in saltwater."

"So how do we find what's underneath the waterfall?"

"Oh, it's easy to find, a bit of a swim but easy. Can't we enjoy this lovely waterfall for a bit?"

"Sure."

Alex took a dive underwater in a quick splash, and no bubbles emerged to reveal his location. I turned my head in every way, looking for any sign of him.

"Alex, where are you?" I asked in a serious tone. I started to panic as it had already been a minute and he still hadn't surfaced. Suddenly, I felt something brush my leg and I screamed when something grabbed my leg. A massive splash later, Alex picked me up by my legs and hips and held me in a comfortable holding position.

"Jesus, Cato, you scared me."

"I'm sorry."

Alex kissed my forehead and made me giggle again.

"You can put me down now."

"As you wish."

Alex threw me three feet into the air, and I landed on the water face and belly first.

"What the hell was that?"

"You told me to put you down."

"Maybe you could be a bit gentler next time."

"Do you want me to be gentle right now?"

"Well, it doesn't have to be now but perhaps sometime in the near—"

I was cut off by a kiss from Alex. The only issue was that I couldn't stop and I didn't want to. I wrapped my arms around his neck and felt his hand slip behind mine. I embraced him as an innocent kiss melted into French, and suddenly his hand latched on to my waist. I loved it as he lifted up my legs to wrap around his waist. It was nice that the mist of the waterfall sparkled and deflected off my warm back. I couldn't resist the chance of feeling human once more in the water without my tail. The cool current of the water flowed through my toes, which I missed dearly. When he stopped kissing me, he simply smiled, staring into my eyes that were simply smiling back at his. He gently put me back down in the water on my own two feet, treading in the water; he was taller than me and was standing on a rock's edge—towering over me. I looked down to my right and back at Alex, who had begun to blush. I smiled even bigger when he blushed as I swam back to the bag on the shore.

"Where are you going?"

"To get the bag."

"Why?"

"Because the way back to the cabin is down."

"What?"

"You'll see."

I hopped up and out of the water and put all the fruit into the bag so the saltwater wouldn't ruin them. I quickly packed them all and threw the bag into the water, happy that it would float.

"Won't that ruin the fruit?"

"Not if I put all the fruit in bags."

"Oh, that's smart."

He grabbed the bag and threw it on his bare back.

"Oh and a piece of advice. Take a big breath before going underwater because it's quite a swim before we reach saltwater."

"I'm not scared."

"Then follow me!"

I took a massive breath before diving underwater, leaving only bubbles and Alex behind me. I kicked with all my might down to get to the saltwater cave faster and faster, and since I kicked so hard, I reached the cave in a shorter amount of time. I looked back and watched my tail form, and I took a breath of freshwater. It was more refreshing than a cool drink of water.

"Check it out!"

I pointed at the wall of the cave, still coated in infinite gems and jewels. Alex gasped and swam straight for a ruby he couldn't pull out of the wall. I opened the bag for a moment to get the chisel I had brought and caught the floating pomegranate bags that made their way to the roof of the cavern. Alex smiled and thanked me for the chisel before swimming up to and gently hammering a ruby the size of my fist. The ruby popped out after a few chisels and Alex put the ruby in the bag. He smiled as he chipped away at an opal, topaz, and emerald, all of which popped out of the wall with ease. I was behind him, keeping the bag from floating away and watching his technique in getting jewels out of the wall. He was so precise and measured in finding the right spot to gently chisel away at the crystals. It was an art form I had yet to perfect. Alex finished after he took one more gem out of the wall, a total of five crystals taken from it. I told him he could take some more if he wanted, but he didn't feel that it was right to take any more crystals from me.

"Cato, you can take a hundred crystals if you like. I have enough crystals here to last a lifetime."

"I can only fit five in the bag."

"I can fit forty crystals in this bag, Cato, really."

"There's no use in taking so many crystals, Jillian. I'm perfectly content with what I have."

"Okay, let's go back to the cabin then."

"How?"

"Just follow me."

I took a turn into the darkness of the cavern toward the familiar claustrophobic tunnel ahead.

"Is that a current I feel?"

"Yes, it is. Make sure the bag is zipped up."

"Why?"

"You'll see."

The current got stronger until Alex and I were being pulled by a force faster and faster forward. The current was getting ridiculously strong, pulling me like a train car and thrusting me forward. The anticipation for the drop off was unbearable, and finally we were shot out of the tunnel and into the water below—or so I hoped; what really happened was that Alex made it to the water first and I slammed into the wall accidentally. The next thing I remember I was coughing on the shore of the entrance of the cavern with Alex hugging me tight.

"What happened?"

"You had better lie down. You're not going to believe what happened."

"I'm sure I can handle it."

I tried to get on my feet but my ankle was too sore to walk on, and all of a sudden, I fell back down onto the cold sand below.

"Let me help you. You took quite a hit on the wall."

"Yeah, I remember that part."

Alex picked me up in his arms and flipped me onto his shoulders, putting me on my feet onto my one good leg. I was sore and had no clue why I suddenly had the inability to walk.

"I'll explain everything when we get back to the cabin."

It seemed like the walk back was longer with me limping every wobbly step. What I would've given to remember what had happened. If it was so bad I couldn't walk, it must have been bad. I hadn't had the best of luck in that crystal cabin; last time I had nearly died. I swore if a shark attacked us I was going to be so upset with myself.

"Here, I'll get the door for you."

I leaned against the side of the cabin for support while Alex opened the door. He came back swiftly and grabbed my arm and threw it over his big, strong shoulders to get me into the cabin. I didn't mind my gimping leg as much as I had done a while ago.

"I think I better lie down. I don't really have the strength to stand up for much longer."

I tried to stand on my own while Alex closed the door, but failed miserably and fell with a loud thump on the hardwood floor.

"Ouch."

"I was closing the door! You couldn't have waited one minute for me to help you?"

"Nope, now help me up."

Alex laughed as he helped me up to my feet and put my arm over his shoulder again for support.

"Please tell me what happened now."

"I'll wait until you're lying down."

I carefully leaped up the stairs and made my way to the top, tripping over the last step. Alex caught me before I could fall and I thanked him for it. Finally, I reached my room and threw myself onto my bed.

"Well, I might as well tell you now."

I flipped over onto my back and slid onto my soft pillow with my leg up on the cover sheet.

"I'm sure you remember that when the cavern ended you smacked your head on the opposing wall before the drop off."

"Yep."

"Unfortunately, it knocked you out cold and left an open scratch on your forehead."

Alex lifted the hair away from my face to examine it.

"But that's not the worst part. After hitting the wall, you splashed down into the water and floated down into my arms with a touch of blood leaving your scratch. I panicked and asked if you were okay, but by the time I asked a shark had made its way to us."

"No!"

"Yes! I swam as fast as I could away from it with you in my arms, but the shark caught up and launched at you, so I had to distract it. So I used the chisel to painfully cut my finger to get the shark away from you. The shark bait worked and the shark headed for me instead, and I defended myself with the chisel and eventually it swam away, until another one showed up."

"You're kidding."

"I can assure you I'm not. He grabbed my arm a bit, but I'm all right since I had a weapon."

Alex showed me several bite marks on his arm that had started to bleed, when I looked over at him.

"Alex, you're hurt."

"Don't you worry about me. I'll find the first aid kit, and you just lie down until I find it."

"It's downstairs. Your story still doesn't explain why I have a sprained ankle though."

"Oh, I sort of dropped you when I fought off the second shark."

"You dropped me?"

"I am really sorry, but with my CPR card, I'm sure that ankle will be just fine by tomorrow."

"What good is CPR on a foot?"

"Well, I can make sure it doesn't fall asleep."

I laughed as I fluffed up the pillow behind me to make it softer and put my other foot up adjacent to my sprained one. My ankle still ached, but I was feeling slightly better when I put it up on the bed. I wondered if the sore scratch on my head would leave a scar after this mess. I heard the thump-thump of Alex going down the stairs while I waited patiently for his return. I whistled to myself while zoning out, gazing at the sun setting outside the window, still showing the brightness of day. I pondered how long I had passed out with Alex and if he was scared at all when I was unconscious. I didn't think I was out too long if I woke up on the shore of the cavern. I could see why he must have been worried sick when I didn't wake up right away. How would he feel if I was unconscious for the rest of the date? I felt a lot safer in his arms for a hug, and I hugged him back when the opportunity presented itself. Why was I always the one to get attacked by sharks? What if Alex couldn't have fought off the second shark and got eaten? This was my fourth encounter with sharks and I was so mad at myself for not being there . . . consciously to help Alex. A great feeling of guilt came over me, and I drowned in its sorrow. Don't get me wrong, but the pain was hurting as much as the growing soreness of the scratch on my forehead. Alex returned with the first aid kit and dug out some alcohol swabs.

"I'm so sorry this happened to you, Cato."

"Don't be sorry, Jill. It was an accident."

"Yeah, an accident caused by me."

"Please don't blame this on yourself."

"Why not? If I wouldn't have hit that stupid wall and cut my head to attract two sharks, the rest of this date would've been great and I wouldn't have to see you get hurt like this."

"Please, Jillian, I'm fine. I'm just glad you're okay."

He reached for an alcohol swab and gently placed it on my scratch; it burned like hell.

"Oh, it burns!"

"Sorry."

Alex delicately dabbed the scratch with the precision and touch of a surgeon. After dabbing at it, he took a cotton swab to soak up the blood that ran down my forehead. I grinned as he examined and wiped away with ease the blood coming off my forehead. He wiped it all off finally with a disinfected cloth from the kit. It amazed me how well Alex treated the wound; it was as if he had done this a thousand times before. When he finished, he stuck a band aid on my forehead to make sure the wound wouldn't get infected.

"Feel better?"

"Yes, thank you."

"You're welcome."

He clicked the first aid kit shut after taking a disinfected cloth out and wiping his bleeding arm with it.

"Surely you can do more than that for your arm."

"Oh, I don't think it's necessary for a tiny bite mark."

"But you're still bleeding."

I lightly touched his arm and examined the wound; it really was still bleeding and the bite marks seemed to rise up out of the skin to really pop out of his arm. Gracefully, I touched the edge of one of the wounds at the edge.

"Careful, it's still a bit tender."

"Sorry, Cato, I think you're going to need stitches on this one."

"You are not going to give me stitches."

"Don't worry. There are instructions, so I can't screw this up, I promise."

Alex tentatively moved his arm closer to me, most likely worried I was going to screw up those stitches somehow. I pulled out the stitching kit from the bottom of the first aid kit and memorized the instructions on giving stitches in five minutes. Carefully, I inserted the freezing needle into Alex's arm.

"Ouch."

"Of course, it hurts. It's a freezing needle."

I leaned down and kissed the spot where I had inserted the needle.

"Better?"

"I suppose."

The instructions indicated I disinfect the wound once more before I sew up his arm. That was the easy part. I had to find a point at which I could insert the needle and stitches.

"This might hurt a little."

I jabbed the needle into his arm just above the wound and sewed as I would one of my shirts at home. The skin pulled together just fine and I only had to give him four stitches; even so, my work looked really good.

"That's it."

I put away the needles and sewing line in the kit, and Alex looked satisfied at my stitching work. He smiled and coughed, probably because he had something caught in his throat.

"Thank you."

"You're welcome, Cato. I don't think it'll scar though the stitches will have to come out in a few weeks or so."

"Aw, I was hoping it would scar."

"And why is that?"

"Every scar has a story to tell."

I smiled at Alex as I cleaned up the rest of the med kit.

"I must say, thank you for the stitches."

"Anytime, Cato. I'm so sorry our date was ruined by a shark attack."

"Hey, don't think that because of two little sharks that this date was ruined. It's not even over yet."

"I hate to tell you this, but I don't think I can do too much else on a sprained ankle."

"Of course, we can. We can still chat and I can make us dinner."

"You want to make me dinner?"

"Of course I do. I'm a great cook. What are you in the mood for?"

"Sushi? California rolls?"

"Coming right up."

Alex bent down over me—I wondered what he was up to—and placed his hands behind my back and under my legs and lifted me up off the bed. He made his way down the stairs, gracefully stepping down each stair despite the counterbalance of my weight. Once we reached the bottom of the stairs, he placed me down gently on the couch in the living room.

"Supper should be ready in about an hour and a half."

"I didn't know it took so long to make sushi."

"It's going to take a couple minutes for me to catch some fresh crab."

"You don't have to catch fresh crab if you don't want to."

"Oh, but I do."

Alex bent down and kissed me on the cheek before going outside and into the water for crab. It was no less than ten minutes later when Alex walked in with two large crabs not moving at all; they must have been knocked unconscious by Alex since they weren't snapping at him. He walked with pride to the kitchen where I heard him slap the crabs onto the table.

"That didn't take long."

"Sure didn't."

He did what he could to clean the crab before rinsing it off some more and cleaning out its major organs. Delicious! He tossed the crab into a pot and set it to boil. He threw some sticky rice in another pot and grabbed the avocado and cucumber out of the fridge. He quickly ran outside to grab some fresh seaweed for the wrap of the sushi and let the pieces dry on the stove. He checked to see if the crab was ready and stirred the sticky rice a bit. Alex seemed to look as if he had done this many times before. It was an art form to watch Alex cook in the kitchen; the grace and precision with which he cooked was enjoyable to watch as my stomach started to rumble.

"How much longer until supper, Cato?"

"Not much longer. About half an hour or so. Is that okay?"

"That's just fine."

Alex took a break from his cooking and took a seat next to me.

"Tell me more about yourself."

To make a very long story short, I told him my entire life's story. I told him everything I could possibly recall about myself from my first time on a plane to how I got here.

"So my mom spontaneously decided that we should take a tropical vacation on our lottery won yacht and take a family vacation cruise. We even went with my boyfriend's family on the cruise to Hawaii. Our first time was on that yacht."

"Anyways!"

"Anyways, a hurricane came through the following night and the yacht sank. I never saw my boyfriend or family again. I'd prefer not to go on anymore."

"Hey, don't feel too bad." Alex gave me a big hug and squeezed me tight. "It's not your fault."

"I just wish my boyfriend and family were still alive."

"There's nothing you could've done, Jillian."

"I watched them float away, Cato. I didn't even get to say good-bye."

A tear had once more escaped from my eye; I didn't give a damn at this point if Alex saw me cry. I missed my family more and more the longer I thought about it. I sniffled for a second before Alex handed me a tissue to blow my nose and wipe my tears. Before I could wipe my tears, Alex beat me to it by wiping away my tears with his hand and thumb that gently cradled my face. I nuzzled into his warm hand that wiped away another tear on my face and closed my eyes. He held my face in the palms of his big strong hands and I opened my eyes to see his inviting brown eyes staring back into mine. I leaned forward and so did he, but before our lips could barely touch, the timer for the crab went off.

"Sounds like the crab's ready."

I smiled as he released my face and ran off to the kitchen and took out the crab from the pot. The crab had turned beetroot red and looked delicious. Alex looked around for the bamboo sushi maker and found it in one of the drawers. He quickly put together the sushi and rolled it all together.

"Supper's ready," Alex called out to me. I tried to stand up on my own, but I still couldn't on my sore ankle. Alex ran up to my side for support and I thanked him.

"Supper smells good."

"Nah, that's the crab that smells so good."

"Well, whatever it is, I'm glad you went through all this for little old me."

"In the words of L'Oreal . . ." Alex handed me a perfectly placed heart-shaped sushi on a little plate. "Because you're worth it."

"Aw! It's shaped like little hearts! That's so cute!"

"I thought you would like that. Now I couldn't find any wasabi, but I found plenty of soy sauce and pickled ginger."

"Pickled ginger and soy sauce is fine. I never liked wasabi anyways."

The first bite of the sushi tasted even better with fresh crab. I thought it may have been some of the best California rolls I'd ever had.

"Cato, this California roll? Incredible."

"I'm glad you like it."

"Oh, and since it's getting dark soon, I was hoping we could maybe go for a walk on the beach and have a nice little bonfire."

"That sounds great! I'd love to."

I tipped the soy sauce onto my ginger-covered sushi and ate it in one bite. The avocado in the sushi was so fresh and sharp with the ginger tart aftertaste; it was great sushi. Alex had made himself some sashimi in the kitchen with tuna, salmon, shark, and red snapper. His plate was quite colorful and I stole a piece of red snapper sashimi; it was delicious.

"Red snapper is my favorite."

"Sorry, it was delicious."

Alex laughed and stole a piece of my California rolls.

"Hey! California rolls are my favorite."

"Sorry, it was delicious."

He smiled as he chewed my California roll and I ate his red snapper; it had a certain raw snap to it. I didn't enjoy it nearly as much as California rolls. I finished my last three rolls quickly, washing it all down with some fresh cool water. I put the glass and plate on the table since I had trouble getting up.

"Cato, can you do me a favor?"

"Sure thing, angel."

"Can you grab my—? Wait, what did you just call me?"

"What? Angel?"

"Yeah, why did you call me that?"

"You can't see it, but I see a pair of blue angel wings on you."

"Well, aren't you sweet? Do you think you can grab my crutches from my room so I don't have to lean on your shoulder the whole time for our walk?"

"Sure."

Alex took a drink of his water before rushing up the stairs and returning shortly with my crutches. He helped me up to my feet when I finished my meal and placed the crutches under my arms. I was fast on my crutches and challenged him to a race to the door; for obvious reasons, he won. The weather outside was cool and the stars were already popping out of the pitch-black sky. The full moon shone of a white sun in onto the sandy beach. Even on crutches, the cool sand felt nice as it squeezed up through the openings of my toes. My crutches didn't click on the sand as they would in the cabin. The walk was silent for a short time as the waves washed over my sandy bare feet.

"Don't you just love the stars?"

"I do! I can't believe how much we have in common."

"I love that about us! I'd point out the little dipper for you, but I just can't find it these days."

"Me too. However, I will show you where the Big Dipper is."

I stopped walking on my crutches and pointed straight up into the sky directly at the Big Dipper, leaning in slightly closer to Alex. He leaned in closer since he couldn't quite see it, and I had to point it out once more. I looked over at Alex and asked if he could see it yet and he nodded in return, but I was so close to Alex I practically kissed his cheek.

"Can you point out Orion for me?"

"Of course."

I easily found the belt of Orion not too far from the Big Dipper and pointed it out to Alex.

"Oh yeah, cool."

"Darn right cool."

Alex laughed as we continued to walk along the water's edge until I found the spot where Seth and I had made a fire last time.

"Over here! I made a fire here last time."

"There's even a log to sit on. Good job, Jill."

"Thanks, Cato."

I sat down on the log, patiently waiting for Alex to return with some firewood. He returned rather quickly with an armful of firewood.

"Did you bring some matches by chance?"

"I did."

I smiled as I handed him the matches, and he quickly ignited a fire with some dry underbrush.

"Aren't you cold wearing only shorts?"

"Well, I'm a little cold."

"Wait here! I'll be right back."

Alex sprinted off into the distance where we had come from. He was gone for thirty seconds, one minute, two minutes, three minutes, four minutes, and five minutes and so on.

"Sorry, I took so long."

I heard Alex shout from a short way. It looked like he was carrying two things in his arms, but I couldn't quite make them out. Finally, I recognized in the light of the fire a guitar in one hand and a blanket in the other. He even had a minute to make me a steaming hot cup of cocoa.

"You brought me cocoa and a blanket?"

"Yes, you said you were cold."

"Cato, you're so sweet."

"Thank you."

He wrapped the blanket around me and handed me the cocoa. It was perfectly hot and wonderful to drink.

"I hope you don't mind if I play a few chords on the guitar, do you?"

"Not at all."

I recognized the chords he played right away.

"Are you playing 'I'm yours' by Jason Mraz?"

"Maybe."

"Sing it for me."

Alex had a beautiful singing voice; it was quite heavenly, I assure you. His low voice tied in beautifully to the music of the guitar; his soothing voice could put me to sleep. I smiled as he continued to sing in the low voice of an angel as he sang.

"But I won't hesitate no more, no more. It cannot wait, I'm sure. There's no need to complicate. Our time is short. This is our fate. I'm yours."

Alex finished the final chords while I applauded and laughed as he continued to strum the chords singing.

We made a lovely duet of the song; both of us sounded so good. Alex started strumming along to another song I knew; it was called "Savior" by LIGHTS.

We sang together perfectly the chorus of the song.

I laughed as we continued the rest of the song, and the words flowed like water between Alex and me.

"We make an awesome duet."

"It's only because you have such an amazing singing voice."

"Are you kidding? Your voice when you sing is the most beautiful thing I've ever heard."

"Really?"

"Really, really, I never lie when it comes to good singers."

"Thanks, angel."

"Anytime."

Alex continued to strum random chords that had turned into a beautiful song without words. He had a real talent for playing the guitar, and even though it was just chords, it still sounded beautiful to me.

"May I make a request, Cato?"

"Sure."

"Can you play 'Summer Paradise' for me?"

"Of course, it's one of my favorites."

Alex played skillfully and sang it pitched perfectly to the song. I giggled to myself as he messed up one of the chords of the song. I could care less that he wasn't perfect.

I stopped him before he could finish and kissed him; he was warm and inviting as he gently placed the guitar on the sand and put his hands on my hips. I didn't want to let him go as I wrapped my hands around his warm neck. He squeezed my hips closer to him and I knocked down my hot chocolate onto the sand.

"Aw."

"Aw what?"

"I knocked down my hot chocolate on the sand."

"Do you want me to make you another one?"

"No, it's all right. One hot chocolate should be enough for tonight."

"All right, I'm going to get some more firewood."

"Wait! Put out the fire. I want to show you something."

"Okay."

Alex grabbed a few handfuls of saltwater to put out the fire until the coals of the fire sizzled to black. Once the fire stopped steaming, he picked up the guitar and threw it over his shoulder. He put his hand on the now empty cup of cocoa and tried to pick it up the same time I reached for it, forcing our hands to collide.

"My bad."

"Your hand is freezing."

"Yeah, sorry about that."

"Here, take the blanket."

Alex picked up the blanket and dropped it over my shoulders, wrapping it around me with an alluring grin on his face. He put his arm around my shoulders and I placed my arm on his.

"In case the blanket isn't warm enough," Alex whispered in my ear. I smiled, looking off to the side as we walked forth into the darkness ahead. I started seeing stars ahead of us in the light sky, lit by the bright full moon. It was already getting dark around nine or so I guessed since the clock was in the cabin. I immediately stumbled on a wet rock that forced my crutch to slip and Alex caught me before I could fall to the ground.

"Careful, I got you."

"Thanks, Cato."

I got to my feet once more and continued with each fast click of my crutches. Alex took his arm off me to open the door to the cabin.

"So what is it exactly that you wanted to show me?" Alex asked before closing the door with a click.

"It's not exactly here. It's somewhere special."

"Special?"

"Just follow me."

I opened the door by myself and sped outside toward the cavern in the water.

"Wait up," Alex yelled from behind me. I slowed down on my crutches and waited for him to catch up. His steps could be easily heard from behind me as he sprinted to my side. It didn't take long to reach the cavern, where I took off my shirt to show my bikini top underneath.

"Uh, Jillian? What are you doing?"

"We're going for a quick swim."

"But it's night."

"So?"

I laughed and heard its echo in the cavern as I stepped in the cool water and watched Alex take his shirt off. He pounced into the water with a small splash and dived down; I followed the light of the crystal on my neck in the blackness of the deep dark water.

"So where are we going?"

"Remember where I showed you the view of the island today?"

"Yes."

"Well, that's where we're going."

Alex knew the way and lit the path ahead for me to swim, reaching the small tunnel to the cavern. It was still smoking hot in there.

"I was hoping it would have cooled down by now."

I don't mind. I like it hot."

I glanced over at Alex and smiled before jumping out of the water, and my crippled ankle returned to its sore and useless state.

"You're going to have to help me up the stairs, Cato."

"No problem."

Alex came to my side and slowly but surely we made it up each step with a simple hop of my good leg. Once we reached the top, I leaped for the hammock and got comfy.

"Any room for me?"

"Of course, pop a squat."

I moved over to the left to make room for Alex as he snuggled in next to me.

"So how are you enjoying our date?"

"Love it. I've had an amazing time."

"And may I say, thank you for letting me steal some gems from your crystal cave?"

"My pleasure."

"And for what happened by the waterfall."

"Yes, I rather enjoyed that."

Alex smiled as he began to rock the hammock back and forth with his foot on the ground. His warm arm stretched over my shoulders and kept them warm as we gazed out at the stars.

"Check it out, a shooting star."

Alex pointed out to a spot in the sky where a streak of light danced over the stars.

"Well, make a wish then, Cato."

"I already did."

"What did you wish for?"

"I can't tell you!"

"Why not?"

"Because it won't come true if I tell you."

"Well, can you at least give me a hint?"

"It's about you."

I paused and smiled, looking at Alex's hazel eyes whilst still rocking the hammock that swayed in the warm tropical breeze. The rustle of branches on the side of the hammock was no surprise as it meant that Miko was coming. Shortly after the rustling sound, Miko leaped up and over the rocky edge and sat down on top of Alex and me.

"Hey, Miko, what are you up to?"

Miko shrugged his tiny, furry shoulders—the international symbol for I don't know.

"Is someone tired after a long run? Aw."

Alex petted the top of Miko's head and scratched away at his stomach. Miko began to yawn and curled up in a ball between Alex's and my legs, parallel to each other. Miko was fast asleep in a matter of minutes and snoozed happily on the warm hammock.

"He's a bit like a child, isn't he?"

"More like a hungry teenager. All he does is eat and leave the house."

"Good point."

Alex and I sighed when Miko stretched out and returned to his ball-like position. Miko made a great pet to have; he'd been my priority for over a year now, and caring for him was easy. He fed himself; he did his business in the forest and he visited from time to time for attention. I loved Miko as I would love my own child. He was there for me during the bad times and the good times, and he was even there through the whole mess and even saved my appetite for fruits by showing me the pomegranate tree. He was not just a pet in this case, but a friend, a very close, very special, and furry friend.

"What time is it?" Alex asked me.

"No idea. I'm guessing around nine forty-five, if we've been out here for ten minutes at least."

"We only have fifteen minutes left of our date?"

"I suppose so."

"Aw, I was having so much fun."

"Me too! But the date's not over yet."

"Hey, yeah, I feel a little bit better."

"How about I make you feel better?"

I turned over to Alex on my side and gently swayed the hammock.

"Close your eyes, Jillian."

"Why?"

"Just close your eyes," Alex whispered. I did so in quiet anticipation for whatever on earth Alex was up to. I waited patiently for a solid two minutes before I heard Alex say, "Open."

In front of my eyes was a carved peridot the size of his hand, the same shape of a heart and carved in precise straight lines.

"Oh, Cato, it's beautiful."

"The peridot is your birthstone, right?"

"It is. Thank you so much."

"I'm glad you like it."

Cato kissed the top of my forehead and looked down at my grinning face. He placed two fingers and thumb below my chin. I smiled again before he gently kissed me, and I placed a hand on his neck. His tongue twisted with mine in harmony as he pulled me closer to his chest. I embraced him happily and turned my head so my neck wouldn't get sore. I felt his hand slide behind my neck and felt a playful pull at the back of my hair; I loved it. Time passed faster than I had hoped when he stopped and gazed in my eyes. I smiled once more and nuzzled into his chest.

"I don't want to go," Alex said as he wrapped his arms around me.

"Me neither, but I think we only have about ten minutes left or so."

"It's not long enough."

"All good things must come to an end unfortunately."

"Mind walking me to the cabin then?"

"Of course."

Alex helped me up, and sweet Alex helped me down the stairs, step by step. He threw me in the water the second we reached the edge and my scream echoed in the cavern.

"That was rude!"

"It wasn't rude . . . I was just tired of carrying you."

I smiled as I splashed water at Alex. He splashed back. I flipped up my shimmering tail and splashed him with it. Alex said, "Stop," as he was coughing and laughing that I had beaten him. I laughed as he whipped his head back into the water and whipped his blond hair forward. He whipped his head from side to side, getting water droplets all over me and making me laugh harder.

"What's so funny, Jill?"

"Nothing, I love the way you whip your hair back and forth."

"Thanks, angel."

I smiled and kissed Alex. I heard a chuckle before I did so. He was just as warm if not warmer than the water. When I stopped, he had the biggest grin on his face and I grinned in return.

"I suppose we should head back."

"I suppose."

I dove underwater first and quickly reached the cavern before Alex was even there. I patiently waited for him to return before I saw the glow of his crystal emerge from the darkness below. Alex was smiling, although I didn't know why; he swam up to me and laughed.

"You have seaweed in your hair."

Alex pulled a piece of seaweed out from my long flowing hair.

"Oh, thank you."

Then he glanced down at my lips and lifted my face closer to his. He kissed me in the cool water, his lips hot as the cocoa that he had made me earlier today. My tail began to twist with his and I wrapped my hands around his neck one last time. The taste of saltwater tempted my lips, but Alex pulled me closer, and saltwater didn't touch my lips when he pulled me closer to him. A current came unbeknownst to me and twirled Alex and me upward toward the roof of the water. We stopped kissing just before we reached the top of the water, and I took a fresh breath of air at the top of the water and swam to the water's edge. As I got out and waited for my legs to return, Alex looked sad.

"What's wrong, Cato?"

"Are you going to choose me?"

"I don't know yet. Depends on how the other dates go, sweetie."

I moved some hair out of Alex's eyes and watched him smile back at me. He walked me back to the cabin, now reunited with my crutches. The second I reached the kitchen he grabbed me from behind and flipped me around in his arms. I laughed and saw the clock on the wall, which said it was ten o'clock sharp.

"Cato, it's ten."

"I wish this date wouldn't end."

"All good things, Cato—"

"I know must come to an end."

"It was a pleasure, Cato."

I snuck a kiss on his cheek before he put me down and gave me a hug, and then he left. I walked up to my room and changed into my pajamas, satisfied with tonight's date; there were only six more to go.

Chapter 26

I returned to eat a fruit in the kitchen and cracked into a juicy pomegranate. A few seeds popped out as I snapped it into half and a few drops of pomegranate juice dripped on the table. I took my time eating the pomegranate; I was in no immediate rush. Once I finished, I headed off to bed and crawled into it for the rest I needed for my date tomorrow.

The morning was warm and pleasant when I got out of bed and opened the closed curtains on the window. The sunrise lit the sky with a bright orange and pink hue that made my day even better than the last. I got dressed in my bikini and headed downstairs to make a banana pomegranate breakfast smoothie. I threw all the ingredients in the blender and turned it on to smoothie while I patiently waited for the fruit to blend. Once it finished blending, I turned it off and poured its contents into a fancy glad with a wedge of banana on the edge; it was delicious. I walked outside by my own, and I was half expecting a wake-up call from Seth, but he never came. If the order of seeing these guys was alphabetical, I'd be seeing Damian today. The only reason I picked him was because he had an amazing body. I don't think of it as shallow if I'm spending my day in the depths of the sea. Oh, what I'd do to that man if he were a hybrid. Anyways, I dove into the water bright and early, and the cold sea immediately woke me up. I was greeted by a school of fish that I hadn't seen before and a small baby dolphin and its mother on my way to Atlantis. I managed to make it there just fine to find Seth waiting at the gates for me. He waved with a smile on his face as I swam up to him.

"So how was the date?"

"Oh, just fantastic. He was so sweet and kind and a great kisser."

"I didn't need to hear that last part."

"Well, it's true."

"So what did you guys do?"

"I showed him the island and he saved my life from sharks."

"He fought off a shark attack?"

"He sure did."

"Nothing I haven't already done."

"Actually as I recall it, I saved myself from a shark and nearly died while you didn't hear me screaming for help."

"Did I mention I was sorry and eventually saved your life?"

"Whatever you say, Seth."

We reached the castle shortly; the castle was still as brilliant and decorated as before. Damian was looking amazing as always with ripped shoulders and arms and a bodybuilder's eight-pack under his pecs. Every man should look like Damian, especially with his caramel skin tone and perfectly sculpted jaw. He made my heart melt just looking at him.

"Nice to meet you again, Jillian."

"Nice to see you too, Damian. Are you ready to go?"

"You bet!"

Damian leaned over me and kissed me on the cheek. I blushed as he put his arm around my shoulders and swam forward. I did the same, waving back at Seth, who was still green with envy and jealousy.

"So, Damian, what do you do for fun under the sea?"

"I'll show you, but first I was hoping we could go treasure hunting."

"I love treasure hunting! Where are we raiding, hmm?"

"A sunken pirate ship off the edge of Atlantis."

Damian and I stopped at his place to grab some raiding bags, and then I followed him to the edge of Atlantis, not too far from his neighborhood actually. Damian told me he had been stealing treasure for years; he and his father couldn't get any work, and so they turned to a life of treasure hunting. Damian and his father got so good at treasure hunting they were assigned to find the king's lost treasure, but they couldn't ever find it. When the treasures were found after my arrival, the king rewarded them anyways and they repaid their debts.

"Now we just raid treasure as a hobby and we don't have to raid to survive."

"Cool story. How much longer until we get to the ship?"

"It's right there."

Damian pointed ahead, and sure enough, a massive ship was on the ground ahead of us. The ship was barely decomposed to be a pirate ship. It looked as if the ship had only sunk a few years ago.

"Just watch out for the sea mines."

"What sea—?"

I almost ran into a massive black ball with spikes coming out of it. Damian grabbed my hand and guided me through the maze of sea mines. But you see, these were no ordinary sea mines; they were much larger and therefore would lead to a bigger explosion. Once we reached the ship, Damian opened the door and three skeletons floated out. I screamed and grabbed on to Damian.

"Someone's a little jumpy. Relax, it's just skeletons."

"I'm fine, thanks for asking."

"C'mon, this ship isn't going to raid itself."

It was dark inside, but Damian had packed a flashlight so we could see. It was really spooky after we found more skeletons around the ship. One still had some decomposing flesh on its bones. We reached a dining room area that had a crystal chandelier that was hanging from the ceiling. It was beautiful, and Damian grabbed my hand and started dancing.

"Damian, what are you doing?"

"What does it look like? Dancing!"

"I never said I wanted to dance."

"Too bad! We're dancing!"

He grabbed my hand and started to tango in the dark. I played along, trying to salsa, but I didn't dance it all that well. His moves were stellar and blew me away. Meanwhile, I tried to dance; I looked as graceful as a jellyfish.

"Ta-da!" Damian said as he twirled me around in a circle. We finally stopped dancing and returned to raid the dining room. The dining room had jewels encrusted in everything you could find—a dining room, chairs, tables, candleholders, and even the fire poker. I went to work on the chairs, and Damian started working on the many candleholders on the tables. I had some difficulties in getting the gems out of the chairs, so I asked Damian for help.

"You just have to gently tap the top of the gems, like this."

Damian came up behind me and grabbed both my hands and picked up the chisel. He gently moved my hands to chip around the edges of the gem and eventually it popped right out.

"I did it!"

"Yeah! You did."

Damian snuck a kiss on my cheek, which made me smile. Underwater, the touch of his warm kiss on my cold skin was inviting and sexy. I looked back at all the gems I had to chisel out and sighed in early exhaustion. I chipped away at over two hundred gems in under an hour, all of which were in my raiding bag.

"How's it going over there?"

"Just great, Damian. I got over two hundred gems."

"Great!"

I chipped away at thirty more gems before Damian told me his bag was full to the brim with gems.

"Already?"

"Yep, I'm faster than you are."

"Oh yeah? I'll race you to the door then."

"It's on like Donkey Kong!"

My laughter echoed throughout the ship as I sped through the water. I was the first to touch the door and did a small celebration dance as Damian reached the door after me.

"Aw."

"You should owe me something for winning."

"How about I buy us dinner?"

"Sounds good."

Damian opened the door for me, and I swam out with caution toward the field of sea mines. I swam past them carefully, and for some reason I nearly dropped my bag.

"Careful, Jill, one little mistake and we'll be blown sky-high."

"No!"

A gem had fallen out of my bag and was headed straight for a sea mine.

"Watch out!"

Damian grabbed me and swam up and out of the way of the soon-to-blow sea mine. A small tink on the sea mine and I watched it blow to pieces, starting a chain reaction to blow up the other mines. Sure enough, Damian and I were blown out of the water. I must have flown one hundred feet in the air out of the water. Damian was having difficulties breathing in the air, as it was his first time out of the water. Eventually, I landed with a huge splash and so did Damian; he took a big gasp of water and immediately hugged me.

"I'm so glad you're okay."

"Thanks, Damian, I'm glad you care."

"Of course I care. What kind of person would I be if I didn't care?"

"A bad person."

"Ha-ha, lucky for you I'm a good guy."

He kissed me on the forehead before putting my bag over his big shoulders and swimming away with a smile on his face. I followed him back to his home in Atlantis and placed the bags on the couch in the living room. For a house underwater, it looked quite nice. Damian invited me to his room to put the bags of gems there instead.

"So this seems like a nice room."

"Sorry, I never got a chance to clean it."

Gems and treasure covered the floor, hiding the color of the carpet. It was beautiful to look at, but his room was still messy.

"So are you ready for dinner?"

"Sure am."

Damian opened the door of his room for me, letting me exit first. Atlantis looked brighter today in the light of day; children were playing in the park and people chatted along the paths, with bright blue crystals glowing on their necks. Damian and I walked along the paths and chatted about our lives. I told him how I got there, and just like Alex, he gave me a hug.

"It's not your fault."

"I know. It just hurts sometimes to know that my family is gone."

"I know what will make you feel better."

"And what is that exactly?"

"Food!"

I laughed as we approached the restaurants of Atlantis.

"What are you craving?"

"No idea."

"How about I pick?"

"Sounds good."

We passed the many sushi and Chinese food places, so it looked like I wouldn't be having any sweet and sour chicken or sushi tonight.

"How do wings sound?"

"Sounds great, Damian."

How on earth wings could be eaten underwater was questionable, but I could care less as this would be the first time I'd be having wings in over a year.

"Something tells me you haven't had wings in a while, have you?"

"How did you know?"

"Well, you've been living on an island for a year. Something tells me you don't get much chicken wings."

"Well, you hit the nail on that one."

Damian was a gentleman in opening doors for me, as he opened the door to the wings restaurant. It seemed like a bar-like atmosphere with two fights going on in the corner, a couple making out on the side, and oh yes, there was a bar.

"Are you sure this is a restaurant?"

"Well, it does look more like a bar."

"I'll say, do you want to go somewhere else?"

"Nope, we came for wings and this place has the best wings in Atlantis."

"All right."

I cautiously sat down at a table, and a friendly waitress came over and introduced herself.

"Hello, my name is Sarah and I'll be your waitress for this evening. What can I get you to drink?"

"Pepsi," both of us said at the same time. I hadn't had a soda in a year and I could sure use a Pepsi.

"So tell me whatever else you forgot to mention to me," Damian said with a smile.

"I can play the guitar and piano."

"No wonder you can sing so beautifully."

"You haven't even heard me sing."

"I was in the park when you first sang. You were fantastic."

"Well, thank you, it takes a lot to get me to sing though."

"Maybe you can sing for me later."

"Sounds like a plan."

Our drinks arrived shortly. How on earth they managed to stay in the glasses confused me.

"How come our Pepsi isn't floating away?"

"It's a crystal thing."

Maybe that was how the food didn't get soggy under the water. I thought about it for a few seconds on how the crystals could do such a thing as I took a sip of my ice-cold Pepsi. It was refreshing to have a soda pop after so long; I'd forgotten the joy of sweet carbonated goodness.

"Do you sing at all, Damian?"

"A little."

"Really? You should sing for me while I play guitar."

"Don't you know?"

"Know what?"

"I know how to play guitar."

"Why didn't you say so? We should jam out at your place after we eat."

"Aren't you supposed to wait half an hour to go singing?"

"I think that's for swimming, sweetie."

"Whoops, even so I'm not the best singer."

"Oh, pish-posh, I'm sure you're a great singer, Damian."

"We'll have to find out."

I smiled as the waitress Sarah brought us our two orders of wings quickly.

"Mind explaining how our food doesn't get soggy underwater?"

"Crystals."

I bit into my first spicy wing, and it was delicious. The crunch on the outside, the heat of the sauce, and the tender chicken that was torn right off the bone—it was good beyond words.

"This maybe the best damn chicken wing I've ever had."

"I told you this place had the best wings!"

"You were right."

I ate three more wings happily before asking Damian what kind of wings he had ordered.

"Trade a wing for a wing?"

"Sure."

It looked like he had ordered sweet and sour honey mustard wings; they were so good.

"I didn't know there were sweet and sour honey mustard wings."

"There are in Atlantis."

Damian took a bite of my wing and immediately took a drink of his Pepsi.

"Wow, yours are spicy."

"I like my wings hot."

Damian finished his last wing as I finished my second last, and I was just about to grab my last wing when Damian snatched it up and ate it before I could even gasp.

"Hey!"

"Got to be quicker there, JJ."

"JJ?"

"I hope you don't mind me calling you that. It suits you."

"Not at all."

He wiped his fingers with a complementary cleansing cloth and so did I; my fingers were coated with wing sauce.

"So what now?"

"We could go see a movie?"

"Sounds good."

"I already decided what we should see."

"And what movie did you pick?"

"*Paranormal Activity 4.*"

"Oh, a scary movie."

"I hope you don't mind scary movies."

"They're my favorite."

"Good, because the movie starts in half an hour."

"That's just enough time to get some popcorn!"

"Exactly!"

I followed Damian out of the restaurant, and we had started walking toward the movie theatre when he held my hand. I didn't mind because he was a lot more confident than I had hoped, but I loved it. We reached the movie theatre in no time and grabbed our tickets to see *Paranormal Activity 4*. Luckily, I had seen the last three movies, so this one had to be good. Damian bought the popcorn while I grabbed some cotton candy and Skittles to munch on with the popcorn. I held the drinks while we entered the theatre and found our seats, and I immediately sat down and ate some Skittles.

"You had better save room for dessert."

"I thought this was dessert."

"Nope."

I munched on some more popcorn and Skittles as the movie started and ate some cotton candy. The ominous crunch of me eating popcorn echoed through the theatre, even though I wasn't the only one eating popcorn. The movie was really good as the ending blew my mind. I just about had finished the cotton candy.

"That was a great movie."

"I was hoping you would say that. Ready for dessert?"

"I think so. What's for dessert?"

"Ice cream!" Damian threw his hands in the air, making me laugh. He invited me to the ice cream parlor where I ordered three scoops of triple tornado ice cream. Damian ordered the same thing; he had good taste. He ate the ice cream with me in the parlor, while he told me some of his favorite songs that he wanted to play on the guitar.

"I'd really like to play 'I'm Yours' for you tonight."

"I'd love to hear you sing it for me."

"Oh, I will."

I finished my ice cream quickly, which gave me a brain freeze, but the ice cream still tasted great.

"Oh, and thank you for buying dinner, and the snacks, and the ice cream."

"My pleasure."

He smiled as he finished off his ice cream cone. He had such an incredible smile to go with that sexy six-pack; my heart melted every time he smiled at me.

"So are you ready to go then?"

"You bet."

He continued to go on about how his father had taught him to play the guitar, and I didn't mind as it was easy to talk to Damian. This date was going really well for being completely underwater.

"What other songs can you play for me on the guitar?"

"You're going to have to find out."

His house was right around the corner, and Damian invited me up to his messy room once more. He grabbed the guitar and sat down on his bed and sang "I'm Yours." He had a beautiful singing voice and sang wonderfully.

"You have a wonderful singing voice, Damian."

"Thanks, JJ. I'll sing you one of my favorites."

I recognized the first lines of the song, but it wasn't until the chorus that I finally remembered that this was my favorite song at one point in my life.

"I started to sing the next part of the song while Damian happily played along on the guitar. We sang the chorus together beautifully when it came around, as he strummed the last few chords.

"Any other songs you want to play for me?"

"Just one."

He sang the rest of the song 'Wildflower' ever so nicely and strummed the last chords softly.

"What time is it by the way?"

"Nine thirty."

"Nine thirty? We only have half an hour left of our date?"

"Looks like it."

I quickly kissed him as he set down the guitar. He was a great kisser, as it turned into French in a short time span. He placed a hand behind my neck and gently pulled at the back of my hair, but it felt so good. He continued to kiss me for an easy twenty minutes before he stopped.

"You're a great kisser," Damian whispered in my ear before kissing my neck.

"Thank you. You're not so bad yourself."

"Thanks, I haven't exactly had that much practice."

"Damian, am I your first kiss?"

"Maybe."

"Don't lie to me, Damian."

"Okay, yes, you were."

"Well, congrats there, Damian. I'm proud to have been your first kiss."

"Thanks, JJ, I'm glad you were."

He tucked some free hair behind my ear and placed his large hand on my face. It was warm and I nuzzled into it; he kissed me softly once again. With his one hand still on my face, I wrapped my hands around his neck.

I embraced his final kiss before the date ended; ten came around far too quickly.

"Is it ten already?"

"Unfortunately."

"This was fun though."

"I sure had a good time, Jillian."

"Me too, Damian."

I kissed Damian on the cheek before swimming out the door on my way home. I wasn't greeted by Seth on my way out, so I swam back all alone. It was already dark when I emerged out of the water onto the sandy shore in the darkness. The moon was covered in clouds, so I could barely find my way back to the cabin. The light of my necklace was the only thing that lit the way to my room. Seth was already in there.

"Jesus, Seth, you scared me."

"So how did the first dates go?"

"Wonderful. Actually, my date with Alex was magical and Damian was a real gentleman."

"How so? I want details."

"Well, if you must know I showed Alex the island and in return he saved me from a shark attack while I was unconscious."

"Why were you unconscious?"

"Oh, I just smacked my head on a wall. The point is he made me dinner after I rolled my ankle and we sang on the beach together. He had such a beautiful singing voice, and then he kissed me."

"Was he a good kisser?"

"Yes, he was. Jealous?"

"Not at all. I already saved your life twice, so he's got nothing on me."

"Well, he certainly knows how to show a girl a good time."

"And Damian?"

"Well, we stole some gems out of a pirate ship and got blown out of the water by a giant sea mine, which was fun. Then we saw *Paranormal Activity 4* and had dinner and ice cream. Then he sang to me at his place."

"You didn't have sex, did you?"

"No, of course not! I don't even know how with a tail. But he was a skilled kisser."

"So far so good then?"

"So far so great."

"So any idea if you'll choose one of them?"

"Depends how the other dates go, Seth."

"I can't believe you can't date me."

"There isn't an eighth day in the week, Seth."

"You have no idea how bad I want to date you."

"Is that so?"

"It is. I would blow you away on just the single date and you'd love it."

"Unfortunately no."

I kissed Seth on the cheek and changed into my pajamas in the bathroom.

"If you're saying no to that you wouldn't love it, you'd be wrong."

"You've done all you could to blow me away, what could you possibly do on one date that would change that?"

I popped out of the bathroom in my pajamas.

"I wish I could get a chance to show you who I am."

"I already know who you are, Seth, and there's no need to get to know you any better if I know you so well."

"Can I stay with you tonight?"

"Of course, Seth."

I got into bed comfortably, and Seth snuggled right into me. I placed my hand on his bare chest and cuddled into him, falling asleep in his big strong arms.

Chapter 27

I woke up still in Seth's arms; he was sound asleep. I carefully lifted his arm off me and crawled out of bed to put on my bikini. Seth was still asleep when I walked out of the room and down the stairs to the kitchen. I was in the mood for something other than a smoothie until I realized that we had mangoes, and I threw one in a blender with some pomegranate juice and a banana with some yogurt in and hit blend. I heard the sound of Seth coming down the stairs and cut up some oranges to eat with my smoothie. I probably could've thrown them in.

"Good morning," I told Seth.
"You weren't there when I woke up."
"That's because you were still sleeping."
"Well, then you should've waked me. I hate not waking up next to you."
"Don't fret. I made breakfast for us."
"Oooh! What's for breakfast?"
"Mango pomegranate banana smoothies with oranges and eggs."
"Sounds great."
"How do you like your eggs?"
"Over easy."

I cracked three eggs into a hot frying pan and put some water in the lid and flipped it on the pan. I heard the sizzle of the eggs below the lid as I chopped up some more oranges. The spritz of the citrus jumped into my left eye, and I felt the burn and sting of the orange juice; it was safe to say it really hurt.

"Ouch."
"What's wrong?"
"Oh nothing, I just got some orange juice in my eye."
"Aw, you gonna be all right there, angel?"

"Yeah, I'll be all right."

Seth hugged me from behind and kissed me on the neck. I stopped him before he could turn around and kiss me as I walked over to the blender and turned the blender off.

"Seth, I can't do this."

"Can't do what?"

"How am I supposed to date five more guys with you on my mind?"

"I'm sorry if I'm on your mind, Jillian. Why am I on your mind exactly?"

"Because you're distracting me by kissing me on my neck and always hugging me all the time. It distracts me a lot from my goals."

"And what goals are they?"

"Marry one prince and live happily ever after."

"And you're sure of that?"

"Absolutely. I know for sure I'll be marrying someone soon, and I'll be glad he chose me too."

"If you say so."

I placed the perfectly cooked eggs on some plates and quickly seasoned them with some salt and pepper. The pink smoothie looked great as I poured the contents of the blender into two tall glasses and garnished the smoothies with whipped cream and a cherry on top.

"Breakfast is served."

"This looks great, angel."

"It is. I guarantee it."

Seth took a sip of the smoothie first and gave me a thumbs-up for the drink.

"This smoothie is incredible."

"I'm glad you like it, Jay . . . err, Seth."

"What did you call me?"

"Seth."

"No, before that."

"Jay."

"That was your old boyfriend, wasn't it?"

"Yes, he's been on my mind a lot lately."

"I'm sorry to hear that."

"It's not your fault, Seth. He's gone, and there's nothing I could've done about it."

I ran up to Seth for a hug as I began to cry.

"I miss him, Seth."

"Everything's gonna be all right, Jill."

Seth kissed me on the forehead before he returned to his breakfast.

"It kills me to see you cry, angel."
"I know, I'm sorry."
"Can't we just have a nice breakfast together?"
"Sure."

I stopped crying and returned to the table to eat my breakfast. The eggs had turned out perfect and the smoothie was fantastic. I started cleaning off the dishes when I finished my breakfast and waited for Seth to join me by the door.

"C'mon, I have a date to attend."
"I'm coming."

Seth ran past me and out the door, leaving a trail of dust behind him.
"Hey! Wait up!"

He was sprinting for the water and beat me there. In a waterless splash, Seth was gone. I jumped in quickly after him and then saw him waiting for me at the drop-off for me.

"Aren't you supposed to be rushed?"
"Who said I was in a rush to meet Lucas?"
"He's a really cool guy. I think you'll like him."
"Good to know."

We swam in silence all the way to Atlantis and reached the city in a short amount of time. The people of Atlantis greeted me cheerfully, and two kids wanted to play ball with me.

"Sorry, kids, I have a date."
"Are you going on a date with Seth?"
"No, no, I'm going on a date with Lucas."
"You should go on a date with Seth," the little girl told me.
"Sorry, I never picked him."
"Well, you should've. Seth's a swell guy."

The two kids ran off to the park with their ball and played together.
"Do you know those kids, Seth?"
"Nope."
"Well, they seem to like you."
"Everybody loves the princes."
"True."

We swam up to the palace, where Seth opened the door for me; Lucas was waiting patiently for me inside.

"Lovely to see you again, Jillian."
"Nice to see you too, Lucas. You ready to rock?"
"Hell, yeah, let's roll."
"Have fun, you two."

Seth waved to us as we left. He wasn't green with envy for a change; something was different about him today.

"So what are your plans for today?"

"Our plans, Jillian, are first I thought we'd hit a hybrid nightclub."

"Doesn't that imply that we go at night? It's quite early to go dancing as it is."

"Oh well, we can go later, I suppose."

"That sounds great."

We left Atlantis quickly and swam for the island. The water was cool and clear, perfect swimming conditions for a hot day like today. The second I walked out of the water I dried out, it was that hot. I raced Lucas to the cabin but lost. I muffled around the medicine cabinet for sunscreen. I did manage to find some 100 SPF strength sunscreens which were just fine for me.

"I'm gonna pack us a little lunch for a hike, if that's okay."

"Sounds good."

I made some peanut butter and jelly sandwiches, though I doubted I'd get the same reaction as last time. Lucas grabbed a mango off the counter and began to eat it; I realized that was the last mango in the house while I finished packing the lunch. I finished packing in less than five minutes, and it looked like we were completely out of mangoes.

"I'm going to have to make a pit stop at a certain fruit tree for some mangoes, if you don't mind."

"Not at all."

I finished packing the last of the lunch as I snuck a chisel into the bag, while Lucas finished up his mango.

"Let's go."

I looked for Miko in the house, and lo and behold, he was in the kitchen, eating the last mango.

"That's the last mango, Miko."

Miko immediately ran for the door I had just opened as I gestured to Lucas to follow me. I ran to catch up; the sudden rustle of bushes signaling Miko's entrance into the forest. There were many bushes and trees I ran into, but we finally reached the mango trees.

"Thanks, Miko. Help yourself to as many mangoes as you wish."

Miko grabbed two out of the tree and walked away on his two feet. I was still too short to reach the fruit, and Lucas immediately ran to my side to help. He did so with ease, filling my bag with lots of mangoes.

"Five more."

"How many mangoes do you need?"

"A lot, Miko and I eat a lot of fruit."

"I can tell here." He handed me a mango. "Just for you."

"Thanks, Lucas."

I took a bite into the juicy mango, its warm juices running down my chin and neck. I was a hot, sticky mess after I finished the mango. Lucas finished pulling the last of the mangoes as I desired.

"That's perfect, Lucas, thanks."

"Anytime, angel."

"Why does everybody call me that?"

"Well, it's true. You are an angel."

"Thanks, Lucas, you're so sweet."

"Thank you."

I picked up the bag which was now twenty pounds heavier, and I ran up into the bushes.

"Where are you going?"

"Follow me!"

It took a much shorter time to find what I was looking for; it only took us about ten minutes to find the crystal oasis.

"Behold, Lucas."

I pulled back the bushes that were hiding the incredible view.

"The crystal oasis."

"It's beautiful."

"It is, isn't it?"

"I wasn't talking about the waterfall."

I blushed as I found the same shady spot where Alex and I had lunch the last time.

"I made peanut butter and jelly sandwiches, if that's okay."

"That's just fine. I love peanut butter and jelly."

He reached into the bag and pulled a sandwich out of the bag and scarfed it down in the same time it took for me to eat a mango. As soon as I threw the core away, I took my shirt off, walking toward the water.

"Umm, Jill, why are you taking your shirt off?"

"I do it . . .," I took my pants off, "to feel human again."

I gave an inviting smile toward Lucas, then walked away in my sexy bikini.

"Wait for me. I want to feel human too!"

I jumped in with a splash and an ahhh, tipping my head back into the cool water.

"Why is my tail not forming?"

"We only grow tails in saltwater, silly."

"I didn't know that. It's so nice to swim with my legs for a change."

"I know, right?"

Lucas suddenly dived underwater and didn't surface right away. Knowing Lucas, he'd probably swim up behind me and scare me, so I turned around. When he didn't surface, I panicked.

"Lucas, where are you?"

I turned in a circle twice and there was no sign of Lucas. I felt something brush my leg before I was lifted out of the water and eventually thrown into the air.

"What the—?"

Splash! I crashed down into the cool water and surfaced as fast as I could.

"What the hell was that for?"

"My arm slipped."

"You jerk!"

I splashed him with my hand and I heard him sputter with freshwater in his mouth and in his hair, making me laugh.

"Hey, take it easy."

"That's what you get for throwing me."

"What? Do you want me to be a bit gentler?"

"Yes, actually, you would be a better man if you were—"

I was cut off by his kiss. He dropped his hands in the water quietly and placed his hands on my submerged hips. I in turn wrapped my arms around his neck as he French-kissed me and lifted me out of the water and onto his hips. A hidden smile crept out from under my kiss, the water deflecting off my back from the waterfall. After he finished, he stared into my eyes and a grin grew on both our faces.

"So are you going to put me down or what?"

"I don't think I will. I kind of like you sitting on my hips."

"Well, you have to put me down at some point."

"When?"

"Like now."

"Aw, do I have to?"

"Yes, Lucas."

"Aw, okay."

Lucas gently set me back down into the water, and I swam for the edge and grabbed the bag.

"Why did you grab the bag?"

"Because the way back to the cabin is down."

"What?"

"Just follow me."

I placed the bag on my back and dove down into the water below. I kicked with all my might and reached down to the crystal cavern in a short amount of time. My tail formed as I welcomed Lucas to the crystal cave.

"Wow, is this cave all yours?"

"All mine, but you're welcome to take some crystals for yourself."

I pulled the chisel out of the bag and put it in Lucas's hand; I was thanked with a smile. He chiseled away at every single type of gem that was in the cave and put them all in the bag. He chipped off a peridot at the last and put the chisel back into the bag.

"Thanks, Jillian, this means a lot to me."

"Don't mention it. Seriously though, I don't want people stealing from this place."

"Your secret's safe with me."

I swam ahead of him, and with the flick of my hand, I asked him to follow me.

"Is that a current I feel?"

"Yes. Is the bag zipped up?"

"Yep."

"Good, because it's going to be a bumpy ride."

The current pulled both Lucas and me forward as fast as a train. Soon, I was being thrust forward at such a fast speed I almost fainted. Keeping our consciousness, we popped out of the cave—without hitting my head—just fine and splashed into the water below.

"That was fun!" Lucas commented. I laughed as I swam up around Lucas, flicking my tail at his before swimming away.

"And just what do you think you're up to?"

"Nothing, just a little love tap."

I swam back and kissed him on the cheek before swimming back up to the surface of the cavern. It was hot as usual, and I dove back under to return to the much cooler entrance behind the cabin.

"Well, that was a nice little adventure. What's next?"

"Dinner."

"Oh good, I'm starving."

We walked out of the water, me in my bikini bottom and Lucas in his colorful swimming trunks. We walked back to the cabin hand in hand, discussing what we could have for supper.

"How about steak?"

"We're out of steaks."

"Chicken alfredo?"

"Out of chicken."

"Taco salad?"

"Sure."

"Finally!"

Lucas opened the door to the cabin for me and got the beef out of the freezer.

"It's rock hard, Jill. It'll have to thaw for a few hours."

"Let's have a bonfire on the beach then."

"Sounds good to me."

I secretly grabbed the guitar, but Lucas spotted it right away.

"What are you grabbing the guitar for?"

"I was going to surprise you with some music."

"I don't get surprised easily."

"I can tell."

Lucas opened the door for me, and I stepped out with the guitar in my hand. It didn't take long to find the spot where Alex, Seth, and I had a fire.

"Right here, Lucas. Go get some firewood."

"You got it."

Lucas disappeared into the bush of the forest and returned shortly with an armful of firewood.

"So are you going to play any songs for me?"

"As soon as you sit down I will."

Lucas quickly made a fire and sat down by my side with his chin on his hands, staring up at me. I laughed as I began to sing "I'm Yours" to him.

"Please sing another song. You have such a beautiful voice."

"Thanks, Lucas. I'll sing you one of my favorites."

""That was fantastic. I love that song."

"How about you sing a little something for me?"

"I can't play the guitar though."

"I'll play you sing."

I was strumming along to a song called "Loving You Tonight." Luckily, he knew the song.

I clapped as soon as he finished the song and kissed him on the cheek.

"Thank you for singing, Lucas."

"Anytime, angel."

I laughed to myself as quietly as I could, but Lucas caught me.

"What's so funny, angel?"

"Oh, you just look adorable when you sing," I told him as I moved some hair out of his eyes. He warmed his hands close to the fire and slid a bit closer to me.

"Any other songs you can sing for me?"

"Just one. It's called 'Shadow of the Day.'"

"I close both locks below the window, I close both blinds and turn away, sometimes solutions aren't so simple, sometimes good-byes the only way, oh," Lucas began to sing."

"I didn't know you knew that song 'Shadow of the Day'."

"There are lots you don't know about me."

"Oh? And what's that?"

"It's a mystery."

I laughed as he put my head on his shoulder and put his arm around me. His arm was warm on my skin of this day on shoulder, and in his arms, I sighed and closed my eyes as he pulled me closer into his chest that I happily embraced. I felt him kiss my forehead and I silently smiled; we both sighed, looking into the fire.

"Jillian?"

"Yes, Lucas?"

"I think the beef should be thawed by now."

"Okay, let's go."

Lucas unarmed me, laughing as I did the same, and we put out the fire with handfuls of sea water. Once the fire was out, Lucas took my hand as we walked back to the cabin.

"Hey, angel? Things for singing tonight."

"No problem, Lucas. It was my pleasure."

"So now we make tacos?"

"Yep."

"And then the nightclub?"

"Sure."

It didn't take long to reach the cabin, where I touched the cold beef that was now thawed. I gathered all the ingredients out of the fridge with Lucas throwing the beef in a pan. I started chopping tomatoes and bell peppers as I heard the sizzle of beef that had begun to cook. I felt Lucas wrap his arms around my stomach and kiss my neck.

"Shouldn't you be watching the beef, Lucas?"

"Not really. I put a lid on it."

"Oh good, then you can start chopping up some lettuce."

I handed him the head of lettuce and knife. He sighed as he took the knife and started chopping lettuce. I looked around the food cabinet and found some tacos.

"How would you feel about having some tacos tonight?"

"Doesn't matter."

"Tacos it is then."

I grabbed the tacos and threw them in the oven to cook up a bit. Lucas finished chopping up the lettuce and asked me what else he could do.

"You can get the Ranch dressing out of the fridge."

"Yay!"

Lucas threw his hands in the air like an idiot and made me laugh.

"I love your laugh, Jillian."

"Thanks, Lucas, you're the first person to tell me that."

"You're welcome."

Lucas turned to the beef to stir it. The beef smelled so good and its aroma filled the entire cabin. Lucas focused on cooking the beef just right; he was doing well.

"I think it's done, Lucas."

"Perfect timing too. The timer for the tacos is going off."

"Wonderful."

A stop the timer and pulled it up with some of the oven. They were perfectly hot and ready to eat as Lucas poured the taco meat into a bowl.

"Grab the shredded cheese out of the fridge, would you, Lucas?"

"Sure."

I grabbed a taco from the cooking palette and started to place meat on it. I grabbed about a handful of shredded cheese and sprinkled it on the hot meat so the cheese would melt. I added the tomatoes, more cheese, bell peppers, lettuce, and Ranch sauce. I sat down at the table with Lucas Huard. He had finished making his taco and was already taking his first bite. My taco was delicious and I finished quickly as I wanted another taco. The next taco was equally good. As soon as we finished our tacos, we both cleaned up the dishes together. Lucas watched while I dried the dishes that I had washed, and I was a little upset he didn't help out at all.

"You know you could've helped me with the dishes a little."

"I'm saving my strength for dancing, baby girl."

"Sure you are."

It didn't take long to finish up the last of the dishes and put everything away. Lucas cleaned up in the back before he came back downstairs. He looked very handsome, wearing one of the necklaces I had made. He was wearing the wolf totem which represented strength, kindness, wisdom, and a loving nature.

"So are you ready to go dancing?"

"You bet."

Lucas opened the door of the cabin for me and let me exit first. It wasn't long before we reached the water and I dived into the cold water; as it was now night, the water was colder than usual.

"Do you find the water a bit cold today?"

"It is a bit cold, but I think I'll warm up on the dance floor."

"I hope you're right because I am freezing."

"Don't worry, the club will be a lot warmer."

It didn't take long to reach Atlantis though it was already dark in the water. Lucas's necklace lit the way and in no time at all we reached the club.

"You ready to party, Jillian?"

"You bet your ass I am!"

"Awesome."

A bouncer at the front gate asked us if we were hybrids, and I guaranteed him I was a hybrid.

"You know that if you are lying you will die from lack of water within our club."

"Don't worry, sir. I am a hybrid."

"Then come on in."

The club was completely full of air, and the second I walked in my legs returned. It was nice that I would be dancing on my legs tonight.

"Oh, I love this song. Let's go dance."

I grabbed Lucas's hand and ran over to the dance floor to dance to "Cotton Eye Joe." I hadn't danced to that song in over a year. It was nice to dance with Lucas on my legs; oh, how I missed dancing!

"You don't mind grinding, do you?"

"I love it."

The next song was perfect to grind to, and Lucas put his hands on the inside of my legs and pulled me up on him. I had missed the sensation of grinding with a guy for so long; it was relaxing to be with another guy doing what I loved. The grinding topped the rest for the evening, but it was so much fun. I saw Seth in the club and asked him to join us; he took the front and Lucas took the back. My heart raced as I was grinding up as Seth after I wanted to do it for so long but to make Seth a little jealous. Lucas kissed my neck while Seth was standing right there. I could see the color in Seth's face change from caramel skin tone to green with envy. I laughed as the next song came on and Seth decided to go.

"Sounds like you two are having a good time. I don't want to spoil it."

"You're not ruining anything, Seth, in fact making this night even better."

"Are you sure?"

"I'm positive, Seth. Stay a little longer."

"Okay, I will."

Seth stayed for the next couple of songs, grinding with me while Lucas was temporarily in the bathroom.

"You've no idea how long I've wanted to grind with you."

"And how long is that exactly?"

"Quite a while now."

"That's good to know."

Seth leaned down and tried to kiss me, but I stopped him and told him I was on a date.

"Don't even think about it, Seth."

"Why not, angel?"

"Because I'm on a date with Lucas. Just because he's gone, does it mean that you get to kiss me?"

"We don't have to tell anyone."

"No, Seth, maybe another time."

"Okay."

Seth continued to grind with me until Lucas got back.

"I'll take it from here, Seth."

"You got it, bro."

Seth and Lucas pounded their fists together, and Seth finally left.

"He tried to kiss you, didn't he?"

"Yeah, but I stopped him."

"That's my girl."

Finally, after couple of hours the grinding song started to slow down and slow music started to play.

"How about it, angel, you save the last dance for me?"

"Of course, Lucas."

Just then, the song known as "save the last dance for me" began to play and Lucas invited me to dance. We started to tango; we were both very skilled in this type of dance. When each twirled me, I felt like a professional dancer on the dance floor and clapped as I finished.

"That was great, Lucas."

"Yeah, that was fun."

"What time is it?"

"Nine thirty."

"What do you say we head to the back of the club and make the best of our last half hour?"

"Sounds good to me."

We walked to the back of the club, where he kissed me aggressively. I didn't mind because he was a great kisser. His skill was nothing like those of Alex or Damian or in fact any other guys I'd kissed; he was spectacular. I wrapped my arms around his neck as he pulled me closer into his chest. He was so warm and inviting it was just a bonus that he was a great kisser. He kissed me for half an hour before I looked at my watch and realized it was ten.

"Lucas, I have to go."

"Please don't go."

"I have to, Lucas. It's ten."
"I don't want to leave."
"I don't wanna leave either, but the date's over."
"I want to spend more time with you."
"Don't worry. You'll see me soon at the choosing of the future husband."
"Are you going to pick me?"
"We'll see, Lucas."

I kissed him good-bye and waved as I left Atlantis. The date with Lucas had gone really well. I couldn't believe his kissing skills. I wasn't going to forget about that kiss anytime soon. I reached home safe and sound, and Seth was waiting for me there once more.

"God damn you, Seth, you scared me."
"Aw, did I scare you? I'm sorry."
"No need to apologize. You always scare me."
"Oh, ouch, that hurt."
"I can't help it. It's true."
"If I scare you so much, why am I still here then?"
"Because you invited yourself in. I think you should go, Seth."
"Why?"
"Because if I kiss you, something bad could happen."
"What could possibly happen if I kiss you?"
"I might love it."
"Is that a bad thing?"
"Yes, I can't fall in love with you because I have three more dates to attend and the husband I choose can't be you."
"And why not?"
"Because I can't choose you."
"You could've picked me, you know."
"No, I don't choose guys who save my life."
"And why not?"
"Because I feel I owe them some sort of debt."
"One kiss won't kill you."
"I know it won't, but I don't want to take the risk."
"Risk what?"
"Our friendship."
"Now, you know I want to be more than friends."
"I know you do, Seth, but I just can't, not tonight."
"Just one kiss."
"No."
"Just a tiny kiss?"
"Nope."

"And why not?"
"I just can't, Seth."
"Like it or not, I'm going to kiss you."
"No, you won't."
"I will."
"Why you pushing this?"
"Because I love you!" Seth shouted.
"I can't, Seth. You know that."
"I've always loved you, Jill."
"I know you have, but I don't."
"I don't care. I just want to be with you."
"You can't, Seth."
"I know I can't. Just please let me kiss you."
"I already said to you no."
"Just a quick kiss."
"Fine, whatever."

Seth lifted my chin up closer to his and placed his hand on my neck. Placing his other hand on my face, he pulled me close to him. He gently kissed me and was about to put his hands on my waist to get comfortable when I pulled away.

"Now was that so bad?"
"No, it wasn't."
"See, now I feel a lot better."
"Glad to know."

I looked up at Seth and smiled as I started walking toward the stairs to go up to my bedroom.

"Wait!"
"What is it, Seth?"
"Can't I stay one more night?"
"I suppose."

Seth ran up the stairs before I could move and jumped right into my bed. He got under the covers and got comfy while I changed into my pajamas in the bathroom. He was already half asleep by the time I got back and crawled in next to him. I felt his arms wrap around my stomach and pull me close to his chest.

"Night, angel."
"Good night, Seth."

I was comfy and warm in Seth's arms and snuggled in close for another good sleep. Tomorrow, I would attempt to talk to Peter on another date, with a total of four more dates to go.

Chapter 28

I woke up in Seth's arms once more for the second time. This time I stayed with Seth until he woke up.

"Morning."

"Good morning, Jillian. Ready for your date with Peter?"

"Ready as I'll ever be."

Seth rolled over and off the bed, landing with a thump on the ground, an "ouch" following it.

"Are you okay, Seth?"

"Yeah, I'm all right."

Seth got up from the floor and immediately put his hand on his hip.

"Seth, you have a bruise."

"Really?"

"Is there anything I can do to help?"

"There is actually. Bring your crystal over here."

I got out of bed, grabbed my necklace, and brought it to Seth.

"Shine it on my bruise, then place your hand on it."

I shone the light of the crystal on to his bruise and gently placed my hand on it. He groaned; the moment I took my hand away, the bruise was gone and a blue handprint melted into his skin.

"That was freaky."

"It is a little bit, but hey, it works."

"I better get dressed."

"Or we can get undressed."

"No, Seth."

"Aw."

I ran off to the bathroom to change from my pajamas into my bikini. I changed quickly since Seth was already making breakfast downstairs.

"Any idea what Peter will do for you today?"

"No idea, but rumor has it there's a carnival in Atlantis today."

"Who told you?"

"Lucas."

"Aw, it was going to be a surprise."

"You mean to tell me that the carnival is for me?"

"It is. They're throwing a party to celebrate the choosing of your future husband."

"Maybe Peter will take me to the carnival."

"Maybe."

I headed downstairs to the already made breakfast awaiting me. Seth had made bacon and eggs; where he got the bacon, I did not know, but I was glad he had got it.

"Where did you get the bacon, Seth?"

"I slaughtered a pig this morning."

"But you just woke up."

"While you were up there, I killed a pig on the island and brought back the bacon."

"Well done."

I ate the bacon happily as I hadn't had bacon in over a year. Oh, how I had missed bacon.

"Excited?" Seth asked me.

"A little. Peter is really shy."

"Yeah, but he's cool once you get to know him."

"Really?"

"Yep."

"Thanks for the tip."

I finished my breakfast, cleaned up, and threw the dishes in the sink. Seth said he would clean up the kitchen for me while I was gone and demanded that I go off on my date. I agreed as I walked out the door toward the beach.

"Have a good time!" I heard Seth yell from the kitchen.

"Thanks, Seth," I yelled back. The water was cool as I dove in and my tail formed quickly. I thought, "The colder the water is, the quicker my tail forms." Seth was mysteriously behind me for a while. I didn't know it until I noticed a shadow over me and spotted Seth.

"Some people call that stalking, Seth."

"I like to call it sneaking."

"Well, stop sneaking up on me."

"Sorry."

The Tail of an Angel

Up ahead of Seth, I saw Atlantis; it was looking rather bright today, as I saw the lights from the carnival. I couldn't wait for my date with Peter if he was going to take me to the carnival. The palace looked very nice today, decorated in rubies. Peter was waiting inside, wearing a shark tooth necklace today and looking good in it.

"Good morning, Jillian."

"Good morning, Peter. How are you?"

"Great now that you're here."

I blushed as Peter grabbed my hand, and we walked out to the palace.

"I hope you don't mind, but I was hoping we can go to the carnival."

"I'd love to, Peter."

That was the most one could ever hear Peter say. It was good to hear him talking some more; he had such a beautiful voice.

"I'm gonna buy some cotton candy. Would you like some?"

"Definitely."

Peter walked up to the food booth and grabbed two cotton candies, one blue and one pink.

"Blue or pink?"

"Blue."

"If you want purple, I can always go buy some more."

"One bag should be plenty, Peter."

Peter pointed at a roller coaster and insisted I'd go on it.

"Peter, I'm scared of roller coasters."

"I'll be right with you. You won't be scared."

"You promise?"

"I promise."

Peter raced over to the roller-coaster line and got us tickets. I was scared to death to go on the roller coaster.

"I'm scared, Peter."

"You'll be fine. Don't be such a chicken."

"I'm not a chicken!"

"Then come on!"

He grabbed my hand and pulled me toward the roller coaster, and we buckled ourselves in and prepared for the ride.

"I want off."

"Too late now, the ride is about to start. You'll be fine."

"I sure hope so."

The ride took off very quickly and swept my hair back; the ride had twists and turns. Sometimes it went up, down, sideways, and at other times below, and it launched forward at an incredible speed. Finally, there was a huge drop at the end of the roller-coaster ride, which made me grab on to Peter.

"Someone scared?"

"A little."

He kissed me on the cheek just as the camera took a picture of us.

"Here's your souvenir photo. Have a great day," the man at the end of the roller-coaster ride said.

The photo was timed perfectly to catch Peter kissing me on the cheek and it caught a smile.

"Good thing we got two photos."

"Yeah, good thing. We look so cute together."

"We do make a good couple."

"What's next?"

"The haunted house."

"That sounds like fun."

We swam toward a haunted house nearby and entered with caution.

"I'm scared. I have never been to a haunted house before."

"Relax, you'll be just fine with me."

We entered the haunted house where the first thing that popped out was a ghost that scared me and made me latch on to Peter.

"You frighten easily, don't you?"

"Yep."

Next popped out a witch that scared me once more. After the haunted house, we headed over to the tunnel of love.

"I don't know if I want to head in there."

"Oh c'mon, we're on a date. It should be in the fine print for a date."

"Well, okay."

There was a boat that we got into, which went into a dark tunnel. It was so dark that we both couldn't see a thing.

"I can't see anything here."

"Me neither. Isn't it wonderful?"

"You were so weird, Peter."

"You like weird guys, don't you though?"

"You're right, I do."

Peter gently kissed me in the dark and I kissed him back. The kiss surprised me as I thought it was an obstacle in the tunnel hitting me. Peter French-kissed me until the tunnel lit up with cupids all over the tunnel.

"Oh boy, cupids."

"I hate cupid."

"Me too, always hitting arrows at people."

"Exactly! That's dangerous."

"I know, right!"

And I felt something hit me on my back, and I pulled an arrow out. It wasn't even in my back. The hanging by a string and gently stabbed me. The arrowhead and engraved cupid name on it until I threw the arrow away which accidentally hit Peter.

"Did you just throw cupid's arrow at me?"

"No!"

"Because it hit me in the arm."

"Is it not bad luck to get hit with cupid's arrow?"

"I think that means you fall in love."

"Well, I ain't falling for you."

"I think I might."

"You really think so?"

"Yes, I do."

Peter kissed me once more before the tunnel ride ended. At the end, he gave me a rose he had found in the tunnel.

"For you, my dear."

"Thanks, Peter."

I smelled the rose, while Peter kissed me on the cheek and returned to eating his cotton candy.

"Your tongue is blue."

"Your tongue is red."

"Let's make it purple."

I raised my eyebrow as he looked at me, his big green eyes staring back at mine. He kissed me until my tongue turned purple. It only took about five minutes.

"There, your tongue is now purple."

"So is yours."

"Wonderful."

Peter gently kissed me once more before we went on the carousel. Peter figured that I'd been through a lot today, so he thought I should take something a little easy.

"I've never been on a carousel before."

"Well, congratulations on your first time."

"Thanks, Peter, you're so sweet."

"Anytime, JJ. I hope you don't mind me calling you that."

"Not at all."

We get our tickets to ride the carousel and I found a horse that was available. Peter found a horse that was right next to mine.

"You ready to rock?"

"Hell yeah!"

The carousel started moving very slowly, then started to speed up over time.

"Rock and roll!"

"Yeah, Jillian, you ride the pony!"

"Woo! It's not the only thing I can ride."

"Oh?"

"You know what I'm talking about."

"Oh, that's hot."

We continued to ride the carousel until it stopped and Peter and I got off.

"That was awesome!"

"Maybe you could show me the other thing you ride."

"I'd love to."

"How exactly do mermaids have sex?" Peter coughed and sputtered a bit.

"Just like fish do. The women lay eggs and the men fertilize."

"Ew."

"Yeah, then the eggs are grown into mermaids."

"So every mermaid is a virgin?"

"Basically."

"Damn, you're really missing out."

"Is sex really awesome?"

"Oh yeah."

"And you'd know this because . . ."

"One I'm a hybrid, and two, I've had sex before."

"Seriously?"

"Seriously."

"Damn."

"Were you hoping to sleep with me?"

"Well, I sort of can't without giving you a child."

"Yeah, and no one really wants that."

"Yeah, I'm too young to get a girl pregnant."

"Me too."

"What?"

"Ha-ha, let's go."

We went to the food booth to get some supper and had hot dogs.

"I haven't had hot dogs in literally a year."

"Good to know."

I ate the hot dog in under a minute I was so hungry. Peter laughed as I finished the hot dog and licked my fingers.

"What time is it?"

The Tail of an Angel

"Nine forty-five."
"We only have fifteen minutes left of our date?"
"Yep."
"Finish your hot dog, Peter."
"Okay."
He took the last bite of his hot dog and swallowed it, as I gestured to him to follow me. When I found a good, I stopped. I grabbed him and kissed him. For fifteen minutes, I kissed him to the best of my abilities and felt his hand on my waist. The other hand of his was behind my neck and pulling me close. Peter was a good kisser too. When ten rolled around, we had one final kiss and said good-bye.
"Thanks for the kiss."
"Thanks for the rose."
"Wait."
Peter brought the rose closer to his crystal and then the rose turned blue.
"A blue rose will never whither."
"Thank you, Peter. Have a good night."
"You too, JJ."
The day had gone well, I thought as I swam back home. It was dark and Seth was waiting for me back in the cabin.
"How many times are you gonna scare me to death?"
"As many as it takes for you to say you love me."
"That's never gonna happen."
"You can't resist me, Jillian."
"Yes, I can."
"Just admit it, you care about me."
"As a friend."
"Only a friend, Jilly Bean?"
"Don't call me that!" I snapped.
"Sorry for giving you a cute nickname."
"No, it's not that. It's what my boyfriend used to call me."
"I'm sorry. Do you like JJ better?"
"I do."
"JJ it is then." Seth came up to me and gave me a hug. "I'm sorry if I keep reminding you of your old boyfriend."
"It's not your fault."
"Yes, it is. I can't help it."
"Just call me JJ from now on."
"I will."
"Thank you."

"So how was the date?"
"Great, Peter is a really sweet guy."
"So it looks like Shawn is next."
"Yep, I'm looking forward to my date with him."
"Oh?"
"He blew my mind with the flower trick. I'd love to see what he can do on a date."
"Is that so?"
"It's true."
"Well, I hope you two have a very nice date."
"Thanks, Seth."
"Can I sleep here again tonight?"
"Sure."

Seth held my hand as we walked up the stairs to my bedroom and invited me to come sit on the bed in my bikini.

"I have to change, Seth."
"How about I take it off?"
"If you think we're going to have sex, you're dead wrong."
"Just spend the night with me and I guarantee you'll never forget it."
"No, Seth."
"C'mon."
"No means no."
"And I say yes."
"No, Seth."
"Fine.
"The only thing you can do to me is kiss me."
"Can I kiss you right now?"
"Of course."

Seth kissed me on the lips gently as I lay down on the bed with him on top of me. I felt Seth reach behind my back and attempt to unhook my bikini top, but I stopped him from doing so.

"Not so fast there, Seth."
"Please let me unhook your top."
"No, Seth."
"Fine. I'm gonna unhook that top sometime though."
"In your dreams!"
"Whatever you say, JJ."

He kissed me again, but a lot harder this time and French. Seth was an incredible kisser, and he blew my mind as I melted in his mouth. I wrapped my arms around his neck as he lifted me up off the bed. I was off the bed

The Tail of an Angel

completely under Seth. I lowered myself back down, and he quickly flipped me over on top of him.

"Your turn on top."

"But I like the bottom."

"That sounds dirty."

"I like it dirty."

"Oh, that's hot."

He kissed me once more and just as hard; he was the best kisser I knew as my tongue twisted with his while we lay on the bed. I couldn't stop kissing him; he just wouldn't stop and neither did I. He attempted to pull his shorts off, but I stopped him before he could.

"For the last time, Seth, stop trying to get naked!"

"You're worth seeing naked."

"Well, you're not gonna see me naked anytime soon."

"I know you want to see me naked," Seth said as he kissed my neck.

"No, I don't."

"Yeah, you do."

"No, I don't."

"Oh, let's have sex."

"No, Seth."

"Please?"

"Nope."

"You're so mean, Jill. Can't you play nice for a change?"

"I could give you a massage."

"Oh yes, please."

Seth rolled onto his belly, as I crawled onto his back and gave him a massage; I gave him a shiatsu massage as best as I could for a whole hour.

"My hands are too sore, Seth. You're done."

"That was incredible JJ, thanks. My back feels great."

"You're welcome. Now I want one in return."

"But I'm so comfy."

"If you do, I might get in the mood to—"

"Massage it is!"

Seth rolled me over and he sat on my butt to give me a massage. He had really soft hands as they worked into my skin.

"If you want me to give you a great massage, I have to undo your top."

"Fine."

"I told you I'd undo that top."

"Whatever, Seth."

He undid my top and worked his hands into my back and gave me a mind-blowing massage.

"Oh, that feels good."
"Of course, it feels good. I'll make you feel great in about an hour."
"Sure."
"So you agree to sex?"
"I never said that."
"I said I'd make you feel great and you said sure. I was talking about sex."
"Well, I agreed to feel great, so finish up this massage and I'll think about it."
"In an hour."
"Yep."

Seth continued to work his hands into my back and it made me wanna have sex, but I didn't want to have sex with Seth now. I couldn't break down and fall for him. I just couldn't. Sex would do that to me. I always fell for whoever I slept with and I couldn't do that with Seth. An hour later, Seth lay down next to me and told me he was done.

"Thanks, Seth, I feel great."
"I can make you feel even better if you let me have sex with you."
"Not tonight, Seth."
"Pretty please?"
"I said not tonight, Seth."
"Aw, why do you have to be so mean and a tease?"
"I'm not mean. I'm an angel, remember, and I'm not a tease. If I were a tease, I'd show you my ass and then say you'd never get to hit that."
"I will hit that at some point."
"Whatever."
"Ah-ha! So you do want the D."
"I said no such thing."
"You're thinking it though."
"No, I'm not."
"Admit it, JJ. I'm on your mind like cheese on a cracker."
"I like pickles on crackers, Seth, so you're not on my mind."
"Maybe I can be the pickle and you the cracker."
"No, Seth."
"But—"
"Ask me to have sex with you again and I never will."
"My lips are sealed, JJ."
"You can still talk, just not about sex."
"Okay, good, because I like talking."
"So what's new, Seth?" I asked him as I grabbed a mango off the counter.
"Oh, just jealous that all those guys get to date you, but I don't."

"Oh well, we sort of have a date as it is."
"We do?"
"Yeah, didn't you say you and I were going to see the reef in bloom?"
"Hey, yes, we did. That means that you can choose me!"
"Nope, the date has to be in the week."
"Aw, I was really looking forward to that."
"You will, Seth. I'm sure that the reef in bloom is going to look beautiful."
"Why look at a reef when I already know something more beautiful."
"What's that?"
"You."
"Oh, Seth, you're too sweet."

I kissed him before heading upstairs to put on my pajamas. Seth followed me up the stairs and to my room, where he crawled into my bed. I changed quickly since I was tired and crawled into bed next to him. He pulled me up onto his chest; although I was half awake, I didn't care. He wrapped his arms around me, as I kissed him good night and placed my hand on his chest. He was warm and perfect to snuggle up to. "Two more dates to go," I thought.

Chapter 29

Today I would be going on a date with Shawn, someone I'd been looking forward to dating for a while. I waited for Seth to wake up, and then his big hazel eyes opened, looking at mine.

"Good morning, JJ."

"Morning, Seth, how did you sleep?"

"Great, how did you sleep?"

"Wonderful."

I kissed him on the cheek as I got out of bed and went to the bathroom to change into my bikini. I heard Seth go downstairs and start up the blender in the kitchen. I knew he was making me a breakfast smoothie. How sweet of him!

"Seth, what are you doing?" I asked as I walked down the stairs.

"Making breakfast and thank you for that massage last night. It was fantastic."

"My pleasure, Seth. You work so hard to make me comfortable in Atlantis I figured you deserve a little treat."

"Well, then I should get another treat tonight."

"We'll see."

Seth made a mango banana smoothie and scrambled eggs; it looked delicious.

"This looks great, Seth."

"Just wait until you try it. It's my secret recipe."

"For eggs?"

"Yep."

I tried the eggs and loved them; there was something else in the eggs that made them taste so much better.

"You added cilantro, didn't you?"

"Shhh! That's the secret ingredient."
"Your secret's safe with me, Seth."
"I hope it is."

Seth handed me the smoothie, and it was really creamy and delicious. I didn't think that Seth could cook, but it looked like he could.

"I hope Shawn and I have sex before we do."
"Yeah, have fun with a child on your hands."
"Shut up. How did you know about that?"
"Common fact, everybody knows that."
"I was hoping to make you jealous."
"I already am that those guys get to date you willy-nilly."
"Well, then I've succeeded."
"In what?"
"In making you jealous, silly."
"Oh, you're such a tease."
"Am not."
"We'll discuss this later."

I finished my breakfast and headed out the door. Seth was right behind me and followed me to the water. I dove in happily, excited about my date with Shawn. Seth nudged me with his tail once we were in the water.

"What is it, Seth?"
"You look beautiful today."
"Thanks, Seth. We're still not going to have sex."
"Dammit."

I laughed as we reached the palace in Atlantis and swam inside.

"A pleasure to see you again, Jillian."
"The pleasure is all mine, Shawn."

Shawn leaned down and kissed my hand, while I blushed. No one had kissed my hand since the party and my first date. Shawn was sweet; he grabbed my hand as we walked out the door. Shawn made a rose out of a ball of fire and put it in my hair.

"So, Shawn, tell me your deepest secret?"
"I am a hybrid."
"Are you serious?"
"I would never lie to you, Jillian."
"Why didn't you tell me this before?"
"I didn't think it would interest you."
"Of course, it would interest me. You're interesting."
"Thanks, Jillian."
"Let's go to the surface and party it up."
"Okay!"

I led the way to the surface with Shawn right behind me. His crystal looked great on his bare tanned skin. I couldn't believe Shawn hadn't told me this before; I had been hoping he would be a hybrid.

"So what's on this island anyways?"

"You're going to have to find out."

I led Shawn to the cabin where Miko was waiting for me in the kitchen.

"Have a mango, Miko. I want some alone time with Shawn."

I threw a mango at Miko and he caught it. Miko screeched at Shawn and ran away with the mango in his hand.

"You have a pet monkey?"

"Yeah, his name is Miko."

"That's so cool. I wish I could have a pet monkey."

"Miko is quite friendly, I assure you."

"Oh, I hope so, so what did you mean by alone time?"

"Maybe I just wanted you alone."

"And why is that exactly?"

"Because I like being alone with guys I just met."

"Is that so?"

"It's true."

"Well, then you leave me no choice but to do this."

"Do what?"

Shawn kissed me before I could say another word. I didn't stop it because I loved it. Shawn lifted me up on the counter onto his hips and pushed me up against a wall. He was a rough guy, but I didn't mind. He slammed me up against a wall again and made me laugh as he kissed me again. I was on his hips on the wall as he French-kissed me with his roughness and power that I couldn't resist. When he stopped, he simply smiled and snuck a kiss on my cheek before putting me down.

"Did you get that all out of your system?"

"Most of it. Oh, c'mon, you know you loved it."

"Yeah, you're right, I did love it. There's something I want to show you though."

"What's that?"

"It's a surprise."

"I love surprises."

With the backpack on my shoulders containing only the chisel, I led Shawn out the door and walked out to the forest. I had memorized the way after visiting the fruit trees twice and finding the falls on my own. It didn't take long to find the fruit trees, where I quickly grabbed a mango and took a juicy bite. Shawn grabbed a mango too, and then I told him to follow me again into the bushy forest. I almost reached the falls in under five minutes, oh yeah. I stopped before pulling back the bushes and halted Shawn from walking any farther.

"Behold." I pulled back the palm tree bushes to reveal the view. "The crystal oasis."

"That is so beautiful."

"It is, isn't it?"

"Mmmhmm."

I ran up to the water, taking my shirt off and pants off.

"Whoa, Jillian, looking good."

"Join me, Shawn."

"Okay!"

Shawn ran after me and grabbed me before splashing into the water, both of us crashing into the cool water. I arose right in front of Shawn and splashed him, standing there with a stupid grin on his face. He laughed as he splashed me back until we were in a splashing war, and then he suddenly disappeared.

"Shawn?"

Shawn was underwater obviously, and I could see the bubbles approach me. I crossed my arms and waited for him to surface and scare me, but then the bubbles stopped.

"Shawn!"

I felt around the water for him, but I couldn't find him. I started to grow worried. Shawn was nowhere to be found and I was simply worried sick. One giant splash and Shawn launched out of the water in front of me, yelling a roar as he did so. I didn't even flinch as I wiped the splashed water off my face.

"Nice try, Shawn."

"Drat, come here."

He wanted me to come closer to him next to the waterfall. I could easily guess that he wanted me to kiss him. I accepted. He pulled me closer to his chest and lifted my chin with his fingers to gently kiss me. I wrapped my arms around his neck as I always did and embraced his warm kiss. He didn't lift me out of the water like the others did, probably because he had one hand on my neck and the other on my submerged hip. He was a skilled kisser but needed a bit of practice to really be a master. He tried to unhook my bikini top, but I stopped him before he could. I giggled as I kissed him once more. When he stopped, he smiled at me as he saw a small grin grow on my face.

"So where's the surprise?"

"Right below us."

"What?"

"Just follow me."

I told him to dive down with me, and he did so happily. It didn't take long to reach the saltwater part of the cavern, and I felt my tail form. Shawn's did as well. I took a breath of saltwater and introduced Shawn to the crystal cavern. He was really excited to be in the cavern and tried pulling the crystals out of the wall until I gave him the chisel. He smiled as he chiseled away at a few crystals while I sat back and chipped away at a large peridot. I had a backup chisel. Shawn finished up quickly and handed me the chisel when he was finished.

"That's it?"

"That's it."

"Okay, let's go."

I swam up ahead of Shawn and asked him to follow me. The current pulled Shawn and me forward until I spotted the drop-off shortly ahead. I turned in a position where I wouldn't hit my head and splashed into the water below. I swam once I was in the water and headed toward the cavern above. It was still hot as hell in the cavern, and the second I surfaced I began to sweat.

"Wow, it's hot in here."

"It just keeps getting hotter."

"Was it hot like this before?"

"Yep, but something's not right. It's getting hotter in here."

"Damn right, it's getting hotter in here."

Shawn grabbed me from behind and threw me into the water.

"You bastard!"

"Ha-ha!"

He grabbed me and held me to his hips in the water. He moved some hair out of my eyes, putting his hand on my face. I nuzzled into the warmth of his hand and gently kissed it.

"Did I ever tell you how beautiful you are?"

"No, I don't think you did."

"And that I have a thing for brunettes?"

"Is that so?"

I playfully teased his hair, still wet from the warm water. I smiled at his tanned face as he leaned in closer to mine. I kissed him before he could get the chance, while I treaded the water in front of him. I didn't kiss him for long as he stopped a little earlier than I had hoped. When he stopped, he gazed into my eyes and gently kissed me once more before diving underwater and going back to the cavern behind the cabin. I led the way to the cavern with Shawn right behind me. It didn't take long to reach the cavern and crawl out of the water. Shawn stepped out first with me right behind him, and we walked toward the cabin.

"So what can we do now?" Shawn asked as he grabbed my waist and kissed my neck.

"I know where we can go, but it involves going back in the water."

"Okay."

He followed me out the door toward the water again, where I dived in first. I took a breath of water and swam toward the heated cavern. I emerged first and waited for Shawn to catch up. When he caught up, his hair was spiked up like a Mohawk, which made me laugh. I fixed his hair before climbing out of the water and hopping out onto the hot rock. It almost burned the hot rock was so warm, but it simply warmed my bottom while I waited for Shawn to hop out. He hopped out quickly, and I asked him to follow me to the stone staircase. I walked up with Shawn's hand in my hand and reached the top of the staircase to see the setting sun.

"This is where I come to watch the stars."

"Cool."

"And do other things."

"Oh?"

"Yeah."

I sat down in the hammock and moved over so Shawn could fit. We snuggled up in the hammock which Shawn rocked back and forth, and we watched the sunset.

"What's the time?"

"Nine forty-five."

"This date went by way too quickly."

"I know."

I kissed Shawn for the last fifteen minutes in silence, as I wrapped my arms around his neck one last time. I embraced the fact that his hands were on my hips and wrapped all around me. It felt so good to kiss Shawn; he was a skilled kisser as I said before, and he was worth it. Ten rolled around really fast and Shawn had to leave.

"Good-bye, angel."

"Really, you're the third person to call me that."

"It's true."

"Good-bye, Shawn."

He left in no hurry as I walked him down the steps and back to the cabin. He kissed me good-bye before he left and returned to the ocean in the night. I returned to the warmth of the cabin. It was a pleasant date with Shawn; although 60 percent of it was making out, I didn't mind. I tucked myself into bed for the night and had sweet dreams.

Chapter 30

I woke up with the sun on my face. I got dressed in my bikini and went downstairs. I made myself a banana pomegranate smoothie and chopped up some oranges to go with it. I heard Seth whistling outside and let him in.

"Good morning, Seth, it's open."
"Good morning! So today you date one of my brothers!"
"Yes, I do. I'm meeting Sedrick."
"Awkward!"
"It would only be awkward if we went on a date."
"I think we can after the week."
"I can't choose you though."
"I know. It sucks!"
"Oh my God, I don't care!"
"Oh, I know you care about me, JJ."
"In your dreams, Seth."
"Whatever you say."

I finished my breakfast while Seth ate a mango off my counter. I looked over at Seth when he took a sip of my smoothie while it was unguarded.

"Hey!"
"Finders keepers."
"Mine!"

I grabbed the smoothie out of his hands before he could take another gulp and finished my breakfast. I headed outside with Seth right behind me and moved toward the water. I jumped in and dove down toward the drop-off with Seth by my side. We found Atlantis quickly and rather quietly; there wasn't a word said the whole time on our way to Atlantis. I think it was because I was dating his brother instead of him that he was so quiet.

"Are you okay with me dating your brother?"
"Oh my gosh!"
"What is it?"
"There are only six guys you chose!"
"Alex, Damian, Lucas, Peter, Shawn, Sedrick, Skylar, no, that's seven."
"Well, since you'll be so bored with all these guys why don't you go on a date with me on Sunday?"
"Well, I suppose."
"Oh, thank you, JJ. It's gonna be the date of your life, I swear."

He kissed me on the cheek and gave me a hug. I hugged him back. I swam up to the gates and waved back to the waving citizens. We reached the castle shortly, where Sedrick was patiently waiting for me.

"Hey, Sedrick."
"Hey, Jillian, you ready to go?"
"Can't wait."
"Sounds good."

Sedrick put his arms around my shoulder, making Seth turn green once more with envy. I laughed to myself as Sedrick and I swam out of Atlantis in the direction of the island. We reached it in no time and emerged on land with our legs in a short amount of time. I took him to the cabin, where the second I turned around he kissed me. I didn't hold back, though he slammed my back against a wall. He shoved me up on the wall on his hips, as I French-kissed him some more. He tasted like cherries and I found him irresistible as he kissed me with all the skills he had. He was a skilled kisser, but a few hours with me and he could be a master. I French-kissed him a little more before he stopped and gazed into my eyes and smiled.

"Mind putting me down, Sedrick?"
"Oh, of course."

Sedrick gently set me back down on the ground, as I smiled back at him.

"Are you up for a hike?"
"Of course."

I packed the chisel into the backpack and told him to follow me. I was walking with ease toward the forest when Sedrick suddenly picked me up and started running into the forest, screaming as loud as he could.

"We got to find cover! They're shooting at us."
"Ha-ha, put me down, Sedrick."
"I can't. They're still shooting."
"Who, Sedrick?"
"Oh, don't worry. They're gone."

"You're so weird, Sedrick."

I kissed him on the cheek as he sat me down and let me continue walking toward the surprise of the crystal oasis.

"Behold, Sedrick." I pulled back the bushes hiding the view again. "The crystal oasis."

"Wow."

"Wow is right."

I raced over to the water and jumped in. I had my shirt soaking wet before I took it off and threw it on the land, while Sedrick slowly walked toward the water.

"Sometime today would be nice, Sedrick."

"Well, good, because I have all day with you."

I laughed as he jumped in shirtless and swam up to me.

"Would you mind if I kissed you?"

"Not at all, Sedrick."

He gently kissed me and placed his one hand behind my neck. I felt him tug at the back of my hair, which I loved as I wrapped my arms around his neck. We were in the center of the oasis, so the water from the waterfall wasn't even close to hitting my back. I didn't mind. He was a master by now and gracefully French-kissed me; it was amazing. I couldn't stop kissing Sedrick; he was too addictive and I didn't want to stop. When Sedrick stopped kissing me, a small "aw" echoed in my head, as he backed away and placed his forehead on mine, smiling once more. I grinned in return and kissed him gently once more; it was quick and quiet.

"Now for the main event."

"And what's that exactly?"

"You'll see. Just follow me."

I dove down into the water that was cool and inviting, and I kicked with all my might toward the bottom; I reached there quickly and took a breath of fresh saltwater. My tail formed as I waited for Sedrick to catch up; when he reached there, he said, "Wow! It's beautiful in here."

"It is, isn't it?"

"And it's all yours?"

"All mine."

He swam up to the wall and tried to pull out an emerald from the wall until I handed him the chisel, and I observed him quickly pop out the crystals. He took out an aquamarine, emerald, ruby, and more. I got slightly bored and looked at the rest of the crystals on the wall. He finished up quickly and handed me back the chisel when he was done. He didn't take much of the gems, but I didn't question him as I swam down the tunnel. It was darker today as the current pulled Sedrick and I forward, but it didn't last as long as the last time as I splashed down peacefully into the water below. I swam around the water for a minute while I waited for Sedrick to fall into the water; he did so about two minutes after I did. Why he took so long I do not know. I was just glad he was here.

"Just a quick swim and it's back to the cabin."

"And then what?"

"We'll have a nice little dinner."

"Sounds good."

I swam up to the top of the steamy cavern and turned around quickly to reach the other cavern with Sedrick right behind me. It took a very short amount of time to reach the cavern behind the cabin. I walked out of the water with Sedrick behind me; he grabbed my hand as we walked back to the cabin. I placed my head on his shoulders on the way back, and we reached the door his hand was on my hip and my body was in his arms and chest.

"What should we have for supper?"

"No idea."

"How about I make us sushi?"

"Sounds good."

Of course, I already had sushi this week, but I could care less; he was making me dinner as it was. I was looking forward to dinner being made for me, and it would be made with the fresh crab I still had in the fridge ready to go, so supper wouldn't take that long. Sedrick put the rice on the stove and microwaved the crab to warm up. I sat down in the living room, patiently waiting for the rice to finish, which didn't take long at all; it only took about ten minutes. He immediately started making the sushi with the fresh crab and rolled all the ingredients together.

"Supper's ready!"

"Coming, Sedrick."

The sushi was fantastic and shaped in little hearts.

"Oh, Sedrick, the sushi looks like little hearts! That's so cute."

"I thought you would like it."

"Oh, but I do."

I told Sedrick as I ate one of the miniature heart-shaped sushi pieces. It was so good I thought that was the second best sushi I'd ever eaten. Alex's fresh crab sushi was better. I couldn't complain though; the sushi was fabulous.

"So how do you like it?"

"It's great, Sedrick, thanks."

"Anytime, JJ."

"How did you know that was my nickname?"

"My brother tells us everything, angel."
"Ah well, you can call me JJ. I've grown to like that nickname."
"JJ it is then."

I finished up my last piece of sushi as did Sedrick, and then I ran upstairs to get the guitar. Unfortunately, Sedrick caught me with the guitar.

"What are you doing with that, hmmm?"
"I was going to play it for you."
"Oh, that's sweet."

He kissed me on the cheek and grabbed the guitar out of my hands.

"Let me carry that for you."
"Well, aren't you a gentleman?"
"That's what I do."

We walked outside the living room toward the outside door and then toward the beach. The walk toward the fire spot was fun as I told Sedrick my life story.

"So your first time was on a yacht?"
"You bet."
"That's kind of hot."
"Thanks, Sedrick, it was."
"I didn't need to hear that."
"Sorry."
"What else can you tell me?"
"That our spot to make the fire is right there. Go get some firewood."
"Okay."

He ran off into the bushes to get the firewood while I pulled the log closer to the spot where the fire was. I was cold and could use a warm shoulder when he returned.

"Got the firewood. Did you bring matches?"
"Yep, here you go."

I handed him the matches as he took some bark and lit the underbrush to start up the small logs and eventually start the large fire.

"So what can you sing for me?"
"How about Rhythm of Love? By Plain White Tee's?"
"I didn't know you knew that song, Sedrick."
"There are lots you don't know about me."
"Like?"
"I can play guitar too."
"Why didn't you say so? Play me a little something."
"Mind if I sing 'She will be Loved' by Maroon 5?"

"That was beautiful, Sedrick."

"Thanks, Jillian. That means a lot to me."

"You mean a lot to me, Sedrick."
"I do?"
"Why do you sound so surprised?"
"I didn't know I meant something to you."
"Oh, but you do, Sedrick."

I pulled his face closer to mine with my hand and gently kissed him. He kissed me back, French of course, as I wrapped my arms around his neck. Kissing Sedrick was addictive and I couldn't stop. I was too addicted. Sedrick placed his hands on my hip and pulled me closer to him, close enough that I could lay my head right on his chest if I wanted to. When he stopped, he exhaled and smiled at me in the most charming way I'd seen so far. He had one sexy smile as far as I knew, and I'd seen nothing but shining white smiles for a week or so. I smiled back and kissed him gently on the cheek. I had barely touched his cheek with my lips, hardly even a peck, but his skin was soft and warm. He kissed me once and backed away before putting his forehead on mine and grinning. I liked this forehead thing that he always did after kissing; it made him stick out, and I liked this about him. I wasn't guaranteeing that I'd marry him, but at this rate I would.

"Oh, there's something I want to show you, Sedrick."
"Sure."
"First, we got to put out the fire though."

I grabbed some water from the sea and threw it on the fire; Sedrick did the same until the coals of the remaining fire went out in a blaze of steam and smoke. It didn't take long to get back to the cabin with Sedrick, his big strong arms around my shoulders and me against his warm chest. When we got back, I raced out of the cabin toward the cavern in the back with Sedrick running to keep up to me.

"Wait for me, Jill!"

I continued to run with Sedrick behind me and made it to the cavern. Sedrick was laughing and trying to catch his breath, and then he dove into the water. He emerged shortly afterward to ask if we were going into the water at all.

"Yes, Sedrick, we're going in the water."
"Oh, okay, good."

I walked into the water and dove in after Sedrick, swimming up to the hot stone steps and the steamy cavern. I got out of the water and waited for my legs to form, and Sedrick also got out, his legs forming immediately.

"What is it you wanted to show me?"

"Follow me."

"Okay."

Seth followed me up the stairs into the starry night above, where I sat down on the hammock with him next to me.

"Where's the surprise?"

"Look up."

Stars were everywhere in the night, and there were even a few shooting stars that passed by.

"Make a wish, Sedrick."

"No, that's quite all right. You can have it."

"No, I insist you have it."

"I wish this night would never end."

"You shouldn't have told me that."

"Why not?"

"'Cause now it won't come true."

"I think it will."

He smiled at me and gave me a quick kiss. I smiled back at him as he moved back and handed me a margarita.

"You made me a margarita?"

"I sure did."

"You're so sweet."

"Aren't I? Ha-ha."

He clinked his glass with mine and then took a sip of the margarita, while I took a sip of mine. He reached into his shorts, looking up at me.

"I have a little something for you."

"Is that so?"

He reached down into his pants pocket and pulled out a ruby carved in the shape of a heart, the size of my fist, and gave it to me.

"Just a little something to remember me by."

"Sedrick, I don't know what to say."

"Thank you?"

"Well, yes, thank you, it's beautiful."

"Carved it myself with a diamond."

"You have a diamond."

"Yeah, I found it in a shipwreck and took it."

He showed me the diamond that was the size of his fist; I'd never seen one so big before.

"What time is it?"

"Nine forty-five."

"We only have fifteen minutes left?"

"Looks like it."

I immediately kissed him and flipped him over until I was on top of him. He seemed surprised as his eyes were wide open when I looked at him, but they closed a second later when I French-kissed him. I heard the crash of my margarita on the ground as he flipped me over on my back, leaving him on top. He lay down on top of me with pleasure, as I felt a smile on his lips that were currently locked on to mine. He continued to kiss me for a full fifteen minutes until I heard my watch beep, signaling the end of our date.

"It's ten, isn't it?"

"Yeah, Sedrick, it is."

"I guess my wish never came true."

"I guess not, but I'll walk you to the water though."

"Sounds good."

We walked down to the water and dove in, returning to the cavern behind the cabin shortly. I stepped out of the water and walked him to the shoreline.

"I guess this is good-bye."

"Don't worry. You'll see me again at the ceremony."

"Right, good-bye, JJ."

"Good-bye, Sedrick."

I kissed him on the cheek before he dove into the water of the night. I returned to the comfort of my cabin, my home. I was still adjusting to that phrase about this place. I walked upstairs to my warm room and changed into my pajamas quickly because I was quite tired. I crawled into my bed and tucked myself in as I had done for over a year, waiting for my last two dates coming up in the next few days.

Chapter 31

I woke up with the sun in my eyes, which was what woke me up in the first place. I didn't mind because today was my official last date of the week—sort of. I had to ask the king today if I was allowed to date Seth after I already chosen among the men before him. I would consult Neptune today when I went to meet Skylar, the second youngest son of Neptune's. I was looking forward to this date with Skylar; he was a really sweet guy. I couldn't wait to see him again. I headed downstairs to make myself some sausage and eggs, then headed outside, having already changed into my bikini that was under my pajamas. I walked toward the water and dove in; today the sea was warm and inviting, and Seth was up early to greet me off at the drop off.

"Good morning, Seth."

"Good morning, Jillian. How did you sleep?"

"Great, thanks for asking."

"So today you date my second brother."

"Yes, I do."

"Ew."

"Why do you say that?"

"You're dating both of my brothers. Kind of freaks me out."

"Don't freak out. I'm going to date you tomorrow."

"I know. I'm so excited!"

"So what are we going to do tomorrow?"

"It's a surprise. It's going to be amazing."

"I hope it is."

We swam back down to Atlantis, and the people seemed a bit happier than usual today. I was greeted much more today than I was any other day. I was waved at and even whistled at.

The Tail of an Angel

"Can you play ball with us, miss?"

"Sorry, kids, I'm dating Skylar today."

"Rumor has it you're going on a date with Seth tomorrow."

"That rumor is true."

"Well, I hope you have a good time. Seth rules!"

The kids swam away, and I laughed as one swam right into a pole. Seth and I swam up to the castle where I caught Skylar scratching his neck and smiling at me.

"Hey, Jill, you ready to go?"

"Can't wait."

"See you, Seth."

Skylar pounded the fist of his brother, and I watched as they made an exploding noise when their hands fanned out. I rolled my eyes and walked out on Skylar's arm, telling him my life story.

"Really? Your first time was on a yacht?"

"You sound surprised."

"No, I'm not. A classy girl like you deserves to lose her virginity on such a fine vessel."

"It sank."

"Damn."

I told him how I ended up here, and he gave me a hug too.

"I'm so sorry for your loss."

"Thanks, Skylar, how about we go clubbing?"

"Only if you'll grind with me."

"Deal."

We swam to the nearest hybrid club and went inside.

"Hold up, are you a hybrid?"

"I've been here before."

"Oh right, proceed. Hey, Skylar."

"Hey."

We walked inside and the place was packed. I couldn't believe how full it was and it was only the morning. Skylar and I were waiting for a good grinding song to come on when I spotted Seth at the bar having a drink.

"Hey, Seth!"

I waved and swam up to him to say hello.

"What are you doing here?"

"Just thought I'd have a margarita in the morning, a toast to me no longer being single."

"Would you be freaked out if I asked you to come grind with me and Skylar?"

"Freaked out? I'd love to. Me and Skylar grind on girls all the time, and I remember this one girl—"

"Less talk, more grind."

I grabbed his hand and pulled him over to the dance floor, and he took the front and Skylar took the back and we grinded for hours. I was starting to get sweaty and a bit smelly, so I ran to the bathroom to grab some perfume. As soon as I smelled of "Pure Seduction," a scent from Victoria's Secret, I stepped out and seduced Skylar.

"You smell incredible."

"Thanks, Skylar."

Seth stepped out to grab another drink while I kissed Skylar in secret. He was an incredible kisser and was a master by the taste of it; he tasted like spearmint and was tasty. When we stopped, Seth returned. I smiled at Skylar and returned to grinding. He was a good dancer, but I was better and Seth was as skilled a dancer as me. We continued to grind for a while, Seth in the back and Skylar in the front. I turned around every now and then to jazz it up. When the club was absolutely full to the brim with people, I told Seth good-bye and left with Skylar, his hand on my waist. The second we reached the surface, I kissed him again and walked over to the cabin. It was empty with the exception of Miko on the table, eating a mango. I shooed him off, as Skylar lifted me on the table and French-kissed me. Oh my God, he was an amazing kisser, indeed a well-rehearsed master, and it felt amazing on my tongue. The taste of spearmint lingered in my mouth like a breath freshener. This continued for about ten minutes before he finally stopped and looked into my eyes.

"So what should we do now?"

"I want to take you somewhere fun after I pack us a quick lunch."

I found some baloney in the fridge. How it got there I had no clue, but I made baloney sandwiches anyways. After I made the lunch, I put it in a backpack and walked out the door with Skylar right behind me. The forest was darker than usual, which made me suspicious, but the forest lit up the deeper we went in. It took about a fifteen-minute walk to reach the oasis and I forgot to do the big reveal, but Skylar was still surprised. I found a shady spot and sat down to eat my sandwich, and Skylar joined me.

"Good sandwich, Jill."

"Thanks, Skylar, it's just baloney."

"Well, it's darn good baloney."

"Thanks."

I finished my sandwich and walked toward the water, taking my shirt and pants off.

"Umm, Jillian? What are you doing?"

"I do this to feel human again."

"How?"

"Join me and I'll show you."

"Well then, hey, wait up!"

I jumped into the cool water and Skylar jumped in right after me, nearly landing on me.

"Mind showing me how to be human again?"

"Notice how our tails haven't formed?"

"Hey yeah, why is that?"

"Because our tails will only form in saltwater."

"That's cool! Anything else you can do to make me feel human?"

I gently kissed him as he lifted me on his hips, and I wrapped my arms around his neck. I couldn't get enough of Skylar's kisses; he was so addictive like a drug. I couldn't stop kissing him, and I didn't think he wanted to stop either. We kissed for at least fifteen minutes. I didn't have a watch, but somehow I just knew. When he stopped, he gazed into my baby blue eyes and grinned. I smiled in return.

"I'm starting to feel a bit more human."

"Me too."

He gently set me back down in the water and cleared his throat.

"So where's the surprise, or was the oasis the surprise?"

"No, no, the surprise is down below."

"Umm, sex?"

"No, stupid, I mean it's literally below us. Dive down and follow me."

I dove down and kicked hard, almost kicking Skylar in the face. Eventually, we reached the cave and our tails formed simultaneously. I showed him the crystals on the wall and handed him the chisel; he thanked me with a smile. He chipped away at a lot of crystals, some I couldn't even name, and he chipped away at all of them. I laughed as he accidentally chipped at his finger. I grabbed his hand and kissed his finger better; he smiled as I did so.

"Feel better?"

"Much."

He finally handed me back the chisel after a few minutes and smiled again; he had an amazing white smile. We swam along the current and shortly reached the drop-off and splashed down into the water. It was warmer than usual and the cave was also just as warm. Skylar kissed me on the cheek before diving back under, toward the cavern behind the cabin. I followed obediently behind Skylar and emerging behind the cabin I walked out of the water. Once we reached the cabin, Skylar attempted to kiss me, but I stopped him.

"There's one more surprise, Skylar."
"Sex?"
"Nope, even better."
"What's better than sex?"
"You'll see."

I grabbed his hand and pulled him outside the cabin, toward the water in the back. I jumped in and it was perfect timing because when we came up to the steamy cavern I could see the darkness of the night above. We got out of the water and watched our legs form, and then we headed up to the hot stone steps. How long was this heat going to last?

"The surprise is right up here."
"And it's better than sex?"
"Well, probably not."
"We should have sex instead."
"Maybe not, Skylar. It's only our first date."
"Okay."

I held his hand as we walked up the steps and reached the top, where the stars awaited us. I lay down on the hammock and Skylar snuggled in next to me.

"The stars are beautiful tonight."
"Yeah, they are," I told him, agreeing. He kissed me under the stars for ten minutes or so. I wrapped my arms around his neck once more before asking for the time.

"It's nine fifty."
"Let's make the best of our last ten minutes."
"Sounds good to me."

I kissed him this time, but he was much more aggressive, and I loved it. For the last ten minutes, he French-kissed me, leaving the taste of spearmint in my mouth once more. I didn't know why he tasted like spearmint without having a chewing gum or a breath mint; all I knew was that I didn't want to stop. When he did stop, another "aw" echoed in my mind and he grinned once more.

"It's ten, isn't it?"
"It is."
"I don't want to go."

Skylar placed his hand on my face.
"Oh, Skylar, you have to go."
"Do I?"
"Unfortunately."
"Unfortunately indeed."

I got out of the hammock and so did Skylar; we walked down the stairs quietly and reached the steamy cavern once more. The second we jumped into the water and emerged out, Skylar kissed me again. I turned to French-kiss him in return as he placed his hands on my hips.

"I don't want to go."

"I'm sorry, you have to go."

"Please don't let me go."

"The date's over, Skylar. I'm going to have to ask you to leave."

"But I don't want to go."

"If I have to ask you again, I won't choose you."

"I'm out of here! Good-bye, JJ."

"How do you know that?"

"Sedrick told me."

"Oy."

He swam up to the open cavern and walked out of the water. He walked to the water's edge and dove in, leaving nothing but a good-bye and a splash in the water. I walked back to the cabin alone, where Seth surprised me again.

"Jesus, Seth, you really got to stop that."

"Sorry, I was just aching to see you."

"You're going to see me tomorrow."

"I know, but I couldn't wait."

"Something tells me you want to spend the night."

"Yes, please," he told me with a grin.

"Oh, Seth, of course, you can spend the night, but no sex!"

"Aw, why not, huh?"

"Because I said so."

"Oh, I know you want to."

He hugged me from behind and kissed my neck as I held on to his arms and sighed.

"We'll see."

"Yay!"

He hugged me and spun me in the air, and then he gently set me down and kissed me.

"Are you trying to seduce me, Seth?"

"Yes, I am. Is it working?"

"A little."

I kissed him back as he lifted me onto his hips and kissed me harder. He was a master kisser as well and tasted like mint on my tongue. I couldn't stop kissing Seth as he laid me down on the couch. Then he was on top of me, French-kissing me.

"Seth, I don't know if I can do this."
"Do what, JJ?"
"Sleep with you tonight."
"Sure you can."
"No, I don't know if I can."
"I know you can do this, JJ. If you don't think you can, it's a lie."
"Are you sure?"
"I know it."
Seth carried me upstairs to my room and took off my shirt.
"I don't think I want to do this, Seth."
"Sure you can."
"No, Seth, not tonight."
"Okay."
I put my shirt back on and walked to the closet to get my pajamas, only I didn't have any clean ones available.
"Uhhh, Seth, do you mind if I sleep in my clothes?"

"You can just sleep in your bra and underwear with me."

"I don't know about that, Seth."
"Really, I don't mind."
"Okay."
I stripped down to my bra and underwear and crawled into bed with Seth.
"I love your bra."
"Thanks."
He placed his hand on my waist and pulled me closer to him. I actually enjoyed it as he ran one hand over my stomach and put the other one under my stomach until he was squeezing me tight.
"I'm really excited for tomorrow, Jillian."
"Me too."
"We're going to have so much fun."
"Is that so?"
"It's true. I have the entire day planned out for tomorrow."
"Mmhmm."
"I'll let you get some sleep now."
"That would be nice."
"Night, JJ."
"Night, Seth."
I fell asleep tight in his arms; a kiss on my forehead was the last thing I remembered before falling asleep.

Chapter 32

I slept in happily, in the morning with Seth behind me, snuggled in close and keeping me warm. I felt him get up and leave the room to use the washroom in the middle of the night, and the warmth I felt behind me quickly disappeared. I missed the warmth behind me, and when Seth returned, I nuzzled into his warm chest and placed my hand on its bare warm goodness. I felt Seth sneak a kiss on my cheek and returned to go back to sleep. I grinned in my sleep as I turned over and felt him wrap his arms around my stomach once more. His big strong hands almost took up my entire belly, but I was probably just exaggerating. I woke up with the sun on my face, keeping it warm when Seth smiled down at me.

"Good morning."
"Good morning, Seth. How did you sleep?"
"Fantastic."
"Good, I'm going to make us some breakfast."
"You might want this."
Seth lifted up my bra from the bed.
"Seth, you jerk!"
I put my bra back on and ran downstairs to make myself some breakfast. I made a quick chocolate banana smoothie and gulped it down quickly before running back up to my room to put on my bikini; I thought I would wear my red one for today. Seth got out of bed. I heard a thump on the floor and knew that he had fallen off the bed again. Still in his shorts, he got up and knocked on the bathroom door.
"How much longer are you going to be in there?"
"Not long. I'm just putting on my bikini top."
"Need some help?"
"I'm good, Seth."

I put on the top just fine without Seth's help and walked down the stairs to clean up. Seth was already in the kitchen, eating a pomegranate for breakfast.

"I don't know if my father will let me date you."

"He might, you never know."

"I know my father. He'll probably say no."

"Let's hope not."

I kissed Seth on the cheek before racing outside to the cool water and the hot sun above. I dove in with Seth right behind me and swam down into the darker water. Seth laughed as he saw a jellyfish swim into a wall, and I laughed too when a dolphin did a flip out of the water. The ocean was full of life today, a perfect day to spend with Seth. Maybe he was going to take me to the club again or we would go back to the oasis and kiss, who knew? We reached Atlantis quickly and had fun on our way there. Atlantis shone brightly today like a shooting star and the city seemed to glow in the midst of the water. I could see Neptune's chambers from the bottom of the gate and swam toward the castle. Seth was right beside me, holding my hand as we swam to the guarded gates of the castle.

"We wish to see King Neptune," Seth boldly commanded.

"Proceed."

In no time at all, we reached the castle doors and walked inside. It was bright in the castle, and Neptune was sitting on his throne as he normally was.

"Father, I have come to ask you something."

"What is it, Seth?"

"Since Jill has dated the seventh man, I was hoping I could go on a date with her."

"And what makes you think you have earned the right to date her?"

"I've saved her life twice."

"Good point. All right, I suppose you two can go on a date."

"Thank you, Father."

Seth and I walked out of the castle and did a small celebration dance the second we got outside the castle. I gave him a hug and we walked over to the nearest club to party. The club wasn't as packed as it was before and there was plenty of room on the dance floor. Seth immediately requested his favorite song to play, called "Low" by an artist called Flo Rida. Seth and I got low and grinded until noon or so. We had a couple of drinks at the bar, and I felt a little tipsy.

"I'm only having one more drink, Seth."

"Okay, one more."

The Tail of an Angel

I ordered a martini and sipped on it while Seth chugged on his beer. How on earth he could like beer puzzled me; I hated beer.

"How can you enjoy that beer? It's nasty."

"I think it's refreshing."

"Whatever you say."

"How about one more grind before we go up to the island?"

"Sounds good."

Another good grinding song came on by the DJ and we got down and dirty. Seth was swaying just right behind me and it felt so good. Once the song ended, Seth turned me around and kissed my hand. Seth was such a gentleman.

"Ready to go?"

"Yep."

We swam out of Atlantis toward the island, encountering a friendly dolphin on the way there. It was following Seth and I and turned back once we reached the island. I walked into the cabin with Seth, and something was on the counter.

"It's a Dr. Pepper."

"Oh my God, Seth! I haven't had a soda in ages!"

"Surprise!"

I hugged Seth and grabbed the soda and pulled it open; it was a king size and that first sip was the best.

"How can I thank you, Seth?"

"A kiss."

I quickly kissed him for a few seconds before backing away and smiling as I finished the entire soda in under a minute. I belched and giggled and apologized for burping in front of Seth. I couldn't help but notice that when I threw away the can, Seth reached for another Dr. Pepper in the fridge.

"How many Dr. Peppers did you get?"

"A few."

He opened the fridge for me a little more and revealed a whole two cases of Dr. Pepper and a special six cherry Dr. Peppers besides the packs of regular Dr. Pepper.

"Thank you so much, Seth. I missed Dr. Pepper."

"I thought you would. So what do you want to do now?"

"How about I take you to an oasis?"

"Sounds great."

"Perfect."

I headed outside the door toward the forest with Seth right behind me. I worked my way through the bushes and ferns that constantly hit me in the face and body. I was sore by the time I reached the oasis, and I think

I had a bruise on my stomach from running into a branch. I was sore and slightly tired, so I could really use a dip in the cool water.

"C'mon, Seth!"

I jumped in with a small splash and resurfaced happy and wet with freshwater in my hair and a smile on my face. Seth jumped in with a huge cannonball and splashed water everywhere, getting cool water all over me. He surfaced right in front of me and smiled.

"I love this oasis."

"I know, me too."

He lifted my face closer to his and smiled once more before kissing me. He French-kissed me before lifting me out of the water and onto his hips.

"Ah."

"What's wrong?"

"My hip and stomach got bruised on the way here. It hurts."

"I'll kiss it better."

"Nah, it's fine, Seth. Whoa!"

He gently lifted me out of the water and kissed my stomach and hip. It did feel a little bit better, I must admit.

"Better?"

"Better."

He smiled and kissed me once more, but only this time he pulled me underwater and kissed me there. There was something about kissing Seth underwater that made it all that much better than kissing on the surface. When he stopped, we rose out of the water and laughed because of reasons I didn't really understand. We just sat there and laughed like idiots. Finally at one point, he just lifted me out of the water and threw me toward the waterfall.

"You jerk!"

"Ha-ha, that's what you get for not sharing that Dr. Pepper."

"You had your own!"

"Still, I love to share."

"Me too. Why don't I show you something I want to share?"

"Sounds good. Where is it?"

"Below us. Follow me."

I dove and swam to about halfway down the tunnel while I waited for Seth. I couldn't believe how slow a swimmer he was. I only had to wait about ten seconds for Seth before he caught up, and then it took another twenty seconds to reach the cave. I almost ran out of breath, but I made it to the cave and took a breath of water while my tail formed. Seth's tail took a second to form, but it formed eventually. Once there, I showed him the wall and handed him the chisel and told him to go nuts.

The Tail of an Angel

"Really, Seth, take as many as you like."
"Are you sure?"
"I'm sure, Seth. Go nuts!"

He worked on a lot of aquamarine and peridot and emerald, but I didn't judge. He could take every single crystal in that cave and I could care less, just as long as he had fun. Seth finished up quickly and efficiently, taking a handful of gems to carry and putting the rest in the bag I packed. He put all the gems into the bag and swam toward the tunnel ahead, letting the current pull us forward. In no time, the tunnel ended with a quick splash and we were back into the water where the steamy cavern was. I reached the top where the cavern was still steamy as heck. I started sweating the second I surfaced and took a gasp of fresh air. Seth emerged right behind me and gave me a hug from behind.

"We could do it, you know."
"Do what, Seth?"
"Fall in love."
"I don't know about that, Seth."
"Why not?"
"I can't fall in love with my best friend."
"Why not?"
"I just can't, Seth, really I can't. Last time I fell for my best friend, he died. I can't go through that again."
"I'd never put you through that, Jillian." Seth kissed my neck. "So how about it?"
"I'll have to think about it."
"Okay, let's go back to the cabin."

I dove down into the water once more and swam back to the cavern behind the cabin. It was warm out and I was comfy in the air, when Seth and I walked out of the water. We walked back to the cabin hand in hand as I hoped we would and walked up to my room to make out. The second we reached my room, Seth picked me up in his arms and set me down on the bed gently. He lay down on top of me and kissed me with all his masterful skills. His tongue tangled with mine inside his minty mouth and it tasted so good. He reached down to take off my bikini bottoms, but I stopped him.

"For God's sake, Seth, stop trying to get me naked."
"I can't help it. You'd look so much better without any clothes on."
"In your dreams, Seth. We should go make some supper."
"What would you like for supper?"
"Fresh crab."
"Oh, I love crab."

Seth ran out of my room, leaving nothing but a kiss on my cheek and a smile on his face, down the stairs to catch some crab. No less than ten minutes later, I heard Seth come back inside with the crabs in his hand. I was in the kitchen waiting for Seth, a mango in my mouth and a grin on my face as I finished off the mango. Seth threw the crab into a steaming pot and cooked up some garlic butter in a pot; he then returned to kiss me in the kitchen. I didn't mind Seth kissing me; I actually enjoyed it quite a bit. He lifted me carefully without banging my hip against the counter and kissed me again. I wrapped my arms around his neck as I always did and French-kissed him as hard as I could. I think I tasted cherry on my tongue. "Where the heck did that come from?" I thought. It surprised me, but I could care less with the breath mint in front of me. Maybe I could learn to love Seth; it wouldn't be the end of the world to fall for my best friend, but could my heart handle it was the real question. Seth French-kissed me some more until the alarm for the crab went off.

"Got to get the crab, JJ."

"Go get it then."

Seth pulled the crab out of the pot and threw it on the plates, ready to eat. He put them on the table with the garlic butter sauce. Supper smelled so good, and I couldn't wait to eat with Seth. I sat down at the table and immediately dug in. The crab was so juicy and hot and delicious; it was incredible.

"Thanks, Seth, for this wonderful crab."

"You're welcome, JJ."

I enjoyed every single piece of the crab and dug out the extra meat in the body with a tiny fork. The meat was so juicy that it dripped crab juice when I pulled it out of the crab shells. Some garlic butter dripped down my face and chin, and Seth licked it off. I laughed as I felt his tongue on my neck and face. I smiled when he wiped the butter off his mouth and returned to eat his crab. I finished up the crab with a grin on my face and butter on my face again. I proudly gave Seth my finest piece of crab in exchange for his and traded just fine. I smiled as I did so, dipping the final piece in the last of the garlic butter sauce. I put my dishes in the sink and hugged Seth for supper.

"Thank you, Seth. I love crab."

"I love crab too."

He kissed me on the cheek and headed outside.

"Where are you going?"

"Come with me."

The Tail of an Angel

He held out his hand. I walked outside with him and saw that he had grabbed the guitar. Something was telling me we might be singing by a bonfire tonight.

"So are we going to sit by a fire and sing, I'm guessing?"

"Good guess, it's exactly what we're doing."

"Awesome."

It didn't take long to reach the fire pit and start a fire. Seth sat down next to me and started strumming away to the rhythm of the guitar.

"Would you like me to sing Fireflies for you?"."

"I love that song, Seth!"

"I love a man who can sing like you, Seth."

"Is that short for I love you?"

"No, I said I love the way you sing."

"Well, thank you. Always a pleasure to hear how much you like my singing."

"You're welcome."

Seth strummed along to "River" by LIGHTS, one of my favorite songs. He strummed along and kissed me on the cheek again. I lightly touched my cheek and grinned.

"You missed."

"Missed what?"

"This silly."

I kissed him while he held the guitar and he kissed me back. He set the guitar down on the sand and placed his hands on my hips, pulling me so close to him I was in his chest. He French-kissed me as he always did, as I wrapped my arms around his warm neck. A smile crept out on my lips as I kissed him some more. When he stopped, he placed his hand on my neck and quickly kissed me one last time.

"Are you up for watching the stars, Seth?"

"I'd love to, JJ."

We walked over to the ocean to grab handfuls of water to put out the fire; slowly but surely, the fire went out in a large puff of smoke and steam. We walked back to the cabin and toward the cavern in the back. I took off my shirt and pants and dove into the cold water. I emerged from the cavern to the steamy area above and climbed out as fast as I could out of the ice-cold water.

"Jesus, that water is cold."

"I know! I'm freezing!"

Seth hopped out of the ice-cold water and sat down next to me, waiting for his legs to form. It didn't take long for our legs to form, and we could walk up the warm steps to the tropical breeze above. I held Seth's hand as I observed the island; Seth pulled me down to join him on the hammock and watch the stars.

"It's beautiful out tonight."
"It is."
"Do you think we'll end up together?"
"We'll see. You'll have to find out at tomorrow's ceremony."
"I don't wanna wait until tomorrow. Can you tell me now?"
"No, Seth, it's a surprise!"
"I do like surprises."
"See, it'll work out for everyone."
"Except the guys who aren't chosen."
"Yeah, they'll be pretty sad. All the dates have gone so well."
"Even this one?"
"Especially this one."
"What's that supposed to mean?"
"Just that I'm glad this date is going so well."
"It's not over yet."

Seth kissed me in the hammock, and he still tasted like mint, for reasons I didn't quite understand, but I loved it either way.

"So are you going to choose me or not?"
"Seth, you'll have to wait until tomorrow."
"But the anticipation is killing me."
"Seth, be patient."
"But I don't want to be. Tell me, tell me, tell me."
"No, Seth."
"Please?"
"Nope, ask again and I won't choose you."
"Got it."
"So is there anything else you wish to ask me?"
"Will you marry me?"
"No."
"Damn."
"How much time do we have left anyways?"
"About fifteen minutes."
"Well, let's make the best of it, shall we?"
"Sounds good."

I kissed Seth for the last fifteen minutes in silence. The only sound that could be heard was the cool breeze and the sound of Seth and I breathing in and out. It was so peaceful and calming to kiss Seth, I could spend an eternity like that. Ten rolled around way to quick and I asked Seth to spend the night.

"I'd love to, JJ."

"Wonderful."

We walked down to the stone steps and toward the cold water; I jumped right in and swam down as fast as I could since I was so cold. I reached the cavern in under a minute with Seth right behind me. He knew exactly that I was in such a rush because of the ice-cold water. Why the water was so cold I didn't know, unless it was the winter season and the water gets colder, then it must be getting close to winter. I emerged from the water with Seth right beside me and picked up my clothes, and I ran back to the cabin since I was freezing. Seth ran up and grabbed me once we got in the cabin, making me laugh and squeal when he threw me over his shoulders and carried me up the stairs. He threw me on the bed and climbed on top of me.

"You wanna have sex?"

"Not tonight, Seth."

"When, JJ?"

"Soon, but not tonight."

"Okay, I'll let you get into your pj's then."

"Thank you."

Seth got up off me and let me run to get my pajamas, only I hadn't done laundry yet, so I didn't have any clean pj's. I guessed I would be sleeping in my bra and underwear again.

"Guess I'm sleeping in my bra and underwear again," I told Seth as I took off my shirt and pants.

"My favorite."

"It's only because you get to see me half naked, perv."

"Hey, hey, who said I was a perv for liking women half naked?"

"Says me."

"Oh ouch, I deserve a back massage for such a comment."

"Fine, but only for half an hour."

I massaged his back with all my amazing skills and heard him thank me for the massage when I was finished.

"That was awesome."

"You're welcome, Seth."

I got down off his back and rolled over on mine, sighing in exhaustion. I wiped some sweat off my head because of the heat of the night and pulled the covers over my half-naked body.

"Well, good night, JJ. I hope you enjoyed the date."

"I did, Seth. It was fun."

"Good."

Seth reached around my stomach and pulled me close into his chest. It felt nice to be in Seth's arms and fall asleep in them. He was so warm and smelled of smoky cologne which was intoxicating. I fell asleep with the feeling of a kiss on my cheek and forehead, drifting off in his big strong arms.

Chapter 33

I woke up snuggled into Seth's chest; I must have flipped around in the dead of the night. He was dead asleep, and I found no reason to be in such a rush, so I fell back asleep and snuggled closer into his chest, feeling Seth put his hand on my back and rub it. Oh, how I loved back rubs. Seth knew what I liked. I woke up again about an hour and a half later and decided to get up out of bed. Seth had me in a death grip, and I couldn't move an inch; the only way to escape was to slither down Seth's body until I was out of his reach. I carefully inched down Seth's body and slid out of his grasp, sneaking downstairs to make myself some breakfast. I made a mango milkshake and eggs with bacon for breakfast, wearing just my underwear and Seth's shirt which was just long enough to cover my, but just barely leaving a little to stick out. It was damn sexy to be wearing Seth's T-shirt over my underwear. I heard Seth coming down the stairs, so I dished up some waffles and bacon for him.

"Good morning, Seth."
"Is that my shirt?"
"Yes, it is. Hope you don't mind if I wear it."
"Not at all. You look great in it."
"Thanks. I made you waffles and bacon by the way."
"You made me waffles?"
"Of course, I did. Why wouldn't I?"
"That's so nice of you."
"Oh, you're too nice. You're not going to believe who I'm choosing for today."
"And who's that?"
"It's . . . classified."

"Aw, please tell me," Seth said as he kissed my neck. I shook my head and turned to eat my delicious breakfast. I enjoyed my hot eggs perfectly seasoned. Seth gave me a thumbs-up for his waffles, covering them in whipped cream and chocolate sauce. I ate quickly because I was so excited to pick my future husband today, the man with whom I'd spend an eternity. I knew exactly who I was going to choose today, and I was 100 percent sure he would choose me too. I finished my breakfast at the same time as Seth did and threw my dishes in the sink. I then ran outside, anxious to get in the water and toward Atlantis. Seth grabbed my hand as I ran, and we both jumped into the water hand in hand. We separated as we swam toward Atlantis; the glow of the city could be seen from the island's edge and drop-off. I was thinking that King Neptune would be throwing a party for me for the ceremony today. I swam up to the gates where the crowds were cheering and applauding at my arrival. I encountered the two kids that had asked me to play ball, and they were screaming, "Choose Seth, choose Seth!" And I laughed as the parents of the kids smacked the kids on the heads and told them just to clap. I couldn't wait to choose my husband. The castle was decorated in peridot, my birthstone. I stepped into the castle, and all the men were there inside, waiting for me along with Akari and her friends, as well as half the kingdom that were invited to the party.

"Nervous?"

"A little, but I am sure the guy will choose me in return."

"Let's hope so."

Seth swam and got in the line with the guys, smiling at them all. I giggled as I stepped up to Neptune. His hair was combed back and he was wearing a tie for the occasion.

"Everyone, please be quiet. Jillian will now choose her husband, one with whom she will spend an eternity. Choose wisely, Jillian, because once you choose there's no turning back."

"I choose . . .," I paused for effect, watching all the guys lean forward in anticipation, "Seth."

I heard Lucas gasp and Shawn sniffle for a minute. Peter broke down and cried, and Alex tapped him on the arm, saying everything was going to be alight. I was close to choosing Alex, but I felt that Seth was more worthy.

"Me?"

"Yes, you Seth. I chose you because you saved my life twice. One reason is that I wouldn't even be here right now if it wasn't for you. Do you choose me?"

"Of course, I do."

I hugged Seth and felt him kiss my forehead when he set me down.

The Tail of an Angel

"It's settled then. She has chosen my youngest son, Seth, and so I grant her the gift of immortality."

Neptune lowered his staff down at me and pointed toward my crystal necklace, and a shot of blue launched out and punched right into the crystal. The necklace glowed so bright I had to cover my eyes, and suddenly the crystal turned dark blue, almost a navy blue, then returned to the normal light blue afterward.

"Congratulations."

"Thank you, Neptune."

I felt fantastic, and I felt that I could take on the world and that nothing could hurt me. I had Seth on my hip as I requested something from Neptune.

"King Neptune?"

"Yes, Jillian?"

"Is it possible I could get married when I'm eighteen? I don't want to get married young."

"I suppose you could get married a year from now. It'll give you and Seth more time to spend together."

"Thank you."

The audience cheered as Seth and I walked out of the castle. Before I left, I had one thing left to say.

"To all the men I didn't choose, I expect you all to be at my wedding in one year's time, as you are my closest friends. Thank you for the opportunity to date you all. I had an amazing time with each and every one of you."

"Bye, Jillian!"

Lucas waved to me from the crowd, and I waved back at him with a big grin on his face. The rest of the guys waved in silence except for Alex, who said good-bye as well. Seth and I waved back and left the castle. The second the gates to the castle closed, Seth kissed me. I quickly wrapped my arms around his neck and played with his hair. It was easy to play underwater and I loved it. When he stopped, he kissed me on the cheek and whispered thank you in my ear.

"You're welcome," I whispered back in his. Seth recommended we go to a club to celebrate and I agreed; a night of dancing before a year with Seth sounded great. We arrived at the club not too far away from the palace and walked right in.

"Congrats on getting chosen, Seth."

"Thank you."

"Do you know that guard?"

"Never met him before."

"He must have been at the party."

We walked right up to the bar and I asked for a margarita. Seth asked for the same.

"A toast, Seth."

"A toast!"

"To us and a happy future."

"A wonderful immortality and eternity together."

"And that no matter what happens—"

"We'll always have each other."

"Always."

We clinked our glasses and took a sip, and surely Seth must have asked her to put more alcohol in my drink because there was no way that there was only one ounce of vodka in my drink. If Seth was trying to get me drunk, he was succeeding. Six margaritas later, I was absolutely wasted. I could hardly stand up, and Seth had to hold me up for a minute before I could stand on my own again.

"I'm okay, really."

"Says the woman who just fell down."

"I'm fine. Now let's go dance."

I grabbed Seth's hand and pulled him to the dance floor to grind. I grinded up on Seth quite hard, pushing my derriere up onto him, which felt so good. I felt him push up on me hard, and I pushed it right back along to the song "Low." I hummed along with the song, wearing those apple bottom jeans. I wish I was wearing boots with fur. With the whole club looking at me, I hit the floor and got low. When we were finished, Seth kissed me, before we left the club and made our way back to the island which I had yet to nickname. Maybe Seth and I could give the island a nickname over the next year. I was looking forward to the next year with Seth; it would be a good time to really bond with Seth. We reached the island and walked up to the cabin, where Seth grabbed me and pulled me up the stairs in his big, strong, and tanned arms. I laughed as he stepped up the stairs and threw me on the bed.

"I'm glad you chose me, Jillian."

"See, I knew you'd like it, and now we can spend eternity together! Yay!"

"I know, right? I'm so excited! So how about it?"

"How about what?"

"Sex. With me."

"Maybe."

"Can I get a hell yeah?"

"Hell maybe."

"Can I get a yes please?"

"Yes."

"Yes . . ."
"Hell, yes, Seth."
"But first I want a back massage."
"Oh, okay."
I climbed on his back and gave him the massage of his life. I heard him mumble something, but I couldn't understand it.
"Could you say that again, sweetie?"
"You're amazing."
"Thank you, sweetie."
I continued to massage his back until I couldn't feel my fingers anymore, which was short of one hour. Seth must have felt good because I was sore beyond belief.
"Oh, Jill, I feel so much better."
"I'm glad you do."
Seth rolled over from his stomach to his back and placed a hand on my face.
"You're so beautiful."
"Oh, Seth, you're not so bad yourself."
"Thanks."
I kissed Seth while he was on his back, then he rolled me over onto mine. He placed his hand at the back of my bikini top and unhooked it. I pulled his shorts off in a snap as he pulled off mine, leaving us both completely naked. I felt no shame in front of Seth. I raised my eyebrow and kissed him. He lifted me off the bed and closer to him until I was thrust up against him. It felt just so good. I was glad I was having sex with Seth. He continued to thrust himself against me over and over again and rocking me back and forth while doing so. He never stopped kissing the whole time. He French-kissed me with all his amazing skill until he stopped for some reason.
"Why are you stopping?"
"I just was wondering why your eyes are glowing blue."
"Oh, Jesus, not again."
With just my housecoat on, I got up and looked in the mirror and saw my eyes glowing the same shade as my crystal. I closed my eyes and opened them, hoping I was hallucinating, but I wasn't and they were still glowing.
"Why are your eyes glowing?" I heard Seth say from the bedroom; my eyes wouldn't stop glowing.
"This happened once before. I'm not too fond of what follows."
"And what's that?"
I felt a great pain in my back as I grabbed my clothes and put them on; it made me scream.

"Jill, are you okay?"
"Yeah, I'm all right. Just don't look at my back, okay?"
"Why not?"
"You'll see."

I stepped out of the bathroom with just my bra and underwear on and Seth put his shorts back on. Then I felt my wings touch the door. Seth gasped and put his hands on his head.

"You have wings!"
"I know. Freaks me out too."
"But why?"
"This happened on the yacht with my boyfriend because he wished for it on a shooting star."
"Oops."
"Don't tell me you wished for this?"
"Maybe."
"Seth, tell me the truth."
"Okay, I wished I could sleep with an angel."
"Well, here you are, angel wings and all."
"Can you fly?"
"Yep."

I jumped out of the window and flew outside, soaring high above the island so high that the island looked like a speck. I suddenly stopped flying and fell freely almost all the way to the ground until a single beat of my wings made me soar once more. I cheered with a woot and flew back to my room in the cabin; my wings were so big I just barely fit in the window. I opened my wings when I got inside and stretched, spanning out my wings from tip to tip. The tips of my wings touched both walls of the room; Seth looked at my wings in awe.

"Well, aren't you going to un-wish it?"
"I don't know if I want to."
"Seth, you know I can't stay like this forever."
"Okay, just let me kiss you first."

Seth ran up and kissed me, making my wings drop to the ground. His tongue slipped into my mouth and melted on my tongue. He tasted like the bubble gum I'd been saving that I had found downstairs until I accidentally felt his gum slip into my mouth.

"Can I have my gum back?"
"Sure."

I took the gum out of my mouth and handed him the gum.

"Actually, it's my gum that I found, and lo and behold, there's a piece missing, Seth. That was my gum."

"So I stole a piece. Kill me."
"Maybe I will."
"Ooo, I'm so scared."
"You should be. I'm a bad girl."
"Oh, that's hot sex. Now."
"Okay!"

I hopped into the bed with Seth x and rocked his world with my bra ripped off and underwear slowly pulled down. He thrust himself into me and made me give an inhaled scream, and suddenly it felt amazing. I think I was done. Seth screamed and lay down on top of me. Something told me Seth was finished too.

"That was incredible."
"I know. I'm awesome."
"Yes, I know. You were."
"So were you."

Seth laughed and kissed my neck tenderly. I giggled and rolled over onto my side. He rolled over and stared at me with a smile on his face. My wings faded away and my eyes stopped glowing after he kissed me.

"So how was your first time?"
"It wasn't my first time, Seth, you know that."
"Oh right, well, it was mine."
"That's good."
"Good? It was awesome!"
"It was for me too."
"I'm glad it was."

Seth put his arm around my shoulder and pulled me into his chest for the night. I snuggled into his chest and placed my hand on it, bare and warm. I was glad I had slept with Seth. I rolled closer to him, still naked, and cuddled in close for the night.

Chapter 34

I got up bright and early, long before Seth was even close to waking up. I rushed downstairs and started the oven to make some Tater Tots. For breakfast, I would make waffles and Tater Tots with eggs. But first I snuck back into bed with Seth, who was naked as a wee baby. I looked under the covers and slipped under the covers with him. I snuggled under his arms and nuzzled into his warm chest. Seth rolled over and cuddled in closer to me. Seth woke up and I pretended to still be sleeping, but I ended up laughing instead.

"You were pretending to sleep, weren't you?"

"Yeah, I was."

"Why?"

"So I could sleep with you longer."

"Aw, aren't you sweet."

Seth kissed me on the forehead before getting up and putting on a pair of pants, his boxers on underneath. Seth hadn't brought a shirt, which I didn't mind. Suddenly, Seth found a shirt and put it on. Aw!

"Breakfast is almost ready, Seth."

"Okay."

I started making the waffles in the waffle maker and pulled the Tater Tots out of the oven. I called out to Seth to let him know that breakfast was ready.

"So what's for breakfast?" Seth asked as he sat down at the table.

"Waffles, eggs, and Tater Tots."

"Oh, I love Tater Tots!"

"Me too! I found them in the freezer!"

"Yay!"

I finished making the eggs and placed them on Seth's plate and my own. Seth put whipped cream and strawberry sauce on his waffles while I simply buttered mine and put syrup all over them. I licked the butter off my knife, making Seth laugh.

"What's so funny?"

"Maybe you could lick my butter knife sometime, if you know what I mean."

"Yeah, right! Just eat your breakfast."

"C'mon, you're my fiancée. I deserve a little treat."

"Wait till Christmas, sweetie."

"Christmas is so far away though."

"All the reason to wait for such a special occasion."

"Aw."

I finished up my waffles and eggs and left my Tater Tots until last, and then I ate them quickly. Everything was perfectly cooked, and I couldn't be happier that I chose Seth. What I'd do for a full year with Seth on our own private island, an eternity together, and all the time in the world to fall in love; the only problem was I already had.

"So what are our plans for today?"

"I was hoping we could explore the rest of the island, maybe rebuild that little shack you burned down."

"Yeah, about that, I'm not ashamed I did that."

"What?"

"Yeah, I don't feel bad at all."

Seth stood up and threw me against a wall, choking me as he did so.

"You are going to regret saying that."

"Seth, you're hurting me."

"Damn right, I'm hurting you. You'll pay for what you've done."

"Seth, please stop!"

I barely choked out the words as everything started to go dark.

"Seth, I love . . . love."

I heard Seth say, "What?" before I passed out. I was scared as I was totally unconscious and I was aware of it. I heard him say, "What have I done?" Well, I can answer that for you, Seth. You choked me enough to knock me out. I couldn't believe Seth would ever hurt me, but he did and I didn't know if I'd ever forgive him. I woke up in my bedroom with my clothes on and Seth sitting on the edge of the bed.

"I'm so sorry, JJ. I can't tell you how sorry I am."

"What the hell, Seth? I tell you how I'm not ashamed of burning down your shack and you knock me out?"

"I'm so sorry."

Seth kissed me and laid me down on the bed. I didn't resist; he as my fiancé after all. I wasn't going to forgive him anytime soon for what he did. He lifted my hips to press up against his and grinned as he did so. I laughed as he rolled over and lay at the base of the bed, and then I was on top of him.

"I won't forgive you for this."

"Why not?"

"Because how can I forgive you for something as bad as you knocking me out?"

"You'll learn to love it in time."

"Yeah, right. I hate being knocked out."

"Can't you ever forgive me for my little fit of rage?"

"No, Seth, I simply can't."

"Give me a thousand years?"

"Sure."

"What was it you were going to say before you passed out?"

"I love cherries."

"Are you sure it wasn't something else? Maybe I love you."

"Nope, it was 'I love cherries,' I'm sure of it."

"Okay, whatever you say, you'll say it eventually."

"In your dreams, Seth."

"Oh, you'll love me at some point. We have an eternity to spend together, remember?"

"I know. I'm looking forward to it."

I kissed Seth on the cheek and headed downstairs to find that the entire kitchen was clean.

"Umm, Seth? Why is the kitchen clean?"

"While you were out, I cleaned up the kitchen for you."

"Aw, Seth, you shouldn't have."

"Well, I did."

I walked over to Seth and kissed him on the forehead and thanked him for cleaning the kitchen. I walked outside to the warm beach in my clothes I was mysteriously dressed in and tiptoed into the water just to let my feet soak. A small fish glided over my toes and scared me enough to make me fall over and get my clothes soaking wet. I stripped them off and threw them off to the shore. I was wearing a bikini top and thong.

"Seth, how did I get in this thong?"

"It's not like I haven't seen you naked before. Besides, you look good in a thong."

"I'm going to go change into my bikini bottom before we work on that shack."

The Tail of an Angel

"No! Please stay in your thong."
"The only underwear I'll wear for you today is my cheeky underwear."
"I can do that."

I walked back to the cabin and changed from my thong to my cheeky style underwear. I looked fabulous as I walked outside in confidence. I grabbed a hammer that I saw on my way out. I walked toward Seth, dodging him to chop down a tree and another and another and another until I chopped down enough trees to build the shack. I started chopping up smaller pieces to build up the walls, and they were up in no time at all. Once the walls were up, we placed some palm tree leaves for the roof; bright and green they covered and concealed just fine. I stepped inside to find the blank walls I had built up and wondered what Seth might put in the shack this time.

"So what are you going to put in the shack?"
"Pictures of you and I and our eternity together. Say cheese!"

I smiled as a blinding flash clicked, and a photo printed off out of the camera. He pinned it up on the wall and stepped back to enjoy the first photo in the shack.

"Day one."
"First day of forever."
"Exactly."

Seth kissed me and slammed me against the wall that shook when I hit it. I wrapped my legs around his waist as he lifted me off the ground and onto the wall with his hands around my back holding me up. It was rough, but he kissed me just as fine as he always did. When he stopped, he set me down and apologized.

"What are you apologizing for? That was fantastic."
"For slamming you against the wall."
"Oh yeah, that kind of hurt."
"I really don't mean to hurt you. I'm just too strong."
"Not as strong as you think."
"How strong do you think I am?"
"Very strong, but emotionally you're as strong as a mouse."
"Hey, I am very emotionally strong."
"Says the man who cried when I was unconscious."
"How could you know that? You were unconscious."
"I can still hear when I'm unconscious, and I heard you crying."
"You can't tell anyone I cried. No one can know I cried."
"Your secret's safe with me."
"Okay, well, what now."
"Didn't you say you wanted to explore the rest of the island?"

"Yeah, I did. Let's do that."

"Let's go."

We stepped out of the shack; while I put some clothes on, Seth waited outside. I changed quickly into a tank top and shorts and walked back down the stairs. I ran outside, speeding past him, laughing as he tackled me to catch up and spin around. I leaned in to kiss him, but then I felt Miko tug on my shorts.

"Hey, Miko, care to join us?"

Miko jumped up and nodded his head. Seth and I walked along the shore and found a trail into the forest. The trail was paved out as if it had been walked on a lot before, as if someone had been there before. I bet that man who wrote that journal was there and trekked into the forest long before I was there. Only how he could've walked with that bad leg of his confused me. I wondered if Seth was there for a while before I was. Miko led the way into the forest with Seth by my side as we walked along the path. There wasn't all that much to see besides trees and bushes and more trees; it was quite boring, I assure you.

"Someone please show me something of interest!"

As we turned around the corner, an oasis appeared.

"All right, thank you."

"Another oasis?"

"It's freshwater too."

I took a sip of the water from the freshwater oasis, and it was the best water I had ever tasted. Seth dunked his head next to me and slurped up the water.

"Wow, this water is amazing."

"Not as amazing as this."

I took off all my clothes and jumped into the water, skinny-dipping! I came up and hooked my pointer finger at him, teasing him to come and join me. Seth took off everything but his shorts and jumped in.

"Aw, c'mon, Seth, take off those shorts."

"Actually I'm pretty comfortable wearing them."

"What's the fun in that, huh? I'm not wearing a thing and you should too."

"Well, okay."

I felt Seth swim up closer to me without his shorts on, as he threw his shorts out of the water and onto the land nearby. I swam up to him and wrapped my arms around his neck and kissed him. He French-kissed me back, his tongue twisting with mine. He lifted me out of the water for only a second before he pulled me underwater and kissed me there. I accidentally

The Tail of an Angel

inhaled underwater and choked a bit on the water as I resurfaced. I coughed and coughed, and Seth asked if I was okay. I couldn't even breathe.

"Can't . . . breathe."

It was only a matter of time before I started to feel dizzy and suddenly everything got really dark. I saw Seth's concerned face before I passed out and fell back into the water. I woke up on land with my clothes back on and Seth's on as well. I asked him what had happened, and he told me I had swallowed some water and would have nearly drowned if he hadn't given me CPR.

"I almost drowned?"

"Yeah, I couldn't bear to lose you, so I gave you CPR, and sure enough you were just fine. I'm so glad you're okay."

Seth picked me up and hugged me for a solid minute. Once he stopped, he kissed me on the cheek and jumped back into the water. I hopped back in as well and swam down to the bottom of the oasis and found a tunnel to another cave.

"Hey, Seth, I found another cave. Join me."

"Okay."

I swam down into the cavern, and suddenly it ended with a splash into a small air pocket behind the waterfall. It was full of crystals that were shaped just like the crystals on our necks.

"This must be where Neptune keeps the extra crystals for newcomers."

"I never knew about this place."

"I seriously doubt that."

"No, really, I never knew this place existed."

"Why are there so few left? Shouldn't there be lots?"

I counted maybe six crystals in the walls with thousands of holes that fit the crystals all around the cave.

"I guess there isn't much more room to join the people of Atlantis."

"I guess not, but at least I was able to join."

"Yeah, good thing too otherwise I wouldn't have met my beautiful fiancée."

"Good thing."

I smiled and wondered how we'd get out of the cave.

"Any idea how we get out?"

"No idea."

I felt along the wall for maybe a secret door; whether there was one or not, I still looked silly. I saw a questionable rock on the ground and stepped on it accidentally, which opened a door to the left of me. I smiled and looked over at Seth, crossing my arms, tapping my foot and waiting for Seth to go through the door.

"Nice work."

"Thanks."

I walked in, and Seth was right behind me and walked into the darkness.

"Do you have a match or something to light this dark tunnel?"

"There's a torch on the wall."

"Oh, okay."

I grabbed the torch and walked forward into the darkness; it seemed to go on forever. I walked and walked for what appeared to feel like an hour until the tunnel finally ended in a large cave.

"The kings of our past!"

I looked up and saw the kings floating in stone faces around some glowing orb in the center of it.

"Seth, what's that glowing thing in the center of the kings of your past? Seth?"

Seth was on the ground speaking a language I didn't understand and huddled into a little ball.

"Seth?"

He continued to speak in a foreign language until I touched him on the shoulder.

"Seth, what are you doing?"

"It's the ancient language of Atlantis. Long before the reign of my father, Atlantis had its own language made up of four other languages until it was lost to us during the great flood. Afterward, we just decided to speak English, and the knowledge was lost to us forever. But before my mother died, she told me if I ever found the kings of our past I should say the ancient tribute prayer in their presence and honor."

"Ancient Atlantian?"

"Yep, I didn't mean to freak you out."

"Oh no, not at all."

"Yeah, I didn't mind either."

"*Ahhh!*"

I screamed when I saw Sedrick and Skylar behind us with their crystals glowing in the darkness behind us.

"Relax, Jill, it's just us."

"I know. You just scared me."

"Sorry, we came to pay our respects to the kings of our past."

"So you already did the weird praying tribute thing."

"Yeah, we were right behind Seth the whole time."

"So what's so important about the kings of your past?"

"Oh, it's just the kings of our past. It's no big deal. *Of course, it's a big deal!*"

Sedrick yelled at me until his crystal rose off his chest and glowed toward the giant sphere floating above the water. It was cold and I assumed bottomless since I couldn't see the bottom. Sedrick started to walk toward the water, his eyes glowing blue. I tried holding him back, but he was too strong and continued to walk forward. He mumbled something in ancient Atlantian I didn't understand, and Seth translated it for me.

"Mother."

"Mom isn't up there," Skylar told me. It was obvious Sedrick was under some sort of hypnosis by the crystal as he walked onto the water without sinking. I stood there with my eyes wide open as he stepped closer and closer to the crystal.

"Why do I get the feeling I've seen this before?"

"This looks like that one scene from *Atlantis: The Lost Empire* when Kita rose up into the crystal and merged with it, becoming a human crystal."

"Let's hope that doesn't happen to Sedrick."

I watched as he stepped under the crystal and started rising off the water toward it.

"This can't be good."

Once he rose high enough, he stopped near the center of the sphere and starting spinning with the stone kings. They spun and spun until it hurt to look at the brightness of the spinning sphere, and then it finally slowed down and stopped with Sedrick floating in the center. He was glowing blue all over and the sphere with the bright blue crystal was gone. I feared that the same thing that had happened to Kita in Atlantis may have happened to Sedrick, as he came back down onto the water.

"Sedrick?"

He opened his crystal blue eyes and looked right at me, his eyes glowing brighter than I'd ever seen. He started walking toward me, and with every step a stone king of the past fell into the water, and I realized that the water wasn't bottomless but rather quite shallow. I tried to touch his arm when he touched land, but Seth stopped me and said that if I touched him I might turn to crystal.

"I've seen this in a movie. This can't be good."

"Is Sedrick going to be okay?"

"I don't know how to stop this. We'll have to ask my father."

"What are we going to do with Sedrick?"

"There's nothing we can do but get him back to the cabin and stay there."

"There's a trap door that leads back to the surface just across the water."
"Looks like we're swimming again."
"Maybe we could skinny-dip again."
"Seth! Not in front of your brother, especially Skylar."
"I don't mind seeing you naked."
"Sorry, Skylar, I'll only be naked for my fiancé."
"Fair enough."

I walked over to the water and dived in, swimming to the other side. Skylar was behind me and Seth while Sedrick walked over the water with us. We reached a secret door which led to a tunnel and let out into the forest. Once we got out into the forest, Seth led the way back to the cabin. Once we reached the cabin, Sedrick sat down on a chair and it turned to crystal. I didn't mind n the chair turning into a crystal as it looked quite lovely. I put on my bikini and ran out with Seth to the water to go talk to Neptune.

"Do you think your father will know what to do?"
"Let's hope so."

We dove into the water and quickly swam to Atlantis. Neptune was in the castle and was chatting with Akari. I interrupted the king and asked for his assistance.

"Your Highness, I have some bad news. Your son is merged to some sort of crystal and we don't know how to stop it. Can you help us?"

"Ah, this has happened once before to my beloved wife. She was bonded to the crystal when we first got married. I stopped it using the necklaces. We'll need a special one to stop the crystal now as it is growing stronger over the many, many years. Take this. Which one of my sons is it bonded to?"

"Sedrick."
"Just drive this crystal into his heart and he'll be just fine."
"Are you sure?"
"Of course, I am sure. I've done this before."
"And what of the crystal?"
"It will instinctively return back to where it came from."
"Thank you, Your Highness."

He handed us a green crystal, and we quickly swam back up to the surface. Once we got there and ran into the cabin, we found Skylar was simply waiting for us while Sedrick patiently sat in the crystal chair.

"This should do the trick."

I drove the crystal into his heart, and the crystal faded away from his body until his eyes finally stopped glowing.

"What happened to me?"

The Tail of an Angel

"You were bonded to the crystal, and I don't know why or how but at least you're better now."

"Thanks, Jill, I feel much better."

I kissed him on the forehead and walked into the kitchen to grab a mango and eat it. Seth gave a look of concern at my arm.

"Jillian, your arm."

"What? What's wrong with my arm?"

I looked down at my arm, and a huge scratch was up the length of my arm.

"Oh, I am hurt! I am very much hurt."

"Relax, I can fix it!"

Sedrick ran up to me and took off his crystal necklace, and he dangled it over my scar, putting his hand over it. I felt a slight burning on my arm, and as he removed his hand I watched him lift it. His handprint remained bright and blue until it faded away into my skin; the scratch was gone.

"How did you do that?"

"The crystals have healing powers. Didn't Seth ever tell you that?"

"No, he never did."

"My bad. Thanks, Sedrick."

"My pleasure."

We walked upstairs, as Skylar and Sedrick had left, and I sat down on my bed.

"Sorry about your arm."

"Oh, it's nothing, Seth, it's fine."

"Want me to kiss it better?"

"I already told you it's fine."

"Okay, I'm still going to kiss you though."

"I don't mind that at all."

Seth gently kissed me and rolled me over on my back, trying to pull my bikini bottoms off. I giggled and told him no.

"Not tonight, Seth."

"Aw, why not, sweetie?"

"Because I'm just not in the mood."

"Maybe I can get you in the mood."

"Maybe not. I'm just really tired."

"Okay, good night then."

"I had fun today though."

"I did too, besides my brother being turned into crystal."

"Ha-ha, good night, Seth."

Chapter 35

I woke up in Seth's arms once more to begin our forever. It was warm in bed with him, so I decided not to get up and Seth squeezed me tighter. What we would do today I had no idea, what we would do besides laze around the house. Seth got up first as I pretended to be still asleep, and I heard him giggle as he poked my nose with a feather.

"Stop it, Seth."

"Good morning, sunshine."

"Is that how you want to wake me up? Feathers? Not with a kiss or a hug?

"I will kiss you if you want."

"I'd like that very much."

He quickly kissed me before running down the stairs in his boxers and into the kitchen. I tried to keep up, but I ended up tripping while going down the stairs and twisting my ankle again.

"Are you okay?"

"Just grab the crutches."

"Why?"

"I rolled my ankle falling down the stairs."

"Again?"

"Yes, again."

Seth quickly grabbed the crutches from the kitchen and helped me to my feet to get on them. I hopped up and started walking toward the kitchen, sitting down on one of the stools.

"I'll make us breakfast."

"Sounds good. I can't really cook at the moment as it is."

"What are you in the mood for?"

"Bacon and eggs."

"Coming right up."

Seth pulled the bacon out of the fridge and put it in a sizzling pan. The eggs he cracked in a bowl so that if any shell fragments fell off the egg you could pick them out, something I taught Seth. Once he finished, he poured the eggs into a hot pan and split them up with a spatula; since the pan couldn't take metal, he split everything with a spatula. He was so graceful in the kitchen; he stirred the bacon some more and the crackle of grease bounced up and burned my arm from a great distance. He finished really quickly and plated the bacon and eggs.

"And I made Tater Tots as well."

"Thank you, Seth. I'd love some."

He handed me the plate with the bacon and eggs and scooped up some Tater Tots and put them on my plate. The eggs were prepared just the way I wanted, and the bacon was chewy, just the way I liked. The Tater Tots were crunchy and hot and perfectly cooked in the oven. Seth was really impressing me with this meal today. I wondered what we could do today as my ankle was twisted. Something told me that we would have a lazy day at home today.

"So what do you have planned for today?"

"Well, I was going to tour more of the island with you today, but seeing as you're kind of handicapped, I guess we'll just spend the day at home."

"That sounds just dandy."

"Dandy?"

"Fine."

"Oh, right."

"You've never heard the word dandy before?"

"There are lots of words from the surface I've never heard before. You should teach them to me."

"In good time, sweetie."

"Okay, sweetie."

I munched on a Tater Tot and some bacon; the combination was delicious, and I couldn't wait to eat some more eggs. Everything was simply perfect and I couldn't be happier. I finished my meal in silence as my mouth was full of a good chunk of the meal and I couldn't really talk with my mouth full. I only talked once the whole meal to ask for some more salt and pepper for my eggs and Tater Tots. It was strange to put salt on my Tater Tots or Mexi-Fries as some people called them, but who cared? Only Seth would know I was weird, but I guess that was why he loved me. Maybe I could say it today, up by the hammock or maybe on the beach; there were plenty of romantic places I could say, thank goodness for this island. I didn't know if I could make it to the beach on my crutches, but

I had done it once before, so I suppose I could do it again. I finished up my breakfast and handed Seth my finished and cleaned off plate. Seth's plate had a ketchup stain on it, suggesting he had dipped his Tater Tots in ketchup. I think Seth smiled at me when I handed him my plate, but I couldn't tell if it was a grin or a smile. He took my plate and threw it in the sink along with his, which he rinsed off with some water from the tap.

"So I think we'll just have a lazy day at home."

"Sounds good, but at some point I want to watch the sunset in the hammock up by the stone steps."

"Okay, okay."

Seth grabbed me and set me up on the counter and kissed me. I dropped my crutches on the ground with a loud crack and wrapped my arms around his neck, pulling him closer. He shoved up against me and pulled my legs around him. I smiled under my kiss and squeezed him tight with my legs around him until he quickly pulled me off the counter and held me up by my back. He flipped me around to lie down in his arms, and he carried me up the stairs and laid me down on my back on the bed in my room. I embraced the fact that he kissed me the second he laid me down on the bed. The second my top came off I tore off his shirt and took off his pants, and in no time we had sex.

"So how was your third time?"

"Great. Yours?"

"Actually, it's my second, but it was still fantastic."

"Good, what time is it?"

"I think it's around seven."

"Oh my gosh, the sun is going to set soon."

"It doesn't set for another hour."

"All the better reason to get dressed and go get ready."

"Do we have to get dressed?"

"Yes, Seth."

"Aw."

I put on my bikini top and bottom and raced down the stairs while Seth put on his swimming trunks. I raced outside toward the cavern in the back, using my crutches with Seth by my side, and we jumped into the water. It was freezing water and reminded me of my swimming days back when I swam competitively; those were fun days I had with my family. I quickly jumped out of the water and onto the rock that was cool for a change; the cavern had finally cooled down. It was so cold in the cavern I swore I could see my breath.

"It's a bit chilly in here, isn't it?"

"Yeah, it is. I swear I can see my breath."

"I can see mine."

Seth breathed out and sure enough a cloud of fog arose from his mouth. I immediately stood up and balanced on my one leg until Seth got out of the water. He scooped me up off the ground and carried me in his big, strong arms up the stairs until we reached the hammock, in which he gently set me down and joined me.

"Anything you want to talk about?"

"I can't believe you twisted your ankle."

"How long do you think I'll have to be on my crutches?"

"Oh, a couple weeks."

"A couple weeks? How am I going to survive?"

"Don't worry, JJ. I'll take care of you."

"Don't you have duties to perform in Atlantis?"

"They can wait. It's just scraping barnacles off the coral reef to make it look better."

"But it's so important."

"It's not really."

"Well, okay, but I demand that every morning we watch the sunrise on the beach."

"Agreed."

I turned over to face Seth and quickly kissed him for a second as a thank-you for taking care of me. I smiled when I finished and he smiled back. I think it was a mere grin this time. I rolled over on my side to watch the sunset, as the entire sky turned orange and pink. Seth put his arms over my stomach and under my belly and pulled me closer to him. I put my hand on his and watched the sun sink into the sea. It was a beautiful sight and perhaps my favorite sunset with Seth. After the sun set, the stars began to peek out and shine in the night, darkness coated the sky, and the moon appeared over Seth and me. I saw a shooting star, but Seth called it and made me laugh. Seth handed me a margarita he had made; only how he had got it up there I had no idea.

"How did you get these up here?"

"Magic!"

Seth made me laugh again. He pulled me closer into his chest as we watched the stars, sipping on our margaritas.

"Want to go to a club?"

"Sure."

Seth helped me down the stairs and threw me in the water. He jumped in, nearly landing on me, and came up with his shorts floating next to me.

"You might need these."

I handed Seth his shorts as he laughed and blushed a little.

"Are you blushing, Seth?"

"No, of course not."

"It's okay to blush in front of me, Seth. I'm your fiancée. You can blush for me."

"I'm not blushing!"

"Okay, okay, calm down. Let's go to the club."

Seth pulled me closer to him and kissed me quickly.

"I love you."

"I love you too, Seth."

"Hey! You finally said I love you!"

"Yeah, I did."

"I'm so proud of you!"

Seth hugged me and twirled me around in a circle, then set me down in the water and kissed me again. He French-kissed me softly, as I put my hands around his neck and pulled him close. I thought I'd change it up from wrapping my arms around his neck. Once he stopped kissing me, he lifted me out of the water and onto his hips.

"Are you going to put me down anytime soon?"

"Nah, I might just keep you on my hips all night."

"What about the club?"

"Oh yeah, we have to go to that."

"Put me down, Seth."

"Okay."

Seth gently placed me down in the water and swam under into the darkness below. I swam under after staring at the ceiling for a second; it sparkled for some reason today. I dove under and followed Seth down, and I saw his crystal glowing ahead of me. Before I knew it, Seth's crystal disappeared while mine glowed red.

"Oh jeez, I can't let Seth see it glow red."

"What was that, dear?"

"Nothing, Seth, nothing."

I swam a bit slower until my crystal stopped glowing red and caught up with Seth, who was already at the surface. He waited for me patiently while I walked out of the water. Seth was waiting, tapping his foot on the sand, and I smiled and grabbed his hand before running toward the water, feeling Seth trip as I pulled him. He laughed all the way to the water, and I let go of his hand before jumping in. The water was cool but warmer than the water in the cavern out at the back. I swam along, with my tail formed, into a current that I discovered and beat Seth to Atlantis and to the club. I sped past several people since it was really late, and glowing fish locked in little glass balls lit the streets. Once I was at the club, I waited for Seth for about a minute before he caught up and saw me waiting for him.

"Took you long enough."

"It wasn't a race."

"It was to me! Now, c'mon, let's dance."

I grabbed Seth's hand and pulled him up to the bouncer who let us pass by.

"Congratulations, you two, have fun."

"Thank you."

I pulled Seth onto the dance floor and requested that the DJ play a song of my choice since it was sort of our honeymoon. The slow song ended, and "DJ Got Us Falling in Love" came on just as I had hoped and Seth and I began to grind. I felt him push up against me and I pushed right back as we swayed to the song of Usher. Soon after, more songs like "Low," "In the Dark," "Smack That," and "Misery" came on, and Seth and I grinded until two in the morning. After that, we took a break and grabbed about twelve margaritas at the bar, and then I was hammered. I couldn't even walk straight in the club, so Seth thought it was time to take me home. I was held up on Seth's shoulders, while I laughed uncontrollably. I am the type of drunk that laughs a lot and can't stand up for more than forty-five minutes. Luckily, it didn't take long for us to leave the club and head back home. Seth took me up the stairs almost falling down, but he made it up and crashed on the bed, laughing really hard; it must have been contagious. Suddenly, I began to laugh too and the entire cabin filled with our laughter. When we stopped, we snickered for a minute but eventually calmed down, and Seth knocked the lamp off the bedside table with his foot.

"You're going to have to pay me back for that."

"I don't have any cash."

"Well, you have to pay me back somehow."

"How about a two-hour back massage?"

"Can you really do two hours?"

"I can try."

"Okay, I'll take it."

It was completely dark, and the only light in the room was from the crystals on our necks; it was kind of hot actually—in the room that is, not being alone with Seth in a dark room. Seth worked his hands into my back, and it felt so nice after a hard day of dancing with Seth. I tell you it's not easy living the lifestyle I do; lounging around all day and dancing at night is hard work. And yet I still had a flat stomach, yes! I was lying down when I felt a kiss on my back, and Seth returned to massage my back for another hour. I had to unhook my bikini top for him to massage my back, but I could care less. He'd already seen me naked—twice. He was a great masseur and it felt really, really good. I sighed as he worked his hands into my back harder and harder and it felt amazing. One hour passed quickly and the second passed even quicker. I was in awe as he finished and kissed the back of my neck.

"You're drunk, Seth."

"So are you!"

"All the reason not to have sex tonight."

"Why not? I know you want to."

"Yeah, I know, but I'd feel bad in the morning if I can't remember what I did the night before, if that means I was with you."

"That's awfully sweet of you, Jill, but I've had such a good time with you tonight, all I want to do is finish it off by spending a fantastic night with you."

"I'd love to, but I just can't."

"C'mon, please?"

"No, Seth, I've made my decision."

Seth placed his hand on my neck and kissed it, giving me a small hickey. He turned to the other side and kissed it hard. I lay back and let him place his hands on my waist as he kissed my neck just as hard as before.

"Oh, Seth, I'm having second thoughts."

"So what do you say now?"

"Okay, let's do it."

We spent the night having sex and slept in afterward. The sex had improved since last time; maybe Seth was one of those guys that got better at sex when they were drunk. Anyways, after we finished I lay back in Seth's arms naked, and I felt him squeeze me closer to him, holding my hips. I fell asleep in his arms and heard him whisper in my ear, "Please remember this in the morning."

"I'll try. No guarantees though."

"Okay, JJ, good night."

"Good night, Seth."

Chapter 36

I woke up in Seth's arms and couldn't recall anything that had happened the night before. I couldn't remember anything past dinner last night; although I remembered Seth saying something about how I shouldn't forgot something, but I couldn't remember. I saw that Seth was sound asleep and I didn't mind falling back asleep with him. We slept in until one or so. It was around five when we had fallen asleep. I did remember that surprisingly. I woke up at one and so did Seth, kissing me on the forehead to wake me up.

"Good morning, JJ."

"Morning, Seth."

"Do you remember anything about last night?"

"Not a clue."

"Are you serious?"

"Yeah, I'm serious."

"So you don't remember anything about last night at all?"

"Not a clue, Seth."

"So you don't remember what I told you?"

"What part of 'not a clue' don't you understand?"

"All right, all right, well, I told you to remember last night."

"So what did we do last night?"

"Well, we had supper. It was delicious and then we went to a club and danced dirty. You were great. I was a better grinder, then we got drunk and I had to carry you home. I got really drunk and I barely made it up the stairs, but I made it. Then I convinced you to have sex with me, then we slept together and then we woke up."

"Is that seriously what happened?"

"You bet."

"I feel kind of bad that I don't remember anything at all."
"Don't feel too bad. It was fantastic."
"But I missed it. I can't remember a thing!"
"It's okay. We can try again tonight."
"Okay, so what can we do for the rest of the day?"
"I have no idea."
"How about a stroll on the beach?"
"More like a stumble and fall for you."
"Oh shut up, I won't fall."
"Fall for me, that is."
"Oh, Seth, you . . . you . . . you're crazy."
"Crazy about you."
"Oh, you."
"Well, let's go then."
"Can't we stay in bed just a little longer?"
"Okay, for you anything."

I cuddled up to Seth as he put his arm around me and pulled me into his warm chest. He was comforting, and did I mention he was warm? He was hotter than the steamy cavern out back like it used to be. I kind of wish that it would get hot again, because Seth would always kiss me in the steamy heat. I loved it. I wish Seth would kiss me now. I kind of really wanted to.

"Do I get a good morning kiss?"
"Of course, you do."

Seth lifted my face up with his fingers, and he put his hand behind my neck before kissing me as I slipped my tongue into his mouth. He gave it right back, slipping his tongue back in mine for about five minutes before he stopped, then held in for one quicker normal kiss. I quickly kissed him once more before smiling, and he kissed my forehead and laughed.

"What's so funny?"
"You're cold as ice."
"Oh really."
"Yeah, here take some more blankets."
"I'm not warming up though."
"Oh, you'll warm up soon."

Seth walked over the thermostat and turned it up, still not wearing any clothes, and crawled back into bed.

"You know you aren't wearing pants, kind of sexy."
"Really? I thought I put my pants on."
"Nope."
"Well, I'm going to get dressed."

"Aw, okay."

Seth got dressed, and I got up to get dressed beside him. But I fell over onto him as he was putting his pants on, and we fell over with me landing on his chest.

"Ouch."

"Sorry, I didn't mean to fall on you."

"It's all right, I'm okay."

Seth got up and helped me to my feet and put my bikini top on.

"You might need this."

"Thanks, Seth. It's a little important."

"A little?"

"Okay, well, a lot, thanks."

I ran downstairs once I put my bikini bottoms on and went straight for the fridge. I found some yogurt and ate about five for breakfast, as I heard Seth walk down the stairs, wearing his shorts. Seth looked so much better without a shirt on. Once I finished the yogurt, I stepped outside in the sun and basked in its glory; it was wonderful. Seth joined me and put his arm around my shoulder, holding the guitar in his hand.

"Let's walk and play some music."

"Okay!"

I walked beside Seth and heard him strum the guitar beside me, humming along to a song I didn't know.

"Save it for a fire, Seth."

"Aw, why can't I sing now?"

"'Cause I prefer singing by a fire."

"Oh, I see."

"What does that stand for?"

"Oh, I see."

"I know, but what does it stand for?"

"Oh, I see!"

"Oh, okay, no need to yell, Seth."

"Well, you wouldn't get it the first time."

"Whatever you say, Seth."

I kept walking along the shore, splashing my feet in the cool water and getting my feet wet and sandy until I saw a snake pop out of the water.

"Oh, look a snake."

"*Ahhh!* Where?"

"Relax, I have it in my hands."

"Get rid of it!"

"No, I demand you pet it."

"No!"

"Pet it, Seth, or I shall break up with you!"

"Okay."

Seth tentatively moved his hand toward the snake as it stuck his tongue out at Seth. Seth petted the top of his head and sighed, then put his hand on the body of the snake. I thought that Seth had finally faced his fear of snakes, and for that I was proud of him. The snake wrapped itself around my neck and put its head on my shoulder as we continued to search for the fire pit near the shore. Once we found it, I released the snake into the forest after Seth returned with some firewood. I released the snake, but it returned to me and curled up around my leg.

"Come on, little guy. That's your home."

The snake slithered away into the forest where I saw a bird pick it up and eat it. So much for the little snake! But I guess that's the circle of life, from one of my favorite Disney movies—*The Lion King*. Seth found the log we had sat on earlier and pulled it closer. He sat down on it with the guitar. He started playing a song I was familiar with and sang along.

"I love that song!"

"I know! Me too. That's why I sang it for you."

"Well, isn't that nice?"

"I'm glad you like it."

"I did, Seth. Anything else you can sing for me?"

"*How about 'I Wish You Were Here' by Cody Simpson?*"

"How did you know that was my favorite song? I've heard it like two hundred times."

"Just a guess."

"You know what, Seth?"

"What?"

"I'll always be here."

"I know you will."

I kissed Seth on the cheek and grabbed the guitar out of his hands.

"What can I sing for you, Seth?"

"Nothing."

Seth grabbed me, then kissed me. I dropped the guitar with a small thump and twang on the sand when one of the strings hit a small rock. I kissed Seth back and snuck my tongue into his mouth once more. Seth French-kissed me back with all the skills he had, and he melted in my mouth. I smiled under my kiss, stepping back to breathe, then finished kissing him.

"Why'd you stop?"
"Because I couldn't breathe."
"That's why you breathe through your nose."
"My nose is stuffy."
"Sure it is."
"It is, really."
"Let's go for a walk."
"In my crutches?"
"Yep."
"Okay."

I hopped up to my feet, while Seth grabbed my crutches and handed them to me. I started to push myself forward on the wooden crutches. I clicked on a stone, then continued forward quietly in the sand around the island. I saw a whale near the shore, and a dolphin leaped into the air out of the water. I wanted to go join it, but I saw a shark fin nearby and I didn't want to risk going near it. I continued to walk with Seth, my crutches clicking on another stone. I almost slipped on it, but I maintained my balance. Seth spotted another group of sharks not too far from the dolphin, and I hoped it wouldn't get eaten. I saw a lot of blood which worried me, so I jumped in. I saw the head of a man in the midst of the blood and found my father's hand in the air, and I rescued him from the sharks. I dragged him ashore. I saw a bite mark on his arm which was bleeding heavily.

"Dad, are you okay?"
"Yeah, I'm fine, thanks to you."
"Here, I can heal it."

I placed my hand on the bite mark with the crystal and watched it fade away, and I did it again to cover the rest of the bite. My father thanked me, and we took him back to the cabin as he was feeling a lot better.

"So you're going to marry Seth, eh?"
"Yes, I am, Dad."
"I'm glad you did, sweetie."
"So how did you escape my father's prison anyways?"
"One night the guards were asleep, and I broke one of the bars by filing down my toothbrush with a jackknife and breaking two bars, so I could nudge my way out. And then I swam here and ran into a pod of sharks that almost ate me."
"Well, thank goodness, you're okay, but you know I'll have to return you to prison."
"Please present my case to the king. Surely he'll let me out by now."
"I don't know. My father isn't the forgiving type."

"If I can escape his prison, he'll have to forgive me for my innocent crime."

"I doubt it."

"We'll have to find out tomorrow."

"Tomorrow? I thought maybe I could spend the day with you as a free man."

"Umm, okay, is that all right with you, Seth?"

"I don't know."

"Please?"

"Well . . . okay."

"Thank you, Seth."

"You're welcome."

My father clapped ridiculously for a second, which made me laugh. We started walking back to the cabin to get my father something decent to eat, after years of eating the filth of prison food. Ugh, I could only imagine. Once we got back to the cabin, I immediately fired up the oven and baked some Tater Tots, then made him breakfast. I made some perfect eggs and some bacon to go with it for my dad. He smiled and put his hands on his face, when he saw me put the Tater Tots on his plate, which I took out from the oven.

"Do you know how long it's been since I've had Tater Tots?"

"How long, Dad?"

"Sixteen years! Since the day you were born, sweetie."

"I'm seventeen now, Dad."

"I know that. I had Tater Tots when you were one."

"Really? I don't remember that."

"That's because your mother was playing with you."

"Do you miss her?"

"Every day, Jilly Bean, every day."

"Then why don't you go back to her?"

"I would if I could, but I forgot the way. It's been so long since I left our family and jumped into the ocean to seek Neptune's forgiveness for finding love on land."

"It's not your fault, Dad. You can't help falling in love. It just happens."

Seth put his arm over my shoulder, and I placed my hand on it and smiled.

"So have you had sex with my daughter yet, Seth?"

"Dad!"

"Yes, I have."

"Seth!"

"What? We have."

"Yeah, but my dad doesn't need to hear that."
"You're my fiancée. I'm allowed to have sex with you whenever I want."
"Darn right, Seth."
"Dad! Why are you encouraging this?"
"I'm not encouraging this. I'm just . . . okay, I'm encouraging it."
"Dad!"
"Sorry, sweetie, I just want you to be in the arms of a loving, strong guy like Seth here."
"Thank you, sir."
"You're welcome."

My father and Seth pounded their fists together; I laughed when they opened their hands and made an exploding sound. I sat down and served myself a couple of Tater Tots on a plate and put a little salt on them. Once I finished my Tater Tots, I placed the dish in the sink and when upstairs to put some clothes on. I got upstairs and started to take off my top when I felt a pair of hands undo it for me.

"What are you doing, Seth?"
"Taking your top off. What's it feel like?"
"Perv."
"It's not being a pervert if I'm engaged to you."
"I suppose not."

Seth kissed my neck as he took off the top and pulled the bikini bottoms down and off. I turned my head as Seth kissed my neck harder. I held his head and pulled it closer to my neck, as he wrapped his hands around my belly and pulled me closer to him. I put my bra on and underwear with his hands still gripping my belly. I put my shirt on first. I unwrapped his hands from around my belly and put my pants on, falling over with a thump on the hard ground.

"Are you okay?"
"Yeah, I'm okay. I just fell putting my pants on, and it's all good."
"Okay, here I'll help you up."

Seth helped me to my feet, and I accidentally kissed him when I got up too fast. I shyly turned my head away and blushed, but he pulled my head closer to his and kissed me again. I wrapped my arms around his neck as he began to French-kiss me. I embraced it by French-kissing him back while he squeezed my hips closer to him. When he stopped, he kissed me on the forehead and pulled my pants up. I laughed and buckled them up. I walked downstairs to see my dad munching on a mango. I grabbed a mango off the counter and took a bite, then sat down at the table to talk to Dad.

"So, Jill, tell me how you got here?"
"Well, it's kind of a long story, but I'll tell it anyways."

"Go on."

"Well, it started when Mom wanted to take a vacation cruise on the yacht we won to Hawaii. We were to vacation with the Sen family. You remember them, right?"

"Of course, I do, my close friends."

"Well, I lost my virginity to their son whom I was dating."

"Really? Good."

"You're not disappointed it wasn't Seth?"

"Not at all. Jay is a good guy."

"Good to hear. Anyways, together we found some treasure and brought it aboard. It was the treasure King Neptune was looking for."

"So that's where you found it? My father was pissed."

"Yes, he was. Anyways, the night after I spent with Jay we hit a hurricane and the boat sank unfortunately. I got separated from the rest of the family and Jay, where I spent three terrifying days at sea killing a shark and eating it to survive until the last night when I smashed into a rock which knocked me unconscious, and I floated down into Seth's arms below, dead as a doornail. Seth swam to the surface and tried to save me, but I was gone. Seth had no choice but to make me a hybrid, which saved my life. Once I was breathing again, Seth took me up to the cabin which is where I woke up in the first place. Once I woke up, Seth left me a note, and I spent a couple of days on land, enjoying myself, wondering what had happened. My luggage was washed up with me and I had all my things, so I wasn't bored. I played the piano but was interrupted by Seth singing a duet with me. I called out to him and ran outside to see him but found nothing. This happened a few times until one night he confronted me by letting me see only the light on his neck and the glow that lit up his chest. That was the first time I met Seth and it was great, except for the part where he threatened to hurt me if I went in the water. He really did scare me, but I didn't tell him."

"And then what?"

"Well, after that I went against his way and went in the water. I found out I had a tail which scared the bejesus out of me. I freaked out but eventually calmed down, and I swam to find the city of Atlantis, where I met a lovely girl Akari. She introduced me to the king and the rest of Atlantis, which was very nice of her. I met the princes and sang for the city, and they loved it."

"You always had your mother's voice."

"That's the thing, Dad. Somehow I'm related to the queen. By the way, the king said so himself."

"Well, that's great, Jillian."

"Anything else you wish to know?"

"Why Seth? Rumor has it there were six other men to choose from."

"I chose Seth because he saved my life twice, something I can never repay him for."

"Unless you save my life twice."

"Unless I save you twice, Seth, yes."

I pulled Seth against my hip and smiled at him as he put his hand over my shoulder and kissed me on the forehead. I laughed and reached for a mango that was out of reach, and Seth reached for it and gave me.

"Here you go."

"Thank you, Seth."

"You two seem very content."

"We are, Dad."

"Are you going to take me back to prison?"

"Not prison, Dad. You're a free man, and it's about time Neptune sees that."

"I think my father will understand."

"Let's go see him right now."

"Oh, I don't know about that."

"C'mon!"

I grabbed my dad's hand and pulled him out the door with Seth right behind him, and I let go of his hand when we reached the beach.

"Oh, I'm still in my clothes. I'll be right back."

I ran upstairs and ripped my clothes off my body as fast as I could. Little did I know Seth was right behind me and watching me undress.

"Jesus, Seth, you scared me."

"Sorry, JJ."

"Why are you watching me undress anyways?"

"Why not?"

"Good point."

"Don't stop."

"Yeah, I'm going to stop."

"Please don't stop, Jill. I love it when you're not wearing anything."

"I know you do. Would you mind undoing this?"

"It would be my pleasure."

For some reason, I couldn't reach the back of my bra today, probably because I was being too lazy. Seth slowly unhooked my bra, and I heard it click a couple of times. I took my bra off, facing the other way, and put my bikini top on, with Seth's help of course. I pulled down my underwear and traded them for bikini bottoms. I was finally ready for the water and to face King Neptune.

"Ready to go?"

"Ready."

I walked down the stairs and saw Dad waiting for me with Seth at the shore of the island. I ran up to the water. I dove in a little early and cut my hip, leaving a bit of blood to trail out of the wound.

"What happened?"

"I cut myself on a rock."

"Here, let me help."

Seth placed the crystal on his neck near my wound, putting his hand on my hips. It burned for a second, but once he removed his hand, it felt loads better. The scratch was gone and the blood rose to the surface and made a small pool.

"We better go before the sharks get here."

"Sharks?" my father screamed.

"Relax, Dad. They won't get here for a while yet."

"I'm still scared."

"C'mon then, let's go to Atlantis."

I swam toward the city which was lit very bright today and took him straight to the palace. I walked in and found Neptune sitting on his throne talking to his sons.

"Ah, Seth, I was just talking about you. Where have you been?"

"With Jillian, Father."

"And what have you been up to for the last few days?"

"Having sex."

"Dad! We were going to tell him after the wedding!"

"Oh, my bad."

"What!"

"Oops."

"You have had sex with Seth? How dare you!"

"Hey! You can't speak to my fiancée like that!"

"Well, I suppose I can't be too harsh if you're to be engaged."

"Damn right."

"Watch your mouth, Seth."

"Sorry, Dad."

"So, King Neptune—"

"Please, just call me Neptune."

"Okay, Neptune, I'm here on business."

"And what business is that?"

"The business of my father's freedom."

"And why should I free him? He has another year to serve in prison."

"Seriously? That's it."

The Tail of an Angel

"He only had another year in prison? That's not so bad, hey, Dad?"
"Dad? How did your father escape my prison?"
"It's an honor to meet you again, Your Majesty."
"How did you escape?"
"Your prison guards fell asleep, and I let myself out with a sharpened toothbrush on the bars."
"Well, it's back in prison for another year you go. I'll make sure he's out in time for the wedding, Jillian."
"What? But why?"
"Because you only have another year left to go. Tough it out."
"But I don't want to go back to prison."
"Too bad, my mind is made up."
"Wait! Perhaps there's a sort of deal we can make for my father's freedom?"
"And what do you offer in return?"
"Seth and I won't have sex until we get married."
"I'm sorry, what?"
"Seth and I won't have sex until the day we get married."
"I don't know about that, Jill."
"Oh relax, Seth, it's just one year."
"I don't know if I can do that."
"Deal, your father is by this moment a free man."
"Thank you, Your Majesty, thank you."
"Get out of my sight before I change my mind."
"Will do."

Seth and I swam out hand in hand, and my father was right behind us, cheering and celebrating in his own way.

"Oh, Jill, how can I thank you?"
"Tell you what. We'll build you your own place, right by an oasis."
"That'd be great."
"Do you know how long that's going to take?"
"About a few days."
"It took me two months to build that cabin."
"Maybe we'll build him a nice little shack."
"Oh, okay."
"What are you two going to build me?"
"A shack."
"Oh, nice."

We walked up to the land above and gathered the things needed to build a shack—hammer, rope, wood, and other things. Once we gathered enough wood, we dragged it all the way to the oasis we had stumbled upon earlier today. It took forever to drag all the wood down there, but eventually we made it, and a pile of wood stood next to the shimmering oasis.

"You know, we could've just chopped down some wood here."

"Yeah, I didn't really think about that."

I started piling up the wood while Seth tied them together with the rope and with a little help from Gorilla Glue we found in the cabin. It helped when we ran out of glue, and soon enough the shack was almost done. We built some furniture in the two-level shack and a ladder to see the cave from the top of a tree so Dad could watch the stars if he wanted to and keep an eye on us if he wanted to, as if we needed him to keep an eye on us. We were going to be married soon, and I could handle living on my own for a while; eventually I'd get bored, but I'd still survive. Finally we finished all the furniture—a chair, couch, bed, another chair, another chair, a table, and a cabinet.

"If you need any food, feel free to raid our kitchen, and there's plenty of fruit if you head north of here and mangoes."

"Which way is north?"

"That way."

I pointed straight ahead toward north. I had a compass which I had taken from the yacht, and it pointed north when I showed Dad which direction north was. I figured that he could raid our kitchen now so he didn't have to barge in later and interrupt anything important. My father followed us past the fruit trees, where I grabbed a fresh mango and headed back into the dense forest. It didn't take long to reach the cabin, only about fifteen minutes at a walking pace; it would've taken ten if we ran, but Seth was carrying a lot of supplies. Once we got back to the cabin, Dad grabbed all the food he could and a lighter for a fire to cook it all. Once he grabbed everything, he thanked us and said he'd be back for more in about fifteen minutes. I nodded in return, and the second Dad left, Seth picked me up and started carrying me up the stairs.

"Seth, put me down!"

"No."

"Seth, put me down now!"

"Why?"

"Because I said so. Do as I say."

"Only when we get to the bedroom."

"We aren't going to have sex. I made a promise to Neptune, and a Verbicky never backs out on a promise."

"Are you sure? Never hurts to break tradition."

"I don't plan on breaking tradition."

"I doubt that."

"We'll see when my father leaves for the night."
"Got it."
"I'm back," I heard my father say from downstairs.
"You were only gone five minutes."
"I forgot some soup."
"Okay then, I'll see you in a few."
"See you in a few."

My father left finally, and Seth ran up to me and kissed me. Seth was kissing me a lot today. I kissed him back of course, and he French-kissed me for ten minutes. The other five he lifted me onto his hips and kissed me again. I held his neck in my hands and French-kissed him until I heard a knock on the door, and he quickly put me down and I fixed my hair. My father came in and said hello as I made some tea on the stove. He said how much glad he was that he was free as he grabbed some more food. I laughed as he dropped a soup can on his foot. I helped him pick it up and put it back in his pile of stuff. He said he wouldn't bother us for the rest of the evening and left without another word. I smiled at Seth with my back turned to him, and I just knew he was smiling back at me. I walked over to Seth, gently sticking out my hips with each step, and I looked him in the eyes and asked him to follow me upstairs. He did so quietly, and I grabbed his hand before going up the stairs and pulled him onto me on the bed. Seth laughed and kissed me roughly. The tip of his tongue had barely entered my mouth when he stepped back and lay down on his back.

"Is something wrong, sweetie?"
"No, no, I just feel that maybe your dad should've lived with us."
"Seth, think about it. We'd never have sex again."
"Good point, we should make it last."
"Exactly, now come over here and kiss me properly."
"How about you come over here?"
"Okay."

I slid over on top of him and lay down on his stomach and kissed him once more. He started to pull my top off by slowly running his warm fingers on my hips and held my top in his hands. He pulled it off quickly, and when it came off I pulled down his shorts since he wasn't wearing a shirt. I pulled those shorts right off, and he took off my pants faster and unhooked my bra. He ripped off my bra and felt my breasts before, making me lie down and taking off my underwear. We had sex a couple of times before we were both absolutely exhausted. Seth laughed when I rolled off the bed.

"Oh ha-ha, very funny, laugh instead of helping me up."
"I'm sorry, sweetie, here. I'll help you up."

Seth gave me his hand and helped me up regardless of the fact that I was absolutely naked. I fell back onto Seth when he helped me up.

"Really, third round?"

"No, Seth, I'm exhausted."

"Yeah, me too."

I fell down on my back next to Seth as I exhaled in exhaustion. He sighed and snuggled up to me, as I put my head on his chest.

"Perfect."

"I know."

"No, I mean what am I going to tell Neptune?"

"You don't tell him."

"I went back on a promise."

"You are no longer a Verbicky."

"Yeah, I know."

"You'll be a princess of Atlantis and my wife soon."

"Wow, your wife at eighteen. I thought I'd be married a lot later in life."

"How much later?"

"Twenty-one."

"That's pretty late. We could do that if you want."

"No, no. Eighteen is fine."

"Good, because I wanted to get married at eighteen too."

"You are eighteen, right?"

"Yep."

"For how long?"

"Just eighteen."

"When's your birthday?"

"It's today."

"What? Why didn't you say so? I'm gonna make you a cake and get you a present from Atlantis."

"Please, you don't need to get me a gift."

"Yes, I do! As your future wife, I will be buying you a gift and there's nothing you can do about it."

"Well, okay."

"This is going be the best birthday ever."

"There is a party we have to attend though, so the birthday sex is going to have to wait."

"Oh, Seth, I don't know if I have it in me."

"Me neither, but we'll have to find out tonight."

"I suppose so."

I got dressed in my finest T-shirt and jeans. I ran downstairs and made myself a quick vanilla milkshake with fresh ice cream from the freezer.

The Tail of an Angel

Once I finished my milkshake, I called up to Seth if he wanted one too and he said yes, so I had to grab the ice cream again and make another one. I topped his with whipped cream and a cherry with chocolate sauce. I felt his was much more special because of his "hard work" last night. I was about to take it up to him when Seth came down in his shorts; he smiled and picked up the milkshake.

"You're wearing that?"

"Yeah, what's wrong with it?"

"It's so plain and boring. You're going to have to go shopping today."

"I don't have any money though."

"Don't worry about it. As the prince's soon-to-be wife, everything's on the house."

"Great, I haven't been shopping in ages anyways."

"But I'm going with you to pick out a dress for tonight's party."

"By the way, Seth, happy eighteenth birthday."

"I can't believe I'm marrying a seventeen-year-old."

"Seth! Don't you love me?"

"Of course, I do."

Seth gave me a quick cold kiss, as he had just finished drinking his milkshake. He tasted like vanilla and chocolate. He was delicious and I wanted another tasty kiss, but he walked away and put his glass in the sink. I sighed and walked outside, stripping my clothes off as I did so until I was wearing nothing but my bikini top and bottoms. I jumped into the water and swam down into the dark water. We reached the city shortly, and the entire city came out for Seth's birthday. I think I even saw Akari talking it up to another prince whom I had dated, making her moves on him. It was Shawn and it looked like he really liked her as he was whispering sweet nothings in her ear, making her laugh. The key to getting the girl was to make her laugh; well done, Shawn. I walked up and interrupted them to say hello. They seemed a little angry I had interrupted them, so I said good-bye rather quickly, mentioning that it was Seth's birthday.

"So do you guys know its Seth's eighteenth birthday today?"

"Duh! It's a holiday for goodness sake. I'm looking very forward to the party, and it should be fun. I always meet great guys at those parties."

"What about me?"

"Yes, you too, Shawn."

Akari kissed him on the cheek and swam up to the palace with him. I followed, but Seth suddenly tugged on my arm.

"What? I'm going to your party."

"We're going shopping first."

"But the party starts in an hour."

"The party isn't going to start until I get there."

"All right, let's go."

There were lots of hybrid and mere clothing stores to choose from. Seth wanted me to wear a dress to the party, so we entered the first dress store we saw and found a dress in less than ten minutes. It was bright red with small rubies encrusted on the hip and was a mermaid-style dress. It ended just as it reached my fin and showed off my curves nicely.

"You look stunning."

"You really think so?"

"I know so. Now let's go to the party."

"But it's so early. How are we going to kill fifty minutes?"

"I think we should get you a new wardrobe and some pajamas while we're here."

We walked into the first couple of hybrid clothing stores, or regular stores to me. I asked for a change room and found tons of clothes in my style and tried them on. Out of twenty, two didn't fit and one was a golden top I just loved. I walked out with plenty of tops, and the next store had nothing but jeans. I looked around and found ten pairs I liked, including the cutest pair of silver jeans and white ones that made Seth stare at my ass.

"I think that's a yes."

"Hell, yeah! Those jeans, Jill, oh I love them."

"I can tell."

I brought the jeans up to the till to get the tags and security clips off, which were on all the jeans. I walked out with three bags and a big grin on my face. The next store had some funky bedazzled jeans I just loved, and I swiped them up before the lady next to me could; she frowned in disappointment. I found eight pairs of jeans, all of which were adorable. Seth took my hand and walked me to the palace, where the party had already started, but they were all waiting for Seth. We must have been more than fifty minutes. I looked over at the clock and we were twenty minutes late. "Twenty minutes, holy cow, that's late," I thought. I swam up to Seth's room and put my bags in there, and then I noticed something on Seth's bedside table. It was a picture of Seth and me when we were children and one from just a few days ago. I smiled as I picked up the photo of us as children and lightly touched the picture of me as a child. I was so cute, and Seth had his arm around me with a toothy grin on his innocent face.

"That was taken at Christmas. My uncle didn't get me anything, but your family did."

"What did we get you?"

"Oh, a bunch of things, I can't remember, but do you know what my favorite gift was?"

"What's that?"

"You."

"Aw, Seth."

I swam up and kissed him. He smiled and told me we should get to the party since we were already late. We swam down the staircase together and made it down to the party where Neptune was red with anger.

"Where have you two been? We've been waiting patiently for twenty minutes. Now the party will have to be extended."

"I don't mind a longer party."

"For this, you'll have to scrape off the barnacles from the reef."

"Aw, Dad, c'mon, it's my birthday!"

"Very well then. You'll do it tomorrow."

"Can I have help?"

"Just as long as the job gets done."

"Thank you."

Akari waved to us from the crowd, and we swam over to say hello. Akari was giggling at something Shawn had whispered in her ear. I wondered what it was.

"Hey, guys!"

"Hey, Akari, how are you?"

"Great, about time you guys showed up. Where have you been?"

"Oh, just shopping for a new wardrobe."

"I can tell that's a new dress. It was on sale, wasn't it?"

"Yes, it was. How did you know?"

"I was going to buy it for this party, but my mom said I couldn't have it."

"So have you found any guys yet?"

"Well, there's Shawn."

"Just me so far."

I walked over to a familiar face, Cato.

"Hey, Cato."

"Hey, JJ, what's up, girl?"

"Oh, not that much, just got here, so I'm just glad my fiancé can legally drink in Canada."

"Ha-ha, yeah, that's true. You look stunning in that dress, Jill."

"Thanks, Cato."

"Really, you do. I just wish you were mine."

"Aw, Cato, you'll meet a girl someday."

I hugged Cato and saw a girl check him out from across the room.

"In fact, Cato, I see a girl over there checking you out."

"Really? You serious?"

"Yeah, I'm serious. Go get her, tiger."

"Tell you what, I can see into the future, so after your wedding I'll give you a premonition on your future together."

"That sounds great, Cato, thank you. Is that the wedding present for us?"

"No, I got you another gift. It's nice."

"Well, I'm looking forward to it."

"I'm glad you are. It's a really good gift."

"I hope so."

"Well, I'm going to let you get back to the party. It was a pleasure."

"The pleasure is all mine, Cato."

Cato leaned down and kissed my hand, making me blush as he began to leave to talk to the girl who was checking him out. She was kind of cute actually, and she and Cato looked good together as I caught him kissing her hand. I hope they ended up together; Cato deserved a cute girl like her. I walked over to Seth and kissed him on the cheek, then chatted with his friends casually.

"So is Seth getting laid tonight or what?"

"We'll see, if he's good."

"And if not?"

"Even better sex later if he's bad."

"All right!"

Seth's friend high-fived him and laughed along with Seth. They continued to talk while I bothered Akari from getting any more guys.

"So are you after all my princes or what?"

"Anything to become a princess like you. Now if you'll excuse me, Shawn and I are heading out."

"You're leaving so early though."

"Don't worry, we'll be back later. Shawn's taking me back to his hotel, so who knows what might go down?"

"Well, good luck, sister. See you later."

"See you!"

I had returned to talk to Seth and his friends when his brothers came along and said hello.

"Hey, Seth, happy birthday, little brother."

"Yeah, happy birthday, little bro."

"Cut it out, you guys."

Sedrick gave Seth a knuckle sandwich, laughing as he did so. Seth started yelling, "Stop it," but continued to rustle his head with his knuckles. I giggled as Seth turned red and begged them to stop because his head was getting sore.

The Tail of an Angel

"All right, guys, you've had your fun. Let him go."

"Well, okay."

They let him go, and Seth felt the top of his head which was now bleeding.

"You guys are so mean! Look what you did to your little brother."

"Sorry, Seth."

"And on his birthday! I'm ashamed of both of you. Shame on the both of you."

I walked Seth to the bathroom next to his room to rinse off his bloody hair. We walked inside and the bathroom was quite nice, but no matter. I was there to wipe off the blood. Seth told me he was okay, but he looked like he was in pain. I took a cloth from the counter and soaked it in the water from the sink and lightly dabbed it on Seth's now red head.

"Is it bad?"

"Yep, you now have red hair, sweetie."

"Oh, that's bad."

"Just shake your head for a second."

"Why?"

"Just do it."

Seth shook his head and about 90 percent of the blood drifted off his head and into the water. I smiled and rubbed the last of it off the few hairs the blood remained on his head. I cleaned him up a bit with some hair gel, and he looked just as fine as always. I spiked his hair in to a cute little mo-fro and Seth looked absolutely adorable.

"I don't know about this mo fro, Jill."

"Are you kidding? You look awesome."

"I don't know. Hair down has kind of been my thing for the past five years."

"Well, it doesn't hurt to try something new."

"I suppose."

I walked out, wiping some blood off Seth's shoulders. I walked down the stairs to the people below, waiting for our return.

"Look, there they are!" someone from the crowd yelled, followed by a loud cheering from everyone. I spotted Akari and Alex in the audience, who were waving hello from below.

"Happy birthday, Seth!" the crowd yelled all together. I smiled as I lifted Seth's and my hand in the air. I felt like Katniss and Peeta in *The Hunger Games* with our hands in the air. I giggled and walked down the stairs with Seth, feeling fabulous. Seth was looking good, and he waved kindly at the crowd. As Seth's brothers came out of nowhere with escorts on their arms, I saw that the women that the brothers were with were extremely attractive. I didn't know where they came from, but I was jealous of their good looks. I wondered if the crystals could do anything about that. We all lined up on the higher stage, and Neptune gave a speech.

"My fellow Atlantians, as you may already know, it is my youngest son's eighteenth birthday today. So instead of telling Seth's life story and boring every one, I'll simply say happy eighteenth birthday, Seth, and enjoy the party."

"Thanks, Dad."

I hugged Seth and the escorts of the brothers were kissed. I was green with envy, so I kissed Seth on the cheek.

"What was that for?"

"For being amazing."

"Well, aren't you sweet?"

Seth tipped me back and kissed me in front of the whole city, and I knew the girls escorting the brothers were envious as they crossed their arms. I wrapped my arms around Seth's neck as he lifted me up then stood me back up straight. I laughed and gave him another hug, whispering in his ear, "What was that for?"

"For being amazing."

"You're too sweet."

Seth waved to the crowd, and they cheered as I expected. I spotted those two little kids that had asked me to play ball with them, and I finally did. I threw the ball around to them in the palace, careful not to hit anything, and had a blast.

"Thanks, Jill!"

"Anytime, kids."

"Those kids seem to really like you."

"I love kids. We should have some someday."

"What do you think the odds are of one being a non-hybrid?"

"Low. If one is, I can change him or her."

"And spend immortality with them."

"Hell, yeah."

I walked over to Akari and Alex, and they seemed to be having fun. I saw Akari flirting with one of the brothers, Skylar to be exact. She was flirting hard, jiggling her hips and batting her eyelashes; she was going hard core. I had a feeling that they would end up together. I sat down with a group of Seth's friends on a couch nearby and chatted about who they all had met, while Sedrick made out with his escort.

"Jeez, get a room, you two."

"I think we will."

"Gross. I think we all know what's going down."

"Yep."

"Wait, how are they going to, you know?"

"They're hybrids. Where do you think they're going to go?"

"Oh, if they have sex on my bed, I'm going to be so angry."

"We better check it out."

"Yeah, let's check it out."

Seth and I swam out and up to the surface, where I saw Sedrick and his escort get out of the water. We followed them back to the cabin, and they decided to have sex on the couch. I was okay with that, just as long as they didn't have sex in my bed.

"That's nasty."

"We've done the same thing, Seth."

"Yeah, I know, but that's just the way I like it."

"Oh, hot!"

I kissed Seth before he could say another word, and he French-kissed me back. He lifted me off the ground and slammed me against the wall.

"What was that?"

"Time to go!" Seth whispered. I ran as fast as I could to the water and Seth tripped behind me.

"Who's there?"

"No one!

"Seth?"

"Ha-ha!"

I laughed, giving away our position as Seth dove into the water behind me, and we finally disappeared under the water. We laughed as we swam back to Atlantis; the dance had already begun. I didn't even know there was going to be a dance. Anyways, we swam in and people were grinding and making out. Akari was leaving with Sedrick to go to his room. God knows what they would be up to.

"Wanna dance?"

"Hell, yes!"

Seth grabbed my hand and started grinding with me on the dance floor.

"What about your presents?"

"I can open them later."

Seth continued to grind with me; his skills in dancing were improving the longer we grinded. Eventually after eight tiring songs, slow songs began to play. Seth took my hand and started to slow dance with me. He placed his hands on my hips and I wrapped my hands around his neck. He slowly turned me around the dance floor, twisting and turning me all around, almost running into a few other couples. I laughed as he started to wave his hands in the air like a salsa dancer and twisted himself around three times, finishing with an olay! He made me laugh so hard I fell over onto the ground, laughing.

"Are you okay?"

"You're so freaking weird, Seth!"

"Not my fault. I'm born a salsa dancer."

"Whatever you say. It was a slow song though."

"Yeah, I know, but I just had to let my inner salsa out."

"Let's get back to dancing slow."

"Gotcha."

He grabbed my hand and pulled me up to his face so that we got a little too close and accidentally kissed. He laughed under his smile while I blushed and smiled back.

"Well, hey there, kiddo."

"Dad?"

"Hey! Happy birthday, Seth."

"Thanks, Mr. Verbicky."

"When did you get here?"

"Oh, just now. I saw you with Seth and I thought I'd say hello."

"How are you enjoying the party?"

"It's great. Neptune did a great job with this dance."

"Yeah, he did."

I glanced over at Seth and grinned.

"Well, I'll leave you two to dance. I'll see you guys later."

"See you, Dad."

"Thanks for coming, Mr. Verbicky."

"Anytime, Seth."

Seth held my waist, and the second my father was out of sight, he kissed me. I placed my hands on his chest to change up the whole hands behind or on the neck thing. He smiled and kissed me gently again before turning me around again, laughing.

"There's a piece of seaweed in your hair."

"Why is there always seaweed in my hair?"

"I have no idea."

Seth pulled it out of my hair and laughed once. He held me by the hips and swayed me back and forth on the dance floor one last time. When the song ended, he kissed me on the cheek and quickly rushed over to his presents. From Seth's brothers, there was a box of condoms, which made me laugh.

"Practice safe sex, guys!"

"Oh, you guys."

The Tail of an Angel

"Just thinking about the future."
"We have. Don't you guys worry."
"Oh, they're lubricated."
"Seth, stop reading the package!"
"Oh, okay."

I took the package and hid it behind the chair I was sitting on. Seth unwrapped the second gift and it was a package of peanut butter filled pretzels. Seth looked so excited when he saw them; he handed them to me and opened the next gift and so on. Seth got a lot of good stuff—a laptop, a couple of computer games, a TV, a receiver. We could finally watch TV! I hadn't watched TV in a year. Maybe we could rent a couple of movies, even though we didn't have any money; that could be a problem. Seth thanked everyone for the gifts and shook all their hands and hugged his brothers. After that, people started leaving as the party was basically over. I walked out with Seth, and he whispered in my ear, "You wanna try those new condoms tonight?"

"Maybe."

We swam back to the cabin and greeted Neptune on the way out. Akari was up with Skylar, doing whatever they were doing, and I caught Sedrick and his escort swimming back, his escort fixing her top.

"You know, you guys missed the dance."
"Aw, really?"
"Yep."

We got back to the cabin fine and walked ashore to find my dad fishing.
"Hello!"
"Hi, Dad."
"Don't mind me. I'm just fishing."
"Have fun, but all the fish are on the southern part of the island."
"Thanks for the tip."
"Jill, the only fish over there is salmon."
"I know. He deserves some salmon."
"Maybe he'd like our smoker."
"Yeah, let's go drop it off."

We grabbed the smoker from the kitchen and walked out in the middle of the night; then we headed into the dense forest and walked on. It took a while to find the shack in the dark, but we eventually found it. And we left the smoker on the upstairs floor and quickly walked out without a trace. The next thing I knew we were lost in the forest. Wandering past the fruit trees, I grabbed a mango from one of the trees, Seth did too. We eventually found our way and were back on the trail after five minutes of confusion. We got back to the cabin and it was nice and dark.

"So how about it?"
"How about what?"
"Sex."
"I don't know, Seth. I'm a little tired."
"Tomorrow then?"
"Sure. Oh shit, I forgot to bake you a cake."
"Well, I already got one today."
"I know, but I didn't bake it."
"Well, it was tasty."
"I know, but it wasn't my cake."
"You can bake one tomorrow."
"But it won't be your birthday."
"Well, pretend it is."
"Okay."

    I walked up and hugged Seth as he placed his hand on my wet hair. It started to get wavy and curled a little with the humidity of the island. I walked upstairs and blow-dried my hair and changed for hair.

"Jill, it's only eight o'clock."
"I know, but I'm tired."
"I'll join you then."
"But you're not tired. How are you going to fall asleep?"
"Oh, I'll fall asleep eventually."

    I crawled into bed wearing my slutty pajamas, and Seth crawled right in next to me. He put his arms around my belly, giving me butterflies which I'd always loved. I held his arms in my own and rolled over, looking into his eyes wide open and staring back at mine. I leaned in the same time as he did and kissed him once more. He French-kissed me as he always did; only this time, it was different. He twisted his tongue differently, kind of 180 degrees, and it felt amazing.

"Where did you learn that?"
"I was saving it for my birthday."
"Well, I love it. You should do it more often."
"I will."
"Good night, Seth."
"Good night, JJ."

    He kissed me on the forehead and put his arms around my back, pulling me closer into his chest. I fell asleep with the words "I love you" whispered in my ear as I drifted off.

Chapter 37

It was cold the next morning. It must have been winter; the inviting warmth no longer existed, and my new wardrobe was prepared for this. It was about time winter came around; I didn't even remember it the last year. The sun was shining bright through, which was a good thing, but Dad had no blankets, so I figured I should bring him some. Seth was still asleep, so I thought if I took some blankets to Dad and came back he wouldn't even know that I was gone. I grabbed some blankets from downstairs and quickly put on a hoodie, zipping it up downstairs since Seth was a light sleeper. The slightest sound would wake him up. I remember I had sneezed one night and it woke him, so I wasn't taking any chances. I snuck out and quietly closed the door behind me, and I ran into the forest and made it to my father's shack in no time. It was early, so my father wasn't even awake yet. I threw the covers on my father and the blankets on top and kissed him on the cheek. I ran out quietly, of course; my father was a light sleeper too. When I ran out, it began to rain, and the rain was ice-cold. The rain hit me like a knife; it was piercing cold, and it felt as if it was freezing my skin with every drop.

I ran as fast as I could through the forest and the rain still hurt. I made it to the cabin and I could tell I was going to get a cold because of this. Seth was still asleep, and I snuck into the kitchen and starting making breakfast. Seth was asleep, and then I dropped a pan. I feared it would wake Seth up, but it didn't thankfully. I starting making waffles with some pancake batter left from the last time, but it was a little old, so I threw it out. I made a new batch easily and poured it into the waffle pan, making lots of waffles so the extras could be microwaved later on. I made about twenty waffles with the batch I made. So there were plenty of extras for at least a week. I thought I heard Seth coming down the stairs, but my mind was playing tricks on me. I heard Miko come in through the window, and he shook just like a dog and dried himself off. I yelled at Miko to get his muddy monkey hands off the counter, which I'm sure must have woken up Seth, but it didn't, which was weird. Seth must have been really tired last night. Liar. I finished bringing out some fruit from the fridge, including strawberries, blackberries, blueberries, saskatoons, and some chopped up mango. I just wished there were some cherries.

Finally, I heard Seth stirring on the stairs and the thump-thump of him coming down the stairs. I saw him trip and fall down the stairs, and I rushed to his side to find him unconscious. I immediately tried lifting him to get him on the couch. I was a strong girl, and I lifted him easily on to the couch. I rinsed a cloth in cold water and brought it to Seth and pressed it on his forehead. It helped me whenever I passed out; it should help Seth. I pressed it on his flushed cheeks that were ice-cold.

"Oh, please don't be dead."

I felt his neck for a pulse, and I found one which was at a normal pace. I quickly grabbed his hand and kissed his forehead which was slightly warm. I pressed the cold cloth on his forehead again, a tear in my eye that dropped out onto the floor. I cried in front of him and prayed he'd wake up. I found my faith again, miraculously. I hoped he wasn't in a coma, but who knew? One hit to the head hard enough and he could be.

"Please wake up, Seth. Please for me."

Seth remained with his eyes closed as I pressed the cloth against his forehead again. I kept on pressing the cold cloth on his forehead until it got warm; then I rinsed it again and repeated the whole process at least five times. He still didn't wake up, and I began to get even more worried.

"Seth, *wake up!*"

I screamed at the top of my lungs for him to wake up, and yet he remained in a coma-like state. I carried him upstairs, whacking his head against the door.

"Sorry, Seth."

I laid him on the bed and placed his hands on his chest, and then I sat by his side, still patting the cloth on his head and cheeks. Some color returned to his face as I kept patting his face with the cloth. I smiled and wiped the tears off my face. I wondered what was going through his mind—whether he was aware of the cloth or that I was there. I had a crazy idea that I thought would work, so I took the crystal that was on my neck and placed it near his head and lips and kissed him. I backed away and stared at him as I watched him open his eyes.

"Oh my gosh, Seth, thank God you're okay."

"What happened?"

The Tail of an Angel

"You were knocked out on the stairs, and I was here the whole time with a cold cloth on your head. You were so pale, baby."

"I was?"

"Yeah, you were, but I used the crystal to wake you up."

"How?"

"Well, I waved the crystal around your head and sort of kissed you to wake you up."

"Well, I'm glad you did."

"You're welcome. I'm just so glad that you're okay."

"I know you are, baby girl."

"Maybe you should just take it easy today. One more slip and you're in a coma."

"I hope that's not what happens."

"Well, that will be the reality if you fall again."

"I won't, I promise."

"You better be right."

Seth leaned forward, stretching out his back, and I was about to leave when Seth pulled me back onto the bed and kissed me again. I leaned back, and he lay down on top of me and started to pull my pants down.

"Not so fast there, tiger."

"Why not?"

"Because you just woke up, silly. You need a full day of rest."

"A full day?"

"A full day, sweetheart."

"Aw, c'mon, I'm not going to sleep for a full day."

"Yes, you are. I'll get the cough syrup if I have to."

"You better get the cough syrup then."

I ran to the bathroom and grabbed the cough syrup from the medicine cabinet and gave it to Seth. He chugged a little bit of the bottle and immediately told me he was sleepy, and right then and there after putting the lid on the cough syrup, he passed out on the bed. I put his legs under the covers and kissed him on the forehead.

"Night, baby."

I closed the door to the room and shut off the lights. I walked downstairs and set up the TV. It miraculously worked; where Seth got the power from confused me, but I swam to Atlantis and asked Skylar if he wanted to watch a movie with me.

"Care to watch a few movies with me? I'm so bored and I know you have the best collection in Atlantis."

"I'd love to. I'm bringing *Tangled!*"

"Yay!"

Skylar grabbed a bag of movies and swam back to the cabin with me, where Seth was in a cough syrup induced coma. I snuck back downstairs where Skylar was setting up *Tangled* on the TV and I heard the intro music starting.

"Hey! Wait for me! Aren't you going to at least make some popcorn?"

"Oh my gosh, how could I forget the popcorn? Could you pause this for me?"

"Sure."

I paused the movie, and Skylar quickly ran up and made some instant microwave popcorn and the popping could be heard from the living room. Once it finished, Skylar made one batch for me in a glass bowl with extra butter—just the way I liked it. How Skylar knew that I had no idea. I sat down with Skylar on the couch as the opening scene started. As Rapunzel sang about cleaning up the kitchen and sewing dresses for her chameleon Pascal, I thought how much I had missed watching movies. I laughed when Pascal appeared in a dress, and so did Skylar. The first movie was good as Skylar and I munched on our popcorn and sipped on some Dr. Pepper. It was a good day to watch movies as the rain flicked against the window pane. *Tangled* finished up, and I was out of popcorn and so was Skylar. He put his arm around my shoulders and I didn't really mind. I put my head on his shoulder just seconds before he got up to change the movie. He put in *Tarzan*, as I wiped happy tears from my eyes at the last scene where Rapunzel and Eugene live happily ever after. I hadn't watched *Tarzan* in at least a year, and I was a little rough on the details but it was still good.

"So, Skylar, how was your little get-together with Akari?"

"I slept with her."

"I knew it!"

"Yeah, she was great."

"I'm sure she was."

"Nah, I mean she was epic. I've never met someone like her."

"Sounds like someone's in love."

"I think I might be."

"Well then, hey, what are we sipping on soda for? We should be drinking champagne!"

"Yeah, we should. Get a little drunk maybe."

"Whoa, I said we'd get a drink, not get hammered."

"I'm just saying."

"I'll get the champagne."

I grabbed some champagne from the liquor cabinet and popped out two champagne glasses, and I handed one to Skylar after he paused the movie.

"Here's to love."
"To love!"
We clinked our glasses and took a sip. It was delicious champagne, and I took another glass right away. Pretty soon, I had drunk five glasses and I was a little tipsy.
"Take it easy, Jill. You don't wanna get drunk, do you?"
"Maybe I changed my mind."
"All right! We're getting drunk!"
"Hell yeah!"
I took another five glasses and read that the drink had 47 percent alcohol; anymore and I might get alcohol poisoning.
"Yeah, I think I'm a little hammered."
"Really?"
"Yep."
"What the hell? I'm not even close to drunk yet."
"You got a tough liver, my friend. Drink up!"
He drank six more glasses and was easily drunk by now, but no, he was just tipsy. This guy must have been to some real parties in his time in Atlantis. After five more drinks, he was drunk finally. After we got drunk, we watched *Tarzan* and it was hilarious.
"I mean like really, how could you fall for a guy wearing a loincloth? Honestly!"
"I totally know what you mean, like who does she think she is? Queen of the jungle?"
"Well, she does end up with *Tarzan*."
"Aw, no way, spoiler alert much!"
"Oh, Jesus, I'm so sorry. I didn't know, Skylar. Why didn't you tell me?"
"Just kidding."
"Oh you!"
I burst out in laughter and so did Skylar; he must have been a laughing drunk kind of person too. After I finished laughing my ass off, I added more commentary to the movie.
"What's the name of Tarzan's mother?"
"Zaazoo."
"That's the bird from *The Lion King*."
"Rafiki."
"That's the monkey."
"The monkey that steals the drawing?"
"No, stupid, the monkey from *The Lion King*."
"Hey, I didn't spend three years in med school to be called mister."
"I didn't call you mister. I called you stupid."

"Well, don't call me stupid. Man, are we drunk? I just thought I went to med school for a second."

"Yeah, we're wasted."

"Totally."

I burst out laughing again and so did Skylar, almost spilling his last glass of champagne. We were absolutely hammered and I didn't care who knew it. Skylar stopped laughing and chugged the last of his glass, lightly burping.

"Excuse you."

"Sorry."

Skylar then leaned in to kiss me, but I fooled him by kissing him on the cheek. He smiled and looked down slightly disappointed.

"Hey, you had your chance to kiss me. And it was fun while it lasted, but I'm engaged to Seth. I can't kiss you anymore."

"It was worth a shot."

"I suppose."

I kissed him on the forehead, and I put my head on his shoulders to finish up *Tarzan*. Once it finished, Skylar popped in *Bambi*.

"Did you only bring Disney movies?"

"Maybe."

"Skylar!"

"Okay, I did with the exception of some movies I bought yesterday."

"And what movies are they?"

"The *Last Exorcism* parts one and two."

"Oh, I love scary movies."

"You wanna watch it after *Bambi*."

"Sure, I can't wait to see you cry."

"I can't wait to see you cry."

"I won't cry."

"Oh yes, you will."

"Okay, I might."

"I always cry when Bambi's mother gets shot."

"Don't say that! I hate that part."

"Gets shot, gets shot, gets shot!"

"Stop that."

"Okay."

"Let's watch the movie already."

"You want some more popcorn?"

"No, I'm good."

Skylar quickly made himself some more popcorn and "accidentally" made some for me, though I'm sure he did it on purpose. I grabbed another Dr. Pepper out of the fridge and sat back down with Skylar and his popcorn. I opened my soda pop and asked him to start the movie, and the intro even got me a little teary. In the movie, a cute little deer is born named Bambi and a proud mother shows him off to the whole forest. The movie was fine until the damn mother had to die. I started to bawl and so did Skylar. I cried in his chest and he cried in my arms, until there was a small puddle of tears on the hardwood floor. I grabbed some Kleenexes from the bathroom and handed them to Skylar.

"Thank you."

"Anytime, you look like you need it."

"I think you need some too."

"Yeah, I do."

I grabbed some tissues and blew my nose a few times. I wiped my nose and dried my tears as the movie went on.

"Why did she have to die? She did nothing wrong!"

"This damn movie should have won an award."

"I think it did."

"Good! I can die in peace."

"Me too!"

The movie ended with Bambi as the king of the forest, and I applauded the movie, and so did Skylar. With a few teardrops running down my cheek, I wiped them off and sighed.

"That is the best damn Disney movie there is besides *The Lion King*."

"You said it, sister."

Skylar hiccupped and I giggled. He leaned to kiss me again and I shoved my hand in his face, but he still managed to kiss my neck. It felt somewhat good until he started biting into it like an animal.

"Skylar, cut it out."

"Sorry, I'm a little rough, aren't I?"

"Yeah, I'll have bite marks on my neck, and Seth will kill you."

"Nothing a little crystal can't fix."

"The crystal can fix hickeys and bite marks?"

"You bet. It's worked tons of times for me."

"Show me."

Skylar pulled off his crystal and held it close to my neck, and it started to light up the bite mark as Skylar was telling me. He put his hand on it and then lightly kissed it. When he pulled back, the bite mark was gone and a grin was on his face.

"Yeah, yeah, shut up, thanks."

"You're welcome."

"So let's watch a scary movie already!"

"Part one or part two?"
"Part one!"
"Part one it is then."
He put the DVD in the TV since it had a built-in DVD player. "How sweet it is!" I thought. The movie started, and the first thing that popped up was the news reporters going over exorcisms and the myths and truths about them. I had already seen the movie, but I just wanted to hear Skylar scream. The ending was the worst part because the girl who is possessed gives birth to a demon baby and her brother murders everyone with an axe. It gave me the shivers every time I watched it.
"Are you scared yet?"
"Nothing scary has happened yet!"
"All right, just checking."
I put my head on Skylar's shoulders again and snuggled up to him with a blanket on me and a Dr. Pepper on my lips. I sipped my soda slowly as I watched the first night of the exorcism, and it frightened me a little, but not enough to make me scream. I thought I would scream during the ending. I always did, and if I screamed, Skylar would definitely scream back. And that was exactly what I was dying to hear. The ending was still one hour away and I almost fell asleep, but I held in till the ending. Oh boy, the ending, I was patiently waiting for the scariest part to come up and then it happened!
"*Ahhhhhh!*"
"*Wahhhhhh!*"
"What the hell was that?"
"A scream."
"More like a wail for help."
"What? That's how I scream."
"That's hilarious."
"Well, your scream is stupid."
"Ooo, tough guy. Says my scream's stupid. You scream like a girl."
"Shut up."
"It's true."
"I said shut up."
"You know I made your brother scream. He didn't sound at all like that."
"You say one more thing and you're unconscious."
"You scream like a woman aloud too."
"That's it."
"What you gonna do, Skylar? Choke me till I pass out?"
"Watch me."

"I'd like to see you try."

Just at that moment, Skylar launched for my neck.

"You're just like your brother, Skylar. He did the same thing when he got angry."

"I don't care."

"This is between you and me, Skylar. Please stop."

"You'll be unconscious soon anyways. Why should I stop?"

"Because we're friends and friends don't choke each other."

"I still don't care."

"Skylar, please just listen!"

"I'm not going to listen."

Everything started to go dark again, and just before everything went black, I made out one last remark.

"Skylar, please just . . . just."

Everything went black, and I smacked my head down into Skylar's soft lap, in a dead like state. When I woke up, the movie was over and he was about to get up, but he looked down with tears in his eyes at me and lifted my head off his lap.

"Ouch."

"I'm so sorry, JJ. I can't even tell you how sorry I am."

"You better be sorry. That's the second time I've been knocked out this week."

"Seth and I, we have really bad tempers."

"You're not kidding. I hate being knocked out."

"I know you do. You told me like twenty times at the party."

"I think I did."

"You did believe me."

"I should probably tell you while I'm conscious. I've already seen the first part."

"Really?"

"Really."

"Well then, what was the point of watching it?"

"To make you scream."

"Oh you, dog, you."

I laughed as he kissed my cheek. I laughed again when he kissed the other side, and he put in the other movie. I was a little more scared to watch this movie as it was said to be the scariest movie of the year last I had heard. It was advertised so when I had left; a year later I wondered if it was still the scariest movie of the year.

"So are you scared yet?"

"Nothing scary has happened."

"C'mon, Skylar, I know you're gonna get scared."
"I am not."
"Are too."
"Are not."
"Are so."
"Says who?"
"Me."
"If you want to scream, that's okay."
"I'm not going to scream."
"Suit yourself."

I continued to watch the movie as I started to get more and more scared. At the ending, I was huddled into Skylar's chest.

"Aw, you scared there, JJ?"
"Yeah."
"Aw, come here then. I got you."

I snuggled into Skylar's warm chest. I tried not to enjoy it, but I really did. I was in the arms of a friend, and that's how it was going to stay. Once the movie was just about over, I screamed, but Skylar didn't scream back. I looked over and saw Skylar was dead asleep, so I snuggled closer and kissed him on the cheek.

"Thanks for the day, Skylar."

He smiled and opened his eyes. He looked over at me and kissed my neck.

"You really thought I was asleep, didn't you?"
"Yeah, I did."
"Well, I'm not, and I appreciate the kiss."
"It was just on the cheek. It's no big deal."
"It is to me! The future princess of Atlantis kisses me softly, it's kind of hot."
"Take it easy there. It's not like we made out. And it's not I want to."
"We should."
"No."
"Why not?"
"Because I'm going to be married to Seth soon."
"And?"
"We've been over this, Skylar. I can't."
"I'm still going to kiss you on the neck whether you like it or not."
"Fine, whatever."

I crossed my arms as Skylar sucked on my neck like a vampire. A small inhaled scream escaped my mouth as I put my hands around his neck.

"Doesn't that feel good?"

"Unfortunately."

"Is something wrong, JJ?"

"No, no, it's just that this doesn't feel right."

"Hey, it's okay. You're not cheating on your future husband, and it's just a little kiss."

"I suppose."

Skylar kissed my neck again as he laid me down, holding my hips in his hands. I enjoyed it briefly until he bit down on my neck again.

"Easy there. You're going to give me a hickey."

"Nothing a little crystal can't fix."

"Are you sure?"

"Positive."

He returned to suck on my neck with me lying down, finally stopping once he had enough.

"Enjoy yourself?"

"Yeah, I did. Now kiss me. I'm so turned on right now."

"No, Skylar, I can't kiss you."

"Just one little kiss? It doesn't have to be French."

"No, Skylar. What if Seth comes down, huh?"

"He won't."

"How can you know?"

"I just know. Now come here."

"Fine, but just one kiss."

Skylar leaned in and so did I for one tiny kiss. He kissed me gently and it felt somewhat good, and then I made the mistake of opening my mouth just a tad. He had made his promise not to French-kiss me, and he didn't thankfully. Once he stopped, he simply sat there with the most adorable smile on his face.

"Oh, c'mon, it wasn't that good."

"It was for me."

"That's because you love kissing me."

"You're right, I do."

"Whatever."

I put my head on Skylar's shoulders and fell asleep in his arms, accidentally of course. Something about Skylar made me want to fall asleep on his shoulders, but I couldn't name what it was. Skylar recommended that we watch *Mulan* so he could sing along to the army song.

"But I'm so tired."

"C'mon, one more?"

"All right."

"Yay!"

Skylar threw *Mulan* into the TV and started the movie with the push of a button. I waited for my favorite part about the man song:

I sang every part of that song, and the second it finished I fell asleep in Skylar's arms. I was snuggled into his chest and warm under the blanket. I couldn't help but fall asleep as I felt a kiss upon my forehead. I smiled and snuggled into his neck and fell asleep. He put his arm around me, pulling me closer into his chest. I snuggled into Skylar for the night; surely the cough syrup would last the night.

"Well, that was a great mov . . . oh."

Skylar must have noticed I was sleeping and stayed for the night.

Chapter 38

I woke up and Skylar was gone. I frowned and got up to put on my clothes and check on Seth. He was still sleep, and I kissed him on the head before I got undressed and put on a change of clothes. Seth was still sleeping by the time I got dressed, and I realized I must have given him too much cough syrup. I walked downstairs and made myself breakfast—a berry smoothie with a hint of vanilla and sugar. I decided I would go to Atlantis for some more food while Seth was out like a lightbulb. I changed into my bikini and dove into the water, cutting my leg. I let out an "ouch" as my tail formed and I swam to Atlantis. I went shopping and got the basic food I wanted: chocolate, ice cream, strawberries, blueberries, apples, oranges, celery, Clamato juice, and a few other things. I put everything in about seven bags, including a whole bag of Lindt chocolates. I swam back to the surface and drained the bags of the water in them; the fruit was protected by a barrier created by the crystals, therefore preserving the fruit. I walked in and set the groceries down on the counter. I had started putting them away when I noticed Seth was on the couch, watching satellite TV.

"Good morning, Seth, how did you sleep?"
"Great, thanks for asking."
"Think you're going to have to sleep for today?"
"No, I was thinking we could—you're hurt."
"Oh, it's nothing. I just cut my leg."
"It's bleeding."
"It's fine really."
I had to hold myself up on the counter, as suddenly I felt really dizzy.
"You lost a lot of blood. I better heal it."
"Yeah, I think you should."

I suddenly fell over and passed out again. I felt Seth's hand on my cut; he must have been healing it. He then carried me upstairs. I could tell because I heard the sound of Seth going up the stairs and the thumps of his feet on the steps. He laid me down on the bed, kissed me on the cheek, and then let me be. I figured he'd wait till I woke up and then cheer me up a bit afterward. I must have been there for a couple of hours because it felt like forever that I had passed out. I woke up and Seth was right next to me.

"What happened?"

"You lost so much blood you passed out. I'm so glad you're okay, baby girl."

"Yeah, I'm a trooper."

"You sure are."

"So what now?"

"Maybe now we could go for that walk on the beach."

"What time is it?"

"Almost seven."

"What? I've been out for the whole day?"

"Yep, I just watched TV."

"You didn't even check on me?"

"Yeah, I checked on you, during every commercial."

"Oh, I picked up groceries by the way."

"Yeah, everything we need for a girl."

"Woman."

"Whatever."

"Seth, I'm a woman and you better damn well know it."

"I know I was just messing around."

Seth pulled me up to make me sit up and kissed me. I French-kissed him back, as he lifted my shirt off.

"How about that walk, Seth?"

"Okay."

I got up from under Seth and walked downstairs, where Sedrick and Skylar scared me.

"Jeez, you guys scared me."

"We have a crisis, Seth. You and Jill better come with us."

"Why? What's the problem?"

"You had better come and see."

I ran upstairs and quickly changed into my bikini. Then I ran back downstairs and met up with Seth and his brothers. I ran outside and dove into the water, swimming down. I looked up and I saw the monster I had thought was extinct, but as I was seeing it with my own eyes, it meant it was very much alive. It was a shark.

"Megalidon."

Chapter 39

It was a shark I had feared since I had heard of it when I was a child. It was bigger than five whales combined; this thing could eat whales if it wanted to. I saw it notice us and I screamed, but Seth covered my mouth as the monster started to swim for us.

"We have to go!"

The shark opened its gigantic mouth and swam for us; it was fast and almost bit my tail off, but Seth pulled me forward and it just barely missed eating me. I swam for Atlantis as fast as I could and raced straight for the palace to warn the king. I marched down to the main room, where the king sat looking bored on his throne.

"Your Majesty, there is an emergency."

"What's the emergency?"

"A shark threatens the safety of the citizens."

"Send a few men to kill it with spears."

"You may need an army to kill this shark, Father."

"What kind of shark is it?"

"Megalidon."

"No!"

"Unfortunately."

"Send all the men we got with spears and swords."

"Yes, sir."

"Jillian, I have a special weapon for you."

"What's that, Your Majesty?"

"I have a spear gun in my room I want you to have. You can kill the shark instantly if you shoot it in the heart."

"How will I know where the heart is?"

"It's right by the fin on the right side. Kill it and you'll be a hero to all of Atlantis."

"Right away, sir."

"Don't disappoint me."

"I won't."

I grabbed the gun and swam out to where the shark was. Seth was out there fighting with a sword. I watched in horror as one of the men was eaten alive in a single bite. I swam under the distracted shark that was being speared to death, and I fired the spear gun directly at the heart and the shark died a painful death. I could sleep peacefully tonight.

"Let's hear it for Jillian, who killed the shark!"

I could hear the men and all of Atlantis cheering for me, and I smiled and waved, as Seth swam up with a huge cut on his arm. He told me the shark had almost eaten him, but he punched it and it let him go.

"Let me heal that."

"I don't know if I'm gonna make it."

"Oh, shush, you'll be fine."

I grazed the crystal on his skin and placed my hand on it, and it disappeared just fine.

"See? You're just fine."

"Thanks, I can always count on you."

"You can always count on me, Seth."

Seth lifted my chin up to his face and kissed me in front of the entire city and army of men Neptune had sent out. I smiled and placed my forehead on his as Neptune swam up and interrupted us, "I don't mean to interrupt, but I want to give Jillian something."

"What is it, Your Majesty?"

"It's a diamond Atlantis necklace. It's a replica of my wife's, only it's a diamond instead of a peridot."

"How many karats?"

"Twenty-four, the highest possible."

"Thank you, Your Majesty."

"You're welcome. Enjoy it. It glows white and blue, whatever mood you're in."

"Awesome."

I put on the necklace, and it was glowing bright blue.

"It was going to be an engagement gift, but I figured I'd give it to you now."

"Thanks again."

I swam up to Seth and hugged him, holding his healed arm. I was glad he was okay. The shark was chopped up with swords and fed to the people,

The Tail of an Angel

after being cooked on the lava vents nearby that created the island. It was delicious and I had some; there were plenty of leftovers since there was so much of the shark that it could feed the entire city. I had about a plate of shark, and that was enough to fill me up. But Seth had two; jeez, that guy could eat. After we finished, we swam back to the island. There, Seth picked me up and congratulated me on killing the shark. He grabbed me and slammed me up against the wall, which I just loved. He roughly kissed me, pressing himself against me. I laughed when he almost dropped me as I slipped through his hands. I kissed him regardless, and he wrapped his hands around me. It felt so good to be in his arms on a wall; when he let me down off the wall, he carried me upstairs and kissed me harder on the bed. I wrapped my hands around his neck, and he slipped his hands to my hips. As he kissed me, I started to pull his shorts down, and his hands instantly reached for my bikini top. It felt so right for him to pull off my bikini top, and he pulled off my bikini bottoms then when I kissed his neck. He flipped me over so that I was underneath, and we had sex right then and there. When we were finished, Seth smiled at me and placed his big strong hand on my face.

"I love you, Jill."

"I know you do, sweetie."

"Do you love me?"

"I do, I love you, Seth."

"Good."

He kissed me on the forehead and tucked my hair behind my ear; Seth knew just what I liked. Afterward, it was about supper time and I made spaghetti with chunks of the shark on the side. I had saved some from my plate to go with the meal. After supper, I cleaned up the dishes that had built up over the past few days. Seth joined me and dried the dishes.

"Well, that was fun not."

"Yeah, isn't doing the dishes a pleasure?"

"I can think of something more pleasurable."

"Me too."

Seth immediately grabbed me and placed me on his hips, kissing me. I grabbed his neck and pulled it closer to mine. I heard a crack and I hoped I hadn't just snapped his neck. I didn't, but he grabbed his neck in pain.

"Ouch."

"I'm so sorry, Seth. I only meant to pull your neck closer to mine."

"As nice as that is, oh, I better lie down."

"I'll help you upstairs."

I helped Seth upstairs and helped him lie down, though I tripped and landed on him.

"Looks like someone's still in the mood."
"No, I'm not. I just tripped."
"Sure you did."
Seth attempted to kiss me, but he pulled back because his neck was so sore.
"Oh, I'm so sorry Seth. I shouldn't have done that."
"No, no, it's not your fault."
"Yes, it is."
"Nothing is your fault, JJ."
"Then why do I feel so bad?"
"You just feel guilty for something that wasn't your fault."
"And yet it's still my fault."
"No, it's not."
It took all of Seth's strength to lean forward and kiss me on the cheek.
"You need rest."
"Again?"
"I just have to learn how to be gentler."
"I could get used to that."
"Do you need the cough syrup again?"
"No, I'm plenty tired, thanks."
"I'll change and join you."

I ran to the bathroom to quickly change into my bra and underwear. I knew Seth would like it if I was in my bra and underwear tonight; it would cheer him up a bit. I walked out and I knew it had worked as I walked toward the bed.

"Wow."
"Thank you, Seth."
"You look fantastic."
"Thanks."
"Really, time has been good to you."
"I'm glad I'm going to look like this for the rest of my life."
"Me too."
"Flat stomach, bigger chest, long legs."
"Beautiful soul."
"Yes, that too."
"Great sex drive."
"Yep."
"Great sex, period."
"The sex is good."
"Good?"
"Okay, fantastic."

"More like amazing."

"Okay, amazing."

"And so beautiful, everyone's itching for beauty, but just scratching the surface. You're all that underneath."

"Thank you, Seth. You're so sweet."

"Even better on the lips."

"You bet."

"We should probably go to sleep."

"Yeah, it's getting late."

"Good night, Seth."

"Good night, JJ."

I snuggled up close to Seth and pulled the blanket up to cover us. It was a little cold in the cabin, and Seth had his arm around me before I knew it. I snuggled into his chest and placed my hand on it, warm and inviting. I fell asleep in his big strong arms with the last memory of a kiss on my cheek.

Chapter 40

I woke up next to Seth as I always did, and his eyes were staring at me, wide open.

"Morning."

"Good morning, Seth, how did you sleep?"

"Fantastic."

"Good to know."

Seth leaned forward and kissed me as he always did. His neck must have been feeling better if he leaned so quickly.

"How's your neck?"

"Much better. I think it's healed."

"Great!"

"I know!"

I laughed at Seth's hair that was sticking straight up. I tried matting it down, but it was still sticking up; it sure was weird looking. I grabbed some water from my glass and matted down his hair with it, and it worked. It still looked terrible, but at least it wasn't sticking straight up anymore.

"How's my hair now?"

"Terrible but better than before."

"Cool, let's have some breakfast."

I smiled and ran downstairs with Seth where we made the last of the Tater Tots and some eggs. It took less time to make the eggs and a little longer to make the Tater Tots, about ten minutes. We ate silently with casual interesting conversation about what we should do today.

"How about surfing?"

"You have a surfboard?"

"Yeah, it's in the closet. You mean to tell me you've been here over a year and you didn't think to open the closet?"

"Never had a reason to."

"Well, why don't we? The waves are high today and I have an extra board."

"Sweet, let's do it."

I finished my breakfast quickly since I was eager to go surfing. I placed my dirty dishes in the empty sink and raced upstairs to go change into my bikini. I figured I'd wear my red bikini for a change, and as soon as I changed, Seth walked out of the bathroom wearing black and red trunks with a red skull on them.

"Nice trunks."

"Nice bikini."

We went downstairs and grabbed the surfboards, walking outside to the bright sun above. I noticed that the board was the same as the one I had when I went surfing with Jay.

"Hey, Seth, where did you get this board?"

"From a hippie in Florida, why?"

"No way."

"Why? What is it?"

"I used to have the exact same board when I was surfing for the first time with my boyfriend."

"Cool."

"You're not interested at all, are you?"

"Not even slightly."

"You jerk."

I pushed Seth over, and he fell onto the sand, laughing. I helped him up with a loving smile on my face and raced him to the water. I won for a change and swam out on my board. The waves were high today, thankfully, as I caught the first wave. It was heaven gliding on the water as I placed my hand on the racing water. Mist fell on my face and my back as I was swallowed by a wave. I didn't mind as I felt the top and side of the water above and beside me. Seth caught up to the wave and snuck up behind me once I got out of the wave. He laughed as we high-fived and caught up to the end of the wave. I turned down to the edge and sat back down on my board. Seth gently bumped into my board and screamed, "Woo-hoo!"

"Aw, yeah, that was awesome. You're a very skilled surfer."

"Thanks, Seth, can't wait for the next wave."

"Me too!"

The next wave came along shortly. I caught up before Seth, but hit the wave head-on and got sucked underneath by the wave. I grew my tail and swam back to my board that was almost washed ashore. I grabbed it and hopped back up, waiting for my legs to return. They eventually returned after a while, though why it took so long I couldn't understand. It must have been a higher concentration of salt in the water today. I saw Seth swim up to me and he asked if I was okay.

"Yeah, I'm fine. I just fell off my board."

"Your crystal."

I looked down and saw that my crystal was glowing bright red. I instantly covered it with my hand to hide the light as Seth lined up his board with mine.

"Don't hide it, Jill. I've been waiting forever for this to happen."

"Why?"

"It officially means you love me."

"Is that so?"

"Yeah, see? Mine's glowing red too."

I looked over at Seth's necklace and it was indeed glowing red. He lifted his face up to mine, and then lifting my face with his fingers closer to his face, he kissed me. The taste of saltwater was on his lips, and though they were dry and warm, he was sweet. He tasted like cherries again, though I never knew why.

"Why do you always taste like delicious cherries?"

"My delicious cherry-flavored toothpaste, of course!"

"I might have to try some."

"Be my guest, but you're already delicious to me."

"Aren't you sweet?"

I kissed him again with the same sweet cherry aftertaste. Once I finished, I swam up to catch another wave, and I actually caught it this time and surfed along the tide once more. Seth and I surfed until we couldn't surf any longer and we were both absolutely exhausted. With my arms feeling like noodles, I barely made it to the shore and crawled to the sand ahead. Seth had to swim to the shore with his board keeping him afloat. I helped him onto the shore, then lay down on my back with water washing away at my feet.

"We surfed the shit out of those waves."

"We sure did, Seth."

I grabbed his hand, still lying on my back. I hadn't been this tired since the night Seth and I had an endless night of sex. That was tiring, but so was surfing all day. I crawled up to a chair on the beach and lay down; Seth took the one next to me.

"That was fun."

"Yeah, it was."

I grabbed his hand again and held it until the sun went down. It was quiet and peaceful with the only sound of tropical birds and the waves crashing against the shore.

"I suppose we should go inside."

"But the stars aren't out yet."

"Aren't you cold?"

"Well then, let's go inside."

"I don't have the energy to walk."

"Then I'll carry you."

Seth picked me up from the chair and carried me into the cabin, where he almost hit my head on the wall going up the stairs, but I was just fine. He threw me onto the bed and walked to the bathroom to change into his shorts, while I quickly changed into my bra and underwear. I looked like a Victoria's Secret angel with my flat stomach. I hopped into the bed, as I felt Seth snuggle in behind me.

"You wanna mess around?"

"Not tonight, babe."

"And why not?"

"I'm exhausted."

"Yeah, I'm tired too."

"Then why did you ask?"

"Just curious."

"You're always curious."

"You know it."

I turned around and snuggled closer to Seth, placing my hand on his chest.

"I love you, Jill."

"I love you too, Seth."

I fell asleep in Seth's arms as he kissed me good night on the forehead with nothing but the red glow of our crystals in the night.

Chapter 41

I woke in Seth's arms again. This year was going by really slow, but after a couple of weeks, it sped up and Christmas was just around the corner. I had already got a bunch of action comedies for Seth including *Red*, *Red 2*, *Scott Pilgrim vs. the World*, *Rush Hour*, *21 Jump Street*, *Mr. and Mrs. Smith*, and *Tropic Thunder*, all for us to watch. I wondered what Seth would get for me; I wouldn't dare look in the attic, because Seth told me that's where he hid all his gifts for me. I hid all my gifts for him in the closet, including a Wii with Mario Kart and all the Just Dance games and Wii fit. It was free, and I had picked it up the day before while I got the games for free. I was so excited about Christmas this year, even though I wouldn't be able to be with my family this year. I missed them terribly. I wondered if they were okay in heaven. I started to cry when Seth heard me and asked if I was all right.

"I just really miss my family, Seth."

"Hey, I'm your new family now. You can tell me anything and do whatever you want with me."

"Thank you, Seth. You're always there for me."

"And I'll always be there for you. Always."

He brushed back my hair and kissed me softly. I wrapped my arms around his neck, the usual. He unhooked my bikini top and I hooked it up again.

"Not right now, Seth. We just woke up."

"I know, but I'm already in the mood."

"You can wait till tonight."

"You're such a tease."

He kissed my neck and walked upstairs, as I ran outside to go surfing. I grabbed the board from the closet and picked out the other so Seth

The Tail of an Angel

wouldn't discover the presents and find all the gifts I had got for him. I ran outside but found the waves were too small today to surf; I frowned and walked back inside, disappointed. I told Seth the bad news, and he was about to put away the surfboard but I stopped him and put away the surfboard in the closet. Seth looked at me suspiciously and shrugged his shoulders. I ran upstairs and changed into my new outfit for Seth, the new white jeans. I walked downstairs, feeling damn sexy, and watched Seth's jaw drop. He stared at me until I lifted up his chin and kissed him. I really was a tease. I finished and smiled at him as he pulled me up onto his hips and kissed me again.

"I love those jeans."

"I know you do."

He set me down and gave me a knockout smile. I smiled back at him and kissed him on the cheek, and I ran outside. I stripped off my clothes and jumped into the ocean with Seth behind me, skinny-dipping. I kissed Seth underwater as my tail formed, and I realized I'd forgotten to keep my bra on, oops!

"I forgot my top."

"Yeah, you did."

"Well, go fetch it then."

Seth swam up and got my bra for me and brought it back underwater, where I put it on.

"That's better."

"I don't know. I kind of liked you without the bra."

"You always like it when I'm wearing nothing."

"Yeah, I do."

I swam back out to Atlantis to grab some lunch with Seth; it was lunchtime anyways. I wondered where Seth was going to take me for lunch. I turned around and asked him just before we reached the gates of Atlantis.

"We're going to New York Fries."

"Oh my gosh, Seth! Poutine is like my favorite thing ever. I've been dying for one."

"I know! I haven't had one in ages."

"I love New York Fries!"

"Me too!"

We swam up to the restaurant part of the city and swam into New York Fries. It wasn't even busy, and we swam right up and ordered our food. Seth got the loaded poutine and I got the original. His poutine looked good, but mine tasted better. After we finished, we left the restaurant full but satisfied. Then we left Atlantis and swam back home. Once we got home, Seth and I were bored. Seth had the great idea to run over to the oasis and harvest some crystals from the crystal cave. I thought it was a fantastic idea, and I could also spend some "quality" time with Seth. I gathered some munchies for the trip and walked out hand in hand with Seth. He carried the snacks, while I simply walked normally as we marched into the forest. It was darker than usual, which was weird, but otherwise the trip was okay. We reached the oasis and it looked just as beautiful as ever. I jumped in, wearing as I was my bra and underwear underneath. I invited Seth in, and he took off his shirt and jumped in right on top of me.

"Seth, watch where you're jumping! You hit me!"

"I'm sorry, babe, you should've moved."

"How was I supposed to know to move?"

"When I was over top of you."

"Ugh, you're such a jerk."

"Would a jerk do this?"

"Do what?"

Seth swam up and kissed me, French of course. He lifted me onto his hips, unhooking my bra and taking off my underwear. I took off his shorts and pulled him underwater, continuing to kiss him. He smiled and kissed me again under the water. I enjoyed the pleasure of having my legs underwater as he French-kissed me and I French-kissed him back while bubbles from our noses rose to the surface. I finally ran out of air. The bubbles stopped, and I swam to the surface. Seth remained underwater and I started to worry until he emerged from the water, smiling and throwing me into the air. I splashed down into the water, laughing. Seth picked me up once more in his arms.

"Would a jerk do that?"

"Maybe."

"See? I'm not a jerk."

"For throwing me, yes."

"I'm sorry, baby girl. My arms just twitched upward."

"I'm not going to forgive you."

"Aw, don't be like that."

"I am."

"Aw, babe. Would a kiss fix it?"

"Perhaps."

Seth let me out of his arms as I floated on my back and he held me up to kiss me. It was gentle and warm, just the way I liked it, and he still tasted like cherries. That was some mighty powerful toothpaste. I had to try it out.

"Let's go get some crystals now."

"Okay, let's get dressed."

I handed Seth his shorts and I put on my bra and underwear. Seth and I swam down into the abyss of the water and found the crystal cave. Once we reached it, I started collecting crystals right away. I handed Seth a chisel and started throwing the crystals in the bag. Seth was collecting a lot of rubies, so I told him to collect a little bit of everything. He started chiseling. I was also chiseling; in fact, there was a lot of chiseling going on in the cave. It didn't take long to fill the backpack; since I had forgotten to eat the snacks, I simply tossed them out to make more room. Seth filled up the last of the bag with the thirty gems he was holding and threw them in. Finally the bag was full; we must have fit at least two hundred gems in the backpack. It was full to the brim and it was really heavy, so Seth had to carry it as we began to leave. The current pulled us forward, and eventually I saw the drop-off, but I hit my head again. I remember hitting my head on the rock, and when I woke up, I was on the shore of the cavern, coughing up water.

"Oh, I'm so glad you're okay, JJ. You hit your head again."

"Son of a bitch, I promised I wouldn't do that again."

"Well, there's that, and when you cut your head, your legs came back which was really weird, and you nearly drowned."

"Really?"

"Yeah, but you're okay and that's what matters."

"Well, thank goodness. Let's get the crystals to the treasure cavern."

"Whoa, hold on there. You're going to go straight back to the cabin and going to rest up."

"Make me, Seth."

"I'll carry you."

Seth picked me up as I crossed my arms, and he gently brought me back to the cabin. He put me down on my bed upstairs and kissed me on the cheek.

"Get some sleep, okay?"

"But I never had supper."

"I'll make you something quick, okay?"

"All right."

"But first I have to put those crystals in the cave."

"Yeah, you better get that done."

Seth ran outside and I heard the splash of him jumping into the water in the cavern; it was really quiet. I laid my head down and closed my eyes, taking a deep breath and exhaling a few times. It was quiet and peaceful; the sounds of the birds echoed through the cabin. Then Miko came to visit.

"Hey, Miko, how you doing?"

Miko nodded his head and gave me a thumbs-up. I smiled as I handed him a mango and told him to have a good day. Miko spoke in his monkey language and left in a flash. I waited for Seth at least ten minutes, then twenty. I ran outside to go look for him and found him floating in the water in the cavern.

"Seth!"

I ran into the water and pulled him out in a second. I saw that he was as pale as snow.

"Seth, speak to me."

Seth didn't move any inch, and I feared he might have drowned. I looked down at his leg and saw a shark bite. He must have bled to death. I looked down at my crystal and remembered what the journal said about turning people into hybrids—a twist of the crystal in the heart and a kiss to seal it. I didn't know if the kiss was necessary, but I was willing to try anything to save Seth. I stabbed the crystal into his heart, turned it, and kissed him. I watched as the color returned to his face, and the water that washed up on his legs temporarily turned them into a tail, but washed away as quick as it appeared. Seth took a breath, but remained paralyzed on the ground. I figured I should take him inside and clean up his wound. I carried him to the cabin and set his body on the couch, and then I placed my crystal near his bite mark. I put my hand on it afterward and watched as my handprint disappeared into his skin.

"Seth, please wake up."

Seth didn't wake, so I thought that maybe I should put him in bed after a shower. I carried him upstairs and put him in the shower, still in his trunks, washing the sand off him with soap. Once he was completely clean, I pulled him out of the shower, dried his hair, and carried him to bed. I covered him in blankets and covers to keep him warm, changing into my pajamas myself. I crawled into bed and covered myself in blankets to keep myself warm; it was a little cool tonight. I looked over at Seth's face which had even more color than before; he looked very human again, I was glad. I guess I only had to save Seth's life one more time for us to be even, who knew? I continued to look at Seth, hoping, wishing he would wake up. I got up and looked out the window at the stars and saw one from the sky right next to the full moon.

"Please let Seth wake up," I whispered under my breath. I saw many stars fall that night, but I only made one wish. I returned to bed and crawled under the covers with Seth still dead asleep.

"Please wake up, baby."

I leaned over and kissed him on the forehead. I sat there and stared at Seth since I couldn't sleep without him. "And there," I thought, "we were going to have sex tonight. It looks like that's not going to happen anytime soon." I held Seth's face in my small hand, warm at last. I let go of him and held his hand on my heart. I smiled and held it there. I continued to stare at Seth until I saw his eyes flicker open.

"Oh, Seth, thank God you're okay."

"What happened?"

"You died, Seth. A shark must have attacked you and your either drowned or bled to death, and I'm not sure which one."

"You saved my life?"

"Now I just have to save your life again so that we'll be even."

"Yeah, you do."

Seth leaned up and held my face in his hands, touching his nose to mine. I closed my eyes and barely opened my mouth. He leaned in, still holding my face, and kissed me. I French-kissed him back. Then I pulled his trunks off, and he slowly unbuttoned my top and pulled my pants off. He took my underwear off and we had sex once more. Only this time, it was different; he was much more passionate and sweet, not as dominant and aggressive as he usually was. He was really a changed man, and I loved it. When we finished, he smiled at me and kissed me again. This had to be the best sex I thought we had. I fell asleep in his arms, much stronger than before. Something must have happened to Seth when I changed him back into a hybrid. He was a completely different man, but I still loved him.

Chapter 42

I woke up next to Seth, alive and well. I was naked and I needed to put some clothes on. After putting on my clothes, I walked outside, feeling the sand squeeze between my toes. I stood on the shore until the tide washed up on my warm feet, cooling them in the sun. I smiled and looked up to the sky, thanking God and my faith for bringing Seth back to me. I heard Seth close the door and come outside.

"What are you doing out here so early?"

"Oh, just thought I'd soak up the sun."

"There's plenty of sun inside, sweetie."

"I know, but I just wanted to feel the sand between my toes."

"Yeah, that's a pretty great feeling."

"Not as great as what you did last night."

"Yeah, that was pretty great too, ha-ha."

I kissed Seth on the cheek, and then with my hand on his hip, we walked inside and made some breakfast. This routine had begun to bore me, and I felt we should visit my dad today. I think he needed some more food anyways. I finished up my cereal for breakfast. Then we filled a backpack with food, which Seth carried, and we walked into the forest. It took a couple of minutes, but we made it to Dad's oasis and walked into his little shack.

"Hey, Dad!"

"Hey, Jilly Bean, how have you been?"

"Good, thanks for asking. I brought you some more food."

"Aren't you sweet?"

Dad grabbed the backpack and started emptying it and putting it away.

"So why the visit? You never visit."

"Just thought I'd drop by and say hello."

"Well, that's nice."

"How have you been, Dad?"

"Very good. I went to that fishing spot and caught a bunch of salmon and ate those pretty quick. Then I caught some crabs off the edge of the island, though how they got all the way out here I don't know, but anyways those were delicious. Then I spent a few days exploring the island which is huge by the way. I then spent a day in the oasis, which was fun, and then I snuck into Atlantis and met your friend Akari, who was very friendly."

"You met Akari?"

"Yeah, I did. She's really nice and showed me around and took me on a tour of the rest of the city I didn't get the chance to see. Atlantis has a lot of restaurants by the way. I went to New York Fries with Akari and had some lunch with her and chatted about what might be going on for the wedding. Apparently, there is a photo shoot before your wedding for the magazines."

"Wow, that should be fun."

"I'm looking forward to that," Seth commented.

"Anything else you wish to tell me, Dad?"

"Who's Seth's best man?"

"Alex."

"Really?"

"Yeah, he's like my best friend."

"What about your brothers?"

"Groomsmen. Lucas is also a groomsman."

"Great, I love those guys."

"What about you?"

"Akari will be my maid of honor, of course, and as for bridesmaids I have none."

"I'm sure Akari will introduce you to her girlfriends."

I pondered if she would, but knowing her, I thought I would rather have my bridesmaids. I thought long and hard on what we wanted for the wedding, whether it should be under the sea theme or an island theme. Who knows? All I knew was that I wanted this to be the best wedding ever. I had a feeling that Seth wanted to get married as soon as possible; we could be getting married in January for all I knew. I was looking forward to Christmas for now. Christmas came really soon, and before I knew it, I was waking up on Christmas morning. I woke Seth up and ran downstairs to the living room and saw the presents under the palm tree. We couldn't find a pine tree, so we had to make do with a palm tree. Seth had chopped it down a few days ago, and we made some ornaments out of wood and painted them all sorts of colors. I picked up the first gift and put my ear to it, wondering if it made any sound. It didn't, but that was okay because it was a rainbow crystal bracelet. I gave Seth the big present containing the Wii, and he just lit up when he finished unwrapping it.

"Oh my God, a Wii."

"I hope you like it."

"I've always wanted a Wii."

"Well, now we can play together."

"I'm looking forward to it."

I opened my next gift, and it was a matching set of rainbow gem earrings.

"Did you just get me jewelry for Christmas?"

"Open your other gifts and find out."

Seth opened his other gifts that contained games and some clothes I had picked out for him. Meanwhile, I had got a teddy bear and a blanket, and as I unwrapped the last gift, I held my hand over my mouth as I unwrapped a diamond tiara.

"My father's idea actually, it's for when you become princess."

"Princess?"

"You bet. You'll officially become princess of Atlantis once you marry me, the first in about twenty years."

"I never thought I'd become a princess."

"Well, now your childhood dream can come true."

"Well, I guess every girl wants to be a princess every now and then."

"And you will, in time."

"This is the best Christmas gift I've ever received."

"So is this Wii."

"Wanna set it up?"

"I'd love to."

We ran over to the TV and set up the Wii in under ten minutes and we were then playing Just Dance in no time. We were pretty good too, getting at least nine thousand on all the songs and the duets were ten thousand; we were on fire. Seth and I had a blast playing Just Dance 2, 3, 4, and 2014. Once we finished playing all the songs on the games, we played some Call of Duty, a bonus gift I had snuck in the DVD package. I played on an online team against Seth's. We played for hours and I kicked Seth's ass. I killed him just about every way you could be killed in the game—headshot, knife, grenade, neck shot, chest shot, rocket launcher, you name it. I only died once, by Seth of course, and he just went nuts when he killed me, but I could care less. Once we had finished a couple of more games, Seth decided to make supper. Tonight we were going to have tacos, and I helped chop up some veggies for the tacos while Seth cooked the meat as I looked, standing behind him as he spiced the meat.

"How's the meat coming?"

"Good, it's almost done."

I had put all the veggies in some bowls when I cut my thumb on the knife and got blood all over the knife; it dripped like a leaky faucet.

"Ouch."

"What? What happened?"

"Oh, I cut my thumb on the knife."

"Here, I got it."

Seth placed his crystal near my thumb and covered it with his hand, smiling at me. I smiled back as he removed his hand which was a little bloody, but the cut was gone and healed completely. Seth wiped the blood off on his trunks and finished up the meat, pouring it into a bowl.

"Thank you."

"Oh, no problem."

"We should eat those tacos now."

"I agree."

I fixed up my taco and ate it as fast as I could. I was starving. I ate another taco just as fast and had room for one more. The tacos were delicious and I savored my last taco. Seth had about four and I could tell he was really hungry. As soon as we finished, we did the dishes and cleaned up the kitchen. Seth put away the dishes, and I smiled at him, thanking him for doing so.

"So you wanna have a little Christmas sex upstairs?"

"Maybe."

I walked over to the stairs, grabbing his hand and pulling him up the stairs.

"Got a pretty tight grip there."

"Seth, you've always known I've had a tight grip."

"Yeah, I have."

I closed the door and walked over to Seth and kissed him with all the skills I had.

"Wow, you're a great kisser."

"You're not bad yourself."

"Thank you."

Seth came closer to me, as I looked into his bright eyes, and he held my neck in his hands to lightly kiss it. Then over the next few minutes, he sucked on my neck like a vampire and laid me down on the bed. I could tell I was going to get a hickey from this, but I could care less because it just felt so good. Seth pulled my shorts down, but I stopped him.

"Seth, it's too early to have sex."

"No, it's not."

"Yes, it is."
"Okay, we should have sex later though. We haven't in so long."
"I know, babe. It's just that I haven't been in the mood in a while."
"And why not?"
"I have no idea."
I stepped out from under Seth and felt my neck as I stood on the side of the bed. I rubbed it with my hand, feeling a slight pain.
"Is your neck sore?"
"Yeah, it is. You're a lot stronger than you used to be."
"I know it's so weird. After I died, a lot of things changed in me."
"But not the way you feel about me, right?"
"Of course not."
Seth held the crystal to my neck and placed his hand on it, and sure enough it disappeared when he removed his hand. He gently kissed where the hickey was, smiling up at me. Seth kissed me on the cheek and laughed to himself.
"What's so funny?"
"Your hair got in the way."
I felt on my face and sure enough a piece of hair was in the way of Seth kissing me on the cheek. I removed it and Seth gave me a peck on the cheek. I smiled and felt the spot where he had kissed and then giggled. I sounded like a child the way I giggled, which made Seth laugh. A few sleeps and it was New Year already. I had another dress to wear to the New Year's party, a little black dress with diamonds encrusted in the hips as a beautiful gem belt. I ran out to the kitchen to grab a quick snack while Seth watched TV. I grabbed a mango off the counter and handed Miko a mango as well. He smiled and ran out the window to eat his mango, and I sat down with Seth to watch TV. Seth put in an action movie *Red* and I popped some popcorn to eat with Seth. We shared a bowl and watched the action movie in silence. I only heard the sounds of the movie and us munching on the popcorn as John Malcovich shot at a woman holding a rocket launcher. It exploded and killed her, as he said, "Old grandpa, my ass," my favorite line in the whole movie.
"How are you enjoying the movie?"
"It's great."
"I know this movie is fantastic."
"I love it!"
We finished watching the movie. We finished eating the popcorn as well and I cleaned up the bowl in the sink. It was almost time to head to the party and I was ready to go, but Seth wasn't even wearing pants.
"Seth, you have to at least put on a shirt to the party."

"Aw, do I have to?"
"And a tie."
"Can I wear that black one you got me for Christmas?"
"Absolutely."

Seth ran upstairs and changed quickly, and I helped him with his tie since he didn't know how to tie it. My mother had taught me when I was little, because even though women didn't wear ties it was always good to tie a tie for your man. It was a very important lesson my mother had taught me. I just wish my mother was here for this New Year. Once done, Seth was looking sharp and I fixed up his hair with hair gel; he looked great. I shaped it into a Mohawk again and he looked quite handsome.

"What's with you liking this Mohawk thing?"
"You just look better with it, sweetie."
"Thanks, hun."

I kissed him on the cheek and walked outside to the warm sand on a cool night. I was surprised the sand was warm, but I could care less as I was looking forward to the party. I swam into the cold water; it was freezing and I could hardly bear it. I swam to the surface and Seth followed me, as he was concerned as to why I went to the surface.

"Are you cold?"
"Yes! I'm freezing!"
"Don't worry, you'll get used to it."
"Well, I'm not."

Seth swam over and gave me a warm hug. I instantly got adjusted to the water. I gave Seth a confused look and asked him how he had done that.

"The crystals can warm you up. I just happened to use my crystal to warm you."

"Thank you."

I swam back down into the now cool water and down into Atlantis. There were underwater lights lighting the way to the palace. I walked in, and half the city must have been in that ballroom, including Akari and her friends. I was hoping that her friends would be my future bridesmaids.

"Jillian! Over here."
"Hey, Akari!"

I waved to Akari and swam over to where she was and said hello. She introduced me to her friends with her, all girls of course.

"This is Samantha, Cynthia, Rebecca, Kim, and Jessica."
"Nice to meet you all."
"Nice to meet you too, Jillian."

I shook all their hands and asked them if they would like to be my bridesmaids. They all squealed and gave me a hug, but Akari looked a little sad.

"Akari, would you please be my maid of honor?"

"Oh my gosh, I'd love to, Jill!"

Akari gave me a big hug and squealed along with the other girls. Kim said she couldn't believe she was a bridesmaid and asked me to go bridesmaid dress shopping with them.

"What color do you want the dresses to be?"

"Blue, mermaid style."

"That will make me look so thin!" Samantha said.

"And what about Akari's dress?"

"Baby blue with blue gems encrusted on the hips."

"Oh, and we're so going wedding dress shopping with you."

"Are you sure? I'm really picky when it comes to shopping."

"Oh relax, we're the most patient girls in Atlantis."

"Good to know."

I walked over and kissed Seth on the cheek while he was talking to his friends.

"So how much longer until the countdown?"

"About ten minutes."

"Great, come and get me when the countdown starts. Me and Akari and her friends or I should say my bridesmaids are gonna start drinking."

"So early, hun?"

"It's not that early. You should come join us. We're doing shots."

"I might join you a little later."

I ran over to Akari and her friends and started shooting down some shots. One at a time, I drank the shots in a single chug, drinking every color. There were rainbow shots, and soon I had five of every color and was pretty drunk.

"I'm gonna be the princess of Atlantis."

"Yes, congratulations."

"I can't wait until I get married."

"I know. I can't wait to be a maid of honor."

"First time being maid of honor?"

"Yep."

"Congratulations."

"Thank you."

"Wanna get our drink on?"

"I thought you'd never ask."

I grabbed some more shots until I started spilling them.

The Tail of an Angel

"Take it easy, Jill."
"Oh, I'm fine, Seth. Don't be such a worry wart."
"You've drunk all the shots!"
"Okay, so I'm a little drunk, big whoop."
"You got to slow down, Jill, or you'll drink yourself to death!"
"Well, that's not good."
"Obviously."
"One more shot?"
"Okay, one more."
"Awesome."

I took the last shot and chugged it in a single gulp and I laughed.
"I am awesome!"

I threw the shot glass in the air, and it crashed to the ground, spreading glass everywhere on the ground.

"Jesus, Jill, you need to calm down."
"Why? It's a party."
"Yeah, but everybody's looking and I hate to be embarrassed."
"Sorry, everybody! I'll get a broom and clean it up."

Akari was equally drunk, and she spilled her drink that she had got from the bar. She motioned for me to come over, but I said, "No, thank you." I was drunk enough as it was. Ten minutes went by quickly and the countdown was starting.

"Akari, quit drinking and get your fine ass over here!"
"Coming, Princess Jillian."
"All right!"

I ran over to Seth and put my arm over his shoulder and so did Akari and we counted down till midnight.

"Ten, nine, eight—"
"I love New Years. Everybody gets the chance to start over."
"You said it, Akari."
"Seven, six, five, four, three, two, one . . . Happy new year!"
"Happy new year, Seth!"

I saw Akari swim over and kiss Skylar, and I figured I might as well do the same with Seth. I instantly kissed Seth the second he looked at me. I tasted the cherry from his lips on my own, which made me smile; I must have tasted horrible with alcohol on my breath. I backed away and smiled at Seth. Then I kissed him on the cheek and told him we should probably go home. Seth agreed and grabbed a drink before he left—a margarita. I took a single sip, and he smiled down at me. But then I started to feel a little dizzy and then everything started to get dark.

"I think I'm gonna pass out."

"Really?"

"Yep."

Just then I fainted, and I felt Seth catch me. I woke up the next morning hungover and tired. What a party!

"What happened last night?"

"You passed out as soon as we left, so I carried you home and put you to bed."

"Oh jeez, I'm so sorry about that."

"It's okay. You cuddled up to me when we were sleeping anyways."

"Aw, that's so cute."

"And I kissed you on the cheek good night."

"Aw, you're too sweet, Seth. That's one of the reasons I want to marry you."

"What are the other reasons?"

"The sex, the way you taste like cherries, and the way you're so sweet to me."

"Your body, the sex, your beautiful singing voice, and your cooking."

"Thank you."

I stretched and walked downstairs, and I got some waffles out from the freezer for myself. I microwaved it and got out the maple syrup to put on the waffles. Seth joined me.

"How are you feeling?"

"Hungover."

"Are you going to be all right?"

"I might need to nap it off, but besides that I'm okay."

"You need a kiss, sweetie?"

"Yeah, I need one."

Seth walked over to me and lifted my face up to his. He gently kissed me, holding my neck in his hands. When he finished, he quickly kissed me again, giving me that knockout smile. I smiled back, and my heart just melted when I looked at him. It was officially the first year of 2014, the year I was supposed to graduate. I would be turning eighteen this year and I was really excited about it. Something told me that after my birthday Seth would want to get married right away. The first few months went by quickly and the next few flew by just as fast. Soon it was August, and Seth was preparing for my birthday coming up in the next few days.

"And there's going to be balloons and cake and of course champagne."

"Seth, relax, I'm grateful you're even throwing a party for me."

"Are you sure you don't want any strippers for the bachelorette party? Underwater they can only take off their shirts, but they do it very well."

"No, thanks, Seth. I'd rather see you strip for me anyways."

"I like the sound of that."

Seth kissed me on the cheek; he then made a shopping list for my birthday party. Three sleeps later, it was the day of my birthday. Seth had bought the things on the list he needed and invited me to Atlantis early to get ready for the party and help set it up. Seth basically dragged me outside and into the water. I laughed as he splashed down into the water clumsily, still holding my hand and pulling me toward Atlantis.

"Seth, you can let go of my hand now."

"Oh, sorry."

Seth released his grip on my hand, and I held it with my other since it was a little sore. Seth had a firm grip, but I always knew that. We reached Atlantis shortly and quietly until we got to Atlantis, which was loud and quickly getting louder. I swam into the gates and everyone cheered at my arrival. I smiled and waved at the adoring public and children I recognized in the crowd. I threw them a killer smile once more and walked to the palace for the party. Every one of the princes was inside. Akari was talking up Skylar; he kissed her on the cheek as she waved hello to me.

"Hey, Jill!"

"Hey, Akari, how are you?"

"Fantastic! Skylar just asked me out."

"That's great. You two make such a cute couple."

"Thank you, Jill. You and Seth make a great couple as it is."

"Thanks, Akari. I wish you and Skylar all the best."

"Well, aren't you sweet?"

"Well, let's party! It is my birthday after all."

"Let's get our drink on!"

"I thought you'd never ask."

I ran over to the table and saw my old nemesis, the shots. I hesitated to grab one after the last time and walked over the bar instead to grab a margarita. Akari was already at the shots table, just drinking shot after shot, and she was definitely getting her drink on.

"Now, Jill, we don't want what happened last time now, do we?"

"Don't worry, Seth. I know exactly what I'm doing."

"I hope you do."

"I'll be fine, sweetie, but thanks for your concern."

I kissed Seth on the cheek, then returned to sipping my margarita. I walked over to the princes to say hello.

"So I hear you're the best man, Alex."

"Yes, I am. Excited to get married?"

"Yes, I couldn't be happier with anyone but Seth."

"I'm glad to hear that, but I do have one question."

"What's that, Cato?"

"Why him?"

"He saved my life twice. One time it was so important that I wouldn't even have had the chance to meet you all. That's why I chose him."

"And you love him?"

"With all my heart."

"Well, I'm glad to hear that. Any particular theme for the wedding?"

"Haven't thought of that yet."

"Well, the second you decide you let me know."

"I will, Cato."

Alex smiled and walked over to another girl to chat, but it looked like he was hitting on her. I noticed Shawn was trying to hit on another girl but wasn't doing too well, since she was laughing and pointing at him with a few of her girlfriends.

"Try that flower thing you showed me. She'll love that."

"Thanks."

Shawn instantly did the flower trick, and she swooned big time; she walked up to Shawn and kissed him on the cheek. Shawn blushed a little, making her giggle. Her friends were insanely jealous and I whistled over to them.

"There are plenty of available princes over here, ladies."

The girls walked over and started flirting with the remaining princes, and they looked quite happy.

"So are you a matchmaker now or something?"

"No, Akari, I just introduced them to each other. The love just happens to flow."

"Well, that's nice of you. Those princes look pretty darn happy."

"Yeah, I haven't even said hello to many of them yet, but I think they're busy."

"Yeah, you better give them some privacy with those ladies."

"What's going on over here?" Seth came up.

"Jill's causing trouble."

"I'm not. I just happen to be setting up the princes with some of the hottest girls in Atlantis."

"Well, they look okay. Jill and I look better."

"Yeah, we do."

I put my arm around Seth and asked Akari where Skylar had run off to.

"Oh, he's grabbing some shots and a drink from the bar."

"Oh well, that's good."

I had finished up my margarita and grabbed another one from the bar when Seth shouted that it was suppertime. I rushed over to the main banquet hall and took my seat at the table. It was right next to the king and next to Seth. Supper was brought to us and it was my favorite—boiled crab. It was steaming which made no sense to me. The point was that the crab was delicious and I continued to dip it in garlic butter until it was dripping. Everything was so good while the crab was amazing. Dessert was another favorite of mine: rhubarb crisp with vanilla ice cream and caramel sauce on top. I dived in but Seth told me to wait, and they brought me and Seth a deep-fried Mars bar to share of course. I had just enough room to eat both. I couldn't have had a better birthday dinner; soon afterward it was time to open my gifts. From Akari, I got lingerie, and from Seth, I got a beautiful diamond bracelet. I got many other little things like new shampoo and body wash that made me smell like roses and lots of other things.

"Is there anything else we're going to do?"

"Dance, of course."

Just as I was about to say what, music started playing and Seth grabbed my hand and pulled me into the ballroom. Everyone was in there by the time Seth pulled me in, and it was a song Seth and I knew too well, "Loving You Tonight." Seth grabbed my hips as I put my arms around his neck, and we began to dance. We glided across the floor slowly, letting the water pass us; it was only that grinding wasn't nearly as fun without legs. Seth announced that the party would be moved to the nearest club which happened to be the hybrid nightclub. Half the guests were hybrids, but it was really late, so most of them went home. The other half entered the club with me and Seth, and we burned that club down, not literally of course but we sure knew how to party. Seth and I were grinding hard and so were the other guests, including Akari and Skylar. They were going hard as I waved hello to them, and Akari waved back. I smiled and so did Seth, as he kissed me on the cheek and continued to grind on me. We didn't take any breaks since we both were on an adrenaline rush, and I barely even drank anything. I finished maybe three margaritas, and that was about it. Seth kissed my neck during one of the songs, and I placed my hand on his neck, pulling it closer to mine. It started getting hot in the club, but Seth and I didn't stop, neither did Akari and Skylar. They walked closer to us and started grinding right next to us. Akari gave me a high five and Skylar fist bumped Seth. The lights went out in the club, and the lights flickered some more.

"Don't you just love this?" Akari had to shout over the loud music in order for me to hear her.

"Of course, I love dancing."

"Especially with guys?"

"Especially with guys."

I just knew Seth was smiling without looking over at him; when I did he had the biggest grin on his face. Skylar had an equally big grin on his face as he kissed Akari. I figured I wasn't that drunk and kissed Seth.

"You wanna head back home?"

"Not yet, one more song."

"Okay."

Seth and I danced to another love song, and Skylar waved to us as he danced. I waved back and so did Seth. Once the song ended, Skylar kissed Akari again and hugged her before they left. Seth and I swiftly left after them and swam home. Seth and I were thinking the same thing, so the second we walked in the door we quickly kissed and Seth slammed me against the wall. I lifted my leg up for him to hold on his hip and he leaned on me. I wrapped my arms around his back and ran my nails down it, leaving small scratch marks, I'm sure. He lifted me on his hips as he slammed me against another wall again and again until we reached the stairs and he carried me up the stairs. He opened the door with his foot, and it smacked open against the wall. Seth smashed me down on the bed, holding my wrists above me, making them crack.

"Sorry."

"I like it rough."

"You're so hot."

Seth aggressively kissed me and continued to hold my hands above me. I tried to fight it, but he was too strong. He loosened his grip slightly, just enough for me to slip my hands out of his grasp, and I instantly placed them on Seth's back as he began to French-kiss me. He rolled me on top of him, and I leaned down to kiss him again. He rolled me over again and kissed me on the very edge of the bed, and we rolled right off the bed.

"Ouch," we said at the same time. We laughed together for about a minute before we got up back on the bed. Seth rolled on top of me and kissed me again as he pulled my hips onto his. I smiled under his kiss, pulling his shorts down. He knew exactly what I wanted, and he unhooked my bikini top and pulled my bikini bottoms down. I put my hands around his neck, as he pulled up the covers over me and him. It was good old-fashioned hot, dirty sex and I loved every second of it, and I think we did it about seven times before we were tired out.

"We tired out after eight times last time though."

"It's the deep-fried Mars bar."

"Well, damn."

I cuddled up next to Seth, both of us breathing in and out again and again. We were tired, it was safe to say. I put on my bikini bottoms and crawled back into bed with Seth.

"That was great."
"We should do this more often."
"Nah, let's save it for special occasions."
"Okay."

I put my hand on Seth's chest and listened to his heartbeat and the sound of him breathing in and out; it was so peaceful and relaxing. Once his breathing slowed down and his heartbeat slowed down, his heart rate increased.

"Are you having a heart attack?"
"No, I'm just a little tired and loving you."
"Aw, good night, Seth."
"Sweet dreams, Jill."

For the first time, he put his hand over my own on his chest, and I felt its warmth on his cool chest. I saw the glow of his crystal on my face red and warm; it was like one of those heat lamps on my face. The warmth put me to sleep. Then Seth although sleeping placed his hand on my face and stroked it a few times, ending it all with a kiss on the cheek.

Chapter 43

I woke next to Seth as always. I ran downstairs and turned on the Wii and started dancing. After about an hour, I checked on Seth, who was still sleeping. "Poor thing must have been tired," I thought. I returned to the living room and did some yoga in my underwear; it was quite relaxing, I assure you. After I finished, I made myself some breakfast. I had got some cereal for my birthday: Lucky Charms, Cinnamon Toast Crunch, and my favorites, Nesquik cereal and Reese's cereal. I reached for the Nesquik cereal and grabbed the milk out of the fridge. I chopped up some cheese to go with it after I finished my cereal. I heard Seth coming down the stairs as I finished my cheese, and I quickly ran over to him to say good morning.

"Morning, Seth."
"Good morning, Jill, how did you sleep?"
"Fantastic, you?"
"Just great."
"Good, you want some breakfast?"
"I'll be the one making breakfast for us today."
"I already had breakfast actually, sorry."
"That's cool. I'll make something for myself. Mind if I steal some of your Lucky Charms?"
"Not at all."

Seth grabbed the Lucky Charms and taking the milk from the counter poured on them, eating them rather quickly.

"So when were you hoping to get married?"
"This week, Friday to be exact."
"That's three days, Seth!"
"I know, just enough time to get everything together."
"But I don't know if I'm ready for this."

"Believe me, Jillian, you're ready for this, you always have been."

"Are you sure?"

"I'm positive."

Seth grabbed my hand and kissed me on the forehead, which made me giggle. I kissed him back and cleaned up the dishes. Seth hugged me from behind and kissed me on the neck before walking outside in his shorts. I put away the dishes and ran outside after him. It was stormy.

"Seth, get back here."

"Yeah, I was just going to say that," Seth shouted as he sprinted back to the cabin. He was covered in rain and freezing when he got back; it looked like a crazy bad thunderstorm. It might have been a hurricane, but I couldn't really tell, so I asked Seth.

"Unfortunately, it's a hurricane. We better take shelter."

I rushed upstairs and closed the window before the rain could get the floor wet. I ran downstairs and asked him where we could go. He said to stay in the living room, as it was the safest place to stay for now; there were no windows that would break and hurt us. I ran into the living room after taking a mango from the kitchen and ate it while shaking.

"Are you okay?"

Every strike of lightning scared me and gave me an instant crushing headache. The sound of thunder made me dizzy and gave me a flashback of the night I lost my family. It was like I was there again on the tiny helpless raft, and I fainted. I heard the remainder of the mango in my hand drop on the floor, and Seth instantly yelled over the lightning and thunder if I was okay. I felt Seth pick me up and place me down on something soft, probably the couch, and sit down next to me as I felt the position of the cushions bend down toward where he sat. He placed a cool cloth on my forehead since I was beginning to burn up. I was still thinking of the night I had lost my family, and flashes of Jay flickered through my mind. It was nice to see his face again, even though I was going to be married now. I couldn't bear the thought of it anymore, and I woke up screaming.

"Jill! It's okay, you're safe."

"Jesus, what a terrible nightmare!"

"What is it? Tell me."

"I just had a flashback of the night I lost my family. It was horrifying."

"You're fine. That will never happen to you again."

"I faint too often."

"No, you don't. I just happened to knock you out once and the other times you lost blood. There's no one to blame."

"But me."

"Now don't do that, Jill."

"Why not?"

"Because you shouldn't always blame yourself for things that aren't your fault."

"I suppose I shouldn't."

"That's my girl."

He hugged me as I shivered. I was freezing.

"Are you cold?"

"Freezing."

"Here, take this blanket."

Seth handed me a warm blanket; he had been sitting on it, so it was even warmer. Once I wrapped myself in it, Seth put his arm around me and pulled me into his chest. It was nice and warm in his chest and I snuggled into it, flinching when thunder shook the cabin.

"Aw, are you scared of thunder?"

"Maybe."

"You can tell me."

"Yes, I am."

"Well, I'm right here for you. Don't be scared."

"I'm not that scared."

"You certainly look like it."

"I'm not."

"Your eyes are dilated. That means you're scared."

"Okay, so I'm scared, sue me."

"I'm right here for you."

"You already said that."

"I know, but I mean every word."

"I know you do, sweetie."

I was starting to warm up a lot more now. I was about room temperature, but it wasn't warm enough. Seth read my mind and he made me a cup of hot cocoa and brought it to me.

"Thank you, Seth."

"I figured you might want some more to warm you up."

"How did you know?"

"I just guessed."

"Thanks."

I sipped on the hot cocoa as the storm started to calm; the last crack of thunder subsided and the clouds floated away. I walked outside and the sand was cold and wet.

"My father must be in a bad mood today."

"Your father did this?"

"Yeah, he gets angry every now and then and sends out a hurricane."

"Are you saying that it was your father that sent my family to their deaths?"

"I have no idea if it was my father that sent that storm, probably not because you were too far away."

"Good, because if your father killed my family, I'd kill him."

"Then my brother would become king, and I'd have to wait till the others died for me to be king."

"But they're immortal."

"Ain't that a bitch?"

"You're so weird, Seth."

"You know it."

I laughed and kissed him as he wrapped his hands around me. I instantly warmed up and saw his crystal glow red again, so did mine. I smiled and held my crystal in my hand. It was really warm, and then it started glowing white.

"What does white mean?"

"I don't know. Let's go ask my brothers or my father. One of them should know what it means."

"Let's go."

I walked out of the cabin, leaving the blanket on the couch, and stepped out onto the cold sand. The beach was a mess with crabs stranded on the shore, but they crawled back into the water, solving that little problem. I jumped into the water which was cold but not nearly as cold as last time. With my tail forming, I dove down and Seth swam beside me. The water was murky and dangerous. I could barely see anything ahead of me, and with water like that, a shark could pop out at any second and eat me and Seth. Seth told me not to worry, and the crystals started to glow brighter and lit the way to Atlantis. We had got closer to Atlantis when I saw the horror of a pod of sharks surrounding Atlantis. I hid behind a rock and so did Seth; we figured we'd never get into the city. They must have been feeding on some fish near the city. I panicked as Seth went up to the circle of sharks and threw a rock at one of the sharks; it chased Seth.

"Go, quickly!"

"Seth!"

"Just go. I'll be fine."

Seth grabbed a hidden spear out from one of the rocks and stabbed the shark in the back, but it wouldn't die. It dragged Seth around for a minute, but he pulled the spear out and stabbed it in the eye, killing it. I had bigger problems as five sharks chased me to the city, but the guards killed them before they could eat me. Thank goodness, because I would've been dead if it wasn't for them.

"Thank you, gentlemen."

"Anytime."

I swam toward the palace, but I waited for Seth before entering. He had a wound on his hip; the shark must have nicked him. I told him not to say a word as I placed the crystal near the wound and put my hand on it. It disappeared quickly after I did so, and we swam into the palace. And then I almost ran into a relic on the wall.

"Better watch where you're going."

"Yeah, I will."

We swam up to the king who wasn't doing anything and asked him what a glowing white crystal meant.

"It means your heart is ready for marriage. Congratulations."

"You do know we're getting married in three days, right?"

"Really? Seth never told me, but nonetheless I shall start preparations for the wedding. What is the theme for the wedding anyways?"

"Under the sea, of course. This means fish decorations, bubbles, and glow fish table decorations."

"Right away, Jillian. I'll send men to catch some glowing fish for the decorations."

"But the wedding is in three days. How will they stay alive for three days?"

"I'll feed them until the wedding of course, and I already have your wedding gift."

"Really? What is it?"

"It's a surprise."

Neptune smiled and told me I could leave; he wanted the decorations of the wedding to be a complete surprise and said I shouldn't return for three days. I agreed and left with Seth, and we went out to lunch.

"So where should we go to lunch?"

"I have no clue."

"Why don't I choose?"

"Sure."

"Sushi?"

"Nope."

"Wings?"

"Nope."

"Poutine?"

"Absolutely."

We found the nearest New York Fries and walked in to the smell of gravy and deep fryer. It smelled great in there, and I ordered my regular normal poutine and Seth ordered his fully loaded with sour cream, nacho cheese, onion, and the usual underneath. His actually looked really good, but I liked the original better. Once we finished, we left the table and the restaurant. I was comfortably full, and we swam back without the sharks behind us, leaving Atlantis behind for three days.

"Oh shit, Seth! I forgot to buy a dress!"

"Oh damn, that's right. We have to go back."

"I agree."

I had promised the girls I'd go shopping with them, but this was urgent and who better to go shopping with than Seth? We went into the nearest wedding dress shop without being seen and shopped. I tried on many dresses; all were mermaid style, but none of them were the one. Finally, after twenty dresses I finally found the one; it was tight, but I could drop the weight. It had a diamond belt that made me look slim and a diamond-encrusted top that shimmered in the light. It was perfect, and Seth whistled to show his liking toward it.

"I love it."

"You look beautiful."

"Thank you, I think this is the one."

"Wonderful, let's get it."

I took it off and returned it to the lady to wrap it up for me. It cost $50,000, but I didn't need to worry about the price. We swam out with the dress and left Atlantis at last. We made it back to the cabin just fine, and I tucked the wedding dress back into the closet. Seth picked me up, and carrying me to the kitchen counter, he put me on top of the counter. He kissed me as he unbuttoned my top.

"Bedroom?"

"Bedroom."

I hooked up my bikini top and ran upstairs with Seth, and we hooked up upstairs in the bed. It was still early and we hadn't even had supper yet. It was still light out, and I decided we should have supper then maybe go for a walk on the beach. I made crab left over from the big supper and heated that up. It took a very short time to eat, and right afterward, we went for a walk. It was peaceful and quiet on the beach, and we must have walked at least a kilometer before we turned around and walked back to the cabin. Once we got back, I ran to the cavern in the back and dove into the water, and then I realized Seth wasn't behind me, so I waited for him. I heard him splash in and swim up to me.

"You could have said you were going to the cavern."

"I figured I'd surprise you."

He smiled and swam ahead of me quickly. I caught up with him before we got to the cave, where we got out and walked up the staircase. It was warm tonight; well, it was the middle of summer and it was a beautiful night. The stars came out the second we sat down on the hammock together, and we watched them in silence. Seth rocked the hammock back and forth, making me slightly tired. I sighed the same time as Seth and held his hand. It was warm and a little sweaty.

"You nervous for the wedding?"

"A little. Can you tell?"

"No, your sweaty palms definitely don't give it away."

"Sorry, I am a little nervous."

"Don't be. You're ready for this."

"I suppose you're right."

"Oh, I know I'm right."

"I'm sure you are."

I snuggled up to Seth and placed my hand on his chest, and he placed his hand on mine. I sighed again as I realized that Seth had fallen asleep on the hammock.

"Seth, wake up."

"Huh? Oh sorry, babe, I'm just so sleepy."

"Let's go to bed then."

"Yeah, let's go."

I walked down the steps, still holding Seth's hand, and jumped into the water. It was warm and inviting, and it got really steamy in the cavern. I immediately pulled Seth over closer to me, and he kissed me. That's exactly what I wanted to do. Once he stopped, he gazed into my eyes and pulled me closer for one more kiss. I giggled when he kissed me on the cheek and pulled me underwater. I followed him and emerged out of the cavern, slightly more tired. I walked out to the cabin with Seth, his hand in my hand, wrapped around my fingers. Once we got inside, he picked me up and carried me to the bedroom upstairs. I was so tired I almost fell asleep in his arms, but I needed to change before I went to bed. I quickly changed and almost fell over, but Seth caught me. I smiled up at him. I got back onto my feet and crawled into bed. Seth changed from his trunks into his shorts and crawled into bed next to me. I snuggled into his warm chest and placed my hand on his chest as I always did, closing my eyes for the night.

Chapter 44

Three days passed all too quick, and soon I was getting into my wedding dress and putting on my tiara. I took it off, saying it wasn't quite time yet. I dove into the water to get my hair cut in Atlantis and put in an updo. I pondered how it would stay up in the water, but I thought the crystals would help with it. I reached Atlantis quickly and went straight to the hair salon, and the hairstylist smiled up at me.

"Oh, you look beautiful, Jillian."

"Thank you."

"Now to do something with that hair."

"Sorry, I didn't even get a chance to brush it."

"You know it's bad luck to see your future husband on your wedding day before the wedding."

"Yes, I know. That's why I had to get out of the house quickly."

"Smart girl."

"Thanks."

She rinsed my hair and washed it in the sink. I enjoyed it when she massaged my scalp. When she finished, she put my hair up in a bun with two ringlets on the sides. It looked beautiful and I almost cried, but I didn't want to ruin my mascara. She finished it up with some hairspray and put some bling in the ringlets. I thanked her and left, lifting my wedding dress up so I didn't trip. I ran into the palace to ask the king when the wedding would be; unfortunately, I saw Seth there, trying to tie his tie. I walked over and tied it for him. I knew it was unlucky, but I didn't really care. I finished tying it, then kissed him on the cheek, putting a red lipstick mark on it.

"Ready?"

"I was born ready."

I smiled and walked away to the park. I stood back for Seth to go ahead of me, and then the wedding music began to play. I grabbed my bouquet from Akari and walked down the aisle with my father on my side, holding my arm. I took it step by step and made my way up to Seth, standing by his best men and groomsmen. My bridesmaids were all lined up, waiting for me, and I smiled at them. Seth smiled at me as I walked up to him and handed my bouquet to Akari. The ceremony was beautiful, and we both wrote our own wedding vows. Seth's vow almost made me cry, but then the time came for me to say mine.

"From the moment we first met as children to the moment you saved my life for the first time, I didn't know it but I loved you then. From then on, you brought me food, took care of me when I broke my ankle, and even helped me make a shack for my father. You helped me pick fruit for Miko and for ourselves and even helped me pick out my wedding dress. I love you, Seth, and I can't wait to spend our forever together."

As soon as we put the rings on, the priest said what needed to be said, and so did we, putting on the rings. I smiled and nearly cried when he put the ring on, and it was a beautiful fit.

"You may now kiss the bride."

Seth leaned closer and so did I, and he kissed me. Everyone cheered as we walked down the aisle and went outside to the eager crowd waiting for us. King Neptune came outside and placed the tiara on my head.

"I now pronounce you Princess Jillian of Atlantis."

The crowd cheered even louder when I wore the tiara, and then the bridesmaids and groomsmen came outside. I was about to toss the bouquet when the ladies lined up.

"Everyone ready?"

"Ready!" they all yelled. I threw the bouquet into the water, and it landed in Akari's hands. I laughed so hard I fell to the ground and so did Seth. We helped each other up while Skylar had the most worried expression on his face. I walked to the park with Seth beside me and the crowd following us.

"So what is your first command as princess?"

"Free cake!"

The crowd cheered and sat down in the park with us. I sat and watched the chefs bring out the cake, bright and blue with a fishnet around the first two tiers, and the top layer was a bubble masterpiece; it was beautiful. I put my hands on my face and gasped when they set it down in front of us. Seth grabbed a knife. I smiled and held it with him as we cut the first piece of cake together. I cut a piece and held it up to Seth, and he held his up to me as we both took a bite. It was my favorite type of cake, lemon with vanilla pudding and hint of orange. It was a magical day. I had no idea what we would do for our honeymoon, but I didn't really care because I was a wife now. Being a wife felt no different than when I was Seth's girlfriend/fiancée. It was only now that I thought about the future and us being together and maybe having children and I wondered if they would be hybrids too. I pondered this thought over the wedding reception, but that thought faded during our dance. We danced till the stars became blue and it was indeed magical; the stars had played a large part in my life and I wanted that to be on my wedding day.

"I love you."

"I love you too, Seth."

I hugged Seth after the music stopped, and we returned to our seats at the main table. Akari was sitting next to me with Seth on the other side, and his best man was sitting next to him. I enjoyed the cake and how it was given to anyone who wanted some; it was a very large cake and there was more than enough to go around. Once I finished my slice of cake, I stood up and made a toast to our marriage, taking a sip of my champagne. It was great champagne that the king had been saving for Seth's wedding. It was strawberry champagne with a hint of orange, a great accompaniment to the cake, and it was simply decadent. I had a couple of drinks of champagne but not enough to get drunk; it would be awfully rude to get drunk at my own wedding. Akari was certainly getting her drink on and it was easy to tell. After the first dance, Alex came forward and told us about his promised premonition.

"In the near future, oh yes, I see it now, I see a beautiful baby girl and boy. Their names are too fuzzy for me to see, but it is definitely in the future."

"Thank you, Alex."

I was taken out on the dance floor for the father and daughter dance, and my father nearly cried.

"You look beautiful, Jillian. Your mother would be so proud."

"Don't cry, Dad."

"I'm not crying."

"Good, 'cause I'm the one who's supposed to cry, remember?"

"I know, Jill."

The dance was nice, and I teared up a bit when we finished. My father wiped the tears falling off my face.

My husband looked so cute dancing with a little girl whom we had invited. She was in a little pink dress. It flared out like a tutu, and it looked adorable on her. I smiled and joined them as the music played on. The dance was short since Seth and I wanted to get to our honeymoon as soon as possible. We said good-bye to all our guests and the groomsmen and bridesmaids and Akari and Alex. I hugged Akari and thanked her for being my maid of honor. She thanked me back and told me she had a great time. Alex gave Seth a bro hug and thanked him for coming. I was a little sad that the wedding was over already, but that meant I could be alone with Seth. We talked about our wedding and wedding reception on the way back to the cabin, passing a dolphin on the way back. It was pink, very rare among dolphins, and it was considered lucky to see. I smiled as we emerged from the water and walked ashore. Seth immediately scooped me up in his arms and carried me to the cabin; I felt that this was the right thing to do. As Seth opened the door, I kissed him roughly, and he slammed me against the wall once more. I embraced it as he unzipped my dress and pushed himself up onto me against the wall. I loved every second of it, as he then let me slide down the wall. He picked me up again and carried me upstairs, running as fast as he could, sprinting for the bedroom although careful not to drop me. He closed the door and ran back to my side, and he pulled down my wedding dress and underwear. I wasn't wearing a bra because the dress was so well designed it didn't need one. I started to pull off Seth's tie and unbuttoned his dress shirt. At one point, I just ripped it open, letting all the buttons fly off.

"Hey! That was my best dress shirt."

"Sorry, I just had to rip it off."

"Good point."

I started to kiss him again, but he was sitting straight up, so I pulled him down onto the bed; he started to kiss my neck, then pulled off my necklace, placing it on the bedside table. I took off his and put it right next to mine; they began to glow white together and then red, but the glow didn't stop us as we had sex again and again. We must have done it ten times—a new record for us; even though we just had some cake no less than twenty minutes ago, it didn't stop us. When we finished the tenth time, we were absolutely exhausted and couldn't go on any longer. Seth rolled back over onto his back and breathed out a lot of times. I thought he might have been hyperventilating.

"Seth, are you okay?"

"Yeah, I just need to catch my breath."

"Boy, you really can't handle going ten times in a row, can you?"

"I suppose not."

"Funny, I'm a little tired but not as tired as you."

"You just have a higher stamina. No need to brag about it."

"Who said I was bragging?"

"Me."

"Oh, whatever."

I rolled over onto my side, ignoring Seth, indicating to him that I didn't want to see him.

"Hey, hey, don't be like that, baby girl. I'm sorry, okay?"

"Oh, okay, I can't be mad at my husband forever."

I rolled back over and kissed Seth gently, placing my head back down on the pillow.

"Oh, c'mon, I know you can do better than that."

"You wanna see the best I can do?"

"Why, yes, I do."

"Be prepared."

I kissed Seth as I normally would and then gave him the kiss of his life; it was the ultimate French kiss and I twisted my tongue into his mouth and turned it upside down, melting on his tongue. I enjoyed it when he French-kissed me back, grabbing my hip and squeezing it. I loved every second of it and I lay down on my back and let him fall into me. I really did fall for Seth and everything about him—his bright green eyes like that of a mint leaf and his tanned skin, caramel definitely, his six-pack he'd always had, I loved everything about him. His sex drive, basically any feature you could think of in Seth I loved, including his thin treasure trail. I was crazy about him, and as our crystals continued to glow red, I thought about our future children and what they would look like. Would they have hair like mine or like Seth's, jet black hair? I didn't really care. I was just glad that we would have children together; what better way to spend forever than to have children? I couldn't be happier than I was right now in Seth's arms with thoughts of the future. I was sure Seth was excited to have children with me and just what I wanted too—a boy and girl. All my dreams were coming true with Seth, and there were more pictures to add to the shack. I figured we'd do that tomorrow and maybe visit the crystal oasis again. There was so much we could do together now, and I couldn't wait to spend eternity with Seth. Today had been an amazing day, and it went just as I had hoped; the future looked bright, full of new memories to be made and children to raise and so much more. I kissed Seth good night and snuggled into his chest for the night.

Chapter 45

Well, the wedding day passed and we were officially husband and wife. I got up before Seth and walked downstairs and made myself Red Velvet pancakes. I figured I'd treat myself, and as I reached for a mango, I realized we had eaten them all. Miko was munching on the last mango. I licked my lips, suddenly craving for the taste of mangoes. I slammed my hand down on the counter, scaring Miko, and I ran upstairs and woke up Seth.

"Seth, wake up."

"What is it, baby?"

"We have to get some more mangoes."

"Why?"

"Why do you think? We're out."

"Okay, five more minutes."

"Now, Seth."

"Okay, okay, I'm up."

Seth got up finally and put on his shorts. He then walked downstairs to make himself some breakfast. I smiled at him when he finished, and then I ran outside with the backpack and sprinted for the forest with Seth beside me. I ran into a few ferns and a tree, but I was okay. Seth ran into a tree head-on and got a bruise on his chest. With the help of my crystal, the bruise was easily removed. We continued running to the fruit trees, and once we got there, we started gathering all the fruit we wanted. I picked a couple of pomegranates and lots of mangoes, with Miko's help of course. He shook the trees and the fruit fell like rain, and soon the backpack was full. Once we finished up, we took a trip to the crystal oasis and went skinny-dipping. I was about to kiss Seth when something jerked my leg.

"Seth, something just—"

The Tail of an Angel

Before I could say another word, I was pulled underwater by a live piece of seaweed that had grabbed my leg. I was pulled to the bottom which wasn't that deep, but it left me completely underwater. I tried to pull it off, but it was on my leg for good and it didn't look like it was coming off anytime soon. I tried to wiggle it off, but it wouldn't come off, and I was running out of time. Seth finally dived down to help me and tried pulling it off, but even his strength couldn't get the seaweed off. Finally, he had one last plan, and he tried to cut the seaweed with the crystal. It glowed bright blue as it heated up the water around it and I watched it, accidentally taking a breath of water since I couldn't hold my breath any longer. I took another terrible breath and another, and before I knew it, everything went black and I felt the seaweed come off my leg. Seth immediately pulled me to the surface. He dragged me on to land and laid me down on the grass nearby.

"Oh, please don't be dead. We just got married. Please don't be dead."

Seth started giving me CPR, and I could feel the pressure of his hands on my chest. He started giving me mouth to mouth, and that did the trick as I started to cough up water on the grass, lying my head back down on the grass. Seth put my bikini back on me and carried me back to the cabin while I was in a mini coma. I heard him carry me up the stairs and place me on the bed, still a little wet from the water. He sat down beside me and put his head on my chest.

"Please wake up, just wake up."

I didn't open my eyes because I was indeed in a mini coma, but after a few hours I think, I woke up. I coughed a few times and looked down at Seth.

"Seth? What the hell happened to me?"

"Oh my God, thanks goodness you're okay."

"What happened?"

"After the seaweed grabbed your leg, you nearly drowned, but I managed to get the seaweed off and I saved you."

"That's three now."

"I know. You have to save me two more times for us to be even. I'm so glad you're okay."

"I'm glad I am too. I think we better stay away from the oasis for a while, until that seaweed dies."

"Should take about a week."

"And something else we should also slow down on is the sex. We've been having a lot of sex lately."

"What's wrong with that?"

"Nothing. It's just I think we're getting too familiar with each other's rhythms. Besides, I think last night should last me a couple weeks."

"A couple weeks?"

"Yes, a few weeks, and we can return to having sex as much as you like."

"I don't like the sound of this."

"Relax, we'll be fine."

I kissed him on the cheek and thanked him for saving my life. I got up slowly, but my leg was sore.

"Hold your horses, Jill. You better lie down for the day."

"Really? But I'm such an active person."

"I know you are, sweetie, but you better let that leg rest. I'll take care of you until then."

"So you'll make me soup and take care of me all day?"

"As long as it takes."

"Thank you, Seth."

"Anytime, Jillian."

He kissed me on the forehead and walked downstairs to make lunch. I heard him drop a pot on his foot and yell, "Son of a bitch," but I laughed anyways. I rolled over to look at the window and saw the bright sun outside and a few clouds that were passing by. It was nice to see the clouds again; I hadn't seen them in so long. I stared out the window for at least five minutes until I got bored and started staring at the boards in the ceiling. I counted about twenty boards before I got bored again and rolled on my other side and sat up with my head on the headboard. I heard a thump or two downstairs, and it must have been Seth setting the soup on the counter, but we only had chicken noodle soup packets, so I thought what the heck he was up to. I got up and put my feet down on the floor, but even that was painful. It looked like I wasn't going anywhere anytime soon. I sat back up on the bed and sighed when I heard Seth coming up the stairs.

"Here's your soup."

"What kind of soup is it?"

"Chicken noodle."

"Oh my favorite, thanks."

"You're welcome."

He handed the bowl to me on a little platter so I wouldn't burn my lap and gave me a glass of cranberry juice and milk to go with it.

"It's delicious, Seth, thank you."

"My pleasure, Jill."

He kissed me on the cheek and ran downstairs to have his share of the soup somewhat quietly. I heard him fall down the stairs with a loud crash at the bottom. I laughed before taking another spoon of the hot soup; it really was delicious I couldn't lie. It was just Lipton's Chicken Noodle soup, but it was still really good; he had thrown in chunks of real chicken, which

The Tail of an Angel

was nice. After I ate lunch, Seth carried me downstairs so we could watch a movie together. He put in *Tangled* from when Skylar and I had watched a couple of movies. We sang together my favorite song in the whole movie.

Seth sang along to Flynn Rider's part beautifully, and I sounded just like Rapunzel, but better. The rest of the movie was really good, and he threw in *Red* again, just so he could watch his favorite part. I didn't mind, of course, but I could care less where I was, just as long as I was with Seth. We finished another movie, and Seth put in *Tarzan*. I hadn't seen *Tarzan* in a year or so, and I missed looking at half-naked Tarzan. Once the movie started, I cuddled up to Seth into his warm and inviting chest and watched the movie. It was entertaining and a classic as previously predicted; with Jane by Tarzan's side, they sure made a cute couple. The movie finished just like the others, and he turned off the TV so he could make supper. I didn't know what he was going to make for supper; he told me he was going to make fish and chips. I hadn't had fish and chips in quite some time; he said he was going to fry the fish himself. It was cod and I loved cod; he had caught it yesterday when I was sleeping. I heard him deep frying the fish in the kitchen; he also fried up some tasty home-cut fries. He used fresh sea salt from the ocean he'd been saving for a while. He salted the fries and called me to dinner.

"Dinner's ready."

"Okay, come fetch me."

"Oh, right."

Seth ran over to me and picked me up with ease, setting me down at the dinner table.

"Dinner is served."

"Thanks, Seth, this looks great."

"Just wait until you taste. Your taste buds will be having a party in your mouth."

"I'm sure it will be."

I took a bite of the fish with tartar sauce, and it was incredible. I tried the fries and they were equally as good. The sea salt made it even better than I had hoped. The salty fries melted in my mouth, and so did the fish. I finished supper rather quickly, but I was still hungry so I had some more fish, three pieces to be exact. I was comfortably full, and Seth ate the rest of the fish and fries, another plate actually. Once everything was put away, Seth cleaned up the mess by himself and carried me upstairs to my bedroom, or should I say our bedroom now? Once he set me down, he lay down beside me and asked me how the meal was.

"It was great, Seth, really. Thanks again for taking care of me."

"Hey, I'm your husband. It's my job."

"Exactly."

Seth rolled over on top of me and kissed me. I didn't mind. I thought of it as a way of thanking him for dinner. I rose up to press right up against him and he pressed it right back. Seth turned on the stereo to play "Turn the Night Up," one of the songs we would normally grind to. I thought it was fitting for us to make out as I wrapped my hands around his neck and pulled him down on me. If it wasn't for our clothes, we would be having sex right now. I didn't mind anything at all and I continued to kiss Seth. He French-kissed me amazingly, and he didn't stop. I didn't want him to stop. I rolled over on top of him as he smiled and laughed.

"I thought you liked it on the bottom."

"Someone once told me I should try new things."

"That was a wise person."

I smiled and kissed him again before rolling back over and asking him to carry me to the window. He did so obediently and carried me to the window and let me see the view. I was hoping to see the sunset from another point of view. I asked Seth to take me to the cavern behind the cabin, and he said it was a bad idea but helped me out anyways. He carried me down the stairs and out the door toward the water. I smiled as he set me down in the water gently and I swam ahead. He caught up. My tail was slightly faded and dull and not as bright as it was earlier. I looked at it suspiciously and swam up to the side of the stone edge and pulled myself up on it. Seth carried me up the staircase to the hammock above. He gently set me down on hammock and sat down beside me.

"You can lie down, you know."

"Of course."

Seth lay down right next to me and watched the sunset with me.

"Despite everything that happened today, it was a nice day."

"So falling into a mini coma and almost drowning was nice?"

"Not exactly, but it was nice of you to take care of me and make me soup when I was feeling a little under the weather."

"You know, I'll always be around to take care of you."

"Always?"

"Always."

I smiled and kissed him on the cheek as the sun finally went down and the stars started to peek out. One by one, they popped up in the sky like popcorn and so did a few shooting stars. I already had everything I wanted in this life, so there was nothing I could wish for, with the exception of one thing—my family. I made a wish for them to be okay and happy back on land. A small tear escaped my eye, and Seth immediately asked me what was wrong.

"Oh, I just wanted my family to be okay."

"I'm sure they are, JJ."

"I sure hope so."

I pondered on the thought for at least an hour until all the stars had finally appeared. I said, "Wow," as Seth put his arm over my cold shoulders. Tonight was the most beautiful as it was a rare occasion when you could see the edge of the galaxy; it was breathtaking. I snuggled up to Seth and watched the northern lights come out, which surprised me; even though it was probably impossible, it was still possible in my eyes. I stared out at the galaxy in the sky and it looked like the face of God; it was amazing. Seth was just as amazed as he said, "Wow," the same time as me. I smiled and so did he when the northern lights fluttered above. There were a thousand colors in the Aurora Borealis. I could only count the seven basic colors; the rest I couldn't even name. Seth squeezed me tight and smiled up at the bright sky.

"It's beautiful, isn't it?"

"Breathtaking, Seth."

"I wish we could do this every night."

"Then we'd never had sex."

"So much for that."

"Yep."

I laughed a little and continued to gaze into the sky. The northern lights soon disappeared and the show was over. I got up, but I still couldn't stand on my leg; you'd think by now it would feel better, but no. Seth scooped me up and carried me down the stairs and lightly tossed me in the water. I was a little angry he threw me in, but then again I would've done the same thing in the same situation. I swam up and waited for him to jump in, and he did so quickly. Once he jumped in, I swam under and to the other side. Once we reached the other side, I swam up to the shoreline and pulled myself up on the land. Seth picked me up and carried me back to the cabin, putting me down on the bed upstairs. He lay down next to me and kissed me on the cheek good night. I thought he was going to kiss me a little better.

"Is that the best you can do?"

"You know I can do better."

"Then prove it."

I smiled as he French-kissed me. I thought, "What's this? Mint flavor? He must have been using my toothpaste." I loved it until he turned his tongue upside down, which he had learned from me. But I loved it; it felt amazing on my tongue. He was on top of me, holding my hips on his, and we were so close. If only we could get a little closer, but I had promised I wouldn't have sex with Seth for a few weeks. It was going to be hard, as I couldn't resist Seth. I know he could resist me; the red glow on his crystal said it all. Mine glowed red in return to his, and I loved it. I rolled over onto Seth and placed my hand on Seth's chest and snuggled into his chest. He looked out the window and stared at the starry sky and sighed.

"It was a beautiful night, wasn't it?"
"It was."
"And you enjoyed it?"
"Of course."
"Good, good."
"The galaxy looked so amazing."
"It did, didn't it?"
"How often does that happen?"
"Not that often. I think once every hundred years."
"Well, I'm glad I'll be around to see the next one."
"Yeah, me too."

He kissed me on the forehead and closed his eyes for the night. I did the same and kissed him on the cheek; a smile crept out on his straight face. I smiled back, even though he couldn't see it, and then returned to place my head on his chest. I fell asleep with his arms holding me and pulling me closer to him. I loved this and I wouldn't change it for the world.

Chapter 46

A few months went by and then Christmas and New Year went by; soon it was the next year. I was happy I had spent another year with Seth, but my pain at missing my family was growing and it wouldn't go away. It was literally an actual physical pain that sent me into a deep depression. I wouldn't eat, I wouldn't sleep, and since I was immortal, I wouldn't die from starvation or sleep deprivation. Seth grew worried and did everything he could to stop the depression; he even went to the king for help, who came to visit me. I'd never seen him on land until now. I was a little surprised but still sad and lonelier than ever. The king took a green crystal and stabbed it into my heart. I screamed in pain, and it dissolved into my heart and skin. My eyes glowed green for only a minute, but it quickly disappeared. Suddenly, I felt really amazing, like I could take on the world. I smiled and hugged Seth.

"What did the crystal do?"

"It's a happiness crystal. It sends happiness straight into the heart and it melts to flow to the rest of the body. It's a rare crystal that's hidden away in some caves far away from the city and it's what got me through your mother's death."

"Thank you, Father."

"Anytime, Seth."

I felt great and that I really could take on the world. I felt that nothing could hold me back; I had the sudden urge to surf.

"C'mon, Seth! Let's go surfing!"

"I thought you'd never ask."

"Let's go!"

I ran to the closet and pushing aside my wedding dress grabbed the surfboards. Seth ran outside first with his surfboard and beat me to the water. I ran in and splashed down into the water next and started pedaling toward the upcoming wave. I hit it just right, and I was surfing next to Seth. I felt great as I was swallowed by a wave behind me, but I could care less as I touched the wave with my fingers. I eventually got out. I saw Seth ahead of me and splashed him with my surfboard. I laughed and sped up ahead of him on the wave until I saw it end and slow down until I came to a stop and sat down on my board, which Seth flipped over. I laughed when I got up and back on my board.

"Oh c'mon, Seth, learn to take a joke."

"Oh ha-ha, so funny, Jill."

"Oh, please take a joke, will you?"

"Fine but just this once."

I was wearing the new bikini Seth had bought me for Christmas; it was plain baby blue with sapphires on the top. We certainly dressed according to our class status. I was usually covered in certain gems 90 percent of the time as it was, including some of my new outfits bought by Seth at Christmas: a green tank top with peridot, a white dress with diamonds, and a purple dress with amethyst on it; they were beautiful. Right now though I was in my bikini, catching the next wave which was huge by the way. I could surf it for an hour if I wanted. But at one point I crashed into the wave when my legs gave out and let the water wash over me; unfortunately, it smashed into me and pulled me underwater faster than I could say blub. Once I was underwater, I saw the coral reef shine bright in the light. I smiled as my tail formed, and Seth pulled me to the surface.

"I thought we were here to surf and not stare at the reef."

"I know. I just got sucked underwater, is all."

"I know you did. That's why we should get back to surfing."

"Okay."

I swam up to my board and surfed the rest of the day. It took forever to get back ashore since there was a riptide and I couldn't make it ashore for a while. I was so tired once I got ashore. I just lay down on the sand and washed it off in the sea. Seth came ashore shortly after me and did the same. I sat down on a beach chair and lay back on it, and so did Seth. I was so exhausted I didn't even want to move at all. Seth was breathing heavily, indicating his exhaustion as well. We sat in the sun to dry and we did at some point, and when we did we had just enough energy to get inside the cabin. Once we were inside, we dropped on the couch together and breathed out. It was really steamy in the cabin today. I wondered how I didn't notice that. I almost didn't need my clothes, but the bikini would have to do until after supper. I had no idea what Seth would make for supper and whether we would be going out or just staying in and maybe have some tasty crab, who knew? I wanted to ask Seth, but I was still out of breath, so I had to wait a minute or two.

"So what's for supper?"

"It's up to you."

"Poutine? We haven't had it in like two months."

"Sounds like a plan."

Seth picked me up since I was too weak to use my legs and carried me to the water. I placed my tiara on my head, which I did whenever I was outside to let the people of Atlantis know who the princess was of course. I dived in, almost losing my tiara, and swam toward Atlantis. It was a quick swim, and once I reached Atlantis, I was greeted by the townsfolk kindly. Since I hadn't visited in a few months, I guessed they missed me. I shook the hands of men and women passing by and hugged a few children; I kissed some babies but not too much. Once I passed all the people, Seth and I went out for dinner at New York Fries. My poutine was wonderful as usual, and Seth got a pulled beef poutine, which was different, but it was still good. It tasted great but mine was better; while we were eating our food only a few others came in and recognized me. Of course, I had to shake their hands and say hello. I didn't mind of course, but it did annoy me slightly that I couldn't have my meal in peace. Otherwise, today would've been perfect. Nonetheless, I finished my meal the same time as Seth and left the restaurant. It was quiet after that; I guess the people had their fill of me. We left full and satisfied, though I was a little too full actually. I think I ate too much poutine; usually I ate half or two-thirds of it, but I had eaten the whole thing. That was a terrible idea on my part. I swam back feeling fat, but I still looked great with a flat stomach, even though I didn't feel like it.

We got back to the cabin where Seth passed out on the couch; I frowned as I had hoped we could take a walk on the beach. I told Seth about it with the promise of sex afterward, and Seth got up right away. I smiled and walked outside; it was really hot outside. The sun was setting on the water and it was a beautiful sunset. I didn't see that Seth had brought the guitar behind him. I smiled and pulled him closer to my hip as he strum the guitar held in front of us. I spotted the place where we always had a bonfire, and Seth put down the guitar and ran into the forest to get some wood for the fire. I pulled out some matches and set them down on the log bench. Seth picked them up when he got back and lit the fire and its heat warmed me up right away, but what really warmed my heart was what Seth sang for me.

"Oh, Seth, thank you. I have a song for you too, but I don't need the guitar."

"Go ahead."
". I sang for Seth 'Angels' by Owl City, and he loved it.
"That was great. What's the name of that song?"
"Angels."
"Suits you."
"Thank you."
"I think I know one of your favorites."
"Really, what's that?"
"The Saltwater Room?"
"Oh, I love that one. Sing it for me."
"Wonderful."
"Thank you. Did you like it?"
"I loved it."
"I'm glad you did."
"I'm glad I did too."
"You're so weird."
"Thank you."
"It wasn't exactly a compliment."
"Then what was it? Bubkes?"
"Sure, let's call it that."

Seth laughed and put his arm around my shoulder, kissing me on the cheek. I smiled and put my head on his shoulder. I enjoyed the view of the fire, but it burned my eyes, so I had to turn my eyes into Seth's chest to make them feel better.

"Is something wrong?"
"No, I just stared into the fire for too long."

I started to tear up from the heat. Seth looked down at me and kissed them dry; they must have tasted salty to him. I smiled up at him and kissed him. He gently set down the guitar so he could place his hands on my hips as we made out a little. He kissed me once more before I got up and held his hand. He grabbed the guitar and walked back with me.

"Ever decide what to call the island?"
"No, I never gave it a name."
"Well, why not give it one now?"
"Okay, got any ideas."
"Fire Crystal Island."
"I like it, but why fire crystal?"
"It's where our crystals turned red for the first time."
"Makes sense."
"I know, right?"

I smiled and kissed him on the cheek as a thank-you; so Fire Crystal Island it was. I smiled big on the way back to the cabin. I glared at Seth every now and then to see if he was still smiling, and he was. Both of us knew what was going down the second we got into that cabin—yummy. Seth opened the door for me and I said thank you, and after he looked out the window to make sure no one was coming, he jumped right into me and kissed me, pushing me up against the wall, which I loved. He grabbed my ass and pulled me up against him; it was rough, but I loved every second as he slammed me up on another wall. He French-kissed me in the dirtiest way, and it was incredible. He then lifted me off the ground and carried me upstairs to the bed, where we devoured one another with countless hickeys and bite marks on our bodies, which could be easily removed with the crystals of course. It took a few minutes to remove them all off our bodies, but it was the roughest, hottest sex we've had in a while. It felt so good, and it felt so right with Seth. Once we were finished, we did it again eleven more times, another new record for us; it was faster and more intense sex than before. We were getting good at this. I snuggled up to Seth after all that, and I was ridiculously sweaty and so was Seth. I was practically lying on hot sweaty leather, even though it was simply Seth's chest.

"Eleven times, new record."
"We should be able to get to twelve pretty soon."
"I don't think so. We need more practice."
"We've had plenty of practice, don't you think so?"
"Yeah, you have a point."
"Of course, I do."

I smiled and curled up to Seth, still very sweaty. I could care less. I was much sweatier than him, and I think he was thinking the same thing. Once I was comfortable, Seth leaned down and kissed me on the forehead.

"Yuck."
"Shouldn't have done that."
"Now you tell me."
"Like I said, you're so weird."
"Not my fault. I want to show my affection."
"I think you did that eleven times, sweetie."
"Oh, right."
"Anyways, good night."
"Good night."
"Good night, Seth."

I kissed him on his sweaty cheek and fell asleep in his hot arms.

Chapter 47

Today was going to be a new day. I got up smelling of sweat, and as I was naked, it smelled pretty bad. I was taking a shower when I heard Seth come in.

"You better not come in this shower, Seth."

"I won't."

I waited for him to leave, but he didn't. I heard him brush his teeth and then I was sure he'd leave after that. When he didn't, I stopped washing my body and let the water wash the soap off my body.

"Seth—"

"Surprise!"

"Seth!"

He laughed and kissed me on the cheek from behind. I was angry he was in my shower; I was hoping to shower alone.

"Seth, this is my shower!"

"I know, but I wanted to shower right now."

"Doesn't matter, Seth. Get out."

"Aw, why do you have to be so mean?"

"You serious?"

"Yeah, I'm seriously staying right here."

"No, you're not."

"Well, this is a first."

"What?"

"Getting kicked out of the shower."

"Out."

I grabbed the shampoo as a weapon and threatened to spray it in his eyes. Before I could squeeze the bottle, Seth lowered it with his strong hand and kissed me while the water teased the corners of my mouth.

Seth pushed me up against the wet wall and kissed me again, as the soap continued to flow down my body and Seth's legs. I smiled under his kiss and decided he could stay.

"Fine, you can stay."

"Yay!"

He kissed my wet cheek which was now clean, and then he shampooed his hair. I smiled as I shampooed my own.

"Here, let me help."

"I don't need help in shampooing, Seth."

"Oh yes, you do."

He massaged my scalp, and the shampoo got really foamy and soapy. I smiled because it felt so good. I hadn't had a hair massage in years. Seth conditioned his own hair afterward and so did I, so all I had left to do was wash my face. Seth washed off his body as I exited the shower, and I heard Seth say, "Aw." I laughed. I dried off with a towel and got dressed in the bedroom. Seth was still in the shower by the time I got dressed, and I walked downstairs to make myself some breakfast. This routine had become old for me: sex and eating breakfast, sex and eating breakfast. I was so tired of it. So I ended it for another few weeks. I had a mango smoothie with strawberries. It was really good, I assure you, and I had a BLT to go with it. It was a nice change from bacon and eggs, and I loved it. Seth was a little disappointed that we wouldn't be having sex for a while, but he could handle it like the last time. I thought he could handle it again. The weeks went by slowly, and I was growing restless of not being with Seth, and my body was taking a hit. I started to lose my muscle, and the six-pack I had formed had flattened into a flat stomach. I missed my six-pack, and when we started having sex again, it returned. Sex really worked wonders on my body. I was happier and my serotonin levels were up; it was healthy and it even increased my stamina. There was more stamina for Seth too; it meant he would last longer, which was good. The days passed nice and slow with Seth; we visited the oasis every now and then and my father at least once a month. A few more months went by peacefully until Alex came to visit one day.

"I have urgent news, Princess Jillian. I had another premonition, but I don't know if Seth should be here for it though."

"Whatever you have to say, you can say to both of us," I told Alex as I grasped Seth's arm.

"Remember when I said you would have children? Well, it turns out they're not Seth's."

"What?"

"Yes, you will return to land to have children with another man."

"And why would I do that? I love it here."

"Because your family is still alive."

"Again what?"

"Your family is safe and sound on land."

"This is impossible! How can this be?"

"They were rescued a few days after the sinking, I just saw this. I would've told you sooner, but Seth made me promise not to tell you or he would kill me."

"You're right, Alex. Now I have to kill you."

"I'm ready to die."

"No, you can't kill your best man!"

"I'm afraid I can't break a promise, Jill, you know that."

"I know, but maybe we could make a deal."

"And what's your deal?"

"My immortality for his life."

"Jill, why would you do that? You want to see the galaxy again, don't you?"

"Alex is more important."

"Fine, it's a deal. Let's go to my father."

"Fine."

I left the cabin with Alex and Seth behind me, my head high and a tear escaping my eye. I wiped it and continued to walk forward into the ocean. Once we reached Atlantis, we swam straight to the palace, where Neptune was pacing in the ballroom.

"Your Majesty, Jillian has a bargain to make on behalf of Alex's life."

"What is your deal, Jillian?"

"I wish to give up my immortality."

"Very well then."

He pointed his trident at my neck and lifted the crystal off. The trident glowed bright yellow until I had to close my eyes because of the brightness. I felt a great pain in my heart and then in the rest of my body; it was like I was on fire. Once it stopped, I felt much better, and my crystal was no longer glowing. It just stayed a plain clear white, and I was a little disappointed. I stared at it as another tear fell from my eye, but no one could see it underwater. Seth noticed my red eyes and gave me a hug without saying anything. So I was no longer immortal; it kind of sucked. So I wouldn't live forever, but now I knew what I needed to do.

"I wish to return to land."

"What?"

"I wish to return to land, I said."

"How?"

"Your guards have been to land before I've heard, and so has Seth. I don't want to live here anymore."

"But why?"

"Because my family is alive and well. I want to be with them again."

"But what of the life you have here? You're a princess and you have duties to Atlantis."

"I hate to leave, Your Majesty, really I do, but some things are worth sacrificing."

"Very well. I suppose I can't force you to stay. Does that mean you'll be divorcing my son?"

"Unfortunately."

"What? Jillian, why?"

"It's just not going to work out, Seth. It's not that I don't love you. It's just that I can't be married to you on land. You belong here, Seth. This is your home."

"But what about everything we've been? What about us?"

"I know it's all about us, Seth, but I have a duty to my family and to be there for them."

"I see. Well then, I'm coming with you, no excuses."

"I know you're the one who has to take me there."

"Also, I'm bringing my brothers, Alex and Akari."

"I'm totally okay with that."

"All right, let's pack up some things, and we'll leave as soon as possible."

"Sounds good."

"Farewell, Jillian."

"Good-bye, King Neptune."

I waved on my way out and swam back up to the cabin with Akari.

"I have to wait here. I'm not a hybrid."

"Okay, we'll be down soon."

I swam up to the surface with Seth and packed a few weeks of food and survival supplies and my things. It all fit in a few bags; plus, I put some of the treasure in a few bags, making it a total of six bags. They weren't that heavy since all the sex had made me so strong. I carried two, Seth carried three, and Alex carried one. I took one final look at Atlantis before leaving. I looked down at my necklace and held it in my palm. I grasped it and then let it go, and finally I moved away from the sight of the city. Seth led the way out, and then I saw my father join us.

"Oh sorry, Dad, I almost forgot about you."

"Where are you going?"

"Home, Dad."

"Really? Count me in!"

"Sounds good."

He carried my share of the bags, and we pressed on. I had a feeling this would be a dangerous trip, full of currents and sharks willing to attack at any moment. The open water ahead was a dangerous place, I kept telling myself as we swam in water I didn't even know was that deep. Indeed the water was deeper than I had hoped, which meant a shark could come up from under us at any moment, so I kept looking down. I saw nothing for a few kilometers until a current made it difficult to swim. I fought it well as I continued to swim forward, but it was hard for my dad, and that first day was the hardest. Day two wasn't as hard, and we must have swum a hundred kilometers that day, but we were still far from our target. My dad was hungry, so I gave him a mango to munch on until there was a safe place to eat supper. Up ahead, there was a spot where some coral had died and it was flat on the sand. It must have been an island at some point. We sat there and ate some peanut butter sandwiches, but mine kept getting soggy since my crystal wasn't working anymore. Seth had to feed me since I couldn't eat myself; it was rather pathetic. Once I finished my sandwich and my dad finished his mangoes, we were back to swimming into the blue darkness. Night was coming and there was nowhere to sleep in the ocean yet, so we had to go on. We must have swum for another two hours and I was getting tired. Finally, I saw a flat bit of sand we could sleep on, and we stopped there, careful that sharks weren't there resting. There were none thankfully, and we put down our stuff and rested for the night. I snuggled up to Seth like I always would; I didn't plan on stopping now. I felt his warm arms on my shoulders; I placed my head on his chest and closed my eyes.

"Do you still love me?"

"Of course."

"Then why leave me?"

"Because I want to be with my family."

"I thought I was your family."

"You are, but I have to be with my real family."

"I am your real family."

"Are you my brother?"

"No."

"Then you're not my real family."

"At least I was for a little bit."

"Yes, you were."

I kissed him on the cheek and fell asleep in his arms. I didn't mind sleeping in his arms once more; at least I was with a trusted friend. Then reality screamed in my ear that he was my ex-husband.

Chapter 48

I woke up in the water which surprised me at first, but then I remembered I was on a treacherous journey back to land. Seth was still sleeping, and I had to wake him up as everyone else was getting up.

"Wake up, wake up."

"I'm up, I'm up."

I smiled at him and swam up to the surface, but saw no sign of land as yet. All I saw was endless ocean and a whale. The whale was huge, as it should be, but it surprised me to see a whale this far from krill waters. Anyways, we returned to swimming in the open water and toward land. I saw, on noting the kilometers, we must be getting close by now.

"How much longer?"

"A few more days, three I think."

"I can do three."

"Shark!" Akari screamed. It was a great white shark and it was alone. I swam to the backpack to grab a knife for defense when the shark got closer. It went straight for Dad and bit him right at the waist, ripping him into half.

"No!"

"Let it go, Jill. He's gone."

"That's my father!"

I watched in horror as the shark ate my dad, and I could do nothing about it. His eyes were closed the whole time, so I was glad about that, but it was true; he was gone. All that was left was a pool of blood left around the shark. In a fit of rage, I swam up to the shark, screaming, and stabbed it in the eye and repeatedly in the rest of the body.

"You ate my father, you monster!"

"Jill, enough. It's dead."

"Oh, sorry, I didn't notice."

The shark floated to the surface and birds picked away at its body. Good, the monster deserved a shameful death. After that, we continued to swim on and follow Seth. I looked back and thought I should do something to commemorate him, so I let go of a mango and left it there floating in the water. Dad loved mangoes; I think that's what he would have wanted. The swim was a lot quieter after that; almost no one was talking and I was crying for a solid ten minutes before Seth told me to stop. I carried my bag that Dad had been carrying and swam ahead when I thought I saw land, but it was actually a boat. We swam deep, deep into the water until the boat left, but it stopped and people came into the water. I panicked and wondered what we could do, but we could only wait until they left. They were there for two hours, which really cut into our time, but at least we weren't seen. Once they left, we returned to our course, and even though we lost precious time we were safe. Akari swam up to me and gave me a hug.

"I'm sorry for your loss."

"Thanks, Akari, you're a good friend."

"And a good bridesmaid."

"That too."

The trip was long, but the sun went down again and we had to call it a night. The night was noisy because Alex was snoring for the first time ever. It was annoying and I got almost no sleep, so Seth had to carry me while I slept in his arms the next day. I woke up around lunchtime, which was breakfast for me, and I was told we moved a lot faster after that. Seth couldn't swim as fast with me in his arms, so we had a few more hours to add to our travel time. The day was bright and the water was warm, so travel was nice today. It was just as long as the day before it, only today it was more boring.

"How much longer?"

"Two days."

"Woohoo!"

I grew excited and smiled for the first time today and swam on. Seth looked tired, and I thought we would need a rest break and Seth's brothers agreed. Sedrick recommended he carry him until he had the strength to go on. Sedrick had been to the surface before, so he knew the way. We followed Sedrick as I chatted with Akari about the guys at the surface.

"They're tall, most of them, and they love hot women."

"So you have no problem meeting guys?"

"Not at all."

"Wonderful."

I smiled as we swam on, as you can probably tell by now there was a lot of swimming. It took hours and hours to get bored of talking to Akari, but we were finally getting bored when Seth woke up.

"All right, I'm up. Let's get back on track."

"Actually, Sedrick was leading us while you were sleeping."

"Oh okay, let's keep going, shall we?"

The day ended with me sleeping in Seth's arms again and waking up in the same way. Only one more day until I reached land. I could sum up that day in one day—boring. It was gray and dull, especially above the water. It was foggy and difficult to see, but underwater it was clear as a bell. I swam with a big smile on my face, but Seth had a frown on his face.

"What's wrong?"

"After this, I'll never see you again."

"You can come visit anytime you want."

"Thanks, Jill, I will."

I smiled at him and kissed him on the cheek before returning to my place beside Akari, continuing to smile. It's true, this was the last day I would have with Seth, and I could think of a much better way to spend it, but I couldn't underwater. Yes, I would still sleep with my ex-husband, but then again it probably wasn't that smart. I laughed at the thought, and Akari looked at me funnily. The night went by fast and we swam really fast. I smiled at Akari and continued to follow Seth. Finally, I spotted land after the longest time; it was still quite a swim, but I swam as fast as I could.

"Jill, wait up."

"Okay."

I stopped in my tracks and waited for them to catch up. They caught up, and Akari started crying.

"Oh, Akari, I'll miss you too."

I hugged Akari and Alex, who was tearing up a little. I hugged Seth's brothers. Then Seth pulled me to the drop off.

"I hereby decree by the king of Atlantis," Seth pulled out a scroll from one of my bags, "that you are banished from Atlantis unless you are required for the assistance in saving Atlantis from certain doom. I sent forth my sons to ensure your safe arrival to land. I wish you the best of luck and that you may not enter the water as a hybrid anymore. I have given Seth a crystal to change you back into a human. You will no longer be able to talk, sing, or swim with a tail and breathe underwater. Sincerely, King Neptune."

"Banishment?"

"Sadly."

"So how the heck does the crystal work then? Do I wear it or something?"

"Ummm, I think so. My father never told me how exactly to use it."

"That doesn't sound good."

Seth looked at the crystal and shook it. He twisted it around a bit but nothing happened. He scratched his head a few times and picked up the crystal from his neck. He brought it up to the crystal in his other hand, and the opposite crystal started to glow bright purple.

"Ah, now I think it's working. Remember, you won't be able to breathe underwater anymore, and it might hurt a bit."

"I'm kind of scared! Can you make sure I won't drown please?"

"Of course."

Seth brought the glowing crystal up to my belly, and the crystal dissolved into the skin and disappeared as my waist ripped into half and two legs formed that felt like I was just lit on fire. I screamed as it became more difficult to breathe underwater, and finally I was completely normal again. I couldn't talk to Seth underwater to say I had used up my air when I screamed.

"Are you okay?"

I shook my head saying no and mouthed the word "air" to him. He quickly came up and breathed air into my lungs in a kiss. I held it and swam up to the edge of the drop-off.

"Farewell, Jillian."

I waved and blew a kiss to Seth before swimming to the surface, my bags pulling at me a little bit. I made it to the surface and saw the coast, and I swam to it. I recognized the cabin on the shore and saw my family in it. I swam as fast as I could to the shoreline, making it with my six bags. I ran to the cabin. Then I realized everyone was wearing dark colors.

"Hi, everyone!"

"Jesus, Mary and Joseph, it's Jillian."

"Where's Jay?"

"Should I tell her?"

"Someone should."

My brother said, "Jay died about a week ago. He got in a car accident saying he saw you and was looking for you, but he hit a semi and died."

"Oh my gosh."

"Here's the funeral card."

It was a picture that Seth and I had taken a while back. I was somewhat happy I was on his funeral card, but it was still very sad. I held the card in my hand as my mother gave me a hug. Jay's family was there too.

"What happened?"

"Well, I lived on an island for two years, living off the fruit on the island, and I swam for shore about a week ago."

"You swam for a week?"

"Well, you all know I'm a strong swimmer."

"I'm so glad you're home."

"Thanks, Mom."

I dried off with a towel my brother handed me, and then I said I wanted some time alone by the sea. I walked out onto the warm sand and let my feet get wet.

"I already miss you, Seth," I whispered to myself. I held the no longer glowing crystal in my hand and was just about to throw it into the ocean.

"What are you doing?"

"I'm going to throw this into the ocean. What's it look like?"

"Why would you do that, JJ?"

"Well, I want to forgot this p—"

I paused and looked beside me, and I saw Seth standing on the beach, wearing trunks and a white T-shirt with the blue glow of his crystal visible under the shirt.

"What are doing here?"

"I'm here to stop you from throwing that crystal in the ocean."

"But why?"

"Because I don't want you to forget about Atlantis."

"I have to, Seth, to move on with my life."

"But why would you want to do that?"

"It's what people do, humans do. It's not a hybrid thing. You wouldn't understand."

"Oh well, I can sort of understand. I have to move on without you by my side."

"I'm all alone up here, Seth. My boyfriend's dead. I just missed him."

"You won't ever be alone, Jill. Just hold this crystal close to your heart and that's where I'll always be."

"I don't know if I can do this without you."

"You have to. You're going to meet another man, have lots of kids, and live happily ever after."

"But what about you?"

"I'm sure I'll meet someone again someday. I have eternity to find another girl."

"But it won't ever be me."

"No, it won't ever be the same, but I'll always have the pictures of us to remember you by."

"Oh yeah, we really filled up that shack."

"Yes, we did."
"Anything else you wish to tell me?"
"Please come back with me."
"You know I can't do that."
"Why not? Skylar can make you a hybrid again."
"He's still here?"
"He's in the water over there."
"Hi, Jill!"
"Hi, Skylar."
"I don't want to leave you, Jill. I'm crazy about you."
"I know you are, sweetie, but you have to go on without me."
"I don't know if I can."
"You just said you'd meet another girl someday."
"I just said that to ease your conscience."
"Oh, Seth, you have to go, live in the water. Take care of Miko for me?"
"He'll be fine for a few days with all that fruit."
"How about Akari? Is she happy with Skylar?"
"You know she is."
"Just wondering."
"Can I ask you something?"
"Anything, Seth."
"Can I kiss you one last time?"
"Of course, you can."

Seth lifted my face and pulled it closer to his, and tucking my hair behind my ear, he kissed me. It wasn't anything fancy, just a regular kiss until I French-kissed him; then it turned into a short make out session. I didn't mean for it to turn out like this, but it did and there was nothing I could do about it. I stopped kissing him and looked into his eyes one last time. He gazed into my eyes and kissed me on the forehead, and then he turned away without another word.

"Seth, wait."
"What is it, JJ? It's killing me to see you go."
"You're the one who's leaving."
"Oh right, what is it?"

I ran up to Seth and hugged him; I died a little inside, knowing I'd never see him again. I squeezed him tight and he hugged me back, of course; he held me tight and I didn't want to let him go, but I knew I had to. Once he let go, he opened my hand and gave me the blue pearl.

"Just a little something to remember me by."
"Thank you for getting this, Seth."
"I'll go now. Will we ever see each other again?"

"It's not like I can visit, but you should come back to land someday, and I'll be there in Canada."

"I'll be sure to visit you someday."

"I hope you do."

He placed an angel carving of a shark tooth in my hand and left.

"Oh, Seth, it's beautiful, thank you."

But Seth was already gone, his shirt left behind on the sand. I picked it up and threw it into the ocean; I figured I'd throw something in the ocean. I returned to the cabin and unpacked the treasure for the family and the San Family.

I kept the necklace because I didn't want to forget those two short years of my life. The press flooded me with questions and tips on how to survive on an island and what the location could be of the so-called "Fire Crystal Island." I told them all, that it was abundant in fruit and treasure and was easy to live on, but I kept reminding myself that it still wasn't home. Lies! I thought for the longest time that there was no home to return to or any family to greet me there, which conclusively brought me back to my role in believing in destiny; I believe it more real than a sinner believes he's done for on Judgment Day. What happened on the boat the night before we sank? What happened that my family was rescued and that I made it back to California healthy, well, and for a short time immortal? You will ask, what does this have to do with destiny? Simply the odds and mysterious ways I made it home and what happened to me in the process. It changed my view on life and my view of destiny in my own life. Faith brought me far, but destiny knew it all along, and I couldn't have had a better story to tell than the one of destiny in two years of my life.

The End

Edwards Brothers Malloy
Oxnard, CA USA
March 5, 2015